A Coward's Guide to Oil Painting

by
MM Kent

Author's Proof Edition

This book is a work of fiction. All Rights Reserved.
Copyright © 2020 by MM Kent

Published by Wings and Roots LLC,
P.O.Box 1101, Fayetteville, AR 72702
270-313-9660   publisher@wingsandroots.com

ISBN:978-1-7350812-1-2

Cover art by MM Kent
Printed by Ingram Spark

for Anne Titus,
who was beside me at the beginning,
and has stayed the course.

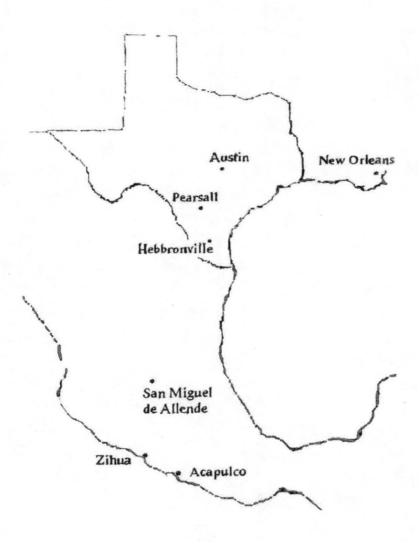

Map

*The first challenge for the artist, even
before picking up a brush, is learning
to see and then retain what is seen.
Over time, these visual memories will
become a library for the imagination.*
                                    -Charlie

CHAPTER 1
CLIFF

*The subject of a work of art is not the
most critical thing. The attitude of the
artist is more important. And attention.
For best results, you'll want to bring
all your faculties to bear on the task at
hand: your mind, your emotion, your
freedom of movement. The work will
take every bit of effort you can muster.*

May, 1969

The windmill stood silent in the dead calm of morning. Two men
walked through the pasture, kicking up a cloud of caliche, one man
tall and crisp in slacks and white button-up shirt, the shorter man
dusty as the Texas hill country, from the sweat-stained hat to the
worn-down boots. A dribble of snuff leaked through the patchy
stubble on his chin as he limped along the two-rut track, recounting
events of the previous evening.

"I'd walked up here to check the water and watch the sun set when I heard the sound of the plane. For a minute I listened, trying to get the direction. I knowed somethin' was wrong. The engine cut out, then started again, like it was runnin' out of gas. I seen the glare as the plane banked and straightened up, headin' this way. By then, I knowed it was comin' in too low so I run over to the bank there for cover, such as it is. I seen it pass in slow motion, like a dream. Read the numbers, N34TZ. Bullet holes in the fuselage. So close I could almost touch it."

The two men stopped fifty yards from the crash site beside the windmill's galvanized water tank. Across the track, a '55 Chevy pick-up sat rusting in the weeds. The rancher paused and lifted his hat to wipe his weathered forehead with a shirt sleeve, leaving a streak of ochre on the faded blue fabric. Then he continued, "I seen a flash and heard thunder. The earth shook, I'm a tellin' you. I hit the dirt flat out. A heat wave passed over me and I got the shivers. I'd been holdin' my breath. *Run*, I thought. *No. Get help! Maybe someone's alive.* I must've froze for a minute, maybe longer. When I stood up, I could see the plane had wrecked my house. Fire everywhere, hot as a pistol. Nobody could've survived that."

Grayson, the tall man, slapped a horsefly on his neck and pulled a handkerchief from his pocket to clean up the mess. He gazed beyond the scorched liveoaks to the pile of ashes where the house had stood. He wasn't eager to move any closer. The muscles around his anus clinched involuntarily, and waves of revulsion passed through his body as he processed the event that had taken place. *Please God*, he prayed, *let it be someone else in that cockpit and not my sons.* Blaine, the older one, had taken combat hits in Vietnam and never lost an aircraft. He wouldn't have screwed up like this.

"Must'a been tryin' to land on the highway up there." The rancher pointed to the top of a low bluff across the creek-bed, then paused to pull a sand burr off his jeans and flick it away. "The thing is, I got a look at that pilot when the plane passed. It was almost dark, and I only seen him for a second, but I'd swear he was a Mexican." The rancher spat on the ground and drifted away toward his pick-up.

Remains of the old farmstead were strewn over half an acre. The plane's wings had been ripped away on impact and the fuselage had blasted straight into the single-story farmhouse, drawing fire along with it. A thin cloud of white smoke still lingered and the odor of burning leaves permeated the air. Beside a smoldering tree trunk someone was bent over a five-gallon bucket, peering inside. The man wore a Stetson and a white western shirt with a star pinned on.

He straightened as Grayson approached and held out a hand. "John Pierce."

"Wayman Grayson, sheriff."

"I notified the FAA and FBI, Mr. Grayson. We have a crime scene unit on the way from DPS. The coroner is coming when he gets loose. Newspaper man will be right behind."

"Can I see the bodies?"

"What with the intensity of the fire, getting an ID will be difficult. I'll show you what I've found, but don't touch anything. Until the state boys arrive, my job is to protect the scene. There's at least one crime been committed here." Pierce turned to the wreckage. "It looks to me like the plane hit the butane tank and flipped over, belly-up. The explosion drove it through the wall of the house and telescoped the engine into the cockpit. What's left of the bodies is under there."

Grayson followed the sheriff's nod to the upside-down fuselage lying among the ashes alongside the remains of a blackened refrigerator and cookstove. The burned and crumpled piece of scrap-metal seemed incredibly small—no protection for vulnerable flesh and blood. Imagining bodies burnt to a crisp, Grayson's gut lurched and he turned away from the other man to empty the contents of his stomach. After wiping his mouth and gathering himself, he sensed the sheriff beside him.

"Sir, I'm real sorry about your son, if it was him in there. You must be as wrecked as the plane." The sheriff held his hat in his hands and fiddled with the brim. "I follow our Texas boys over there, you know. Across the water. Major Grayson was a fine airman. Someone to be proud of . . . an American hero." At that point, Pierce ran out of gas for giving speeches and concluded quickly, "Stay as long as you like. The coroner should be here any minute, and he's bringing coffee and doughnuts. Looks like I'll be around for awhile."

Sheriff Pierce started to walk away, then circled around Grayson to indicate the remnants of a gunny sack. "Sir, I found evidence of smuggling here. These bags of marijuana—what's left of them—were still smoldering when I got here. I've hauled water for days trying to put out the fires."

Grayson cocked his head at Pierce, thinking, *days?* and said, "I thought I recognized the smell of pot, walking down here. You just got here this morning, right?"

The sheriff seemed confused for a minute. "Yeah, well it feels like a week." He took off his hat and scratched his head. "There's one thing about those bags of dope that puzzles me. Some of it's just hay. I don't know much about marijuana, but I'd know Johnsongrass anywhere."

————

They say the part of the brain that stores memories is situated right next to the part responsible for the imagination. That must be why it's so easy for one part to borrow from the other—for an axon or a thought to wander across that scant border in search of freedom or truth or fiction . . . Like a Mexican wetback, say, crossing the Rio Grande to look for work.

My name's Clifford Grayson, or Cliff for short, but since I started flying under the radar, I've been going by CJ MacRae. This story is half mine. At the time of the plane crash in sixty-nine, I'd just graduated from high school in Travis County, Texas, where I was a good student and a fair athlete. I'd always been sheltered from most of the world's harsher realities, but that was about to change. And the troubles that were coming my way? I brought them all on myself.

Before I ever thought about telling a story, I painted, first in watercolor, then oil. Before that, I drew, with fingers, crayons, and pencils—whatever was at hand. It's all the same, really, making a picture, leaving a track. So here I'm learning to paint with words, instead of brushes, looking to capture an elusive trail of light. I expect I'll write the same as I paint, by plunging in and thrashing around until the words start to make sense. But I do know this—before you begin a story, it helps to have a picture in your mind of how the story goes. Then the words just come, like prayers to a believer.

I wasn't there on the scene, so I must have dreamed it, what happened that Saturday in Texas with the rancher and my dad. Or maybe they told me the details later. After my brother's airplane crashed the night before, Mr. Cole the rancher had driven three-quarters of a mile to his neighbor's house. From there he called Sheriff Pierce, who told him to sit tight until morning and keep quiet. Pierce sent a deputy to guard the crash site overnight and had himself arrived at 6 a.m. and sent the deputy home. From the numbers Mr. Cole had seen as the plane passed, they'd checked the registration and discovered the owner was Blaine Grayson, my brother.

Someone knew he was the son of a State Representative from Travis County. The DPS was called in and Hal Watkins, the director, made a phone call to Wayman Grayson, his old college football buddy. Grayson, my father, had taken the call in his office near the State Capitol building in Austin, where he'd gone in on a Saturday morning. He was hoping to get away before noon.

"Wayman, I have some bad news," Watkins had said. "We had an airplane crash yesterday evening down near Pearsall, by the state highway. Two jets from Lackland Air Force Base confirmed the location after dark, when the fire was still burning. It looks like your son's plane. There's not much left of it. I'm sorry. There are two bodies . . . I.D.'s going to be difficult. You might want to get hold of your son's dental records." Watkins went on, "We're trying to shake loose our unit that deals with crashes. Normally we'd be right on it, but my people are slammed and the FAA is busy with two situations right now, one in Hebbronville, and one near Houston. Don't know when they'll get around to us . . .

"There's one more thing," Watkins said. "The aircraft was loaded with marijuana. Probably came from Mexico. The FBI will be involved, so I thought you'd want to get down there. The county sheriff is there now. He'll need to ask you some questions."

My father was already packing his briefcase and planning his next moves while he listened to Watkins. He checked his watch at 8:30 am, made a quick call to his wife, Martha, then called the airport to ask for a plane and pilot . . . Then the dentist, to have records sent. By 10:30 AM, my father had landed at the tiny Pearsall, Texas airport. The deputy who was waiting drove him to the crash site where they met the rancher, Mr. Cole.

It feels like getting my wisdom teeth pulled, exposing this part of my life, with all the remorse around my carelessness and the dire way it affected other people. My nature is to keep secrets, not to spill the beans—that's how I stay safe and maintain control. But at the same time, I feel the urge to lay down my burden, come clean, and tell it all. Maybe not *the* truth, exactly, but *a* truth.

Earlier that same week of the crash, I'd had a minor scrape with the law, and to let things cool off, I'd persuaded Blaine to take me with him to Mexico. We'd flown to Acapulco and checked into a fancy hotel for a short vacation—body surfing in the Pacific, eating enchiladas, playing volleyball in the sand—and I tried to forget about the incidents that led to my departure from Texas. Well, not *all* the incidents. There was a girl . . . a woman, I mean. No chance I'd be forgetting her after what happened at the waterfall that night.

If I could have time-travelled backward three months from the day the plane crashed, and landed in New Orleans a week or so before Mardi Gras, I might have wandered along Magazine street, stopped at Joe's Po-Boy Shop and ordered a bowl of gumbo. If my timing had been right, I might have seen her then—hazel-green eyes, dark blonde hair, spirited and strong.

I know her as Mariah now, but I knew her before I knew her name, and before that I didn't know her at all.

———

CHAPTER 2
MARIAH

*How to conquer a blank white canvas?
And what moves are necessary to
accomplish a finished painting? The
answer will always be embedded in the
questions you ask.*

Feb 6, 1969, three months before the crash

New Orleans is a city of contrasts. Blinding hues are jammed up
against sooty old brickwork, hung-over doormen stand attentive in
tuxedos beside overflowing trash cans, and on a morning trolley ride
you see the dingy underbelly of a culture designed for darkness.

But here in Audubon Park, people are turned out in full color, like
human flowers, with faces to the sun. It's warmer than last week, just
right for my cotton print skirt and scoop-neck peasant blouse. A good
day to celebrate nature with a brisk walk around the grounds. That is,
until I hear an approaching commotion. I cover my ears and skip off
the concrete as the combo streaks past, fast as a photograph—the
scrambling boxer straining at the leash, the skateboard, its wheels
howling, and the afro, blown back in the wind.

"Maniac!" I yell at the rapidly disappearing clamor. But I love it.
The gleeful exuberance. The audacity. The edge.

With the excitement over, gentler sounds return. Last year's liveoak leaves crunch underfoot, and stones clatter in the creek-bed, launched by the hands of children. Near the park entrance, an empty seat beckons. Dappled sunlight splashes onto a fountain where I stop to rest, soothed by the sound of falling water. I don't consider how long it takes to produce the chalky patina of verdigris on a bronze sculpture. I only sense the security of age and culture and permanence here.

Pulling *The Wizard of Earthsea* out of my bag, I allow myself to become part of the scene, vanishing into a world created by Ursula LeGuinn. But I'm not invisible, it seems. I'm turning a dog-eared page of the book when a pair of Converse high-tops shuffles to a stop in front of me. The shoes I recognize (I have brothers), but the voice belongs to a stranger.

"Mind if I sit with you?"

I shrug and shift to make room. "It's a free country."

"I'm Blaine." The guy offers a hand. "From Austin. I call it 'the other' Texas."

I put down my book and shake his hand. "Mariah, from Illinois. I'm actually on my way to Austin, looking for land."

"What brings you here, Mariah?" Blue-gray eyes. Pale skin. Freckles.

"A yellow submarine." I suppress a grin.

"No kidding?" Blaine chuckles. The eyes crinkle at the corners. "Did you drive it?"

"Sometimes. I have a commercial license, but my friends and I take turns. We went together and bought an old school bus."

"So, it's like the song."

"It is," I nod. "We're living in it."

"Hey." Blaine glances down the street. "There's a Po-Boy shop about five blocks from here. I've heard they make a great gumbo. Want to try it?" *He sure isn't wasting any time.*

"Well, why not?" I'm already on my feet. "But only because I'm starving."

The aroma of fried fish meets us half a block away, luring us into the diner. The ancient screen door slaps shut and propells us to the counter, where Blaine orders the chicken and sausage gumbo.

"No gumbo." The voice coming out of the black beard has the treble turned all the way down and the bass all the way up—deep and sort of mushy.

"No gumbo!?" Blaine looks alarmed.

"Can't sell it—too old."

"You have it, but you won't sell it?" I ask, incredulous. *What kind of guy won't sell his gumbo?*

"Right." The man folds his arms across his chest.

Blaine's voice elevates a notch on the decibel scale. "I bet it's just fine."

"No. It's ain't *fine*." The man jams hands on hips. "Chicken's stringy now. Made it three days ago and I can't sell it, *now*." His thick Louisiana accent obscures his words, but one thing is perfectly clear—the man won't sell us any gumbo. I've put a hand on Blaine's arm, wanting to avoid a scene, since the two roosters have their feathers puffed up, and I'm the peacemaker here.

"But I've had a taste for gumbo all week." Blaine has a dreamy look in his eye. "Hot, thick, spicy . . ."

"Wait." The proprietor struts back to the refrigerator, pulls out a big pot, and brings it to the counter. He opens the lid and shows it to us. "You can *have* a bowl if you want, but you can't *buy* it."

"Looks great to me." Blaine gives a thumbs-up. "Fix us up with two bowls, would you, and a sausage Po-Boy to split."

Noticing the two males have bonded, I wink at the proprietor and point at Blaine. "Thanks, he clearly hasn't eaten all week."

Two steaming bowlfuls arrive in a few minutes—flavors perfectly merged, plenty of spice—and the stringy chicken melts in our mouths, bringing sighs of satisfaction.

Blaine wipes his chin, "Earlier, you said something about looking for land."

"Yeah, well, I want to be close to the Earth, away from all the commercial hype . . . somewhere safe."

"That's funny. I just bought a farm in Arkansas—for the same reason. I'd like to be up there before winter comes. Try some fishing. Maybe go deer hunting."

A glint of sunlight angles from the front window across the polished linoleum floor and up on our table. It lands on the wall amid a stunning assortment of feathered masks and a hand-written sign that reads, 'Extra Help Needed for Mardi Gras Week.'

The gumbo grouch appears at our table as I'm taking my last bite. "Where y'at?" His black eyebrows are joined above the bridge of his nose and a blue bandana clings to his head. Dark eyes hover over a long beard. He means, *How are we doing?* in New Orleans speak.

Blaine assures him all's well, then I ask, "Do you still need extra help at Mardi Gras?"

"Sure do, I got *no* help. Can you take orders?"

"I've waitressed a little" Not exactly the truth, but I'm game, and I need some kind of job.

"You're on, then—tomorrow from 10 'til 2. Five dollars a day in cash. You keep your tips an' eat free. I'm Joe, by de way."

"Mariah." I give him the peace sign. "I'll see you tomorrow, Joe."

As Blaine and I turn toward the door, Joe glances down appreciatively, then back up. "Wear that skirt, sister."

———

On good days my braided pony-tail attends me like a pleasant companion. On bad days it feels like a ferret has attached itself to the back of my head. Today it's all piled in a coil on top like some old lady's hair. I've picked my muslin blouse with the ruffled neckline to accompany the print skirt for my first day on the job.

Joe will be pleased. Shoot! *I'm* pleased. My *dad* would be pleased. Thinking of Dad sends a warm shot of feel-good to my heart. He always told me to remember that I can do anything I want. *Not true.* He was the one, really, who could do anything—fix a toaster, tune up a car, build a house. Mother never approved of me. Her standards were unattainable. Still are. I'm positive she'd approve of Blaine, though. Dad, too. Why wouldn't they? Courteous, clean-cut All-American?

Carrying a change of clothes in my bag, just in case, I catch a trolley from the French Quarter to Joe's Po-boys and pull a shift waitressing for the lunch crowd. Then I let my hair down and explore the garden district with Blaine. New Orleans blows my mind—white and black and color all mixed up like Joe's gumbo, a savory stew composed of structure, enterprise and humanity. Somehow it's more alive than other places I've been, and I've never seen a city with more cemeteries. So maybe it's the contrast between life and death.

The Garden district is all decked out, poised for celebration with banners hanging and bright fabrics flying. On Magazine Street I sense the proximity of treasure. It's palpable among the array of feathered masks, stage costumes and gypsy clothes. Sure enough, on a rack in the back of a thrift shop, the jacket awaits—tan leather, interspersed with patches of red and purple velvet, all whip-stitched by hand with heavy gold thread. It reminds me of a print I saw once by Gustav Klimt. *The Kiss,* maybe. The thrill of discovery is intoxicating. And it fits perfectly. *Yes!*

The jacket is coming apart, of course, and some of the fringe is missing. Why else, besides sudden death, would someone give up such a cool garment? I pounce on it, show the imperfect places to a clerk at the register and bargain for a lower price.

"Okay, lady, okay." The clerk makes a face. "Please, take it away. And get outta here."

Oh, happy day! *Did he say Lady? Cripes, I'm only twenty-two.*

Outside, the temperature has dropped along with the sun, and I'm glad to have the jacket as we poke along some other shops. Further down the street is a small hole-in-the-wall art gallery. Closed, but on the door a paper sign reads, 'model wanted for life drawing class— good rates paid.' Thumbtacked below the sign is a line drawing of a nude woman. Always alert for new adventure, I take down the phone number under Blaine's skeptical gaze.

"It's a little naughty, maybe, but it *is* an opportunity for work," I explain. "I have no experience, but you never know." The fact is, I've been so ordinary for so long that experimentation is at the top of my agenda.

We catch a trolley to the Quarter, smoke a 'J' and continue window shopping until the exertion leads to hunger. On Dauphine Street, a white mountain of oyster shells rises beside a tin roof. Under the roof, on the back porch of the establishment, two ancient men are at work, tossing shells into the pile, while an oceanic aroma wafts across the street.

"Oyster Bar," Blaine reads. "They'll be fresh at this joint—you like oysters?"

"I have no idea. Midwestern girls don't have many chances to eat exotic seafood. No oysters in the Mississippi river."

"You better try some, then."

Inside we find a sawdust floor, three high stools at the bar and six tiny tables. On the jukebox, Mississippi John Hurt is playing acoustic blues. Above the dark paneled bar, glassware hangs upside down and sparkles. We take a table and Blaine orders me a coke. He has a bottle of Jax, the local beer. A platter soon appears, and the ill-fated feast begins. Blaine demonstrates, picking up a half-shell and letting the oyster slip into his mouth. I slide one of the slimy things down my throat and gag. It comes back up and I chase it across the table with a napkin, snagging it before it heads to the floor. Thinking everyone in the bar is watching, and trying to be nonchalant, I find a trash can, deposit the offending bite, and take a minute before returning to the table.

"I wonder how much beer you have to drink to appreciate that?" I ask.

"I think that's the idea." Blaine sucks an oyster down, followed by a huge gulp from his glass.

"Well, I'm not impressed. I've no doubt eating raw oysters is what prompted our ancestors to discover fire."

Blaine laughs and further inspects the menu. "Looks like you can have 'em baked. 'Rockefeller,' 'Bienville,' garlic and lemon. . ."

"Now *that* sounds interesting."

"I'll get a sample plate," he says.

The 'Bienville' are my favorite—made with mushrooms, wine, Parmesan and bread crumbs—although the other styles are delicious, too. They're savory, palate charming and sublime. Whoever invented baked oysters is my hero.

"Be some good jazz a little later in the club." The bartender indicates the door at the back of the room. "Five-dollar cover charge."

"Thanks, we'll see." Blaine turns to me, raising an eyebrow.

After another toke outside, we try the door. It opens to a candle-lit room where a host appears, takes our money and leads us to a table beside the stage. Somewhere in back a juke-box plays. The singer keeps shouting 'Salt Peanuts,' or maybe it's 'Soft Penis,' I can't tell. A waitress takes my order for a rum and coke. Blaine orders bourbon.

When my eyes adjust to the dim lighting, I see the place is packed with people, their faces glowing orange and gold in the soft light. Restrained laughter and muted conversation complement the tinkle of glasses, producing an atmosphere of anticipation. Drinks arrive, and we savor them while waiting for something to happen.

Blaine has just asked if I want to leave and find someplace more exciting when the jukebox goes silent, the curtain parts and a huge stand-up bass fiddle creeps on stage. Under it, bent over and grizzled, is a man who looks like one of Snow White's dwarves. He straightens, the bass settles on the floor, and he spins around to embrace it. Sound erupts with notes pulsing and spilling from the plucked and patted strings.

I have never seen anyone make love to an instrument before, but there is no other way to describe the spectacle. *Oh, to be embraced that way, enveloped in a perfect wrap and stroked until music spills from all my seams.* Ten feet away, the man plays a solo—part warm up, part tuning, part melody, all beautiful—all with his eyes closed.

Now a middle-aged woman enters stage left, glances at the audience and sits at the keyboard, rocking back and forth for a measure, like Stevie Wonder, before be-bopping into the beat. My fingers twitch on imaginary keys. A drummer sneaks onto his stool and plunges into the mix, first teasing, then pounding the crowd's collective pelvic floor. *Who ever thought jazz would be like this?* If rock is sex, then jazz must be love.

At the beginning of the second set, a barefoot waif joins the trio of musicians, dragging a battered brass instrument onto the stage. She's wearing a threadbare dress that drapes to her knees. Limp blonde hair hangs on her shoulders. When she looks up at the audience, a grin breaks out on her face, showing dimples and crows-feet that reveal she's not a kid.

"What is that monster thing she has?" I whisper to Blaine.

"I believe they call it a baritone sax."

Just then it breaks wind with a discrete 'blat.' The woman is testing her lip. She grins again, and hollers in a clear voice, "Let's party, y'all."

The drummer pushes the combo into a Dixieland beat, the bass backs it up, and the piano slips in with a melody. When the elfin woman starts blowing her horn, the crowd goes crazy. Notes erupt from the sax like cannon shots. People catapult out of their seats and tables scatter into the corners. I hop up, grab Blaine and drag him into the music, the ragged sound piercing me to the bone.

We end up staying for all three sets and dance until my feet burn. At the end I'm physically altered. Molecules have rearranged. Music has done its work, with a little help from the weed and alcohol. After the show, we take a cab back to Blaine's place and make love, accompanied by the radio. Compared to the combo at the club, this music has no substance, only intensity. Blaine's eyes are closed. Mine are open.

Propelled by hard rock, it's over too quickly, and the condom is ripped. Now I have sperm in me. *I should have gotten the IUD.* This is my first time for sex in nearly a year and I'm too aroused to sleep, so I lie in bed, looking occasionally at the money belt Blaine has casually thrown on top of his clothes and thinking about oysters and jazz.

———

CHAPTER 3
MARIAH

*Since it's impossible to re-create three
dimensions using only two, what you
draw or paint is the illusion of reality
or the feeling of reality, not reality
itself. Don't forget, there's a big
difference between light and pigment—
as much as there is between flesh and
the image of flesh.*

"Bring a robe if you have one" was all William said on the phone
by way of advice. In a moment of courage, I decided to call about the
modeling gig, but now I'm having second thoughts. *Am I nuts?* After
a long soak in Blaine's tub, a joint smoked, razor applied to legs and
armpits, hair brushed and re-braided, I am presentable. I hope they're
not expecting a centerfold because that's not what they're getting.
How about ordinary but healthy? How about clean? How about I
don't show up?

No. I *am* doing this—for the sake of freedom. And money. This is
my chance. There's no way I'm going to cash in the savings bond to
use for living expenses.

When I arrive at the gallery wearing jeans and jacket, carrying a
tote bag, the door is locked and the note about needing a model is
gone. Up above, the stained-glass transom is a nice detail from a
bygone era—nothing fancy, a purple and green decoration with one
red accent. Hundreds of thumbtack holes pock the wooden door,
evidence of prior notices tacked there. I press the doorbell and turn to
look at passing cars. Magazine street seems dirty but benign in the
raking light of the six pm sun.

Across the way, windows glare orange and highlights bounce off a
broken street-lamp. I hope I don't look like a hooker standing on the
sidewalk in jeans and patchwork jacket, braid hanging down my
back. *Nah, I'm definitely a hippie girl.*

The doobie has taken away most of my trepidation about this.
Still, I jump when someone rattles the door behind me. A tall gaunt
man stands in the doorway holding a set of keys in one hand. He's
the image of a funeral director or a riverboat gambler, pale skinned
and dressed in a black vest, crisp white long-sleeved shirt, black
slacks and shined shoes. A large bent nose, wire-rim glasses and a
New York accent just complete the picture.

"Oh, hi." He straightens his glasses, holds the door open, smiles
and reaches out a hand, all at the same time. Thank goodness I catch
myself before cracking up. He has nice eyes, blue and reassuring.
Older than me. Thirty-plus.

"Hi, I'm Mariah. I'm the model."

"Great, ah . . . well, come in." I swear, he almost bows. "I'm
William."

He leads the way down a hallway with plastered walls and dark
polished floors, past gold-framed paintings, dimly revealed. Then up
a twisting staircase to another hallway and into a room with the same
décor. Easels and tripods lean against the wall in one corner. A
couple of low wooden boxes stand in the middle of the room,
surrounded by nine chairs. I'm vaguely aware of bodies in the chairs.
This is like someone's crowded living room.

William looks at his watch. "The bathroom is down the hall. Do
you have a robe?"

"Yes, I brought one, thanks." I rush out the door as a woman
enters, bent-over, head down, making no eye contact. Somehow it's

comforting that my audience will not be all male. After undressing quickly amid antique fixtures, I put on the robe, stick my clothes in the bag, and hurry back to the 'drawing' room. Always wondered what 'drawing room' meant.

Inside, seven people choke the room with bodies and equipment, the solitary woman in an armchair with sketchbook in her lap. Six men of various ages and dress are fussing with drawing boards and arranging easels—way too close to the center of the room where I'll be posing naked. *What if they pack up and leave when I take off the robe? Why are my knees shaking? Why can't I breathe?*

A spotlight shines on the simple tableau. A wooden chair with a rounded back stands on a box the size and height of a small dining table. Two sofa pillows have been tossed on the floor beside the box. William gives the signal and I step onto the stage, sit and un-belt the robe, shrugging my shoulders to let it fall away.

"That's great, can you hold that?" William asks.

I nod, drawing a deep breath, acutely aware of the collective gaze focused on my body, expecting a tingle of excitement, but I feel nothing. The case of nerves quickly passes. My brain, however, is overactive, measuring my intake of air, my exhalation. *How much does my chest rise and fall of with each breath? Do I dare look away from the spot on the window across the room? Even for a second?* No. It will take all my attention to keep from slumping in the chair. *Am I smiling?* Scribbling sounds accompany classical piano on the stereo, along with an occasional tearing of paper. The drama is over, and the anticipation gone with it. Nothing could be more ordinary than this. There are only eight of them, after all.

Five minutes pass, and goose bumps have risen on my skin.

"Okay, next pose," William says. "Is it warm enough, Mariah?"

Is he psychic or what? "I'm a little cold." I tell him, the sound of my voice surprising me amid the stillness of the room.

Without thinking about it, I stand and drape the robe over one arm, steady myself and distribute weight onto both legs. The scribbling and tearing of paper continues. William fiddles with an extension cord and places a small electric heater at my feet. Then someone jams another eight-track tape into the stereo and Van Morrison cuts loose with *Midnight Special*.

As the warmth spreads up my legs, I remember standing nude by a campfire, taking a sponge bath in Kentucky where we'd parked the Sub on the way to New Orleans. The smell of pine. Snow all around, but the fire compensates. Time stops. Poses lengthen. I drift back to December of 1968 and my graduation from Illinois State. Hard to believe that was just a couple of months ago.

> A black torrent of mortarboards spills out the
> gymnasium door and flows down the steps, propelling
> me along in a wave of exultation. Cheers go up all
> around and square hats fly.
> Across the street protesters chant, "Hell no, we won't
> go!"
> On the curb, flames erupt from a cardboard box. Two
> dozen young men have formed a line. I recognize
> some of them from draft counseling sessions I've lead.
> Most of them are holding small cardboard signs that
> say, "Draft Card," since their actual cards haven't
> been issued yet. Only three have real cards. It takes
> guts to do this in public—to go against the flag-
> waving hawks of war.
> One by one the guys advance, and the cards flutter into
> the fire while the group continues chanting. On
> impulse, waving my rolled-up diploma like a baton, I
> join the end of the line. When my turn comes, not
> having a draft card to burn, I march up and toss my
> newly-presented diploma into the fire, surprising
> myself, feeling truly autonomous maybe for the first
> time in my life. A cheer goes up from the guys and
> relief washes over me. Sparks rise with the smoke. I
> relax, buoyant and free, rising with those points of
> light.

The timer bell is going off and people have started moving around, so I wrap myself in the robe and take a break, still thinking about that pivotal day when I assumed the name Mariah. Mary Ellen Justice would never have burned her college diploma, especially after enduring four years of college to get it. *But with Mariah, who knows where the wind might blow?*

I'm careful not to bang against the splayed easels as I weave around the slalom course of the room. Each drawing is surprisingly different, each artist having rendered my form in a unique way— some black on white, some black on gray, some heavy and dark, some thin and delicate. I'm studying one effort in particular that was done in a beautiful reddish-brown tone and wondering what produced it.

"*Conte* crayon," the artist volunteers, reading my thoughts. He looks me over like the robe isn't there, and a ripple of excitement lights up my body from knees to chest. I half expect him to come on to me, a dirty old man who likes to ogle young women. But his mind is focused on art. "I don't really *do* color," he says, "but I like this tone much better than black and white."

The effect is pleasing. From clearly drawn lines to soft blended passages, using a variety of strokes, he's imparted me with a dignity and grace I didn't know I had. Amazing to see what I look like through his eyes. *Not too bad. . .* It dawns on me that I really do like doing this. It feels like a privilege and an honor, being admitted into this exclusive inner circle of life drawing devotees.

"Next pose," William announces, and I'm back on the model stand, finding a new position and speculating whether all memories are seen in monochrome, like drawings with a *conte* crayon. Before long, I'm on the road again . . . re-playing the schoolbus trip from Illinois to New Orleans in my mind.

> Camped with the others in western Kentucky, the cold is bitter, and I sit for a long time beside our little pot-bellied stove, then feed the fire before crawling back to bed . . .
> In a dream, I'm lying in a den surrounded by puppies. They're warm and moist. I'm trying to count them but keep starting over. One of them is trying to find my nipple. It tickles and I'm laughing.

"Ding."
Papers shuffle and chairs scrape. People are putting things away.

"Thanks, Mariah." William hands me a wad of bills, "We don't meet next week because of Fat Tuesday, but I hope you can model for us again. You were great."

"Thank you, I'd like to, but I don't know how long I'll be in town."

I dress quickly in the bathroom then join the caravan of boards, bags and recollections that accompany the artists down the stairs.

———

Outside, I find Blaine leaning against the wall.

"How'd it go?" He asks.

"Fine, I slept, mostly."

"Bunch of guys?"

"One woman."

"I don't think I could stand looking at you naked for hours without, um, you know."

"Yes, I *do* know." He gets a poke in the ribs for what he's thinking. It's weird, sometimes I think guys fall in love with their own erections instead of the person who turns them on.

Nine o'clock at night on Magazine street marks a boundary between the marginal world and the patently criminal one. Doorways reveal lit cigarettes, huddled figures and low voices. Dogs growl and cats holler. Vermin scurry. Their day has just begun, and the ambience here has turned sinister. A scattering of firecrackers perforates the night a block away, and Blaine shoves me against a wall, then looks both ways down the street.

"What the hell?" I'm struggling against his arm, uncomprehending.

"Gunshots. One block over," he points down a side street. "That way."

"Gunshots?"

"Small caliber. Stay put right here for a minute."

"Wait!" I yell, but he's already running to the corner, plastering himself against the building. I follow and take cover behind him. He reaches back and wraps my arm with that big hand of his while he peeks around the corner for a count of two. I wonder who fired the shots, and why? *A robbery?*

He shakes his head. "I don't see 'em."

"Don't give me orders, Blaine."

He looks at me like I'm a stranger. "I was trained to respond, give orders. It saves lives."

He's sort of like a blunt instrument. I *do* feel safe with him, and I'm glad Blaine's here, solid and strong, protecting me from danger in the dark. At the same time, I feel oddly aligned with the nefarious activities of this place—slightly criminal—especially after modeling in the nude. With danger near, my vision is sharp, and my nerves tingle with anticipation. There is warmth in my nether regions.

Running footsteps approach, a panting breath, then a man bursts around the corner. I stick my leg out, tripping the runner, and a handgun clatters into the street. Blaine jumps on the guy and I go for the pistol, slip off the safety and take aim.

It's a kid, maybe twelve. He struggles, says, "Gimmee back the gun," trying to look mean.

I shake my head and smell the barrel of the little automatic, a .22 maybe, the hole just bigger than a BB. I shrug, "I don't think it's been fired."

Blaine drags the kid upright, says, "Get lost," and gives him a shove. The kid hesitates for a second, then he gets lost, but I'm thinking he was lost already, before I tripped him. Blaine takes the gun out of my hand and drops it down a storm drain in the street.

Amazed at my own calmness in the heat of action, but enjoying the physical arousal, I resume the inner dialogue about nudity and art. Am I an exhibitionist? A pervert, catering to perverts? Is being an artist's model gratuitous, like striptease? *Or is modeling in the nude a noble profession that makes an invaluable contribution to civilization? If so, then why? What's the difference?* And where do I get off on the threat of violence?

I get no answers to my questions as we pass a doobie and walk the dark stretch of sidewalk, but we hear no more gunshots, either. I'm at ease, but Blaine is disturbed by the incident with the kid.

"Why'd you do that?" he inquires. "Trip the guy."

"I don't know. Just reflex, I guess. Saw him coming, next thing, he's on the ground."

"You'd make a good free safety," Blaine nods, grinning with appreciation.

"I like that. Free safety. A basketball star."

"Football."

"Whatever. I accept the position." Something like pride or power surges through me and I *am* the wind, not something blown around *by* it. I'm thinking I need to work on my two meager jiu-jitsu moves, to perfect them before trying to put them into practice. But then, I wonder how effective they'd be against someone with a gun. With the dangers in this neighborhood, I feel more naked than I did in that drawing room. "Do you ever carry a gun?" I ask.

Blaine shakes his head. "I've gotten out of the habit. Guns are made for killing, and I've done enough." His stare goes right through me, as though I'm transparent—as though he's struggling to put the war behind him. A pain that's not physical has hold of him, and for a second he seems to be free-falling through space. Then, like a cat, he flips and lands on his feet, coming back from that faraway place to finish his thought. "Besides, I can defend myself with taekwondo."

Maybe Blaine *is a cat. I wonder if he has multiple lives.* My dad taught me to shoot a rifle and a pistol, so I'm comfortable with firearms. Just never thought about needing one before. I can see how a person who lived here all the time might want to keep a weapon.

"You know," I voice my realization, "that kid's without protection now."

"Yeah, we didn't do him any favors, taking his gun away."

I'm sending the kid a prayer, allowing the universal life force to flow into me and directing it through the void to connect with him, like a prayer. It's something my sensei taught me, called *Reiki.* The practice is intense, but pleasant, essentially allowing my body to be a conduit for healing. I keep up the transmission of energy until the stillness comes, signaling that all is as it should be. It's all I know to do.

The dim neon sign in front of us just says, "Bar."

"You want to get a drink?" Blaine asks. "I could use one."

It's no brighter inside the shotgun establishment than it is on the sidewalk. A long bar on the right with a row of gleaming half-filled liquor bottles that seem to be the source of light for the entire place. On the left, a row of tables for two along the wall, a narrow aisle between tables and bar stools. Two customers at the far end and one starched and side-burned barkeep are the only inhabitants. The keep slides over with a towel neatly folded and draped over his hands.

"What'll it be?"

"Something fizzy," I grin. "No alcohol." I'm kind of a lightweight when it come to drinking.

Bartender suppresses a smile, but the mirror beside me bounces a twinkle into his eye. He nods and turns his shoulder a fraction. "And you sir?"

"Jim Beam on the rocks, with a splash."

Our host bows and spins away. Blaine has found a votive candle on the chair rail and sets it alight on the table. He turns to me, "It *was* a nice move back there, tripping that guy and getting his gun."

"I had a good judo instructor."

"You handled him all by yourself. I'm impressed."

"Blaine." I drape a hand on his shoulder and look him in the eye, waiting for his focus. "I like it when you protect me, but just for the record, I don't follow orders."

"Yeah, I understand," he says, and a shadow of anguish passed over his brow. "I quit following orders when I realized they were immoral."

"You didn't re-up."

A deep sigh escapes him. "By that time my hitch was almost up. They wanted me to be a flight instructor, but I said no. Instead I went to D.C., got decorated by Lyndon Johnson and ended up invited to the White House for a private dinner. That was early in '68—last year."

"You met with the president? Just the two of you?"

Blaine nods, "He wanted someone outside the Washington crowd that he could talk frankly with. I think I symbolized all his 'boys' over there. He treated me like an adopted son."

Our side-whiskered host has returned bearing a whiskey glass for Blaine and an ice cream soda for me, with a cherry on top.

I'm grinning, "I didn't know you could get one of these in a bar."

"Full service, ma'am. We aim to please." He couldn't keep hiding his hands while serving the drinks, so even in the candlelight I could see the scars where his skin had been badly burned. A wave of compassion flooded me. Instantly I sent a thread of healing energy to those hands, watching them glow white momentarily before he covered them with the towel. I wondered if he was one of Lyndon Johnson's 'boys,' then took a sip of heaven as he glided away.

I turned to Blaine. "What did you and LBJ talk about?"

"Killing, mostly."

"Killing?"

"Yeah. He carried a ton of guilt. Hundreds of people were being killed daily in Vietnam and Cambodia. He believed he was personally responsible."

"He *was* responsible, wasn't he?"

"He was, partly. We should have never been in Vietnam, though. Wouldn't have been, except all the liberals were scared shitless that they'd be looked on as weak by the Republicans. It's complicated, though. Johnson inherited a tough situation. He didn't know who to trust. When I met him, he'd already decided not to run for president in '68. He was losing his health and his leverage in Congress. Hated the war. We met a couple of times last year before Bobby Kennedy was shot, then again in the fall. Johnson was working out a treaty with the Chinese government to end the war. Had the talks all arranged. I told him what I thought."

"What did you say?"

"I told him what I'd seen of the war from the air. Then I told him to end it at all costs. He tried, but Nixon fucked him over."

The memory of dead bodies shown on television brings me a moment of nausea. Blaine has gone quiet. He catches the bartender's eye and holds up his glass.

"I guess you don't see much of the war from an airplane," I say, measuring out my breath.

"You'd be surprised," Blaine stares into the candle flame. "I flew dozens of missions. We shot up plenty of villages. All for no reason."

"That must be hard on your conscience." I move closer and put my hand over his.

"It is. But what's really hard is accepting that my country betrayed me, my own government. And I'm powerless to do anything about it."

I'm squeezing Blaine's hand, but he doesn't seem to notice, so I leave most of my ice cream soda untouched and head for the restroom. I became a draft counselor my senior year at the university, serving the guys whose numbers might be coming up, helping them resist, keeping current with the anti-war effort. Last year was a bad year all around, with the assassinations of Dr. King and then Bobby Kennedy. I went to the Democratic Convention anyway, to support Eugene McCarthy. Stood in Lincoln Park, yelled myself hoarse, marched with the marchers, got tear-gassed and grazed with a billy club. Then I bailed out before the mob went to Grant Park for further abuse.

I brought back a souvenir scar on my head to show for it all—and a bad case of disillusionment. To top it all off, the damn Democrats nominated that twit Hubert Humphrey. I'd have given a kidney for Bobby Kennedy, but it was too late.

When I slip back into the booth, Blaine has ordered a third whiskey. I take a glass of ice water. Our friendly bartender has brought the jukebox to life, and Ray Charles is crooning *Somewhere Over the Rainbow*. There's a sloppy grin on my date's face, and for some reason, I start pouring out my guts.

"Blaine, the bad guys have stolen our country and stacked the deck against us. The only viable option is to run for the hills, find a safe place to build a cabin, grow our own food and live peacefully. I want a garden so bad I can taste it, but I'm afraid the perfect place is only a mirage, hovering on some distant horizon."

"I know, Mariah," he sighs. "I need to get away from people, forget about 'Nam, raise some horses, go fishing. I hate what I'm doing. Only reason I'm smuggling dope is to pay off the farm in Arkansas. It's not a mirage, I guarantee. Green hills, waterfalls. Lots of deer and wild turkey. I'd like for you to see the place after I finish this deal."

"It sounds nice," I reply lamely, aware that we may actually want the same thing. The smuggling concerns me, but then again, maybe it's no big deal. I've never seen Arkansas. Maybe Blaine and I belong together, sharing a dream. But I wonder if that's an adequate basis for a long-term relationship. *What about the earth-shaking part?* There's no telling where this odyssey will lead, but I have a new part in it now that I've become an official free safety.

Inside Blaine's apartment I find flowers on the table—pungent white daisy mums. A bottle of champagne in a bucket of melting ice, the radio on. He pops the cork and brings me a glass and a kiss.

Seduced already, I slip away to the bathroom and freshen up, grab a handful of condoms. Then I'm back, admiring his well-developed chest and obvious desire for me, responding to his explorations, losing clothing and liking the pure human contact a lot. Needing it. Almost a year has gone by since boyfriend Don headed for grad school in Berkeley. I need touching, skin-to-skin, as much as I need food and water.

I'm prepared for New Year's Eve and the Fourth of July all in one, expecting fireworks, ravishment, even. But Blaine is holding back for some reason. It takes him a week to get the rubber on.

"Let's take it slow," he says. "I want to make this last."

But I urge him on, wanting a connection, picking up the pace. For a minute I feel human again, performing a rite of affirmation, taking my due pleasure. Then he withdraws, wants to kiss and fondle. It feels like we're brother and sister instead of lovers, side-to-side rather than face-to-face, and I'm beginning to lose interest. So I take control, take him in again and move on him, seeking the sweet spot. Two seconds later he's filled up the condom, ending with a moan and a shudder. In a minute or two, he's gone to sleep.

Considering climax and arousal, I'm puzzling on which is more important. Climax is great, when it comes, *excuse me*, leaving you spent. You might as well be dead, in fact. Arousal is better—full engagement, heightened sense of being alive, the feeling that what you're up to really *matters*, more than anything. The debate goes back and forth, but finally I make my peace with arousal. The hell with fireworks. *I tried.*

———————

I really don't like crowds, I've found. Working the lunch rush at Joe's is all the exposure to people I can stand, so I'm content to stroll the city alone or with Blaine, check in at the Submarine every day or two, admire the sights. Now that Fat Tuesday has come and gone and the big party's over, it's turned cold in New Orleans. People are wearing pea coats and wooly hats like they're afraid of freezing to death. *They would die in Illinois.*

One morning, there's a knock on Blaine's door about eight o'clock, waking me up. I stick my head between door and jamb, trying to focus. It's Nan, my buddy from the school-bus. Through bleary eyes I see she's upset.

"What's up?" I ask.

"Someone tried to break into the Submarine during the night."

"No."

"Phil showed his double-barreled shotgun and scared the guy off, but everyone is spooked. John and Phil decided it's time to leave town, and I agree. Bear is okay with it."

"Do I get a vote?"

"Sorry, Mariah. They're dead set on leaving. You coming with?"

"Yes, I mean, of course, I think so, but I need some coffee. Let me wake up, okay?"

"Sure, but we're leaving tomorrow morning."

After cleaning up, I go to Joe's diner and quit, asking for the rest of the day off, so my last day in New Orleans can be spent with Blaine. Later I'll probably remember it as the trolley day. We ride five different routes, talk about life—and plans. He needs money for the farm in Arkansas and I'm committed to my quest for the perfect place. Maybe I should stay with him. *This man has a good heart,* I'm thinking, *and he knows how to eat, and drink, and dance.* But I also want to be useful, to serve the world somehow. I want this lifetime to count for something.

"I'm leaving for Mexico on Saturday," he says. "Come with me?"

"Blaine, I don't think so. But I'll sleep on it."

He drinks a couple of beers, and I toke on a joint. Sex is better this time, since I've lowered my expectations. He's a good man, but this is not true love. We exchange our parents' addresses like people in a fender-bender, with other places to go.

"Let's get together later after Mexico," he says the next morning.

"Sure, maybe so." *Or maybe not.*

———

CHAPTER 4
CLIFF

*You can establish the 'color world' of
an oil painting in different ways. You
can mass the shapes with lots of
opaque paint, then scrape it back off.
You can scrub on a thin coat with an
old brush and dry paint. Or you can
dilute the paint and make a wash—slop
it on and let it run a bit. The idea is to
get a color world going to break the
spell of a blank canvas.*

March

   Colitas is not a disease. It's the Spanish word for 'little tails.' Late
in the decade of the 1960s, these little tails were available to people
all over the country in the form of dried herbaceous material
weighing approximately an ounce and packaged in plastic sandwich
bags. But it was not available in stores. Those who weighed it and
placed it in baggies first removed it from large brown paper bags
weighing approximately one kilogram, called 'kilos.' Most of the
kilos came from south of the border, down Mexico way.

The search for high-quality *colitas* took my brother to Acapulco, by way of commercial airline from Austin to Houston. Then he flew Aeroméxico to the coastal playground of the rich and famous, home of the legendary 'Acapulco Gold.' Blaine had checked into the picturesque Posada la Mar, a yellow stone and red-tile-roofed horseshoe of a building with a view down to the bay.

I remember the place well from my visit a couple of months later, so it's easy to picture the scene where Blaine met his Mexican contact. Bright carmine bougainvillea climbs the walls, dark mission-style furniture crowds the dining room, and low arched doorways threaten to scalp anyone over six feet tall.

Blaine and I had been out of touch for a while, and it would be another while before I saw him again, so the details of his meetings with Ricardo are pieced together from things he told me later. My brother's Bermuda shorts and Hawaiian shirt would have branded him as an American. Two weeks of people-watching on the veranda of the old hotel would have familiarized him with the regular clientele who came for the atmosphere, the coffee, the seafood and tequila. The slender middle-aged Mexican who wore silver-framed glasses, came every afternoon at the same time, but his purpose wasn't clear. He would always take a seat at the same table and unpack his camera bag so the big Pentax was ready for action. Then he would take a notebook and begin to write with a gold ballpoint pen. Same routine each day. The camera remained unused, and Blaine was curious.

One Friday, the lunch crowd lingered later than usual. When the man arrived and found all the tables occupied, he approached Blaine and asked to sit with him.

"Have a seat." Blaine indicated a chair.

"*Gracias*. I see you sit here each day, *señor*," the man said, mixing fluid Spanish and imperfect English.

"Yes."

"*¿Norteamericano?*"

"Yes."

"You don't like much talking."

"Don't get me started."

"Ha, ha. You are comedy."

"And you're a photographer." Blaine indicated the Pentax.

"Reporter. Freelance."

"What do you report about?"

"Oh, this and that." The man pushed his glasses back up his nose. "I write on places, travel."

The Pacífico he'd ordered arrived, and he put a shake of salt and a squeeze of lime in his frosted glass, then added the beer. It filled halfway with foam, then settled a bit. Blaine gave him a curious look.

"The big head makes me drink more slow," he explained, sipping and wiping his mouth with a linen napkin.

"Ah."

"No good working drunk."

"You're working? Now?" Blaine was not convinced.

"I work all the time."

"What's the story?"

"No can tell," the reporter smirked. "I am a secret."

"Nah."

"Yes, really." A spate of vigorous nodding emphasized his assertion.

"Oh, now I get it." Blaine pointed his finger at the man's chest and let his thumb fall. "You're a reporter disguised as a journalist."

"Correct." The reporter slapped two hands on his chest and laughed. "Now you know me."

Blaine downed a third of his beer and reached across the table.

"I'm Blaine."

"Ricardo Silva. *Mucho gusto*."

They shook hands. Ricardo fired up an unfiltered *Delicado*, leaned back in his chair and stretched, the smirk still on his face. He had adequate command of English vocabulary, but his tongue wrapped awkwardly around some of the English sounds. He pronounced Blaine with two syllables: Bay-leen.

Ricardo produced a travel magazine from the camera case and opened it on the table, turning it around so Blaine could read.

"You see, *don Belín*, people see us reading the magazine. Is necessary, no? I show you the pictures. People think this is nothing serious."

"Ricardo, there are words in between your words. Things you haven't spoken." Blaine scanned the pictures with the magazine article, going along with the ruse, putting up an innocent front for prying eyes. Then he asked, "So what *are* you serious about?"

"I am serious . . . about women." Ricardo leaned forward, eyebrows pulled close together and going up and down. Then he winked and tipped his head toward a nearby table. The hotel's café, though off the beaten path, had its share of beautiful people, and two of them were sitting at a nearby table, intimately engaged in a conversation of their own.

Both men laughed. They watched the women for a minute, quietly with unabashed enjoyment, conjoined in the fellowship of a favorite sport. Then Ricardo pointed at the magazine in front of him. "I write *artículos* for *el turismo* and *la agricultura*."

"You wrote this article on agave production?"

"Yes, I am serious about plants, also . . . and about gold. Keep the magazine, *don Belín*. Is for you."

"Thank you, Ricardo. I, too am serious about plants. I'd like to find some gold ones."

Ricardo reached into the pocket of his slacks, pulled out a wallet and extracted some pesos to lay on the table. He packed up the Pentax and touched a forefinger to the top of his forehead in salute. He glanced at the pesos on the table then nodded at Blaine, said, *"Señor,"* and left.

Under the bills on the table was the corner of a white piece of paper that Ricardo must have prepared before sitting down. *Premeditated*, Blaine thought. He slipped it out and read—directions and a time. Two days later, at sunset.

Blaine began walking at noon two days later. Around his waist, a small pack held a camera, a hunting knife and a water bottle. He jogged up the beach for an hour, ghosted through the back door of a hotel, and onto the street where he caught a taxi to the station.

His bus went three hours west and north up the new coastal highway and stopped in late afternoon where whitewashed walls glowed orange against the purpling sky—Zihuatanejo. As he followed the memorized map through the little town to the two-story stone house, thoughts about the imminent meeting with his counterpart went through his head, *Is he trustworthy? Can he provide a quality product? And logistics—is there an empty place to land the Cessna around here? What about security?* Blaine had made a few assumptions.

"*Don Belín!*" the voice called from the upstairs balcony. Ricardo leaned over the railing and pointed to the door downstairs. "The door is open." Ricardo met Blaine at the bottom of the stairs with an outstretched hand, "Welcome to the house of my uncle Víctor."

"I took care not to be followed," Blaine assured him.

"Good, good." He tapped his head. "A man of intelligence."

A small fire crackled in the fireplace, where a cast iron pot emitted the aroma of chiles, cumin and garlic. Ricardo was dressed for relaxation in faded Levis and a black 'Light My Fire' t-shirt with Jim Morrison's picture on the front. Blaine was comfortable in his tourist garb, polo shirt and Bermuda shorts, leather belt and loafers. To him it was just another kind of uniform, something that came with the job.

"You hungry, my friend?" Ricardo asked.

"Yes, starving."

"I prepare a simple meal. We eat, then talk." Ricardo warmed tortillas over the fire on a rounded piece of blackened steel. Blaine took a chair at the table and Ricardo set out bowls and spoons. "Sorry, the tortillas is not fresh."

"They're perfect. Thank you." The *carne guisada* was perfect also, a thick stew of meat and potatoes swimming in dark gravy, seasoned *al Mexicano*. Between bites, Blaine noticed more travel magazines on the table, written in Spanish, entitled *Mexico Desconocido*.

"More of your articles, Ricardo?"

"Yes, I write on *el gobierno's* plan for building a new city, Ixtapa, close to Zihuatanejo." Ricardo found the article he wanted and indicated a page of diagrams. "Is the next destination for the rich peoples."

When they finished eating, Ricardo set a plate of quartered limes on the table. "You like Mezcal?" he asked, producing a bottle and pointing at the worm in the bottom.

"Why not?" Blaine bit a slice of lime and swigged the Mezcal while Ricardo launched into his story.

"I go to *la Universidad Normal*. Start writing for the newspaper. Reporting. First story I write is the railroad strike in 1959. Soon I go to Cuba, write the war for independence. I join the rebels, fight against Batista. The CIA wants Batista gone, sends weapons to the rebels. When Castro gets power, the rebels divide." Ricardo had his hands in prayer mode, then moved them apart. "The CIA sends airplanes with guns for the rebels fighting Castro, but Castro catches the parachutes, gets the guns."

"Fucking CIA," Blaine nodded, knowingly.

"Fucking CIA, is right. The government of *los Estados Unidos* is bad for Cuba." Ricardo took a shot and wiped his mouth with the back of his hand. A dark cloud settled on his brow.

Blaine stared at the bottle of agave spirit. "My government screwed *me,* big time."

"My government screwed me too, *don Belín*." Ricardo's eyelids drooped. With solidarity established between screw-ees, more of the *400 Conejos* mescal disappeared and Ricarco continued, "Last year in el D.F., Mexico City, before the Olympics, I prepare a story. On 2 October, a half-million peoples come to the Zocalo, bring signs— 'Peoples Unite,' and 'Mexico, Freedom.' The army shoots on them, kills many, wounds hundreds. Is a massacre. . . I know a dead woman." He closed his eyes, indulging a memory. "After the massacre, they show her body, half naked on the street. Her breasts is beautiful, even in death, amigo.

"I take the pictures. I write the article on the part of the demonstrators, but *el gobierno* stops the newspaper publishing the article. 'Is too soon before the Olympic Games,' they say. Too much money to lose." Ricardo's eyes darkened, and his mouth went tight. He tapped his chest. "*El gobierno* puts me in prison with a thousand people. *Mi amiga*, Elena, comes in the prison, dressing like a poor old woman, writing a story of the massacre. We talk. I tell her what happens. She writes it, but she don't publish because of Echeverría."

Ricardo took his glasses off and polished the lens with a small square of cloth from his pocket. "I am free after two months in *cárcel*. Echeverría orders me 'don't write no words of 2 October.' Is why now I write articles of travel. 'Come to the paradise of Acapulco, where the beautiful peoples from Hollywood meet the aristocrats from *Europa*.' Is all sunlight and smiles, no?"

"But now, all this is forgotten, right? The massacre?"

The candle shone orange on one lens of Ricardo's spectacles, casting a highlight and his voice took on an edge of passion. "Yes, peoples forget, but Echeverría, *el gobierno's* angel of death, never forgets." He slammed his palm on the table, made a rude gesture and looked at Blaine, his eyes narrowed to slits. "Now, *los halcónes* follow me."

"What's a *halcón*?" Blaine asked.

"Translates, 'the hawk.' Echeverría hires *los halcones* to make enemies disappear in the ocean." Ricardo hung his head. "You, my friend, have power. I, Ricardo Silva, have no power. Because I am the enemy of *el gobierno*, and I can't swim, I prefer going to the North for a time. California needs good reporters, no?"

"You're serious?" Blaine asked. "You mean you want to emigrate to the U.S.?"

"Yes, but I need the cash money. I like to make a little business first—just one time. Go in, go out. Like that." Ricardo snapped his fingers. "You see, is nothing for me here in Mexico. My family in San Miguel de Allende is only my grandmother and my brother, Sergio. I hate my brother. Before I go to *la universidad*, I have a *novia*, Anna. Sergio steals her and fucks her, then throws her away, like is nothing. She visits *la bruja* for the poison and takes her life. Anna is dead since many years. My brother kills her, is why I hate him, *don Belín*. Sergio must die."

Both men observed a moment of silence.

"What about this business you mentioned?" Blaine asked.

Ricardo pulled three eight-inch long 'tails' out of a grocery bag and they inspected the Gold—magnificent clusters of tiny flowers with immature seeds. The aroma was heady. The color, deep green-gold with red-orange highlights. Miniscule transparent droplets of dried resin sparkled in the light of the single bulb in the ceiling. Ricardo called the product, *"mota."* Thunder echoed outside while they sampled it. No question it was good. No question at all. Maybe too good.

———

Sunlight ignited the tops of the coconut palms down the dusty Zihua street while a local rooster announced the arrival of new possibilities. Blaine stumbled out the back door into the cool air of morning, relieved himself against the shaded garden wall and re-arranged the money belt that rode low inside his pants. He liked to carry his stake with him, always said it was safer that way. I don't know how he thought that. It seemed kind of dangerous to me, having all that dough on him, but at least it was handy if he needed it.

From the chimney, a curl of blue smoke materialized and hung motionless above the red tile roof. Garden soil, damp from the previous evening's rain, clung to Blaine's bare feet and accompanied him inside the house. His companion squatted in front of the fireplace, tending a blackened pot, and the sharp smell of burning juniper wood soon gave way to the aroma of brewed coffee. A third cup of it finally penetrated the fuzz in Blaine's head.

Ricardo sipped his coffee. "*Don Belín*, we bring the grower a gift for the favor to see the field. Is a custom. You carry cash?"

"I think I have some on me," Blaine grinned.

"One thousand American dollars is correct for the gift."

"I have a little over $500," he lied.

"Is good fortune. I have the same here." Ricardo handed the wad of pesos to Blaine. "You give it all to Víctor. We go today."

A brisk uphill hike took them toward the field of gold. After several kilometers of jeep trail, a cluster of wattle houses appeared, the low roofs thatched with palm leaves. A wisp of woodsmoke trailed up into the trees. *Truly a third world place*, Blaine thought. *Maybe fourth world.* When they passed the last house in the village, Blaine looked back to see a tall man watching them from the doorway. He was holding a rifle. The man lifted it, pointed the barrel at them and fired off two quick shots.

"Holy shit!" Blaine said, from his position on the ground beside the trail. "What the hell, Ricardo?" He wished right then for the .45 caliber automatic he'd brought back from 'Nam, The one he'd left in Texas.

"Don't worry, amigo. The man is *securidad*—is with us. He is playing with you. Don't worry." Ricardo was standing beside a papaya tree, indicating two holes in one of the green fruits. "Shoots good, no? Kills the Papaya."

"He's a son of a bitch." Blaine spat into the dirt.

"Yes. But the man also is Víctor's guard, with the radio. Has one finger on the radio and one on the trigger, no?"

"Ha, ha, Ricardo." Blaine stood and dusted himself off, catching the eye of the shooter. The man was doubled over, cracking up laughing at him.

"Now Víctor knows we come." Ricardo patted Blaine on the shoulder. "Two shots together means is okay. Friends is coming."

They passed through rows of coconut trees on both sides of them before entering another stretch of forest. Ricardo whistled a signal when they came to a fence where barbwire stretched in horizontal stripes between the trees. At intervals, sheep or goat skulls dangled from the fence, some old, some with hair still attached. A minute later a guard appeared carrying an M14. He unhooked the gate and motioned them through.

"Quite a fence." Blaine pointed at one of the goat heads. "Is this some kind of voodoo fetish?"

Ricardo laughed, "In a way, yes, but this *vodoun* is not for humans. You see, the goat is always hungry, and *persistente*. Fresh blood from his family makes the goat fear for his life."

The old farmer wore cotton peasant pants, an olive-green T-shirt and sneakers. His hatless head was thick with wavy charcoal-gray hair brushed away from his face. His brows were knit together over deep brown eyes. Long wrinkle lines were etched into the weathered cheeks alongside his nose. His underbite thrust his lower lip forward, giving him an ambiguous expression, part bewildered, part pissed off.

"I am Víctor," he scowled, holding out one limp hand. A polished machete dangled from the other.

"*Mucho gusto*, I'm Blaine."

They shook, and the tour began. Blaine understood about the goat heads on the fence. But forget the goats, he feared for his own life after the rifle shots. More precautions would be in order before proceeding with a deal.

"You see the plants grow close to the ground?" Víctor nodded at the healthy looking, well-branched yellow-green cannabis. Interspersed in the field were banana trees maybe ten feet high. "The banana trees cover the *mota.*"

"Camouflage," Ricardo added. "From the air you see only banana trees."

The plants might have been roadside weeds for all the attention they commanded. They were low and bushy, branched and spreading, with only the first signs of blossoming, and the heady aroma of mature marijuana was missing.

"Now I know why we call it 'weed,'" Blaine said.

Víctor reached down and palpated a frond that curled up toward the light. "I cut the plants to make branches. Stop the flowers so the plants want to make many buds." Víctor's menacing face lit up briefly. "Many *colitas.*"

"How big, these *colitas?*"

Ricardo stepped up and held his palms about three inches apart, like he was describing a fish he'd caught. "This big."

"The one we smoked was seven or eight inches long," Blaine spread his hands, indicating the larger size.

"Later, amigo. Another month," Ricardo promised. "The next cutting."

"Víctor, do you have trouble with Federales here?" Blaine asked, to check if Víctor's story was the same as Ricardo's. "Someone took a pot-shot at me on the hillside."

Víctor cleared his throat to answer, but Ricardo interrupted, "The shooter works for us. Is crazy a little, because last year someone steals the man's *mota* crop and makes the son disappear. The man shoots now at everybody."

Víctor cut his eyes toward his great nephew and his face turned hostile. As he walked on, Víctor took great swipes at the foliage of encroaching trees, deftly lopping whole branches with the big knife. "Many sons disappear, mister." He spat, "Echeverría *y los halcones* is murderers. Have no honor. Make no justice."

There was no sampling of product. Blaine and Ricardo's visit with Víctor was all business. The weed they'd smoked the night before was the previous year's crop, which had all been sold. The upshot was, they'd have to wait for the spring harvest in mid-May.

After touring the plot, the three men gathered in a pole shed with banana leaf thatching and opened warm bottles of *Pacífico*. Blaine and Ricardo settled on a price with no difficulty, without input from

Víctor. They discussed landing on a dirt road up the coast and Blaine asked how he could be sure the deal wasn't a scam.

Ricardo answered, "Because I fly with you to *los Estados Unidos* as a hostage, *don Belín.*" And Blaine passed a stack of dollars and pesos to Víctor, sealing the deal. The rest of the money would be paid later, when the kilos were loaded into Blaine's airplane.

Víctor nodded at Blaine and scowled. "The film, amigo, you leave here with me."

Blaine looked at Ricardo.

"Your camera. Give him the film."

"I didn't use it."

"No matter. Is the principle. The rule is for protecting the fields. No film is leaving here. *Securidad.*"

Blaine emptied his camera and tossed the film to Víctor. The man nodded and turned away. On the walk back down the hill, Blaine asked if Víctor could be trusted to deliver the product. Ricardo confided, "Víctor always needs money for the daughter. She goes to the best doctors. Paralyze, you know. Polio. Many years, I give the old man money. To me Víctor owes the value of all his property."

The next morning after sealing his deal, Blaine said goodbye to Ricardo at Víctor's house in Zihua and took one of the canoe shuttles to *Las Gatas* beach where the scuba diver lived—the guy who'd worked for Jacques Cousteau. Maybe Blaine was suspicious about where Ricardo got money to give Víctor. Maybe not, I never knew. I did have Ricardo figured for a smooth operator, but I didn't know then just how smooth he was.

In the next six weeks, before he returned to Texas for his airplane, Blaine would eat fish, learn to scuba dive, and get covered with freckles. He would have plenty of time to think about oysters and jazz and sending a letter to the girl he'd met in New Orleans. But when he told me the story later, he never mentioned he'd been slipping away from time to time to do research on another project.

———

CHAPTER 5
MARIAH

*Lyrical art is about beauty. It's
pleasant. It's about a moment, about
visual space, about how a picture plane
is filled. By contrast, narrative art
presents some kind of intellectual
challenge. There is content that entails
a 'before' and 'after.' The element of
time is involved.*

March

After leaving New Orleans, the bus heads west through miles and
miles of saltwater marshes and endless gumbo. Eating the rich broth
feels like partaking of the marsh itself, part land and part water,
prompting an urge to take root and merge with the primordial ooze.
But the pulse of the gulf itself, more nourishing even than gumbo, is
what resonates.

At the Galveston ship channel, Bear fearlessly maneuvers the
Submarine onto the ferry and the rest of us spill out on deck for the
ride. The boat's diesel motor throbs, the water glares and sea gulls
circle. Freighters blow horns in the distance. Pelicans on pilings
guard the ship channel, and I inhale salt-fishy air, feeling profoundly
satisfied.

On the west side of Galveston, a campground has beach parking, restrooms and showers. As soon as we stop, I'm out of the Sub and at the shore, running barefoot in sand still damp from a recent rain. The surf is choppy with the tide coming in, and gray water stretches to the horizon. Waves break and swish, then quietly recede, challenging me to keep my clam-diggers dry.

Just before sunset, the clouds part and golden sunlight settles onto the beach in broad rays. I follow the sparkle of shells, where water meets sand, until the amber sky turns orange, then magenta, and then deep violet.

The guys went grocery shopping and brought back beer and raw shrimp fresh off the boat—nothing else. I'm pissed they didn't think of side dishes, but so hungry it doesn't matter. We boil gulf shrimp in beer and eat it warm. Never tasted anything better. Sitting here in a folding chair, letting my thoughts drift back and forth with the waves, I sense the timelessness that attends a great body of water. The full moon presides over a calm sea and goes out of focus, becoming many moons stretching to infinity.

Of all the possible me's that were rendered by those artists in New Orleans, which will I become? The dignified physical therapist that uses her training to heal? The passionate warrior who goes to battle, fixing the world? Or the cautious one searching for a retreat, where harmony and peace prevail? Still pondering that question as the moon's aureole edges toward morning, I stroll to the Sub and creep into bed.

―――――

On the second day, I walk the shoreline and practice judo throws in the sand. A gentle on-shore breeze picks up in the afternoon, then yields to a frigid offshore wind that shakes the Sub all night and keeps me rolling around. The next morning, I wake to a Gulf that's becalmed and warmer. A groggy mosquito shows up on the tablecloth at breakfast time. Dark eagles cruise languidly, eyeing the ground. Dandelions bloom among patches of sand and grass. Scrub-oak limbs dangle among the shaggy palms, broken by some wind of the past. It's a natural and perfectly served-up day.

In the stillness, I catch a whiff of lighter fluid and boys' excitement. They're making a big fire at the next campsite. Laughter, as they take turns squirting the fire and watching the flame leap. Then a cloud of toxic black smoke, and the smell of burning plastic overwhelms me. Disgusting jerks—burning milk jugs of all things. I grab a bucket and march away to the faucet. Fill the bucket with two gallons of water, lug it back to the neighbor's fire, heave once and then, *ho!*

"Hey!" one of the boys yells as steam and smoke envelop everything. "Hey lady, what are you doing!"

Too late. The startled teenagers are everywhere, checking themselves all over, looking for injuries.

"Next time you burn plastic garbage in this campground, I'll bring something stronger than a bucket of water." *I have no idea what.*

I give them the eye, then stomp off to mumblings of "crazy lady," "bitch," and worse. Might have been different if they'd camped downwind . . . *No, probably not.* I hit the beach to walk off my frustration and practice jiu-jitsu forms as I go, dropping, kicking and rolling in the sand. *Dumb kids. . .*

One by one, seven white pelicans stream in for a water-ski landing. I pull off my shoes and socks, roll my jeans above my knees and dance along the water's edge while stiff-legged birds scurry ahead, searching for treasure. The pulse in my belly synchronizes with the pulse of earth and water. The sounds and smells tempt me to stay here forever.

I've been expecting my period to come all week, since it usually precedes the full moon by a day or two, but there's no sign . . . and there *was* that broken rubber. I agonized all through college about birth control while I watched three friends get pregnant and drop out of school. Tried the pill but couldn't stand what it did to my body. Thought about an IUD and decided that would be worse. Finally decided to rely on old-fashioned protection, and now it's failed me.

"I've heard they do abortions in Mexico," Nan advises.

I suppose, if I were smart. I'm thinking the question, but don't answer myself—I can't. The thing is, I don't have a ready-made basis for making a decision on this. No natural law dictates and no organized religion holds me in thrall—or no disorganized religion for that matter. I've nothing to go on besides my gut feeling. Having a child *would* be a reason to stay—somewhere. A purpose. An anchor. Blaine *is* in my thoughts, but only in a vague and peripheral way. The genes are good, the memories are mostly fond and I'm happy to carry his child, but this will be *my* baby. I'm the one with an investment in this.

To be a grandmother someday, center of my own family, with future generations running around—I can almost picture it. But it's hard to picture that scene with Blaine in it for some reason. *What if he really is my soul mate? Have I let him slip away, like Bobbie McGee did in the song?* Nah, I would have known. He's an imperfect man and this is an imperfect beach.

Months from now, I suppose I'll remember the ocean as as idyllic place and forget its discomforts. But when the wind blows here, it carries sand and salt that insinuate themselves into your being in irritating ways. Every crevice and crack receives a fine coating of tiny abrasive particles and the cold bathhouse showers just move them around. There is no way to escape the nagging salty itch, especially when it gets into your head, and there's nothing like an itchy brain.

So, after three days here, we have a consensus. It's time to head for Austin. *Time to start a garden. But where?* It's starting to bother me, wandering around like this, chasing a dream. I'm ready for some order and permanence. The spontaneity that seemed like such a positive thing at the beginning of this trip, almost three months ago, has lost its luster and turned into uncertainty.. New Moon will mark the end of my first month, so I'll be due in November. Right now, I want some answers. *Right now, I want a hot indoor shower and a laundromat.*

CHAPTER 6
CLIFF

*The color world may derive from a
simple observation of natural
phenomena—the earth's hue, its
elements, the weather—or it may be the
result of an artist's intention or
emotion.*

Freedom's a funny thing. You might be free to *do* something, or
you could be free *from* something. There's a difference. My brother's
dope dealing was, in a way, his bid for freedom—and his way of
protesting the war he'd been part of. His way of telling the
government they no longer had any power over him. And, in the
course of the preceeding year, the attitude had rubbed off on me. Of
course, what he and I got involved in was illegal, but we didn't think
of it that way. When you believe the top officials of your government
are criminals, you tend to lose perspective on what constitutes a
crime.

Before I got in trouble with the law and lost my job at the dude ranch, life was good, though ordinary. The high point of my senior year in high school was the basketball season. When that ended in early March, I hit the wall. I was too short to play center for a university team and couldn't dribble well enough to play forward, so my daydream of a sports career was snuffed out. The school counselor said I could do anything I wanted. My mother forbade me to become a lawyer or ballet dancer, and strongly recommended I never, ever, ride a motorcycle. But that still left a world of options, so naturally I decided to become an artist.

The painting sessions had started back in January, on Saturday afternoons, led by Miss Edna Faye, who had been teaching watercolor for at least a hundred years. I joined two crotchety old men, a nice middle-aged lady, and a girl my own age to comprise the class.

"You have the eye of an artist," Miss Edna said, "but you need to get your hand and eye to play on the same team . . . it takes practice."

Then she explained contour drawing. "Like on a map, where a line follows a specific elevation with a contour line, your drawing shows the surface of the subject. Relax and let your pencil travel along the contour at the same speed as your eye. Be patient and breathe. Make regular check-ins. Where is your eye looking? Where is your hand?

"I'm old, but I'm slow," Miss Edna liked to say. She may have been slow, but she played tricks that took us outside our comfort zones. "When you draw, hold the pencil by the eraser end." She demonstrated the technique, flipping the pencil around, held between two fingers. "Let the hand move freely, with a mind of its own."

One Saturday in March, our subject was a vase of flowers from the florist. We always did a simple line drawing before applying paint, but I found it difficult to control the soft-lead pencil while holding it on the wrong end. Almost at random, I let my hand vary the tension and speed of the tool, twirling, leading with my wrist, attending the big shapes, developing flower-heads naively, and feeding on the energy of my subject. The pencil drawing was only an arbitrary pattern, so I relaxed, knowing the paint would later spill into its own destiny, same way I would spill into mine.

But others resisted.

"I can't draw it right," the girl complained.

"It doesn't have to be right." Miss Faye patted her shoulder. "You want to draw economically—simply, not perfectly."

"Why are we drawing, then?" one of the men asked. "I thought this was supposed to be painting class."

"Just a way to get started, hon. You don't have to draw at all."

I worked in pencil on my quarter-sheet of paper until I was satisfied with the flower shapes and the symmetry of the vase. Then I applied color freely, splashing red, yellow and purple onto the paper with abandon, excited by the intensity and color of the paint. The ultimate disappointment came when the painting's brilliant hues—the ones that looked so vibrant when wet—dried and faded to something dull and drab.

"More paint, less water," Edna Faye said.

Undaunted, I thought, *How hard can painting be?*

————————

After class I headed downtown and turned on a street lined with mature post oaks. I parked my old Plymouth at the curb in front of a one-story bungalow where the food co-op was housed. As I walked up to the screen door, *Foggy Mountain Breakdown* played on the stereo, a nice change from constant rock and roll I was used to. Inside, the old house smelled like cinnamon and sage, an unlikely combination, with a hint of incense thrown in.

I spooned some natural peanut butter from their five-gallon bucket into a quart-sized mason jar and licked my fingers. Nothing but roasted peanuts and salt. After selecting my other groceries, I paid and stepped outside, wishing I'd worn a jacket. Sunlight sparkled on a patch of daffodils beside the sidewalk. They nodded, looking uncomfortable in the March breeze.

At my car, I looked back at the house and saw a young woman in faded bell bottoms and patchwork coat hurry to the door. Watching her thick braid bounce, a yearning surged through me and I couldn't help but wonder what she was like.. Her image was gone in a flash, though, and when the door slammed behind her, my imagination must have taken over.

She looks over her shoulder, and taking my hand, leads me down a darkened hallway. Laughing, she throws off her jacket and pulls me to her, long hair everywhere, green eyes challenging. I kiss her lips, face, neck . . . our clothes fall to the floor.

HONK!

I jumped, the car swerved, and I lurched back into the real world, holding a bag of groceries and shivering for no reason. Diving into my car, I got the heater going, and with my attention still half-captured by the lingering fantasy, wrestled with the wheel, then cringed at the sound of metal on metal. The Plymouth had scraped— just barely—against the blue and white bread truck parked in front of me. The old truck already had a door missing. *I couldn't have done much damage*, I thought, and left the scene.

When I stopped for a burger and fries at 'Dirty's, there was long blue scar on my passenger door where I'd scraped that truck. Oh well, the Plymouth was thirteen years old, a chrome-less 1956 model two-door sedan. The paint job had turned to pale green chalk, and the bumpers were beginning to rust. No big deal.

Plenty of people were seated inside the diner with beer and burgers in front of them, escaping the unfriendly March weather. Dirty Martin's joint on Guadalupe was an institution in Austin even though Dirty himself was long gone. My parents had dated in the old two-story frame building and, twenty-some years later, it still had a reputation for the best burgers in town. I hadn't yet developed a taste for beer, so I got a coke float with my basket of food and sat in a window booth, flipping through the latest issue of *the Rag*, featuring a Fabulous Furry Freak Brothers cartoon, an ad for draft counseling, and an invitation to an SDS meeting.

"Grayson!" Someone put a hand on my shoulder, and I turned to face James Conner, my nemesis. Red-faced and loud, always bragging, he had the makings of a successful politician. For two years we had battled daily to see who would become the starting center on our basketball team and I'd won.

"Hey man, have you got something to smoke?" He breathed a cloud of Lone Star in my face and said, "I hear there's some killer weed in town from Michoacán."

I would have disappeared that minute, but my super-powers were not yet fully developed. I played dumb. "Conner, I have no idea what you're talking about."

"I bet you've got a bag on you." He stared, red- eyed. "Come on, let's go outside and smoke a joint."

"You're crazy." I shrank down into my seat and wished myself somewhere else—anywhere but a popular greasy-spoon with everyone watching.

"Hey, man," he slurred and slouched into the seat across from me. "I just want to get high, have a little fun, you know."

I had already gathered my burger and fries into the paper basket liner. "I'm leaving," I said, sliding out of the booth, embarrassed by the exchange. I wanted to run but managed to make a slow steady beeline for the door without dumping French fries on the floor. Dirty's had windows all around, even in the door, and the clientele had their eyes on me as I walked by. Or at least it felt that way.

At the car, I wished I'd grabbed my coke float and some ketchup, too, and wondered who'd heard what Conner said. The idiot. You make the mistake of getting high with a shithead just once, and you suffer for the rest of time. As I waited to enter the stream of traffic on Guadalupe, I looked in the rear-view mirror and saw him hurrying to his car. *Oh boy.* My tires squealed when I made the right-hand turn.

———

CHAPTER 7
MARIAH

*Forget what you know. It's what you
see that's important. Bring fresh eyes
to your work every day. Experiment
with paint. Welcome surprises. Depart
a little from the familiar and you
become aware of your vulnerability.*

At the food co-op in Austin, I've just bought nine dozen turkey
eggs for two cents apiece. *Wonder what turkey eggs taste like?* I also
get brown rice, pinto beans, grain-based coffee substitute and splurge
on a new copy of *The Mother Earth News*. Well, the mind needs
nourishment, too. I'm paying at the check-out counter when a
bearded man with a head full of curly black hair backs through the
door, turns and sets a cardboard box on the hardwood counter.

"Whew!"

"Papa Max!" The check-out guy has lit up like a hundred-watt
bulb. "Where you been? We missed you."

"Been moving hives all month! Finished just in time. Acres of
clover in a four-acre peach orchard. Sunflowers just beginning to
bloom. Much to be done." He pulls a two-pound jar full of dark
amber liquid from the box and holds it up. "The bees outdid
themselves last fall. Wildflower honey—lots of flavor."

Max finally notices me. "Oh, I am sorry." He steps aside. "Always
in the way."

"No, it's fine. I'm not in a hurry."

"Looks like the lady is making a big omelet. No?"

"No," I smile, "Well, maybe. But not this big." I look at the huge box of eggs and think maybe I *am* buying too many—such a bargain, though.

"Would you be in need of honey?"

"If I can afford it."

"Here." He hands me the jar. "First one is free." His laugh is contagious, his voice exotic, honey-like.

"Is it legal?" I ask.

"Ninety-nine per cent." No handshake. No introduction.

"That farm with the peach trees sounds amazing. I'll bet it's beautiful."

"It *is* nice. The older couple who work the orchard are genuine treasures. Hey, would you care to go there?" he asks. "It is only thirty minutes away."

I cut my eyes, give him a once-over, consider whether he's coming on to me. He's nice-looking in a rounded, middle-aged and Middle Eastern kind of way. His embroidered shirt looks like it came from India. There's no collar, and it hangs down past his belly. Soft black pants. Leather sandals. I have a good feeling about this honey-man.

"Sure, when?"

"Right now. I am going to check the hives." He reaches for the now-empty honey crate. "It is the most beautiful place. Very colorful."

"I'll just put this stuff in the bus," I say.

Max opens the door to the wind and I step outside with my bag of eggs, feeling strangely beautiful. The tiny bells I sewed on the bottom of my patchwork jacket make gentle tinkling sounds with every step as I hurry to the Sub where my bus-mates are waiting.

————

We're tooling down the road in the bread truck with Max at the wheel and the passenger door open. Actually, it's missing. It seems the last week in March can be chilly in Central Texas and I'm glad to have the jacket with the patches, the warm socks and work boots. The north wind is blowing up my denim skirt, so I've wrapped the extra fabric tight around my legs and squeezed my knees together.

"My apologies for the door." Max reaches behind his seat and tosses me a wool blanket. "I am waiting for it to fix itself."

Only forty miles per hour in a fifty miles-per-hour zone. I would drive faster, eager as I am to see the farm, but being a mere passenger, I sit with my blanket and my impatience and munch on some crunchy granola I snitched from the food co-op. This Mediterranean-style teddy-bear seated beside me is all round and hairy. He speaks in a deep voice—kind of indirectly—as though he's narrating a script or acting on stage. Friendly enough, but there's also something serious about him.

"Approaching the sunflower house and farm," Max announces. "Noted residence of Cindy and the Lost Boys."

"I thought it was Wendy?"

"No, it is Cindy this time. Very soon all shall be revealed," he says. "Beginning with me. I'm Papa Max."

"I gathered. I'm Mariah."

Max turns beside a blue mailbox with a hand painted flower on it. The lane bisects a field where a few scattered yellow blossoms with dark centers punctuate a mass of green. Spreading shade trees flank a pale-yellow house at the end of the lane. Three guys are sitting on a couch on the front porch, passing a joint. The place looks like an album cover.

Max declines the proffered smoke, but I accept, and from that point on, I'm a buddy. A young woman named Cindy emerges from the house to introduce herself and partake of the front porch ritual, a chunky Labrador at her heels. She's about five-two I'd guess, voluptuous, wearing jeans and a plum colored mohair sweater. Her hair's as black as the Lab's.

I present the bag of a dozen eggs I brought along. "I may be bringing coals to Newcastle, but I came on short notice."

"No, no, these are great. Down, Rascal!" The Lab has his paws on my thighs, looking to lick my face, but he obeys Cindy. "We don't have any chickens," she says. "The guys haven't gotten around to fixing the coop yet." She pokes one of the guys in the ribs, then turns back to me. "Want to look around?"

Max leaves to address his chores, and I'm getting a tour from Cindy while Rascal scouts ahead. I shiver as we walk through a field choked with prickly sunflower plants in early bud. It seems like the plants are shivering, too. I learn that Cindy goes to work in town at a diner three days a week. She's a small town Texas girl with a great sense of humor, the only female living at the farm with Otis, Bruce and Peyton.

"I've slept with all of them," she says, then hastily adds, "Not all together!" We both convulse in laughter. "They are so needy," she continues, "but that's not happening now. I mean, we're all friends, but I'm not really attracted, you know?"

"I know. John and Phil and Bear, my bus-mates, are just friends, too. We made a deal when I signed on with the troupe—no messing around. Blaine's been my only lover since college." I notice Cindy's watching me with eyebrows raised. "Oh sorry, I was thinking out loud. He's this guy I was with in New Orleans."

"Tell me."

I sigh, welcoming the chance to share the story, female to female, remembering the guy on the skateboard with the dog, the fountain, and Blaine's sneakers. "It was around Mardi Gras. We met in the park, and you know, we just connected. He was funny and confident . . . and I'm pregnant."

"I knew it!" Cindy yelps.

"I didn't think it showed."

"It's your skin, girl. You're glowing! With skin like that you're either pregnant, in love, or on acid."

"Well, I *have* been getting a lot of sunshine lately," I admit, and we laugh until my belly hurts. I wonder what my tiny hitchhiker feels. A laugh to her must be like riding bareback on a trotting pony—exciting, but a little scary.

"Do you miss him?" she asks.

"Maybe a little." Putting my finger to the tip of my nose helps me think about that. "He was nice enough. But I felt sort of like the generic female, like he wasn't really into me. Like it wasn't anything personal."

"Bummer, that usually doesn't turn out very well."

"No."

"Must have been hot, though, in the sack."

"He was okay, I guess. But when I think of him, it's all mental. There's absolutely no remnant of physical sensation. He never did last very long."

"Uh, oh."

"Yeah. And a lot of the time he wasn't really *there*. He just drifted off, you know."

"I *know*." Cindy's eyes got huge. "Where do they *go*?"

"It's a mystery, isn't it? I don't think he really knew how to have a relationship. Are all men like that?"

"Yeah," Cindy nods decisively. "Most of the men I've known."

"It's like they need lessons or something."

"Now there's an idea. We could start a school."

"We could! I can just see it now, Miss Cindy's Academy of Love."

We laugh out loud again, enjoying the spontaneity of female companionship, but I sober quickly. "Blaine was on his way to do a dope deal in Mexico."

"Listen, Mariah," she says, "Don't argue. You're staying here with me. I need a friend."

"I do too," I admit, reaching out for a hug and clinching the deal.

———

It's another day and the Sub is rolling again. I'm watching two crows harry a chicken hawk over the fields when the blue mailbox suddenly appears.

"This is it," I scream, catching a glimpse of the sunflower house as we breeze past.

"How about a little warning next time," Nan complains, then makes an expert three-point turn at the next driveway. In no time, we've stopped in front of the house. My companions and I pile out of the Sub and get hugs and thumbs-up handshakes all around. Rascal, the resident Lab, greets me like a long-lost friend, then sits waiting for the treat he has sussed out in my purse.

"Good dog." I produce half a peanut butter sandwich. "Shake."

Rascal shakes and dispatches his reward. Then he offers his other paw.

"Sorry, that's all, Rascal." I give him my best head-scratch and a belly rub, wishing I had my own dog.

He sniffs everyone, then follows Cindy and me to look at the 'garden'—a droopy fence, enclosing a healthy plot of weeds. Not a garden, but rather a place for one. Beneath the weeds, though, a glimpse of rich ebony soil gives hope, and the spongy texture of the ground shows evidence of good tilth. Arising from the earth is the rich air of humus, an essence my cells seem to require for nourishment. After four years in a college physical therapy program and three months on the Sub with four others, this is exactly what I need. I've come prepared to move in.

Cindy and I are discussing where to plant beans and squash and corn when Max's antique bread truck appears across the fence. "Hey Mariah," Max calls, leaning out the window. "I have an appointment with the bees. A little ritual. You are welcome to come along."

"Sure." I assure Cindy and Rascal I'll return, then duck under a strand of barbwire and climb in with Max. We pass a white stucco house with a clothesline, blue overalls and white fluttering underthings. Farther back, a woman is bent over in the garden, pulling on a plant. A wide straw hat covers most of her steel gray hair and a bouquet of dark leaves hangs over one arm. Around her, patches of freshly tilled soil alternate with regular rows of pale cabbages and young corn. The young tomato vines look lonely but hopeful, spaced so far feet apart.

"I covet those tomato plants," I admit, remembering the one garden I had while in college, longing for an Earth connection, needing that kind of sustenance, and needing to find a place where I really belong.

Max parks and leads the way uphill between long rows of peach trees, carrying a carpet bag with two rolled up rugs sticking out the top.

"What kind of ritual do you do?" I ask.

"Meditation. You know, 'Be here now.' It keeps me calm."

"*Calm* sounds like a good way to be around bees."

"Yes, with bees, you just *be*."

"Well, I'll be."

We've reached the top of the low hill where a cluster of wooden hives stands in ankle-high clover, emitting a subtle hum. I'm uncertain what to do, but Max reassures me. "It is not how you act, really. More a feeling. Just do what I do and remember, your thoughts are not *you*."

He spreads out the rugs on the ground a little way from the row hives. Then we sit side by side, cross-legged on the rugs.

"Concentrate on your breathing. Put yourself, your attention in your nostrils. Feel the air going in, going out." Max's voice is serene, soothing. "Now, we're going to stretch for awhile, so just follow along the best you can."

I've managed to focus, cross-eyed on the end of my nose when he announces, "The Sun Salutation," and begins a movement so graceful it seems he is swimming on land. As I follow, the gentle movements bring my attention into my body, and the downward facing dog pose burns my hamstrings. My braid flops around, getting in the way, so I have to twist it up on my head. We repeat the salutation three times then sit again. I imagine gracefulness will come at a future time.

"Now you can close your eyes or not," Max says softly. "We are going to sit here for a few minutes. You might imagine sending a root from the base of your spine deep into the earth."

The insistent buzzing settles to a comforting hum as I close my eyes and finally let the sound take over. Another vibration joins the buzz—a deep resonant "MMMMM." Max chants along with the bees and my voice joins in, breaking at first, then settling into a natural harmony.

I've been longing to plant myself, just didn't imagine it happening quite like this. A warm, pleasant sensation vibrates my torso. My consciousness drifts downward, plunging into the soil, anchoring me to earth, searching for the deep place of nourishment. There is water down there somewhere and my roots are thirsty, aching with a desire to merge, to connect. The resonance I feel with Max is invoking intimate predilections. *Is this what it feels like to be a man, sinking his root?*

Max stops chanting, and I open my eyes. He rolls his mat and I do the same, still tingling with sensation. Max pulls a contraption out of his bag that reminds me of the Tin Man in *Wizard of Oz* and proceeds to light it. Then he lets a puff of smoke out the nozzle and sets it on the ground. Approaching one of the hives, he lifts the lid and carefully sets it down before reaching inside to pick up one of the narrow wooden frames covered with beeswax. Bees are crawling on his arm. Lots of bees.

Max smiles and nods, then slowly eases the frame back into place. After gently brushing the wayward bees into the hive, he picks up the lid and replaces it. Unbelievable. While he checks the other hives, I practice Judo forms until there is no thought, just action. Center, breathe, move. Center again, perfecting the technique. Since New Orleans, I've come to identify with my role as a free safety. I'm the last chance our team has to stop the opponent from making a score. Jiujitsu is just one of the tools of my trade, along with *Reiki* and physical therapy.

After Max inspects the last colony and douses the fire in his strange contraption, I ask, "Aren't you going to use that smoking thing?"

"Didn't need it today," he smiles. "Hey, I know a guy with a *furo* bath. It's a wooden barrel filled with water, a Japanese hot tub, with all kinds of wonderful, healthy benefits. There is a fire under it. Takes the water to about a hundred and two degrees. Traditional in Japan for relaxing. There is room for three people. You interested?"

"Interested?" I'm thinking just the two of us would be preferable.

"Yes. Would you want to try it?"

"Is it clean?"

"Sure is. Mark purifies the water with hydrogen peroxide."

"Mark?"

"A gentleman."

"We're talking about coed bathing, right?" It's a rhetorical question, since I already know the answer.

"Yes. Common in California. Not so much here."

"No clothes?" *It might be advisable to look before leaping into this.*

"Optional."

"Sounds like fun, why not?" It means intimacy, not sex—nothing wrong with that. I've always been curious what a three-way would be like, though, and the thought gives me a jolt of electricity. I bite my lip. *No way I'm having sex with two guys.*

"All right. We shall have a vegetarian dinner afterward. If you want."

"Sure thing, Max."

Pretty soon I'll have a bulge, and I've heard guys tend to get nervous around pregnant women. I like sex but wonder how I'll feel about it come summertime, with a big belly and the Texas heat. This may be my last chance to cavort with a man for a long time. So many possibilities . . .

Max drops me back at the sunflower house My bus-mates have all bonded with the boys there over music and marijuana. Cindy has alloted me a spot on the back porch. Arrangements are made to park the Submarine between house and garden. We now have a home.

———————

Mark appears at his door wearing a red silk kimono with blue hummingbirds dipping their beaks into exotic pink flowers. He looks like a Barrymore or Fairbanks—the star of some old movie. I guess he's in his thirties, younger than Max, with hair combed across a narrow head starting to bald. Short trimmed mustache. A twinkle in his eye.

"Welcome," he bows graciously, staying in character.

Max says, "Mariah, this is Mark. Mark, Mariah."

Mark grins and offers his hand which I take. "Mariah, Max, Mark . . . Emmm." He carries the tone in a resonant tenor.

"Hi Mark," I respond, in a clipped alto.

"You've come just in time. The water is perfect. Slip off your shoes here by the door and follow me." He's short on small talk, I notice.

Mark leads us down a hallway into a suite, past a dressing room and glassed-in shower and up three steps to a tiled room where a big steaming wooden barrel is sunk into the center of the plank floor. A matching wood bench sits against the far wall. He holds a hand out to indicate the bath.

"Voilà. The furo."

"It looks inviting."

After sharing a joint, we retreat to the shower area where Mark hands me a robe. "You can change here. I'll get some fresh drinking water and meet you in the tub."

I don't have a change of clothes or a swimsuit, or anything but underwear, so I elect to go topless with panties into the water. My braid gets coiled and stabbed with a hairpin. Maybe it will stay on top of my head. I could still skip out on this, but if I do, I'll always think of myself as a chicken.

Max is already in the tub when I approach and dip my toes. "Ouch!" I stand and let my foot get accustomed to the heat for a minute, then try the other one. "Ouch! Ouch!" I'm amazed by the amount of hair on Max's back. A little unsettling. A little beastly. Still . . . he does have a certain attractiveness.

"It takes some getting used to," Mark says, entering the room with a tray, two pitchers and three porcelain cups. He sets the tray down beside the tub on the bench and removes his robe, revealing a smooth body—with no hair at all. What a contrast. Max has a full pelt. I avoid staring, just, as Mark slides into the tub in one slow easy motion with an "Ahhh."

We are all making noise, but it's pre-verbal. Max giggles, sticks his shaggy head in the water and commences to blow bubbles. Pretty soon everyone is laughing. *That was good weed we smoked.*

I'm sitting on the edge, easing my calves into the water. I eventually yield to the heat and slip into the tub, up to my neck, with a man on either side of me. I'm a little self-conscious with bare breasts in close proximity to a new acquaintance. There's not quite enough knee room for three. Slit-eyed images float through moisture-laden air as I melt down to humanoid jelly.

We adjust for each other. I keep my knees together. Soon the haze of hot steam envelops us all in a drowsy semi-conscious state. Being the shortest, I'm also the deepest, my bottom resting on wooden slats that form an underwater bench. *There's a little footsie going on down below.*

I'm the first one out. In a slow stagger, I find the shower room and turn on the water, mix it cool and enjoy the spray. I lose the wet panties, then towel off and drift into the bedroom where I flop down on top of the bedspread. In a world solely and completely my own, my cells vibrate, and I drift, still hot and steamy. Breathing is my only concern—long, slow breaths.

In a while, the guys come in and join me, exuding waves of heat. I don't know what to expect. This is the closest I have ever come to joining an orgy. Nor do I know how I feel about it—just that Max is a good guy, and I trust it will be okay.

It is okay, but not how I expected. At first there is caressing on the cheek and ear, then I'm kissed on the neck from both sides at once. Slippery lips are sending ripples of energy down my chest, and I'm enjoying the moment, passively. They are gentle and considerate. The kissing has progressed from neck to breasts, one guy teasing a nipple with the tip of his tongue—Max—and this is getting juicy. So far so good . . .

Then something changes. All at once my nipples are abandoned, and I feel the weight of two heads on my ribcage. When I look down to see what's happening, the two men are kissing each other—deeply. They rise up and embrace across my torso, continuing to kiss, and I feel my connection with them cease. The men are both aroused, but not by me. *Okay, then.* When they fall together on one side of me, I take the opportunity to slip out the other way. Max catches my eye as I'm heading for the shower room to find my clothes. He winks. *Of all things.*

I start to giggle, but press my lips together, thinking I'd hate to interrupt their flow of passion. Still, it's hard to keep from cracking up as I'm getting dressed. When I escape into the living room, the guys are moaning and making other sounds, so I drown them out with Vivaldi's *Appalacian Spring* on the stereo.

Since Max is my transportation, I relax for the duration and find a book—*Stranger in a Strange Land*. I'm lost in it when Max appears at the door with a sheepish grin.

"I owe you one," he says.

"You do, and I'm going to collect one day." I stick the book in my bag.

"Dinner anywhere you like, but not tonight."

"I understand. It'll be expensive, though."

"I shall pay, Mariah. I called a cab for you," he says and hands me an Alexander Hamilton.

"Thanks, Max."

———

CHAPTER 8
CLIFF

*Uninspired and unproductive periods
often indicate a search for the right
question. Ask it, and be assured an
answer will arrive.*

April

"This is Cliff Grayson," Bill said. "Our new pool boy."

After basketball season, my coach had given me a phone number and I'd called right away about the job. The dude ranch owner hired me over the phone. I'd showed up at the Bar S that afternoon, wearing denim jams and a Hawaiian shirt, with my new double string of wooden love beads around my neck.

Six people said their names in sequence around the table and I remembered two of them, Snake and LeAnn. Snake had a James Dean haircut and wore a blue corduroy FFA jacket. Leann was a permed and curled brunette with big eyes. She and another girl hopped up and disappeared into the kitchen as soon as I sat down. I admit I watched them go until the swinging door slammed behind them.

"Them's real cute beads, um . . . Cliffy, is it?" The words slid out one corner of Snake's mouth while the other corner curled up in what passed for a smile. Letting his comment slide as well, I sat up straight and let my lungs provide oxygen, but I was bordering on a fight or flight response.

Bill stood up, then. "C'mon, Cliff, I'll show you around."

Leaping at the chance to get back outside, I followed him through the door. The Bar S occupied a short peninsula on the sixty-five-mile-long Lake Travis. It was a destination for families who wanted a break from city life, but with all the conveniences. I'd be working there on Fridays, Saturdays and Sundays until school was out, and then full-time for the summer. Bill showed me the swimming pool, the boat dock and rodeo arena, describing my role in each venue—life-guard and groundskeeper, fishing guide for four year olds and twice-a-week rodeo contestant. Everyone rode the girl's events only, no bronc riding or bull-dogging. Nobody was a pro, but we could all stay on a horse.

Back in the cafeteria most of the staff were sitting down to sloppy joes and coleslaw when I filled up a plate at the buffet and joined them. I listened to their small talk while I scarfed my food then went to meet my room-mate. Bill had assigned me a cabin with a kid my age named Paul. After parking the Plymouth, I carried my guitar case and travel bag into the ice-cold room and right away I knew it wasn't going to work out.

"You'll have to keep your beer elsewhere," Paul sneered, as I placed a single quart bottle of Pearl in the refrigerator. "I don't allow booze in my cabin."

I took the forbidden bottle of Pearl down to the lake and sat in the gravel. Rays of light shot out of the clouds and lit the water in a spot near the far shore. I could see life at the Bar S was going to take some adjustment. After being more or less an only child for the last eight years, I'd gotten used to doing whatever I wanted. It was no big deal about the beer—a quart of beer would have lasted me all week—and I might have adjusted to my roomate's wishes, but our differences ran deeper. On one wall hung a poster that read, 'America, Love it or Leave it,' next to his six-foot wide American flag.

As if it's illegal to criticize something you love.

I suppose a person could love the country *and* leave it, but the way it looks to me, if you go to the trouble to love it, you might as well stay awhile. And if you do leave, I figure you'll probably come back, sooner or later. Although, when I think about it, Charlie never came back. But that's another story and I don't want to get ahead of myself.

My brother, Blaine had been around the world and back several times. When I started work at the Bar S, he was in Mexico—Mom told me he'd sent a postcard from Oaxaca. For all I knew he was taking up residence there. She told me he flew charters for wealthy fishermen, but I had no clue about what he was really into. Blaine and I had made tentative plans for me to go down there for a week at the end of summer. But you know what they say about plans.

I'd learned from my brother to hate the war in Vietnam, and I despised the politicians who perpetrated it. I wanted to stop the war more than almost anything, but for Paul to insinuate I didn't love my country was going too far. My beef was with the President, his cabinet and with Congress, not with America, and not with the flag. One look at that poster could bum me out for hours. I needed to find a creative solution, but I was told that the housing available for staff at the Bar S was all booked up, so I had no choice but to put up with Paul. While I was musing on things, the cook I'd met earlier eased up beside me.

"Mind if I sit with ya?"

"Be my guest." I saw he was empty handed, so I offered him the beer.

He pushed his glassed up and asked, "You sure?"

"It's all yours."

"Thanks." He carefully wiped the rim with his sleeve and swallowed half the remaining beer, handed it back."

I cut my eyes at him, wiped the rim on my shirt and took a long swig myself.

He nodded, said, "Thomas," and held out his hand.

"Cliff," I said.

"They ain't all that bad, you know. Snake, he jus' like him a little fun."

———

Thomas was a big jolly man in his mid-twenties, with a belly that betrayed his habit of tasting all the food he prepared. His race set him apart from the others at the Bar S, and he lived in a cabin by himself. Apparently the owner liked it that way. One night after the kitchen was cleaned up and the swimming pool area lights were out, Thomas and I sat in folding chairs by the lake drinking cold Pearls and watching the moon's reflection. On top of the vague fishy odor by the shore, I got a whiff of onions and hamburger grease.

"You know, Thomas," I said, "I sure lucked out getting Paul for a roomate. He's a real prize."

"Yeah," he nodded. "You sure the winner—big time." Thomas kept a straight face, but I saw his eye twitch through the thick lens of his glasses.

"It's not funny." I kneaded the back of my neck where the pain was beginning. "Yesterday, he told me he wasn't eating 'that colored boy's food.'"

"It don't make me no never-mind, Cliff. I hear things of that sort all the time. Worse . . ."

"I don't know how you can take prejudice so lightly," I said. "If I were black, I'd be so pissed-off, I'd probably get myself killed."

"You got that right, you be dead," he nodded. "Sure would."

I shuddered, and shook my head, trying to ward off something evil. I'd tried to imagine being black, but found it impossible.

"Thomas, I can't live with him."

"I 'spect he would be hard to live with," he said, taking a pull off his beer.

"He irons his shorts." I pictured my roomate all belted, cuffed and creased.

"Well, he do look kind of spiffy. I 'spect he irons his undershorts. Starches 'em too."

We both cracked up then, releasing the tension. I looked out across the lake at the sparkles on top of the water. Fortunately for me, Thomas was easy-going and open to friendship. I knew he was lonely, there being no other black folks at the Bar S, but I'm afraid I took advantage of the situation, and of him.

"I don't suppose you have room for me in your cabin?" I ventured.

"Be pleased to have you as my roommate, Cliff," he smiled, "but you the wrong color."

"What's wrong with pink?" I joked. "You got a problem with it?"

Thomas was far from black. More the color of mahogany or rosewood. I personally belonged to the pink, sunburned race. I had no illusions about my skin color. In fact, more pigmentation would have been welcome—but just a little more, enough for a good tan. Not enough to single me out, like Thomas, among an all-white crowd.

"No sir," he said. "No problem, Pinkie sir. Pink's just fine with me."

"All right then, I'll bring my stuff over tonight."

"That suits me, but what will the others say?"

"Does it matter?"

"Might stir up some trouble is all." The moon suddenly escaped its cloud cover, bathing his face in celestial silver light, and he added, "Nothin' I can't handle, though."

I was elated to be rid of my snooty roomate, but even with all his faults, Paul did do me one good turn. He made me realize there are two kinds of patriot, the blind, unquestioning ones, and the honest ones. I had no doubt both kinds were sincere, but when I went to load up my stuff that night, Paul was shuffling through my record albums. He looked at my favorites by Bob Dylan and Peter, Paul and Mary, and scoffed, "This is communist music."

I can tolerate idiots, and even shitheads, but nobody messes with my music.

That night I horned in on Thomas, oblivious to his better interests. I threw my pillow on his extra bed and hung my toothbrush in his bathroom. The space was tight, so I left my stereo and guitar in the trunk of the Plymouth. I thought nobody would notice my move since Thomas' cabin was hidden in a thicket of live oak, surrounded by sumac. You couldn't see my car parked there, or so I thought.

I pretended like nothing had happened, but next morning as I walked out the door of my new lodgings, Snake and another wrangler rode up on horseback and gave me the eye. *Cedar-whackers*, I thought. But what do you expect from guys who like to get drunk and try to run down jackrabbits at night with a pickup truck? Rural Texas, I knew, was a different kind of place from Austin. Prejudice there is carefully taught, from the cradle on. LeAnn, of the kitchen staff, had flirted with me when I first arrived. We'd made out on the couch a couple of times in the maintenance man's travel trailer, serenaded by the Kingston Trio, but she cooled right away after I moved in with Thomas.

"I suppose you prefer to do it with boys," LeAnn said. "Colored boys."

I got the shivers, then, looking at the wicked arch of her eyebrows. Couldn't believe her tongue had been in my mouth. To complicate matters, James Conner resurfaced, near at hand, driving his '69 Barracuda. That afternoon he came to pick up LeAnn in the Bar S parking lot, then peeled out, throwing gravel. One thing I noticed about that guy—his father had way too much money.

CHAPTER 9
MARIAH

*An 'arabesque' is an expressive dance
move. In two-dimensional work, it's the
gesture of the abstract design, the
pattern of light and dark—the thing we
notice first about a work of art seen
from across the room. An arabesque
incorporates rhythm and thrust and
balance. It is the key to the initial
success of the work.*

April

I'm settled now on the screened-in back porch at the sunflower
house, which I've shortened to just 'Sunflowers.' Early this morning
Max shows up with twelve overgrown tomato plants in gallon
buckets. "Mariah, these came from a friend who works in a
greenhouse," he explains. "They are rootbound, but I thought you
would know what to do with them."

"They're perfect," I claim.

He gets a big hug, and now I'm dancing with delight. I've wanted
a garden since I first picked a ripe raspberry in my backyard when I
was six, and I've already installed three plants when Max returns
from his beekeeping chores.

"I still owe the lady a dinner. Do you remember?" Max picks a blister beetle off one of the tomato plants, throws it over the fence.

"How could I forget?"

"Have you been to the Bo Tree? They serve dinner guests a bowl of short grain brown rice and vegetables, seasoned with words of wisdom."

"Tonight?"

He bows, "As you wish."

————

We're sitting on stools at a table the size of a family-size pizza, crammed with other customers into the front rooms of a house in downtown Austin. Cindy did my hair in a French braid this morning, and I feel elegant wearing my olive-green cotton dress with the boat neck and thrift-store sandals. Max is dressed in a beige shirt with red suspenders, allowing his Buddha-belly ample freedom of movement. He delicately wipes his mouth with a cloth napkin and looks me in the eye.

"Mariah, there is more about me that you do not know."

"Really?"

"Yes, I like to draw naked people."

"Oh my God!" I pull back in my chair with mock alarm. "That's horrible, Max. We need to find you a therapist, or a priest, or something."

"Perhaps, but the compulsion will not be denied. Tomorrow night, in fact, our little group of deviants will meet for three hours," Max declares, as if fate had made an unassailable decree. Then he adds, "We share the twenty-five-dollar model's fee."

"And I suppose you want me to be the model?" I'm pretending to consider the offer, but it's already a done deal. I need the work.

"Would you consider it? Our regular model cancelled, and we are in desperate need."

"The fee *is* tempting." I stall for a minute before letting him off the hook. "Sure, why not? You've already seen me naked, and I *am* experienced."

"Experienced?" Max looks genuinely puzzled.

"Yeah, I've done it before."

"No!" Now Max is getting into the drama, with a room full of chopstick-wielding rice-eaters for an audience. "We were hoping for a virgin."

"Ha, ha. What time do you meet?"

"Six o'clock. I shall provide your transportation. After the session you have the option to stay in town or get a ride home."

"This really *is* a proposition, then."

"In your wildest dreams," he snickers.

I like sparring with Max. After the *furo* experience, I feel like we're co-conspirators in a private joke.

The next afternoon Max presents me with a gift from Mark, saying, "He sends his apologies for the other night." He's holding out the red kimono that Mark wore the night of the unconsummated three-way orgy.

"Wow! It smells like sandalwood." I hold the silk to my face. "And it feels luxurious. Tell him 'Thank you' for me, Max."

The prospect of modeling again has its appeal. I can picture myself, stripped to my essence, returning to that obscure civilization where the human form is revered for beauty and complexity. It's a special kind of high. The end of the session is a downer, though, when you have to go out and re-enter a world where only the ideal bodies are valued, and ordinary people are ashamed of their innate beauty.

In the double garage behind a house not far from the food co-op, two women and two men are waiting. The atmosphere is relaxed, with low lighting, plaster walls, high ceiling, a huge abstract painting hung at the far end of the room.

"Max, we are just getting warmed up." The tall blonde woman turns to me. "I'm Sara."

I find the bathroom and return wearing the kimono and a smile. Feels like I'm getting away with mischief, like stealing strawberries, or being initiated into a sacred rite.

I step up, drop the kimono, and reach for the sky. After a minute, the timer goes off with a buzz, startling me into another pose— quarter turn and change the arms, this time holding one straight out, like Washington pointing across the Delaware—and I realize how quickly an arm can turn to concrete. When the timer goes off again, George Washington is pointing at the floor.

I continue to rotate on my axis for the next fifteen minutes or so without reaching above my head again and without mooning anyone too seriously, I hope. The huge painting at the end of the room reveals its secrets—two figures entwined, close-up, both female.

The music changes to a Mozart piano concerto, and now I'm looking behind me like Daphne fleeing Apollo, frozen in place. I can relate to the classical maiden's plight, but it's not my path. Paying attention to the road ahead is my major objective right now. There are things I need to consider in a conscious way. Strange, how suddenly pregnancy and it's hormones have me all concerned with safety.

For instance, this room with Max and his friends feels safe. I have freedom here to assert myself, to act out my feelings in different poses in a variety of different minidramas. There's no such freedom with a baby, stuck in a single pose for ages, like an oak tree, rooted in the earth forever—attached, in fact, just like Daphne. But now my attention is fading, and I dream.

> A splash beside me, and I feel a presence. Someone
> I've known for a thousand years. A quickening surge
> steals up my spine. Hold it gently . . . his presence.
> And the pose.

"Buzzzz!" It's the damn timer, signaling the end of the pose. *I could have stayed with him all night.*

"Okay, Mariah, let's break for five minutes," Sara says, so I slip into the kimono and stand in front of the box fan, enjoying the feel of silk whispering on my skin. There's plenty of room to glide around and see what the artists have done. I stop in front of Sara's easel and her drawing makes an instant impression.

A coating of charcoal half-covers the light gray paper. She's used an eraser to reveal where the light hit, leaving a shadow where my form meets the wall, and white pencil strokes catch the highlights to make me seem timeless and beautiful. I dissolve into that figure and become the work of art, myself, with edges vibrating.

"Are you ready?" Sara has moved close, brushing my shoulder and hip with a spark of electricity.

Ready for what?

"It's time for another pose."

"Yes, I'm ready . . . Great drawing, by the way."

"Thanks," she says. "Twenty minutes again?"

"Standing?"

"Maybe try sitting this time."

At the end, after I've dressed, she hands me a wad of folded bills, says, "Thank you, Mariah," a question in the tilt of her head.

"You're welcome, Sara. Thank *you*."

"Max said you are a physical therapist. I'd be interested in getting a massage if you'd like to practice."

"Maybe, sometime." We studied approach-avoidance complexes in psychology class, and this is a classic case. Like a good existentialist, I'm trying to be honest. *I know what I'm feeling, but what do I want?*

"Why don't you think about it?" Sara takes a drawing from her board, rolls it up and tapes it together. Then she hands it to me.

"What's this?"

"For you." She smiles.

"Thanks, Sara. I'm honored." It's an honest statement, so I give myself an 'A' for honesty.

"Come back next week? You were an excellent model."

"Sure. Thanks, I enjoyed it." A trickle of perspiration wanders down the side of my ribcage. *Someone must have turned up the thermostat in here.*

"Is the lady ready to go?" Max is standing by the door waiting.

The bread truck has a new door made of heavy cardboard with *The Honeycomb* written on it in large script letters, surrounded by a grid of hexagons all around.

"Max, you've named the truck."

"I have been inspired."

"And thanks for adding the door. It'll keep my butt from freezing off." It's inconvenient, though, getting in on the driver's side and crawling across the seat to shotgun position.

Max climbs in after me, looks at the rolled-up drawing in my lap, and asks, "Did Sara make a pass at you?"

"I'm beginning to get that feeling."

"Yes. I thought maybe so. She's a treasure hunter. Completely upsets the hormonal balance in the room."

"Treasure?"

"We humans are like gold miners, are we not? Finding treasure in each other's bodies."

"You mean pleasure, not treasure."

"That too, but a precious metal, for sure. Neither gold nor silver, I speak of the kind that gives one strength to endure life's pain and hardship. That kind of *mettle*." Max chuckles. He starts to turn the ignition key but pauses to look over at me. "But then, perhaps I should not be *meddling* in your affairs."

He's good with puns, but I'm glad he's finished with the wordplay. It's almost painful.

Max backs out of the parking place and stops to shift gears. Then he adds, "You did very well tonight. I believe you deserve a *medal* for your performance."

"Stop!" I protest.

But he's a true friend. He's managed to lighten my mood and I'm still grinning when he asks, "I don't suppose you could be persuaded to return for another drawing session?"

"Sure. I'm always needing money. Cindy's Corvair lives on gasoline."

"Right on, sister!" Max offers his hand, thumb up, and we shake like brothers.

––––––––

I've taken Cindy's car to Breckenridge Hospital to inquire about work. According to the office manager, in the State of Texas, a degree in physical therapy is useless by itself. The woman says, "You need to complete an internship before you can get a license to practice."

I was afraid of that. So far, my burnt but hard-earned college diploma qualifies me to either work a minimum wage job or be a waitress, so I decide to try the University, where the familiar feel of campus elicits a pang of nostalgia. *I could always go for a graduate degree.* College is a womb, a safe, nourishing place where students can grow toward maturity, but postpone it at the same time. It's almost a compulsion, the drive toward safety, toward this kind of 'neverland.' But no, I have a destiny. . . and my garden awaits.

"We try to fill all our positions with students," says the woman in personnel, "but the Art Department is always looking for models, part time. You can pick up an application over there."

At the Art Department, I pick up a form. Name, age, Social Security number, phone number, nude, clothed, etc. Some rummaging in my bag produces a pencil and my ID. The driver's license stares back at me with the name Mary Ellen Justice.

I hate the name Mary. So ordinary. But an extra syllable gives it movement and emphasis and possibility. Ma-ri-ah. In school I always used just plain Ellen and plain is what I'm feeling right now. Plain and slow and a bit heavy, a Gypsy who's abandoned her wagon and gone to ground. And who's a little bit pregnant. Not at all like the girl who dropped acid one night, listened to a Kingston Trio song and became 'The Wind.' More like a hot air balloon that's losing air and drifting toward Earth. The change is undeniable, though. I need to keep pace and be practical.

I write Mary Ellen Justice on the form with a grimace and a number—the café where Cindy works. Pissed off for some reason, I leave the application on the counter. *Why is there no artwork on these walls? It is an art department, after all.*

———————

"Freedom, freedom, freedom, freedom, freedom, freedom, freedom."

I swear that's what the bird is saying, "Freedom." Looking in the trees, I can't find it . . . the bird, that is. Freedom is another matter. When the baby comes, I'll give up every bit I have.

It's nice and restful along the creek in Zilker Park where big sycamores line the bank. A crawfish scuddles under a bed of gravel, Jesus bugs walk on the water's surface, and I have a sudden urge to run naked through the woods. But instead, I sit here and think, away from the man-made world, glad for some alone time.

Children are playing nearby, their sing-song voices mingling with water sounds, reminding me of Audubon park where I first met Blaine. I wonder how his smuggling trip is going, what it's like in Mexico. Something tells me I'll be hearing from him soon—just a feeling. I should consult with him, since he doesn't know about what's-her-name. It would be the straight-up honest thing to do. The authentic thing. After all, he did have a part in this pregnancy. But I wonder if fatherhood would make a difference in him? Or to him? I *do* feel affection for the man—friendship, but no passion.

At this point, it makes sense to consider all my options. I *do* have a home, but no car and no job. Perhaps I'm not ready to drink from the chalice of motherhood. It's an eighteen-year commitment at least, and being pregnant feels like a burden now, when I'm just barely being born myself. Without coming to any conclusions, I let Cindy's Corvair take me home where the familiar yellow house greets me with open arms. Rascal and Cindy greet me likewise, making everything feel normal.

"Any luck?" Cindy asks.

"Zero."

I allow the dog and garden to nurture me until sundown when lightning bugs come out by the hundreds to make a fantasyland. Before bed, while chanting OM, I imagine a high soprano harmony to my alto voice, a barely audible resonance.

———

CHAPTER 10
CLIFF

Painting on location can be both
rewarding and frustrating. Total
immersion in nature involves
relinquishment of a certain amount of
control.

May

I had to quit Edna Faye's watercolor class because of my job, so I was on my own for a while with becoming an artist. Typically, on my days off, I would drive around the hill country, hike to a secluded spot and make a *plein-air* study, sitting by myself with the birds and bugs and cottontails.

One day I drove around the lake, turned down a gravel road, and found a place where the bluebonnets and Indian paintbrush were still making a show. The twin ruts of a little-used track led to a field of pink primroses that shimmered beneath a limestone outcropping. A few white-tipped bluebonnets poked up through the grass in patches. I'd found the perfect spot.

After softening overnight on my makeshift palette, the pans of yellow ochre, burnt sienna, Indian red, and two blues all clustered together, waiting for action. My paper was tight but I was loose and before I knew it, color was flying. Ochre with green for the grass. Ochre with a touch of red for primroses. Cobalt for the sky. For my part, I sucked in huge quantities of air and dust and gnats, becoming merely another stroke of paint made by a larger hand. I hardly noticed the gnats.

The cobalt pigment had broken up in interesting ways, clumping randomly where I'd painted fingers of sky reaching into the green of the trees. The primroses needed more color, so I wet them and dropped in an extra splash of pink. Then I gave the sky another light wash of cobalt to build contrast with the flowers. Finally, in the shadows beneath the rocks and trees, I added burnt sienna with ultramarine to give them a feeling of weight. *Maybe it's finished*, I thought.

It was time for a break, so I left my painting and climbed the rounded domes of rock down to the lake. After a quick look around, I untied my sneakers, shed my socks and dropped my shorts and shirt. The chilly water took my breath away, so I stroked double time in a crawl for a hundred yards until my chest burned and my legs ached.

I returned to land sculling on my back, watching cumulus clouds make patterns among the treetops, then dressed and walked back uphill to assess my painting. I'd nearly reached my car when up the lane an engine roared, and a teal green Barracuda churned a cloud of dust. Conner. *What the hell?*

My heart rate accelerated from zero to sixty in two seconds flat when I saw what he'd done to my car. 'Nigger Lover' was written on the windshield and doors with black tar. *Damn.* I stared at the lingering dust where Conner had been parked, and realized the bastard had waited for me to see him before leaving. I reached down and picked up a golfball-sized rock and chunked it down the road after the Barracuda. Then another. I rained a salvo at the diminishing cloud of dust, feeling rage and impotence all at once, resisting the temptation to throw up my hands and run screaming over the hill.

I pulled a crumpled joint from my pocket and smoked it down till it burned my fingers, then tossed the roach. I have a daemon that compels me to look for one single go-to answer for all questions.

Some lodestone that philosophers may have by-passed. Some simple formula, like *Yes, and . . .* the way Del Close had taught us at a comedy improv workshop. Something like, *All You Need is Love*.

Along the same lines, as a novice marijuana user, I'd been seduced by Bob Dylan's suggestion, *Everybody must get stoned*. No question smoking pot helped me loosen my inhibitions. For one thing, it became much easier to talk to girls. And I stopped thinking ahead all the time and learned to focus more on what was happening at the moment. These were changes to appreciate, and it seemed to me that everybody *would* benefit from smoking a little weed. After knowing Conner, though, I was beginning to suspect that there were some kinds of fool who just couldn't be helped.

Anyway, my mood lifted. The car was no treasure. Not stylish. Inherited from my grandmother. Only a six-cylinder engine and no air-conditioner. Good radio, though. I had no complaints about that. I wasn't sure about the car doors, but I figured the tar would come off the windows. So no big deal. Only a small taste of the shit Thomas had to go through being a black man. I actually felt lucky for a moment. I still had air in my tires, gas in the tank.

Then, I found my painting of the primroses, wadded up against one of the tires and drenched in muddy water, like a giant spitball. I hauled off and heaved it as far as I could and watched it bounce into the agarita bushes.

––––––––

CHAPTER 11
MARIAH

*In life and in art, it's important to find
out what you really need. So many of us
are all wrapped up in our desire, in
what we think we need. Sometimes it's
good to strip down to the very
minimum.
If you go out to paint and forget your
brushes, make do with just a paper
towel and palette knife. You may turn
out one of your best paintings that day.*

May

The University has called me to model for a sculpture class on Tuesday and Thursday afternoons, Cindy has loaned me the Corvair, and I've done a quick-change in the Art Building restroom. The ladder-back rocking chair waits on a high stand in the middle of Room 310 where twenty or so art students are chatting, expecting their instructor. When I appear in my robe, they go quiet. Before long, a woman I know strides into the room carrying a heavy leather briefcase. She stops in front of the modeling stand, spots me and grins with both eyebrows raised. I nod and grin back, then clamber up onto the stand, trying to keep the robe closed. *Small world.*

"I'm Sara Kruppa," she announces. "Due to Mr. Sparks' hospitalization, I'll be your instructor for the rest of the semester . . ." Sara swings her arm wide, toward me. "And today, Mariah will be our *muse*."

I have never thought about being a 'muse,' or having a 'muse' for that matter. *How would I go about finding one, andyway? I could probably use one.* Aside from trying to draw dogs and horses in grade school, and doodling when I talk on the phone, my only artistic experience is practicing piano. I don't believe I ever met the muse of music, though. There *were* brief moments of bliss, when my fingers danced on the keys, and all the right notes came, but only after I'd practiced the same piece for weeks on end. The bass player at the jazz club in New Orleans? That man *had* a muse.

Sara is fiddling with a tape deck in the corner of the room when I bare my ever-so-slightly swollen body for the young sculptors. I sit, cross my ankles and put my hands in my lap while a Scott Joplin tune plays softly, and my fingers twitch to the familiar rhythm.

"Mariah, if you are uncomfortable at any point, feel free to move and stretch, then return to the pose."

I smile and nod, find a spot on the far wall for a focus. Then I disembody, arriving at once in a crowded, smoke-filled room with chandeliers dangling.

> A few dancers occupy the floor. Hangers-on linger at the piano. I am the entertainer. Across the room a man appears, skin the color of coffee with cream, wearing a flat straw hat and long-sleeved striped shirt with garters on both sleeves. He's twirling some kind of stick, weaving his way through the tables, stopping to nod and smile at people while I struggle to play my notes cleanly.
> A mirror behind the bar reflects the room like a Manet painting. Leather-covered bar stools are filled with clientele. Beer mugs are filled with libations. A girl in ruffled red underwear swings in seductive arcs above the bar. A black fan hangs from the ceiling, spinning in slow motion.

> When I finish the tune and look up, garter man is
> standing in front of the piano. We lock eyes and a
> warm river rises inside me. The nature of time is
> altered, stretching out and slowing down to the pace of
> the ceiling fan. Then he taps both my hands with his
> wand, and I play again—this time like a master,
> flawlessly and without effort. *Who is he?* My fingers
> throb on the keys, and The Peacherine Rag courses
> through my body and blood. The man winks. *I sure
> hope he stays a while.*

When I come up for air the students are still in room 310, working diligently with lumps of clay. I'm still in my pose, so I can't move, but there's a ragtime rhythm in my bones. I blink, thinking peaches, then trees, and it's no sooner thought than done.

> I'm a tree, with what's-her-name sprouting from my
> trunk, a long thin limb like the water sprouts that grow
> from the crotch of a tree. My skin is the rough bark.
> My flesh, the tender green cambium inside. The
> scratchy sensation is focused in my back and hips—
> my bottom.

I startle, with the rough woven chair seat digging into my flesh, compelling me to move. The robe wraps itself around me, then accompanies me off the stand and out the door for a break. When I return to Room 310, Sara is lecturing about volume and mass.

"You've had a whole year of life drawing, and I'm sure part of that was devoted to massing the form. In 'massing' you work in two dimensions, not to show details, or even accurate drawing, but simply to give the illusion of mass and volume." Sara is making snow angels in the air with her arms, indicating a sphere around herself. "In three-dimensional work, we also begin by massing the figure. Always start with too much clay at first. We'll be using a subtractive process here."

I realize she's describing the same concept Sara used in the drawings she did of me. Subtraction—she took away something in order to reveal my form. The students had all been building up forms by adding pieces of clay. The subtractive idea is new to them.

"You have all gone into detail much too quickly." Sara paces the length of the room. "Don't try to get it right, just get the feeling of space being occupied."

This new teaching side of Sara is something I didn't see when modeling for Max's drawing group. She's impressive.

"I want you to carve the negative space," she commands. "But do it gradually, like you were chiseling stone."

She approaches an empty sculpture stand—a circular wooden platform mounted on top of a vertical steel pipe which is embedded in a five-gallon bucket of concrete. She peels back the plastic wrapping from a twenty-five-pound cube of brick-colored clay, hefts the block and upends it on the stand with a 'Whop.' Then she repeats the process and crowns the first cube with another.

"Now!" She breaks into a broad grin. "We've got something to work with." Sara picks up a tool—what looks like a bow and arrow, with a curved metal bow and a wire string—and using both hands, attacks the mass of clay with the tautly stretched wire. Then she peels off a five-pound chunk and holds it up like a prize.

"Exhibit A, class: this is negative space. Now, get into it! You have plenty of material." The students, most of whom have an anemic figure started at their respective stations, rush to the clay storage area and line up to liberate more blocks of clay.

Sara turns to me. "Mariah, we're ready."

I've been gently stretching my back, getting ready to pose again. Silence dominates the last sitting of the day while the students revamp their meager beginnings. Despite my efforts to re-conjure the ragtime muse, he has retreated to another realm. After class I bump into Sara and satisfy my curiosity. "How did you end up teaching this class?"

"The instructor was in a motorcycle wreck and can't teach. He called and asked me to sub for him the rest of the semester. I'll be staying on to teach two summer sessions."

"It sounds like they need your instruction."

"I want them to be bold. They need to break through their inhibitions." With guys, I can always tell if they have sex on their mind. It's easy—they usually do. But with Sara, I don't know. With hands on her hips and head thrown back, she's appraising me, as if the robe isn't there. "You changed your name."

"It's a long story."

"I'm glad you're modeling," she smiles. "You look beautiful today."

"That's what they all say." I'm trying to keep it light, but the honest truth prevails. "I'm pregnant, you know."

"I thought maybe so. And you're okay with that?"

"Well. Yes and no."

"No father?"

I take a deep breath. "No. Not really."

"So you're keeping it?"

"I feel like I should check with him. It's just that he's . . . unavailable."

"That's one I've heard before. Listen, kiddo, I know a place in Mexico called *las hermanas*. It's clean. Not a border-town dump. Down in Acapulco. All staffed by women. The sisters take good care of you."

"I'll keep that in mind."

———

Back at Sara's afternoon sculpture class I'm modeling again. She's had the students collapse Thursday's tentative efforts, pound them into abstraction, and start over with their sculptures. This time, I'm standing, legs about a foot apart, hands laced together under my belly, leaning back slightly. The job is harder than modeling for a drawing class, since I have to hold the same pose for nearly three hours with my knees slightly bent.

There are breaks, but not enough, and my back is cramping with pain each time I get a rest. This is way different, staying in the same position for a long time. Feels like I'm turning to clay or stone myself, becoming fixed—life imitating art.

A sudden muscle spasm in my right calf puts me in agony and I have to sit and pound on it for a while until it settles down. Sara and I negotiate a plan where I use a counter-pose to stretch the hurting muscles. We get an armless chair, so I can model the top half of the pose while my legs and back take a rest.

The students seem to adjust to the change in routine. The job becomes tolerable, but by the end of the third hour, I'm acutely aware that I'm earning my fee—and acutely aware of my hurting feet, back, hips, calves and arms. After the session, Sara offers to give *me* a massage. A trade, maybe, with me giving her one next time.

"You know. That doesn't sound bad at all." She's a strong, smart person and I've gotten over my reluctance to be in intimate contact with her.

"Come on, then." Sara grabs cushions from the sculpture studio, and I grab my bag. She leads the way to her office, a tiny space filled mostly with an oversized desk. She clears the desk and plops the cushions down on it, then rummages in a drawer, producing a pump bottle of skin lotion. We each take a hit from a little pipe she has.

"This is good." I hold it all in for a count of thirty.

"I'm afraid that's the last pipeful," she says. "There's a drought going on. I'm going out to West Texas next week to meet a plane. We'll have plenty to smoke, then."

Could Blaine be this pilot she's meeting? I try to picture him, but can't. It's a moot point, though. There are probably hundreds of pilots smuggling marijuana. Sara is rubbing her hands together, so I belly-flop onto the cushions.

"Why don't you lie on your back? That way I can start with your neck."

Just like that the way is prepared for me to relax. I free my arms and pull the robe over me. This is a change of roles. I'm usually the one manipulating someone else's body. That's what physical therapists do. Something I enjoy. Now it's my turn to receive. I hear the sound of the door locking, then warm, gentle hands slip around the back of my neck and head.

"Okay, Mariah, take some deep breaths and let go of the worries and cares of the day. Take this time for yourself."

I suck in all the air I can, then let it out slowly through my nose. After three repetitions all my attention is focused on Sara's hands. Her fingers are on my clavicles and her thumbs behind my neck, moving up and down. It feels heavenly. Next her fist is sliding on one side of my neck from shoulder to jaw, stroking up and down, lubricated with lotion. She gently turns my head to one side and continues the strokes as I bare my neck. I feel vulnerable, but she is taking care of me. I am clay in her hands. *When did the stereo come on?* My breathing synchronizes with a recording of ocean waves.

Sara turns my head the other way and massages my neck with her knuckles, stretching muscles that never had this kind of attention before. She straightens my head and kneads my upper pectorals and deltoids, then somehow, she is working both her palms underneath my shoulders, alongside my spine and down to the middle of my back, lifting my ribcage. The hands act like pistons, moving up and down my spine in slow, short strokes. I hear a crack.

"Did you hear that?" I ask, wondering if I still have a voice.

"I did. I love the way your body responds to my touch," she croons. "I'll be right back." Sara stops to turn the record over, then her hands are on my feet. "You said something about your calves?"

"I had a cramp in the left one while I was modeling."

"Okay."

Her knuckles are doing things to the bottoms of my feet. Tiny circles. Various parts of me wake up as the magic fingers move from heel to toe, to instep. Then she had taken hold of one ankle, twisting forward and back, side to side. I am at her mercy. If I were face-down I'd be drooling.

"Ready to turn over?" Sara asked.

Uh-oh. Now I *will* be drooling. I manage it without falling off the cushions, and Sara has hold of my heels, pulling. I am being stretched out. My lower back releases the tension it has been holding. Sara begins on my calf muscles, squeezing with both hands on one leg and pushing across the muscle with one hand and pulling with the other. Then she switches to a Swedish chopping technique, and my heel jumps up, smacking her in the face.

"Oops!" She recoils. "Sorry, hon. I got carried away."

"Mmph." I reply.

Before I know it, she's working on my thighs, using long strokes and going deep into the hamstrings. As a physical therapist, I know each muscle by name, so I repeat their Latin names to avoid becoming a human volcano and erupting right there on the table. I have never . . .

"Knock, knock." A voice outside the door.

"Oh shit." Sara whispers.

The music stops. I turn on my side and sit up, grab for my robe and slide to the floor, mildly alarmed, but still pulsating from intimate contact. Sara motions me into the chair in front of her desk, then hides the cushions and lotion.

"Hellooo." Sara's voice sounds funny.

Who's here? I wonder.

After a brisk conversation at the door, she explains, "A student is thinking about dropping my class. I'd better go talk to her."

"I'd better go too," I say, half wanting to stay and finish what we started. The other half wants to run for miles and keep running.

———

CHAPTER 12
MARIAH

There must be a hundred shades of green. The color can be overwhelming, especially in late spring and early summer. Landscape painters have always managed to temper the green, neutralizing it with its complement, red, or making it bluer in the distance.

I've been staying in town at Max's place on Tuesday and Wednesday nights, so I can model for both sculpture class and the drawing group. On Thursday afternoon I catch a ride home to Sunflowers, throw down my bag and run out to the garden where I kick off my shoes and wiggle my toes into the loamy soil. Although Cindy says the owner of this place could put it up for sale anytime, and all my work would be for nothing, checking for squash bug eggs under the zucchini leaves fills a primal need, both for me and the zucchini plants. It gives me the chance to be of service to another being. Besides, it stretches my legs, something I desperately need after three straight days of modeling in town. Intoxicated with the scent of growth, I can imagine my essence seeping out in waves, through unbroken chains of being until I become infinite.

I pamper my plants, taking the time to channel some love to each one while watching out for lethal grass-burrs, those little bastards that linger in ambush wherever you find dirt in Texas. They must be aliens, invading from another planet, like squash bugs—unearthly. So I struggle with the invaders, just like humans have for eons.

After working up a sweat turning the compost, I'm standing *contrapposto* with a shovel in my hand beside twelve healthy-looking tomato plants, looking out across the sunflower field at the sunset. I'm enjoying a pastoral moment, rooted in this spot, belonging, like the girl in a Bouguereau painting, timeless and serene in the dying light of day. I've started to make peace with being pregnant. The little passenger in my belly promises a connection with eternity, and, before dark, the doves on the powerline bestow their solemn blessing.

———

In the morning, I wake to the sound of cattle bawling and galloping. At first the noise seems like part of a dream involving cowboys on a roundup. *Ghost riders in the sky.*

Then Cindy's voice cuts through my imaginings, "Git. Git out of there, go on! Git!"

Jolted from the dream, I orient myself and run to the window. There's trouble in the garden. I throw on a nightgown and race from the house to find Cindy stampeding half a dozen cows up the lane and onto the highway. I disregard the demolished garden fence and catch up with her. Now two barefoot women in short nighties are running down the blacktop chasing panicked cattle, heading off rogue cows, and keeping them all going the same direction. I stop to yank one of the cursed sand burrs from between my toes and vow never to venture off the pavement again.

A quarter mile down the road, the animals bolt through an open gate. We've been focused on the task at hand and didn't see the regular morning school-bus coming toward us, loaded with kids.

Cindy gasps, "We better go back."

"Think we can outrun it?"

"Let's go!"

"Whoooeee!" We scream, and sprint full-out, leaving little to the imagination with our flimsy nightgowns flapping and fluttering, revealing everything, and the bus in hot pursuit. Who knows why the idiot bus driver didn't have the presence of mind to stop and wait for us to clear out? But he didn't.

Still, we almost made it.

As we turn into our driveway, the bus passes, kids faces pasted to the windows. They saw the whole thing, buns and all.

"Think we'll be arrested?" I ask after the excitement while picking more grass-burrs out of my tender feet and trying to catch my breath.

"Nah, why would they arrest us?"

"I don't think we were decent, and those were schoolchildren."

"Shit, we were defending our property, Hon. This here is Texas, don't ya know!"

I'd been putting off looking at the damage done to the garden. A stretch of fence is down, the posts laid over. Tomato tripods toppled. The devastation is widespread.

"Damn cows!" Cindy stands with her fists clinched, "If I had a gun right now, I'd go shoot the infernal beasts. After all that work you did making a garden, and now it's totaled."

While Cindy stomps around ranting, I survey the waste for a minute, then turn back to the house without looking at her again, or at the garden. Too discouraged to talk, I cry for a long time, then put Dylan on the turntable and sing about *the moral of this story, the moral of this song* and how *you should never be where you do not belong.*

The cow episode brought a shift in attitude and precipitated a decision. Although it's my garden that got stomped, and Bear insists on remaining neutral, John, Phil and Nan have decided the tomato and zucchini massacre was a sign that it's time to move on. This evening, the Submarine crew has gathered with Cindy around the kitchen table, perusing the pages of the *Whole Earth Catalog* and looking for clues. Where to go?

We've narrowed the possibilities to either Arkansas or Canada.

"I want my own place," I say, "with a real fence, a real dog and a real man," surprising myself with such detailed wants. *Must be the hormones.*

Phil already has a destination in mind. "You could put a fence around Arkansas and people would survive just fine. It's perfect."

"Arkansas is full of hillbillies," John counters. "I say, let's go to Canada, it's way too hot down South."

Phil asks, "What makes you think Canada isn't full of hillbillies?"

"That's true." Cindy jumps in. "Hillbillies are everywhere. There's more right here in Texas than anywhere."

"Those are rednecks. Rednecks are predictable." John shivers, "Hillbillies are creepier."

Cindy rocks forward and back, taunting him with exaggerated nods. "Sounds like you're just a little bit prejudiced."

"Me?" John points at himself. "I'm just freaked out by people who sleep with goats and chickens.

"That's not fair. Those people you're calling hillbillies know how to make the dirt productive." Cindy flips a page in the Catalog, looking for geographical information. "And how to live without having to buy everything they need."

"Good dirt and plenty of water are all you need to make a homestead," I say. "I like it here ast Sunflowers, except for the damn cows.. I wish we could buy this place."

"This is a twenty acre parcel, and all we can afford around Austin is two acres," John adds, looking defeated. "We need more than two acres."

"Why?" I ask.

"Privacy," Phil says. "The people here live too close together. We should be looking for forty acres in a state with the fewest people per square mile. "

Cindy has found the map with population figures. "That would be Wyoming."

"It's all sage brush out there."

"Not true," Phil argues. "There's a perfect spot outside of Jackson. It's beautiful! We went there on vacation one year."

"No water," John complains. Why is he such a pessimist?

"There is too water. There's a river." Cindy says, lost in the map of Wyoming.

"You can't buy the river," John points out. "There's no water in the West. It's all bought up. Besides, it takes a lot of acres to homestead there." John has a point, but no solutions.

"That brings us back to Arkansas. It's kind of like out West, but not," Phil concludes. "We're going North, no matter. Let's swing through Arkansas and check it out, but my money is on Canada. There *is* that little issue with my draft status."

"You could stop in Fayetteville," Cindy adds. "I have some cool friends there."

"Hillbillies," someone murmurs.

I say screw the garden, anyway. The heat in Texas is beginning to get to me. I dread July here, but what I really dread is living in the freezing cold of the North. Putting on children's snowsuits and mittens and taking them off for eight months every year is not my idea of fun. The West? I like the 'horses' part, but it seems a little too conservative and too cowboy.

My opinion doesn't count, though, since all the others vote to go north. Sometimes I think they'll always be looking for that *something* that's just over the horizon, but never finding it. At any rate, we've given up on buying a piece of land in Central Texas. It's too bad, there's a lot to like about this place. But a force of nature is stirring up my nest, and I'm being pushed along again, right when it felt so good to be settled.

A few things I've collected are spread on the floor by my cedar chest, waiting to be judged worthy of keeping or giving away. Everything else has already been trashed. I've toyed with the idea of calling my folks, but put it off again and decide to address what's directly in front of me—this cedar chest of grandma's.

Grandma Justice always had time for me. We enjoyed being together for the love shared, but also the intellectual stimulation. Thanks to her, I read Emily Dickinson and J.D. Salinger, Ford Maddox Ford and Virginia Woolfe. I could almost do no wrong around grandma, but if I did, she would let me know in a gentle way. I remember the hours we spent reading out loud to each other, and after her death I still feel closer to her than any other person in my life. Her house symbolized comfort and hospitality—a place where kids played, everyone ate their fill, and laughter was the common denominator. I long for a house like that.

In the bottom of the chest is the embroidered pouch that Blaine bought for me in New Orleans. It contains photos of my mother, father, sister, two brothers and myself. There's the envelope with Blaine's parent's address and the one with the treasury bond from Grandma that I've been saving until the right piece of land comes along. The pouch and quilted jacket will go with me, but the chest will have to stay here at the farm I have a feeling I'll be travelling light in the near future.

————

CHAPTER 13
CLIFF

Color has a flavor and a feel, as well as
temperature. We say a color is either
warm or cool, but that distinction is
only relative. There is no absolute rule.
Red is warmer than green. Grays can
be either warm or cool. Temperature is
significant only when one color is
compared to another.

The tar came off the windows of the Plymouth, but the doors were a problem. Gasoline worked to dissolve the stuff, then dish soap washed that off, but there was a ghost message still residing on both sides of the car. I'd have to deal with that later somehow, but in the meantime, I let my anger at Conner subside into the background and enjoyed a bit of independence after all the years of earning nothing but trophies and grades.

One Wednesday during finals when I didn't have any tests, I spent the morning exploring the lake in a canoe, and afterward, I stopped at my cabin. In the mirror was a face flushed from time in the sun and water, the sandy hair bleached toward yellow. A smear of zinc oxide by my nose needed attention. Good enough, I grabbed my serape and guitar case, stood for a minute wondering what I'd forgotten. Then I got into the car and drove away hoping there would be some young ladies out at the cove.

Over the still-green hills to the south, low rumblings and a darkening sky indicated a thunderstorm on the way. Maybe it wasn't the best time to go swimming, but I shivered and drove toward Rock-n-Roll Randy's house anyway, as preliminary raindrops spattered the windshield and cool air gusted in the window. Lightning streaked, thunderclaps shook the earth and I breathed ozone.

Daydreaming about girls, I missed the Mt. Bonnell cutoff, and had to turn around. At Randy's, no one answered my knock, but the shower was running inside, so I sat down on a bench by the door to wait. A sudden flash and boom erupted from the ground and echoed inside my head. Then the bottom dropped out. Rain descended in sheets, covering the hard ground with instant lakes. I sat in the half-shelter of the roof gable, pulled my feet up, and hugged my bare knees to my chest, enjoying the smell of rain, thrilled with the drama of the storm.

It lasted all of five minutes, then Randy came outside naked, trim and white-skinned, drying his long hair with a towel. He looked all around before spotting me. "There you are. I decided to clean up my act. How about this rain? It's like smiling. When you shower, the whole world showers with you." He grinned and disappeared into the house.

In a minute, he came back out warbling a blues riff, dressed in sandals, faded skin-tight bell bottoms, and a denim cowboy shirt. We climbed into the VW bus, and the bus climbed over Mt. Bonnell into town where we stopped to pick someone up.

"How can we have mo-lasses when we ain't got no lasses?" Randy said, and I got bumped from the shotgun seat by a girl.

We stopped again for some others and headed back out of town. The cove was tucked away on the other side of the lake where the bluffs were steep, and cedars were plentiful. Randy turned off the highway through an opening in the thicket, then eased us into a turnaround and backed uphill onto a cleared knoll—a smooth move, one he'd obviously done before.

I opened the door as the sun hovered on the horizon and the amber-edged clouds intensified to orange. Caught in the last ray of the day, I stretched, enjoying the warmth, and let my gaze wander along the ridge-top. Toward the west a distant oak caught a glint of fiery light. We need a better name for sunset colors—something that does justice to the stupendous reality of it, like topaz or carnelian. I'll never understand why people don't drop everything for ten minutes once every twenty-four hours and simply watch the day come to a close.

––––––

With the distant hills still shimmering, our troupe took the path downward, hugging a limestone bluff, and we entered a lush purple-green bowl of mysterious shadow. The recent rain had made the ground slippery, so I was busy watching my feet and managing the awkward guitar case, holding it with both hands over my head while Randy and the others dragged along some firewood. Ancient feathery treetops that hovered within arm's reach on one side, while umpteen varieties of dark fern leaned into the path from the other.

At eye level I caught glimpses of pink and green lichens forming the stone's mottled skin. Bass notes from the waterfall below pulsed in my belly, wood-smoke curled among the branches, and the odor of burning cedar surrounded our little group. Down by the water, cypress roots sprawled over the ground and heavy limbs reached up to a bright pink sky. Human murmurs emanated from the pool below and mingled with high-pitched birdsongs.

I can picture the scene clearly now, as though time and space have warped and I'm re-living it all. Ahead, along the bank, people are gathered around the perimeter of a blaze. I recognize LeAnn, the waitress from work, sitting with another girl, the two of them between two guys. *Oh fuck.* One of them is James Conner. After the shitty message painted on my car, he's the last person I want to see, but I won't let him spoil my evening. I'll just have to steel myself against his bullshit.

Randy hails the group to ask if they have room for a few more, and they wave us into the circle. I back up to the fire and scope out the seating arrangements. There's plenty of room, so I untie my water jug from the guitar case, unpack the Gibson, and strum a song while a joint comes around. I don't play that well, but I know a few tunes and like to sing. What can they say? I brought the only guitar.

Six guys and four girls are sitting around the fire. Two more guys and a girl appear on the path and someone puts out the joint. The new people sit, and the joint re-appears. Five girls and eight other guys, I notice, while I continue to strum and sing. *LeAnn must have changed her mind about me*, I'm thinking as she moves closer and starts to sing along. Conner scowls from across the fire and pulls a beer out of the cooler beside him.

Bruce, a guy I know from school, is one of the new arrivals. He catches my eye after a song and gives a "May I?" sign, indicating the guitar. I gladly hand it across to him and sit back. LeAnn has her hand on my leg, her tit rubbing my arm. Connor's scowl has turned into something nasty, boring through me like a power drill. LeAnn likes it, but I don't. *Dammit!* She's just messing with us, to see what we'll do. To top it all off, I'm getting aroused and not wanting to be. *Red light.*

My turn again to play a song again, so I move away from LeAnn when Bruce hands me the guitar and I sing the one by Jim Kweskin about when the light turns green and you put your foot down on the gasoline. *But when the light turns red . . .*

———

CHAPTER 14
MARIAH AND CLIFF

*Art is about the extra-ordinary
experience. When the creative hand
and mind combine to make a
connection with the 'other,' what
results is a process of communion and
a product called 'art.'*

   Several of us are sitting on the front porch at Sunflowers in post-
prandial, post-spaghetti satisfaction after my final meal here. I'm in
the rocking chair, unbraiding my hair, while cicadas and frogs play
counterpoint in the thickening dusk. The screen door opens, and Otis
asks, "Who's up for a swim? Mariah? Cindy?"
   My mind answers, *It's too late to go swimming,* but every cell in
my body says, *yes, yes, yes.* My mind gets out-voted, so I go looking
for the clean towel I have stashed in my room. I'm packed for
traveling light, so there isn't much to gather. Cindy begs off, saying
she's tired, but others are moving around with varying degrees of
purpose.

I show up on the porch. "You ready?"

By the time Otis is ready, we have a car full.

Out at the lake, half a dozen people have a cozy fire blazing by the shore, and they're singing *Blowing in the Wind*. Beyond them on my right, a waterfall spills over the rock overhang and pounds into the water. To my left, the cove opens into the body of the lake. The others go naturally toward the fire, but I go left, down to the bank. Since this pregnancy began, I dream of oceans and swimming pools—underwater, surrounded, buoyed, supported. Water is everywhere, as if I've entered my baby's world. I feel no distinction between the human and the natural realm.

Out of my sandals to test the temperature—cool, but not cold. I lose skirt, shirt, panties and towel (don't own a bra, or need one for that matter) and enter the dark water alone under starlight. Easing away from the shore, I find my depth, chest deep, and stand on the bottom, soaking up the sweet solitude as darkness descends.

My feet find their way toward the waterfall, past the murmur of conversation around the fire where a single guitar accompanies a baritone voice. He sings, *Relax your mind, relax your mind, sometimes it feels so fine.* I swim to the deeper, cooler, darker place near the fall and tread water, slow and easy, until a flat rock presents a place to sit with my head above the surface.

———

I'm sweating by the time I finish singing, *Sometimes, you've gotta relax your mind.* Someone has piled on the wood, making the fire way too hot. Conner is still glaring, and I have to pee, so I hand the guitar to Bruce and walk up to relieve myself among the rocks. Then, making my way through boulders to the shoreline, I'm pulled by the vortex where the waterfall meets the surface. In a heartbeat, I'm out of shorts and tee shirt, stepping into the water, deeper into the darkness and under the fall, letting it pound me until I'm barely able to stand.

The din has obliterated all other sound. Staggering away from the thunder, I feel purified, and the roar subsides. I'm feeling my way, walking in chest deep water among the rocks when my hand grazes something slippery and warm. There is a surprised "Oh!"—not my own—amid the roar of the deluge.

———

I gasp as something warm brushes me in the coolness below. *A hand?* There's a splash and a ripple. I slide off my perch and turn, at once afraid, then curious, reaching out to see. *Who?*

A dim face in the shadow.

———

My "oops" and "sorry" get lost in the other sounds. I lose my footing and my head goes under. My toes find a rock, so my head is above water, but barely. I've intruded on someone sitting, it seems, on a submerged boulder. We're close together but invisible in the faint glow. Sliding deeper and turning toward me, this person reaches out a hand and touches the side of my face, cheek and jaw. I reach out slowly to return the gesture and feel an ear, covered with long wet hair—an ear with an earring attached. My fingers trace from the large hoop along a delicate jaw to a strong but smooth chin—female!

The exploration continues with me slowly kicking and sculling to keep close to her, then my toes find a better perch below. She's reached a place to stand with her head and shoulders above water. In the muted starlight I strain to see something of her—the brief twinkling of an eye, one earring. Beautiful. She feels my hair, which has grown over the ears since basketball season. Then as if blind, she touches the top of my forehead with palm and fingers, then my nose, the faint bristle on upper lip. Her fingers linger briefly on my lower lip before sliding to my chest. I have the strange sensation that this girl is 'seeing' me the only way she can, and I'm being fully revealed for the first time in my life.

———

He's gentle but responsive, so I'm leading. The ballroom instructor said, "The one who leads must be firm and balanced, in order to show the follower what to do next. The cue should be clear. Leaders, push or pull, or twist, or spin with your hands. Followers, maintain resistance, give the leader something to push against."

My eyes are closed. His hair is not long, curling only once around my finger. There's a place on his neck where the light stubble ends and the skin is smooth. He's holding my neck and feeling my hair in response. Gentle warm hand. We trade touches like this for a while, slowly and carefully, feeling faces, necks and shoulders, maintaining a precarious balance in the water. It is a dance in counterpoint—a ritual call and response. We each maintain distance with pressure, exploring unknown but strangely safe territory.

———————

Everything is held in balance. The only things in my universe are the points of contact—tiptoes on rock, fingers on flesh—and my pulse. I am aroused, way beyond anything or anytime ever before, and subsumed into a tactile feast.

It seems like an accident when it happens, although later I'll wonder. Probably just a lapse in concentration. She has one hand on my heart and the other on the side of my neck. I shift sideways to adjust my footing and in doing so, find higher ground. Stepping up, I upset her balance and both her hands go around my neck. She slides against me and down. All the way down, the angle of presentation, acute. No resistance at all, only warmth and welcome. An accident of timing, lucky but unsought.

We make a perfect fit with her legs around me and my hands under her backside, absolutely still, absorbing the sensation of union and warmth and wetness.

My poor brain, robbed of blood, manages to come up with one word. "Warm."

"Mmmmmm," I hear through my chest. Through her chest, I mean.

———————

I've fallen on to him, incredibly, with the abrupt sensation that I have at last arrived home. Totally calm, totally right, perfect even. A heartbeat swooshing in my ears—*Whose heartbeat?*—feeling the pulse beating with my palm on his chest, and inside, too. I give an internal squeeze, feel instant response, wait . . . and squeeze again, sending everything I've got his way.

———

Back and forth it goes as the touching continues, now with an inner dance. Her movement and my response coordinate, without thought or design, and we both yield to the mystery, allowing the blessing to wash over us in waves that last a lifetime.

The flashing lights seemed like a part of my ecstatic state, but then she tightened on me and said, "Look!" in a loud whisper. What I'd taken at first for fireworks of a personal event were, in fact, the blue lights of a cop car up on the hill. Immediately, a spotlight came on to my right, shining toward the fire. The boat had approached silently in the darkness and was almost on top of us. Luckily, a cluster of rocks shielded us partially from view. I saw the silhouette of two men sitting in the boat, their attention directed on the group on shore.

If I hadn't been anchored so solidly within my new companion, I would have jumped out of my skin. Instead, I marveled at what was happening, and we stayed like we were, snugly joined beneath the surface, keeping our heads low, unmoving. Well, moving a bit—just enough to keep the taut connection. I held her, kissed her and felt her while watching the lights, sustained by the anticipation of her next gentle squeeze. It seemed like we'd been together forever, sharing a perfect moment, and I gave up the need to finish what we'd started, knowing that whatever happened would be okay.

There was another commotion when the boat finally eased away toward the fire and voices on a loudspeaker ordered our friends to freeze and put their hands up. That broke the spell.

My partner pushed herself up and slid off of me, saying into my ear, "I'd better go get my clothes."

As she swam away, only a silhouette against the distant glow of open water, I said something like, "Who are you?"

Then either she yelled or someone on the hillside yelled.

All I heard was "Ai-yah."

———

CHAPTER 15
CLIFF

All our lives we have learned to see the world symbolically. Everything falls into a category: tree, cup, airplane, woman, book, face, hand, etc. As sensory artists, we liberate ourselves from that symbolic way of seeing and look at things in terms of patterns of positive and negative shapes and values.

I was dazed for a minute, and why I didn't follow her while I had the chance, I'll never know. Self-preservation, I guess—didn't want to be caught with my pants down. I watched her swim away, a silhouette circling past the boat and waterfall, growing smaller until her shape disappeared. She was beautiful, she was gone, and I never even saw her face.

Blue lights still flashed across the cove as I made my way to the far side of the waterfall and began to climb up through the rocks. I'd just slipped on my clothes and tied my shoes when lightening struck and a thunderclap shook the earth. Then came rain, single drops at first, followed by a downpour. The full force of the storm caught me on the cliffside and forced me to crouch in a ball and wait it out.

When I got to the top of the hill Randy's bus was gone and I was drenched to the bone. A car started on the far side of the cove and the flashing lights drifted off toward the main highway, followed by the thunder and the rain. Soaking wet, I took off in the other direction and floated along a meandering backroad through a star-lit Texas valley, full of wonder, my body vibrating in resonance with heavenly bodies. Everything had re-aligned in a different order, as though I'd strayed into a parallel universe, thunder-charged and beautiful. And having tasted beauty, I felt a comradery with all humankind. I believed in the essential goodness of the earth and all its people.

When a car noise registered behind me, I eased over to the fence-line, straddled the fence and slipped over it. My shorts caught on a barb and I heard a ripping sound, then felt a sharp jab on the inside of my thigh. *Damn!* The lights of a car appeared then, so I crouched down in the bushes and watched out the corners of my eyes, afraid their glow would give me away. I became a kid again, playing soldier, lugging my old decommissioned Springfield rifle, crawling through vacant lots and sneaking up quietly on the neighbor boys, watching them like a cat stalking a bird.

The car whooshed by and I came back to the present. Not a cop. Just a car. I fingered the rip in my crotch, then, oh my God, I was back at the cove again instantly, feeling the connection with *her*, Aiyah, amazed once more by the abruptness of our joining, the absence of release and the knowledge that my life would never be the same again.

That's when I noticed the pain in my testicles. In fact, my whole groin, thighs and belly ached with the immediacy, the pleasure, the maddening incompleteness of it all. But it was sweet torment. Her skin, slick, and breasts, firm against my ribs. Thighs clamped around me. Liquid inside, like a hot bath—slippery and wet. So alive—like she was inside *my* body instead of the other way around. With the lake patrol only ten feet away and the searchlight swinging back and forth, I'd been on the brink of explosion the whole time.

Another noise and headlights down the road prompted another fence-climbing episode. With the clump of cedar trees providing cover, I pulled down my shorts and gave myself a much-needed release, luxuriating in the best memory of my life. Then my body took charge, my feet took to the road, and movement brought a welcome warmth to my bones.

Hoofing it down the highway, I held a faint hope that my friends would find me, but realistically, I knew it was everyone for themselves. Later, after many miles, a sliver of moon emerged with a glow around it, and not long after that, the sky lightened, and Sunday night turned into Monday morning. I was trudging on the shoulder of the highway when a '58 Chevy pickup slowed down and pulled over. I climbed in and had a moment of panic, realizing way too late that I'd left my guitar and serape back at the bonfire.

At Randy's place I opened the front door, and called out, "Anybody home." Hearing no response, I got in the Plymouth. Damn! Wet seat. I'd left the windows down. A soggy piece of paper was stuck on the steering wheel, and in the Plymouth's dim overhead light, I read the note, "Sorry buddy, I had to split. Back at ya later."

Sometime, I would have to process all the events of the night, but right then I was dead tired, my feet were on fire and I just needed a place to crash. My brother's place in town would be perfect. He was out of the country, but I knew where he kept the key. With my destination close, I entered the stream of early traffic coming off the Balcones plateau and rolled into Austin the instant the sun peeked over the Eastern horizon.

————

I woke up the next afternoon in my borrowed bed, then limped into the bathroom for a shower, only to find no hot water. I made it short with cold water and reached for the towel as footsteps passed in the hall outside. Blaine. I thought he was still in Mexico. He must have been curious when he got home and saw my Plymouth parked in the alley.

The footsteps returned with a question, "Hey bro, you want a shirt?

I emerged from the bathroom wrapped in a towel. "Please."

"Sorry about the water. I forgot to replace the fuse." Blaine tossed me a shirt. "Hey, I'm thinking about El Toro for supper. You know— all you can eat. How about it?"

"I'm in," I said. "Just be a minute."

The blisters on my feet hurt like the dickens, reminding me of walking twenty miles the previous night before getting a ride.

And *Aiyah*. Strange, the improbable way we slid together and joined bodies without any intention. We could never have accomplished it deliberately . . .

First the Band-Aids, then the shirt, then my ripped shorts. The socks were trashed, so I laced my Chuck Taylor All Stars gingerly.

"Let's go, Cliff, I'm starving." Blaine headed for the car.

"I'll take my car, too." I hobbled after him. "I'm going back to the Bar S tonight."

The aroma of cumin, hot grease and corn tortillas was thick in the parking lot as I pulled in beside Blaine, and I was salivating before I opened the restaurant door. We slipped into a booth and the easy, immediate rapport of brothers.

"I met someone last night, but I don't know her name," I sighed.

"You *do* look like you've been rode hard and put up wet."

"I feel sort of like that, but not because of her."

An agile waiter poured our iced tea. Started tipping the pitcher three feet away and a stream of tea arced through the air into the quart-sized glass. The waiter followed the arc all the way to the glass, stopping just above it. Didn't spill a drop. He probably had to pass a tea-pouring test before getting hired.

"You going to see her again?" Blaine asked.

"That's just it, I didn't *see* her."

"How'd you meet her, then?"

"You wouldn't believe it." I'd planned to tell him the whole story, but it was too fresh and too private. When I felt for her inside, she was still there, so I sent a carnal squeeze her way through the universe, like a wish or a promise, the only means of communication available at the moment. Used to be people got to know each other before having sex, but things had changed since the sexual revolution. I guessed I *was* in sync with the rest of the world, but it felt weird, not knowing her.

"You should have seen this girl I met in New Orleans during Mardi Gras, before I went to Mexico." Blaine looked wistful. "She was an art model, you know, in the nude. Wild chick. Funny too. We went to a jazz club and danced all night. If I didn't have this trip coming up . . ."

I drifted back to my own memories of the night before until the waiter came with food and we dug in to plates of enchiladas and tamales swimming in chili. I loved how they put almost-raw chopped onions in their cheese enchiladas. The chalupas were piled high with shredded cheese and refried beans, lettuce and chopped tomatoes. I ordered one of everything, but the chili-con-queso was the highlight of the meal—a puffed, dome-shaped crispy corn tortilla drenched in melted cheese.

It was only the third time I'd seen my brother since he came back from 'Nam. Blaine had mustered out as Major with a Purple Heart after flying sixty-some-odd missions. A bit of shrapnel in his shoulder earned him the medal and changed his mission from the A1 aircraft to a converted C47 after a short stint training ARVN pilots. Blaine had come back from the war with a strange mixture of anger, pain and guilt—along with something softer that I couldn't place. I'd always wanted to go to the Academy like he did. Follow in his footsteps. Until he came back from Vietnam, that is.

I said, "Dad wants me to join ROTC when I start at UT this fall." There'd never been a question about my going to college. It was understood.

"Sure, follow in my exalted footsteps." Blaine trapped his lower lip behind his upper teeth. "Dad served in World War II as an office manager at a magnesium plant. They refined material for incendiary bombs. It was part of the war effort, all right, but he was a long way from the action." Blaine leaned across the table. "He doesn't know the score, Cliff. I've dropped napalm on defenseless women and children. Civilians. Do you know what that stuff *does* to people?"

I tried not to imagine, forced myself to take some deep breaths of *comino*-flavored air, and focused on my jumbo glass of tea.

My brother went on, "You get yourself informed, and watch out for politicians. Stay in school, keep your student deferment. The war in Vietnam will be over before you get out. We're going to lose. You wait and see."

We dug into another order of chili con queso, and over bites of that crunchy, gooey, chili-infused cheese, I tried to visualize the end of the Vietnam war. I couldn't. In my mind it went on for years. For a lifetime, even. I knew there was more to his story than I'd been told, more darkness than I could imagine, and probably more medals than he told me about, but something about Blaine's manner kept me from asking about the war, so I asked him how he ended up in Mexico, instead.

Blaine scanned the empty tables around us and leaned forward. "When I was giving flying lessons in South Texas, sometimes I would slip into Mexico over the Gulf or down by Big Bend when nobody was watching. I started hauling fishermen across the border. At first, my plane ate up all the profits. Then I hit the jackpot. This guy I met in Tampico wanted me to run some pot into Texas for him, so I made a couple of trips and paid off the plane.

"After that, the guys on this end said the pot from Tampico wasn't good enough. Shit-weed, they called it. Said I would have to go deeper in, further South. Now I've got something set up down in Acapulco."

I have to say my appreciation for Blaine jumped up a few notches with the revelation that he'd been smuggling weed. My world expanded a few sizes, too, to include that mysterious territory across the border. Our waiter brought the check and a plate with two pieces of Mexican candy—hard, sugary pralines with pecans—bringing an end to the conversation about smuggling.

"Well, I'd better get back to the Bar S." I grabbed a praline for the road and stood up. "I have to work in the morning.

"I'll get the check. You can take off."

I punched his shoulder. "See you later then."

He laughed. "So long, little bro."

I climbed into the car and saw the beginnings of a meager sunset, a streak of yellow-orange winking at me through a dense cloud layer. Fifteen minutes later I pulled up to the cabin I shared with Thomas at the Bar S. The porch light was off and the door was locked, a strange thing since we never locked it. I knocked and called, "Thomas, it's me, Cliff."

With a rattle, a scratch and a click, the door opened and cool air escaped from the interior. Thomas was looking down at the floor between his size thirteen sock feet, a gloomy expression on his face, a broken LP record and ripped cover in his hand.

"What happened?" I asked, ogling the mangled Buddy Guy album with *Stormy Monday* on it, a new favorite of mine. Thomas glanced out at the Plymouth and saw the residue of Conner's message, still legible.

"Looks like the same polecat been messin' with both of us."

"Who . . . ?"

He just shook his head.

I came into the cave-like room and closed the door behind me, wondering what was up, and saw the record player, upside-down on his floor. "Your stereo," I said.

"That's nothin, Cliff. I'm afraid there's bad news, besides that."

"Uh oh."

Thomas filled me in, "I was working in the kitchen this morning when cops came in the dining room with LeAnn and Bill. Cops say they have LeAnn's boyfriend in jail."

"Conner? I can't say I'm disappointed."

"No, he ain't no good."

"Is that all?"

"They asked LeAnn a bunch of questions about Conner and you. Bill was pissed. He told her to pack up her stuff."

"He fired LeAnn?"

"That's right. She's out'a here. Then Bill came to the kitchen and got me. The cops ask me about what happened at the lake. I told them I don't know nothing. They ask about you by name. I told them I hardly know you."

"Thanks, Thomas."

"No need. You been here, they'd of called you in too. Bill, he wants you up to the office, first thing in the morning." He tilted his head and spread his hands. "Sorry man—weren't nothin' I could do."

Fuck! I said to myself. My chalupas did a little dance in my stomach and threatened to come back up. I drifted down to the lakeshore where guests had brought folding chairs to watch the sunset. It was a nightly ritual at the Bar S. Under my breath I sang

Donovan's words over and over, like a benediction, *Way down below the ocean. . . where I want to be. . . she may be.*

The clouds parted just in time to reveal an orange globe squatted on the horizon like a burning bullfrog. It paused there for three long breaths before plunging into a horizontal band of blue, and I felt like the sun had dropped into a pit of doom.

———

CHAPTER 16
CLIFF

*What is good design? It's the ability
first to attract, then hold a viewer's
attention. All the artistic elements and
tools conspire with the mind and hand
to achieve this result. Value, color,
balance, rhythm, edge, texture, thrust,
not to mention content, emotion and
intention.*

After a restless night, I limped over to Bill's office the next
morning and got fired.

"A deputy came by the office this morning looking for you." Bill
shuffled some papers on his desk, like he'd lost something. "They
found your guitar at your party site and brought it here, asked if it
was yours."

"Where is it then?"

"They kept it for evidence."

"Evidence of what?" I asked.

He looked up at me. "There were two bags of grass in it."

"Oh shit! That's not mine."

"Conner and LeAnn both claimed it was." Bill fixed his gaze on me.

"That's a lie."

"That's what I figured," he said, casually. "The deputy wasn't buying it either. They let LeAnn go and kept Conner. He has a record of burglary and possession of methedrine. They found other stuff in his car, so he'll do some time for it."

"What about me?"

"Cliff, I know the deputy. I told him you were an honest and responsible worker. That I didn't think you were involved. That the dope in your guitar was probably Conner's."

"And he believed that?" I had no doubt that Conner had planted the weed, but there was no way to prove it.

"At least he listened."

"Thanks, Bill."

"You know the score, Cliff. It's nothing personal, but I'm going to have to let you go. Boss's rules."

The rush of emotion itched and smarted, like the sting of a red wasp. I wanted to go, get away, or scratch or something, but the damage was already done. I did know the score. Employees at the Bar S were not allowed to associate with anyone using illegal drugs, even if it was only marijuana. The summer's plans, the job, the people—all shot. To top it off, the cops were looking for me.

I let out a long breath and managed to ask. "So that's it?"

"I'm afraid so. Here's your check."

"They didn't bring my serape?"

"They didn't mention it."

"Well, so long, then." I turned and walked out the door, still feeling the sting, too discouraged and distracted to even shake Bill's hand. That old serape was a gift my great Uncle Nel had brought me from Mexico—I'd had it for years. I looked at the buildings around me and realized how dull everything looked. Paint was peeling everywhere. Pieces of trash were lodged against foundations. Wasp nests cluttered the eaves. I hadn't noticed before, but the Bar S was a dump.

"Canned?" Thomas asked, when I was back at the cabin.

"Yeah."

"That's a raw deal. I just got used to having a roommate, and here the boss tells me I'm not to share my place with nobody. Just as well, I guess." He shook his head. "We're sure gonna miss you, Cliff."

"Same here, Thomas."

"What you gonna do?"

"I don't know. I liked this job. I really liked it." I wasn't liking it any more, though. The pay was meager, the wranglers were jerks, and LeAnn made me sick.

'This place ain't so bad."

"No, it's not," I lied—it *was* bad. Even so, my eyes kept searching for beauty and discovered it in the violet highlights on Thomas' deep mahogany face. Seeing a watercolor portrait there, I had a momentary desire to capture him in paint. *But that'll never happen now*, I thought, and said, "Thanks for everything, Thomas," already missing his gentle ways.

"Sure thing."

"Well, I'll be seeing you." I held out my hand.

Thomas grabbed it with both of his. "Keep the faith, Cliff."

It didn't take long to clear out my stuff—pillow, sheets and clothes. I crammed my bathroom things in the clothes bag and threw it in the trunk of the Plymouth, where my stereo sat beside a pile of records. Remembering the wrecked turntable, I lifted my old Magnavox out of the trunk and turned to face Thomas, who'd followed me to the car.

"Here," I said. "You'll be needing this."

He blinked, and through his glasses, I watched his eyes double in size.

I left Thomas speechless and drove out the Bar S gate into a hot wind that blew across an alien world. The cloudless sky darkened, trapping me in a shadow that I couldn't escape. Every car I passed looked suspicious, and the drivers, unfriendly. On the radio, The Animals echoed my thoughts, singing, *We've got to get out of this place, if it's the last thing we ever do . . . We've got to get out of this place, Girl, there's a better life for me and you . . .*

The girl! How could I forget? . . . *Find the girl, stupid!* I admonished myself. *Find Aiyah.*

But if I found her, what would I do? Ride up on my stallion—a faded old marked-up jalopy—and grab her hand, pull her up behind me and ride off into the sunset like some kind of hero? *Get real.* It was a juvenile fantasy, but then isn't that what all little boys dream of? Not to be *like* the Lone Ranger, but to *be* the Lone Ranger.

———

I had no job and no place to live, no girl and no idea how to find her. My feet were killing me and the cops were after me, so I went to consult the familiar voice of experience, my brother, and found him at home.

"Hey Blaine, I've got a problem. . . well, a couple of problems." Actually, there were more troubles I could have listed, but *What to do about money?* and *What to do about Aiyah?* were the ones on my mind.

"You okay?" Blaine asked, leading me into the kitchen.

I sat down at the table, my fingers toying with loose Formica. "I got fired today."

"Damn!" he winced.

"And remember the girl I told you about last night?"

"Oh yeah," Blaine nodded. "The one with no name."

"I can't find her."

"That's a double damn!"

"When the heat showed up, we got separated." That got his attention.

"Wow! Triple damn, Cliff. What happened?"

"We were, uh . . . swimming. The cops came in a boat. She went one way and got a ride. I went another way and had to walk. I left my guitar there and the cops found it with two lids inside."

"You are royally fucked!"

"I'll say. They want to talk to me."

"What are you going to do now?" Blaine asked.

My troubles sat on me like three hundred pounds of free weights. I couldn't lift them off and getting out from under was not an option. Unless a miracle happened.

"When's your next trip to Mexico?" I asked, hoping for that miracle.

"Actually," he said. "I got the call yesterday. I'm leaving day after tomorrow."

"I wish I could split and magically appear somewhere else," I said.

Blaine was on his way to Barton Springs for a swim, and I was already dressed in jams and t-shirt, so I piled in with him. The spring-fed swimming pool beside the Colorado River is famous throughout Central Texas. The water there will make your nuts crawl up inside your body like a sumo wrestler's, especially in May. Rather than jump right in, we spread towels on the grassy bank and lay heating up in the sun, watching a group of kids turn blue in the water.

After a while, he rolled over on his stomach. "I'll just be gone four days," he said. "Long enough to do the deal."

"Take me along," I begged, shameless.

"I have to fly down and back twice to keep kosher with the official flight plan. Maybe . . . " He thought for a minute, then turned on his side. I could see the wheels turning. "You've got your visa, right?"

"Yep, I got it last week. All I need is shots." We had planned an excursion to Mexico at the end of summer, after my job was over and before I started college in the fall.

"You'll have to talk to the parents, you know."

"I will." *I was in!* I thought, and the melody of *La Cucaracha* began playing in my head.

————

There was no way to avoid going to dinner with my folks. That evening after dessert we sat on the patio and talked. Dad was preoccupied with preparing for a summer session of the Legislature, so at least the timing was in my favor.

"You got fired?"

"Yes, sir."

"What happened, son?"

"Well, the other night I was at the lake with a bunch of people at a campfire. I went for a swim, and while I was in the water, the cops came. A girl I work with and her boyfriend got caught with some pot."

"You went swimming in the lake at night?" Mom shivered.

"The water was nice, Mom."

"Did you talk to the police?" Dad asked.

"No. After all the excitement, I went to Blaine's house. The next morning a deputy came to the Bar S and found out I'd been at the lake."

Dad was nodding, like he'd heard it all before. "So, when the shit hit the fan, some of it got on you."

"That's about it. And, they confiscated my guitar."

"I suppose you were squeaky clean?"

"It wasn't my pot." I walked the razor's edge, holding back critical details but trying not to lie.

"Son, there are drug laws for a reason." Dad had the stern look he always used when dispensing advice. "You need to watch who you associate with." He pointed his finger at me. "I can't risk the press finding out about this. It's embarassing. The voters wouldn't like it."

"I don't think I care what Nixon voters like." I figured they didn't like having fingers pointed at them.

His face flushed bright red and he puffed up like a fighting rooster. "You'd better care. I have to face those people every day, smile and shake hands with them." With that, he deflated a little and his voice calmed. "Besides, Nixon was the best choice we had for the country."

"Not for *my* country. Nixon's a liar and a crook."

"He's a politician, Cliff."

My legs propelled me out of my chair. "He promised to end the war, Dad. He's already sent more troops."

"You're too young to understand, son."

"So, I'm too young to understand that you end a war by keeping it going? You put out a fire by pouring gas on it? Get real. I'm supposed let a bunch of self-righteous old men send me to 'Nam to get my legs shot off for no reason? I'm too young to understand that?"

The winds of war—along with my rant—blew me away, clear off the patio and into the darkness. I stumbled over the stone border on

Mom's flowerbed, barked my shin and fell into the four-o'clocks, landing with a *splat!* The pungent reek of mutilated vegetation pervaded the atmosphere, and dampness seeped through my pants. I guess she must have watered the flowers.

"Stand up and be a man, son," my dad hollered.

There was no personal damage, except to my dignity, so I stood up, brushed myself off, and delicately stepped away from the flowers. I turned back to my father, quivering with emotion, and my voice turned to steel. "It's a stupid war, Dad. It has nothing to do with defending America. Your friend Lyndon Johnson is an ass, but Nixon makes me want to puke."

"You'll never make a persuasive argument using that tone of voice. If you want to debate an issue, you need to act civilized."

"Civilized! So it's civilized to lie, just to get elected? It's civilized to massacre whole villages of women and children for no reason? I don't need that kind of fucking civilization, I'm not joining your fucking ROTC, and I'm not fucking going to Vietnam."

My father yelled, "Son, you're a God-damned coward." With that, he turned, fuming, and strode toward the sliding door, threw it open and went inside. He slammed it behind him, having 'sonned' me so much in one night, I thought the shaking glass would break.

I flashed back four years, to the last time my father had used a belt on me. It was something he'd bring out, not to punish my misbehavior itself, but for trying to cover it up, refusing to admit what I'd done, or for lying about it. As though dishonesty was a fatal flaw that had to be rooted out at all costs. What the belt did was instill in me an obsession with truth and fairness.

I plopped back down in my chair and Mom brought dessert.

"Cliff, he didn't mean it."

"I believe he did," I said.

She shook her head, her voice soft. "You need to be working this summer."

"I'll get another job."

"What are you going to do now?"

"I'm getting out of here." I stood up, leaving my pecan pie untouched. "Sorry, Mom. I've gotta go."

"I love you, Cliff."

Mom kissed me goodbye and gave me a long look. "Be careful and come back soon."

I beat it, still trembling from the confrontation with Dad, caught up in self-righteous indignation. He was dead wrong. I was glad I hadn't actually lied to him, though. I'd only omitted part of the story, the part about the pot in my guitar and all that. Well, the truth is, I'd omitted most of the story.

If Dad knew about the deputies looking for me, I would be in deep shit, but I felt no remorse about that. What I felt guilty about was fudging on my promise to Blaine. He'd expected me to tell the parents I was going to Mexico with him. When I got in the car, my hand was shaking.

In bed, back at Blaine's house, Aiyah called to me before sleep came, and I answered. It would become a nightly ritual, visiting her in that other place. As I slid into her comforting embrace, my troubles ceased, and I made a pact with myself to find her, no matter what.

————

CHAPTER 17
MARIAH

*A painting in monochrome has a
timeless quality and archetypal flavor
of its own. It can effectively depict a
rite of passage—a pivotal event, a life
choice, a crossroads—like a sepia-
toned photograph.*

The Submarine is parked by a shade-tree mechanic's shop in a
laid-back neighborhood just west of downtown Austin. I'm sitting on
a stone wall with a cup of Pero, my favorite coffee substitute, re-
living my escapade one more time—a gift, a sacred homecoming, a
touching base with something true . . . And hot! Oh my God! Way
hot. Who in the world is that guy? Neptune the water god? My body
still feels occupied, like my incubus is still in me, filling me up.

He's here, then gone and I'm swimming along the far
side of the cove, keeping my head down and ducking
underwater each time the spotlight sweeps around. As
soon as I reach dry ground and get my shorts on, Nan
seizes my hand, and I'm pulled up the path to the van,
sandals and shirt still in hand. Otis speeds off with the
rest of us crammed against each other, panting.
Awkwardly, I pull on my shirt in the dark as
lightening turns the night into day. After a count of
two, thunder crushes the air.

It would have been convenient to learn the guy's name, where he's
from, maybe get a phone number. *This is why we have courtships in
our culture, so you'll know the person you've just balled.* But I have
no information, so I'm writing poetry, needing to acknowledge last
night's experience in a meaningful way. *Meaningful? Accidental sex?
Get real!* Last night was a fantasy, a longing, an indulgence. *Be
realistic, forget about romance. Who'd want a pregnant lady?*

To Neptune

*I'm on my way, destiny calls.
No more time for waterfalls.
If you want to meet like we did before
I left a note in the co-op store.
Find the note and pass the test
the clue is in my grandma's chest.
Follow directions, if you will
and I'll see you in Fate-ville.*

From: the Wind

This poem is corny . . . Suddenly coy, I'm afraid I'll appear like
the pursuer . . . Still, I have to do *something* . . . How else will he find
me? Across the street is my friend Arnold's house, staring back at
me, giving me inspiration. There's no answer at his door when I
knock and it's after 10:00 AM, so I knock louder. He appears, his
Norwegian blond hair a mess and his blue eyes puffy.

"Hi Arnold, sorry to wake you up, but I need help. I'm looking for a guy I met last night, and I thought you might know him. He's tall and slim, not skinny though, and he's young, maybe nineteen or twenty. His voice is low, but not bass, and I think he has a Texas drawl."

Arnold's index finger goes to his temple, pointing at his brain where the answer surely lies, but he's unable to place the guy I just described.

"His hair is this long." I'm holding my fingers two inches apart. "And he plays guitar, folk songs like *Blowing in the Wind*. I don't know his name."

My friend's snowy eyebrows have joined together in concentration, as though two eyebrows can solve a problem better than one. But the task is clearly beyond him. He nods slowly and glances to the side, possibly looking for an escape route, and I'm having second thoughts about my choice of messenger. "Look, I have to go," I tell him. "They're waiting on me. If you figure out who he is, would you give him this?" I hold up the blue card with my poem-note.

"Sure." He takes the card and looks around him for a place to put it, finally deciding to lay it on the table.

"See you later, Arnold."

"Yeah, come back anytime, Mariah. Hey, would you like to take something with you?" Arnold is holding up a joint. I'm not surprised. Even when the whole state is looking for weed, he usually has a little something.

"Sure. Thanks." I hug him and turn to the door, take the steps quickly and run to the Submarine.

————

Now that the note's delivered, my perspective has changed. The Sub will shortly be heading north toward Dallas, but I already feel an urge to put my foot down and stay here where Neptune can find me again. I don't know why I always let momentum carry me, as if I have no say in where I go and what I do. All I want is a place where I have my own room—with bookshelves, a garden and fruit trees, outside the city limits, away from the damn television, where I can pee outdoors.

What does a plant feel when it's been uprooted? *Panic, probably.* I was bonded with my garden at Sunflowers until the cow incident, and now my heart's not in it. The worst part about that is deciding who to blame. Cows do not have ethics. They form mobs and destroy vegetation—it's their purpose in life. They do not respect their neighbors. They don't inform themselves about the issues, and they sure as hell don't build fence. To let cattle determine the course of my life is crazy. But so is going back and forth into the past, into the future, leaping around like this in time and space. *Maybe I'm hungry.*

Bear has made the final check under the Submarine's hood, turned the ignition key, and now the customary cloud of black smoke spews from the tailpipe. Knowing I'll have to do something soon or go crazy, I stare out the window at the clear Texas sky, expecting it to solve my dilemma. *What am I supposed to do? Just keep riding on this stupid bus until we come to the edge of the Earth?*

Then I look at my cohorts and announce, "This is where I get off."

"You're getting off?" Nan's mouth is hanging wide open.

"I have to, Nan. I'm going to stay in Austin."

"Well, I'll be. Just like that? You're leaving?"

"Just like that."

Bear drops me off at Max's place, and the goodbyes short and sweet. *What can you say to companions you've lived with intimately for half a year?* It has all been said. We try to re-say it anyway, but soon give up, and I find myself standing on the curb, watching my travelling home disappear. Everything I have is now in my shoulder bag or in my belly—except for memories, that is, the best one being the Neptune character. Here I'm smiling like an idiot, enjoying the current running through my body just thinking about him. *It's silly to be on the brink of climax when he's probably forgotten all about me.* After all, we were never properly introduced. There was nothing proper about our meeting at all.

————

Inside the apartment, Max's cupboard door hangs askew from a loose hinge, but there's a loaf of bread inside, a jar of honey on the counter and butter in the fridge. Kind of eerie here without Max, but at least I won't starve. I'm disoriented, though, with no home, no job, no school bus, no transportation. Oh . . . and there's also no hurry, now that I've made the decision to stay. In a flash I put together a butter and honey sandwich, toast it in a pan. *Sometimes a body has to settle down and let the spirit catch up.*

Once during my last modeling session—against my will and better judgment—I caught the practical Mary Ellen side of me thinking fondly about my time with Blaine in New Orleans. Somehow, I've begun to forget his flaws and remember what I liked about him. The cheerful and confident nature. Not a doofus like most guys I've been around. But there was a darkness around his role in the War. *How had he endured being such an integral part of something he hated so much?* The surge of compassion takes me by surprise. Who knows? Maybe Mexico wouldn't have been so bad.

Exploring the apartment, I feel like Goldilocks, homeless. I'm grateful for a place to stay but it's frustrating, being neither here nor there. While I'm perusing Max's bookshelf, *The Wisdom of Insecurity* jumps into my hands. Maybe I can pick up on some wisdom from Alan Watts, the west coast guru. On page 24, I read,

> "Belief . . . is the insistence that the truth is what one would . . . wish it to be. The believer will open his mind to the truth on condition that it fits in with his preconceived ideas and wishes. Faith, on the other hand, is an unreserved opening of the mind to the truth, whatever it may turn out to be."

I'll try to keep my mind open and look out for truth, so it won't sneak up and bash me over the head, but that's enough philosophy for now. One truth I know is that Max hasn't come home, and it's getting dark outside, so I'm going to cram myself in the shower and then take half an hour to meditate. Afterward, I think Mariah will spend some imaginary time with Neptune.

———

CHAPTER 18
CLIFF

Harmony exists where different
elements respond to, and partake of,
each other. In a painting, letting a bit
of each color spill into the others
creates a resonance.

On my graduation day, after visiting the clinic for travel shots, I stopped at Arnold's house to help him smoke a 'j', and he gave me half a hit of LSD to save for my trip. An old converted yellow school bus sat parked across from Arnold's, with flowers painted on it. A sign on the back read 'Mardi Gras or Bust.' *Bet they have some stories to tell,* I mused. Up the street and around the corner was the food co-op where I stocked up on peanut butter and browsed the bulletin board, where a small blue hand-written note grabbed my attention.

To Neptune

I left a clue where the sunflower grows,
beyond the graveyard, past the peaches
standing in the endless rows.
Famous marbles name the place.
So, follow these directions, please,
Or you may never see my face.

From the Name of the Wind,
Mistress of the Waterfall.

It was *her*, holy shit! Mistress Aiyah! I un-pinned the card and stuck it in my wallet.

"Where did she come from?" I asked, "And who was she with?" But the guy at the counter had no idea who'd left the note.

Sitting outside in the Plymouth, I read the note again and thought about the field of sunflowers, the graveyard, and the peaches. My head spun. It finally came to me, where I'd heard about the marbles. In some previous century, a man named Elgin had saved some precious stone slabs and taken them to England. He was a hero—or a thief, depending on your point of view. The little town where I'd turned south coming from Austin was called Elgin.

There was no time, but I knew where to go and I had to try . . .

Twenty miles out of Austin going east, I turned south at the little town of Elgin, passed the cemetery and the orchard. A field of sunflowers appeared ahead on my left, so I turned in the next drive. The place looked deserted—no cars around. A knock at the front door produced no answer. It was locked. I walked around back, found the other door locked as well, so I explored.

Beside a small weathered shed and a patch of blue plumbago flowers, I found a rusty corrugated metal enclosure where a hose and spray attachment hung on the wall—an an outdoor shower. On the ground lay a wide plank, surrounded by lush grass all around. I found a single footprint in the soft earth—small, probably female, maybe Aiyah's. Kneeling down by the print, I inhaled the green scent of clover, desperate for some scant trace of her, and the plumbago blossoms sucked me in. They're a pure blue, the way gingham is pure, without any red edging it toward purple—pure like the love I felt for the faceless girl.

While speeches were being given and my classmates walked at my high school graduation ceremonies, I lay on the grass and dreamt of the mistress of the waterfall.

> I can almost read the name scrawled on blue paper, but it's fading away. A woman's portrait shimmers, disappearing like the name, morphing into the rear of an old yellow bus, with a message scrawled on the back. A clock ticks, and I hear the beginning notes of a song.

I came to, slouched on the damp grass, my side itching. A couple of bees worked the clover blossoms under my nose. Beside the shed, a blanket of head-high sunflowers caught the setting sun. *If only there were time,* I thought, *I'd take out my watercolors and paint a picture of these blue flowers and the run-down gray shed with its maroon colored roof. There'd be a glimpse of a nude woman taking a shower.*

I jumped up and headed back to the house as the sunset made burgundy fire on the ridgetop. Beside the patched-up fence, a set of wide dual-tire ruts gave evidence that a big truck had been there . . . or a bus, like the old yellow one parked by Arnold's house. The one with 'New Orleans or Bust' written on it.

I got in the Plymouth, thinking I'd solved the mystery, and under the dome light, I scratched out a poem for the mistress of the waterfall. Then I ran up the steps and stuck it under the front door of the house. As I drove away from the place, an old blue and white panel truck parked next door caught my attention. It looked familiar, but I couldn't place it.

A few minutes later I was standing on a second floor landing downtown under the peaceful glow of one of Austin's blue mercury-vapor lamps, knocking on Arnold's door. The Norwegian answered, his clear blue eyes kind of squinty and red around the edges. He always had some of the best weed in town.

"Hey man," he grinned.

"Hey Arnold, how you doin'?"

"Great, "He stood aside for me to come in. "You want to try some killer smoke?"

"Not right now, thanks." I looked at the cookie pan full of marijuana buds on the table. Tempting, but I had to concentrate. "Do you know what happened to the school bus parked across the street?"

"The bus? Got fixed. It's gone." Arnold sat down at the table and began to clean his dope, separating seeds from leaves with a blue card.

Aiyah was gone? I couldn't take it in. I still felt her with me—the Name of the Wind. While I waited for Arnold to say something else, he continued pushing the weed around, flipping over the card, his movements slow and repetitive, kind of hypnotic. Blue cards, blue flowers. *A blue day all around,* I thought. Arnold seemed to be thinking about something, or trying to. Finally, he said, "I think they went to Canada, or maybe Arkansas."

"When, Arnold?" I asked, a little too firmly.

"When what?"

"When did they leave?"

"Oh, they left right after I got up."

"This morning?"

Arnold nodded.

"Hey, I've got to go. Thanks, man," I said, standing up and reaching out for a brothers' shake before heading for the door.

Damn, I cursed, *Like the wind is right . . . She's already blown away.*

———

CHAPTER 19
MARIAH

Your main job as an artist is to remain
passionately interested in making art.
You have to decide for yourself what
your duty is—to yourself and to the
world. To deny it is to miss the mark,
and missing the mark is the original
definition of sin.

Max's lumpy hide-a-bed lets me rest and his bicycle gets me to this café, a regular stop for me on laundry days. It looks like no one's here, but on my way to the restroom, I get a surprise. Otis and Sara and Peyton are in the middle of a huge breakfast—biscuits, gravy, bacon, omelet, coffee cups, orange juice and newspapers. I have a moment of queasiness, remember to breathe and snatch up an untouched glass of water. After a long drink, my stomach settles.

"Sorry, I had a thirst attack."

"Mariah!" Sara looks surprised. "We were just talking about you. I thought you'd left town."

"Hi." I say, a little tongue-tied. The last time I saw Sara, I was covered in massage oil and nothing else. "There's been a change of plans."

So she knows Otis and Peyton—small world. Evading Sara's eyes, I claim an empty chair across from her and turn to Otis. "I haven't seen you in here before."

He points at his mouth and grunts, then finishes chewing before he speaks. "We take a lifestyle break once a month . . . come see how the other half lives."

I laugh. "Believe me, they don't live as well here as we do out there in paradise." It dawns on me that I haven't yet adjusted to the fact I don't live at Sunflowers anymore.

"There's no bacon in paradise," Peyton murmurs, absorbed in his food. He never cooks and hardly talks.

"Well, there's that," I concede, as the waiter hands me coffee in a to-go cup.

Peyton takes a swig from his mug and looks up with a forlorn face. "Hey Mariah, we're down to stems and seeds, waiting on a pilot. He's bringing kilos coming our way, but we need a little something to tide us over."

"I'm afraid I'm in the same boat with you, Peyton. Sorry."

I've decided to linger and see if there's more to the story when Sara asks, "Aren't you going to order something?"

"Just coffee. I only drink a half cup a day, now, but I want it to be a good one." I look over at Otis and try to sound casual. "About that pilot. It wouldn't be Blaine Grayson, by any chance?"

Sara breaks in. "Oh, it's Blaine, all right." I expect her to ask how I know him, but she purses her lips discreetly. "Otis and Peyton are meeting him in west Texas day after tomorrow."

I lived at Sunflowers for going on two months, but never knew what was really going on, right under my nose. After visiting the Ladies', I stop to say goodbye, but my curiosity has gotten the best of me, so I take a seat again and address Sara, "Have you known Blaine for a while?" I'm curious about the nature of their relationship. From across the table, I don't feel any special vibes coming from her. Maybe her interest in me has cooled.

"Not long," she shrugs. "We met in Zihua when I went down for Easter break. Blaine came to scuba class every day. I think he was trying to grow gills and fins." She laughs and leans forward, "He never mentioned your name, but you must be the girl he kept talking about. He had some regrets that you took off on the school bus."

I chew my lip. "He wanted me to go with him. You know, take a vacation on the beach in sunny Mexico. Sit around while he's off smuggling weed, right? Great life for a girl."

Despite my sarcasm, I've managed to invoke the smell of ocean and the sound of surf. Galveston beach emerges in my memory, clear as a freshly washed window. I'll always ache for the ocean and beach, but maybe without the salt and sand.

"No regrets?" Sara asks, face deadpan.

"No, no regrets, but I *am* concerned. I hope he shows up with the weed." I stand to leave, and everyone jumps up to get hugs.

"Well, g'bye Mariah." Sara's hug is more like a snuggle.

"Bye, Sara."

I stop at the bank on the way back to Max's and cash the savings bond that grandma bought for me when I was born. I should probably be saving it for a piece of land, but transportation is on top of my agenda right now.

It is tricky riding a bicycle with a raincoat on and a bag of dirty clothes tied to the handlebars. On a boy's bike, to boot. Good thing my destination is only two blocks away. And it's a good thing I'm only three months pregnant. Bag on my shoulder, I duck into the laundromat where the atmosphere is rife with musty clothes, detergent and bleach, all warm and humid. Machines are spinning through cycles, muted thumps come from the dryers, and outside, tires are flinging water onto windshields. Reminds me of pelicans on the gulf, throwing up a wake behind them when they land.

Anonymous people have taken refuge inside the laundromat, each with a tenuous grip on some marginal lifestyle. Bored men standing alone beside washers. Students accidentally dyeing their underwear pink. Women giving harsh instructions to children who ignore them. All the tables are claimed, even the little one by the window. Rolling wire baskets are piled with dry clothes waiting to be folded and stacked. I set my bag of dirties on top of a washer, then go for change.

The lady behind the counter calls me 'hon,' and says, "The morning rush is almost over. You shouldn't have to wait for a dryer."

It's true. Two women with bags full of clothes are leaving, a noisy dryer stops with a *whump!* and the decibel level drops noticeably. I start my load washing, then go to the pay phone. It's been a while since I called Mother and Dad. I'm glad I haven't warned them yet to expect a grandchild.

Mother answers.

"Hi, Mother, how's everything?"

"Mary Ellen! This is a surprise."

So, now I've surprised her, and it feels like my fault. Why couldn't she just say, "I'm glad you called?" That's why I left home in the first place, to get away from the constant criticism, if not from Mother, from my sister Pam, Miss Perfection. *But, to be fair, it is my fault she's surprised. I haven't called for weeks.*

"Sorry, I've been on the road and haven't been close to a phone." *Now I'm lying.*

"Are you all right? Where are you? Are you still looking for land?"

I forgot how many questions she can ask per minute. "I think I've *landed* for now in Austin, but I'm still looking."

"We worry about you, you know, driving that old bus."

"I'm buying a car, Mother." *Why is my foot tapping uncontrollably?*

"Won't that be expensive?" She continues the inquisition, unable to resist making snide remarks. As a teenager, I had to account for my every move, every decision, but no more.

"I have a job here in Austin," I tell her. "Is Dad around?"

"He's gone to the hardware store this morning. It's his entertainment, you know."

"Shoot, I was hoping to talk to him."

"He's going to your brothers' baseball practice after school. They'll be home for supper. You could try calling again this evening."

"I might." *Should have called at night in the first place.*

"What's your new job like."

"It's just temporary. No big deal." *I refuse to explain myself.*

"Any boyfriends in the picture, Hon? A Vernon Cole called for you. He sounded a little old, Mary Ellen." *There she goes again, sticking needles in me.*

"I don't know a Vernon Cole," I reply, too sharply, wondering who the man is, what he wants.

"Said he wants to talk to you. That it's important."

I take down his number and stick it in my bag.

"When are you coming to visit?" she asks.

"Maybe in the fall." I'm purposely vague, afraid to make a commitment. *Who knows where I'll be in November?*

"I hope you do come. We miss you, honey. The family will be here for Thanksgiving, you know. Like always."

Tired of talking already, I end it. "Mother, I have to say goodbye. I'm out of quarters. Love you."

Why is it so difficult to talk to parents? Mother is all questions about things I don't have answers for. Dad is usually quiet while Mother rattles on. He's a good listener, though. Open minded. I wish I could call him without calling her, but now I'm feeling guilty for wishing that. I miss sitting with him on the branch of the giant boxelder in our backyard, listening to foghorns blow down on the river.

Max is home and the kettle is on when I arrive with a damp bag of laundry. Anxious for dry socks, I stick a pair in the oven and light it with a match. Then, with a cup of tea and a head full of questions, I help Max sort through stems and seeds to gather a meager pipeful of weed.

"This is the last of my smoke," he says, lighting me up. "I like to keep a little stash for special occasions. Well, actually, any occasion." I hold my breath and pass the pipe back. Max's weed must have truth serum in it. *Either that or talking to my Mother has created an identity crisis.* I feel myself going into confessional mode and I'm not even Catholic.

"Max, I'm pregnant."

Max grins and asks, "Is there anything else I might need to know? Mafia affiliation? Running for president? Devil worship?" He's fooling around with the pipe, trying to nurse another hit out of it.

"I don't think so," I laugh, thankful for a friend like him. "But I'm not sure I'm a Christian anymore."

"It's likely you are and don't know it," Max says, turning serious.

"I relate more to Mother Earth than I do to God."

"Is there a difference?"

Max has me stumped, but I let the sleeping question lie. The truth is, I believe in a supreme being, just not one that looks like the old guy on the ceiling of the Sistine Chapel, or for that matter, any guy at all. And I *do* believe in the sanctity of the family, just not in a limited nuclear sense. More like, all people are brothers and sisters, in a bigger family. I'm stuck, though, on letting the jackasses in Washington into my clan. And the Ruskies. Ever since the nuclear bomb drills in grade school I've been leery of them. I know I should work on this problem of non-inclusiveness in my personal sisterhood and brotherhood, but it will have to wait. For the time being I'm focused on clarifying my own identity.

"There *is* something else, Max. Mariah's not my real name."

"Ah, I never suspected. To think you're the first lady I have met who uses an alias—other than performers, that is." Max has that twinkle in his eye, "You are not a performer, are you?"

"Not really. Unless you count modeling for art class."

"May I ask what your true name is, then, if not Mariah?"

"Mary Ellen Justice. Can you believe it? How drab it sounds."

"She sounds like a heroine," Max grins. "A superheroine."

"A pregnant heroine," I concede.

"I suspected your condition, you know," Max says, staring fixedly at my midsection.

"You noticed?" I put my hand on my belly. "I'm not showing, am I?"

"Oh no. Just came to me." He taps his head. "It was an immaculate conception."

"It wasn't immaculate for me," I counter. "There's a father, you know."

Max nods. He's humming, waiting me out. . .

He wins and I sigh, "We got together in New Orleans and had equipment failure. I mean, not *his* equipment. His worked, but the condom broke. Then he took off on a smuggling thing, and now Otis is waiting for him to bring a load of weed from Mexico."

Max leans forward. "The man must have some regrets you and he are not still together. He'd be crazy not to."

"That's what Sara said, but I don't think there's any future in it. Not on my end anyway."

He nods again, "I understand your sentiment."

"Thing is, I feel guilty. He doesn't know."

"Ahhh." He takes the 'Ah' into a full chant, filling the room with a round sound. Strange that by telling him my feelings, I understand myself better. *I wonder why Max has this kind of influence on me.*

"You know," I say, "I like to smoke a 'j' as much as anyone, but the dealing and smuggling scares the shit out of me."

Max goes "Mm hmm."

I add, "The truth is, motherhood scares me even more. I have prepared no *nest*, Max. You're supposed to have a nest. And a nest *egg*. I don't even have a real job. The timing is not good. Besides, being a mother is something other people do. Not me. It feels like the cart is running away with the horse." *What am I supposed to do with this decision?* I'm thinking. *It's too huge.*

"Right."

I can see Max is not going to say it for me, so I take the plunge. "I've been thinking about getting an abortion."

"Ah . . ." Max is encouraging me to unload.

"And I'm not in love with Blaine," I add. "There's someone else."

"Right on, sister." This man is a perfect listener.

"So, it doesn't matter if he's the father. Does it?" *I must be wanting confirmation, rattling on like this.*

"Does it what?" he asks.

"Matter."

"Sure, well . . . as you know, I do not have a horse in this race." Max takes a deep breath, puts his thumb under his chin, his elbow on the table. He leans forward, catches my eye. Then he breathes out slowly, his expression open.

"I should tell Blaine," I admit. After finally giving voice to what's been churning around inside, a weight lifts and I feel strangely free.

He nods again and goes to turn up the stereo. I rescue my singed socks from the oven, put them on, and we settle down into *Goodbye, Ruby Tuesday*, letting the Stones take us away.

Later I think about calling the number for Mr. Cole. *Or maybe I do call, I can't remember.*

———

The world this morning is washed clean, and the sky is a color of blue I have no words for. So heavy and close yesterday, that same sky seems deeper and farther away today, as though my decision about my future has cleared the air. Sara has a day off from teaching university students, and I find her at home in a leotard, with a candle on the floor.

"Do you practice yoga, Mariah?"

"I've done a little with Max," I tell her.

"Care to join me? I was just starting my routine."

"Well, I came to ask you something about Mexico." This feels awkward, like I've disturbed her private space.

"Can it wait? You don't have to be anywhere, do you?" Sara stretches for the ceiling, coming up on her toes.

"Not really, but I'm not dressed, exactly."

"Clothing isn't necessary for yoga," Sara says. "You can get comfortable."

Why not? I kick off my sandals and slip out of my jeans, glad my underpants are clean. Sara has found an extra mat and laid it beside hers a few feet away. At first, the bending and stretching is causing me to make unintentional noises—knees and ankles popping, slight moans or groans. Sara is silent in her movements, and I feel a little klutzy. We do sun salutations until my hamstrings ache and there's perspiration on my lip. Then she leads me through other stretches. We conclude the session lying flat for fifteen minutes on our backs in Savasana, the corpse pose, affording me time to notice the sweet vanilla scent of her candle.

I've also noticed Sara's supple, graceful movements and appreciated her unadorned beauty. I remember the time in her office when we were interrupted during . . . *what?* I don't know why I resist the attraction I'm feeling, she hasn't hidden her interest in me. Maybe I'm afraid of the uncharted territory. But it doesn't make any sense, she's considerate to a fault.

I hear Sara's soft easy breaths and feel warmth exuding from her, only a couple of feet away. My hand extends, reaching for contact, and her hand meets mine half-way. Fingers entwine, grips tighten, we roll together and hold on tight. My mouth seeks hers and the softness of it sends charges through my body as we cling to each other. The contact is heaven, legs wrapping and tongues exploring.

I feel fingers on my head, like whispers. Little brooms sweeping my scalp without really touching it. There's a crackle of electricity, oil comes from somewhere, and Sara begins to work my neck muscles all the way to my skull, causing pinpoints of sensation—not pain, but almost. Then I rise and straddle her as she pulls down her leotard. Yes. Right now, this is what I want. I've found the oil and begin massaging her sternum, circling her heart, and continuing up the sides of her neck. Back down beside and under her breasts with both hands and up again to her heart.

Sara has been unbuttoning my blouse. I shift it off my shoulders and fall onto her, feeling her skin slip along mine, savoring the intimacy. I think I'm beginning to cry just a little. Now I shift downward and straddle her thighs. She pushes the leotard down further. I'm kneading her belly in long slow strokes, firmly, clockwise, with closed fist.

I give the best massage of my life. No words are spoken. At the end I have gently and surely kneaded or stroked every muscle in her body, and we've brought each other multiple climaxes, leaving us limp as a couple of wilted roses.

"How do you feel," Sara asks.

"Greasy."

"Well, let's take a shower."

When I emerge less greasy but more steamy, hair freshly washed and towel-wrapped, she asks again, "How do you feel now."

"Renewed. Thank you, Sara. How about you?"

"If I told you, I'd have to shoot you." We grin at each other like fools. Hungry ones. We take dinner seated on the carpet and, over plates of fresh crab salad, Sara asks what's up.

"I've decided to get an abortion," I say, but the words sound artificial, and there's a catch in my throat.

"Oh my, that must be hard."

"It is. I've heard stories about women who go to a place in Nuevo Laredo. It scares the shit out of me."

"Those sisters I mentioned the other day are courteous and kind, Mariah. And very competent. You needn't worry. Acapulco is not Nuevo Laredo."

"I want to find out about the sisters."

"Well, I can tell you this. There's a fee. The sisters ask for the payment when you arrive. It's three hundred dollars."

"It's okay. I have some money left from the savings bond I cashed." *My land money.*

"Let me get the address. They have a phone if you want to schedule in advance. Or you could just go."

Now I'm crying again for sure. After holding the tension for weeks, this discussion is somehow too matter-of-fact. I've been thinking the decision would be more ceremonial. These stupid hormones have me expecting angels in attendance. Then I notice there's one right in front of me. "Thank you, Sara, really."

She's shaking her head and handing me fresh tissues. Then she comes around behind me on the floor and wraps me up in her arms and legs, just holding me and swaying. I think she is crying a little too.

I leave after a while, equipped with contact information for *las hermanas*, the sisters in Acapulco.

———

CHAPTER 20
CLIFF

*A work of art has the power to shift an
observer's point of view. The ordinary
way of seeing is replaced and we are
entertained or 'taken in'. . . When this
happens, our perception of truth may
be altered.*

With sore feet and sleep in my eye, I dragged myself into the
Cessna 210D and felt the takeoff deep in my gut as we climbed
sharply and merged with the sky. Not like flying in a DC6—which I
had done exactly three times—this was the wild blue yonder.

I read once in some art instruction book that, when designing a picture, it's good to leave a place for the eye to go—a bit of blue. Blue means distance to us—something we've all learned from looking at the same world since childhood. Most people take the opportunity to relax into a blue space and rest their eyes. That's what I did. When Blaine leveled off at cruising altitude, I dozed. I would have slept longer, but my brother had other plans.

Jolted awake, I felt the world go ninety degrees off-kilter, like on a state fair ride, but worse. Or better, maybe. The engine sound increased, and my butt clinched. Gravity doubled and centripetal force pressed me into the seat. Blaine had taken the single engine plane into a horizontal 360. Half-way around, I finally let go and enjoyed myself.

When he pulled us out of the turn and the plane gently came to an equilibrium, I exhaled, "Wow. So that's what flying's all about."

Blaine, always good for drama, just grinned, "Didn't want you to miss the best part. We're almost there, by the way."

That was my cue to drop the half-hit of windowpane acid that Arnold had slipped me the day before. I had only taken LSD once before and was still curious about its power and effect. I let it melt in my mouth, figuring the trip would be a light one. I had no obligations, was just along for the ride, so I thought, *Why not*? I was safe with Blaine nearby.

The frantic activity of the past few days had left no time for art, and I missed it. With my guitar gone, I'd brought along my watercolor box to try my hand at painting the Mexican beach scenery, an appealing prospect. Anything to help take my mind off the anxiety I felt about my future in Texas, with the law on my trail. Without *Aiyah*.

"Almost there" turned out to mean we were still an hour away from Acapulco, so Blaine turned the controls over to me, and I practiced making slight alterations in our course under his guidance. It wasn't long, though, before I willingly yielded the plane back to him. As we started our descent toward the coast, the acid took effect and the picture show began. With coastal mountains below glowing like hot lava, we flew into a setting sun. The Pacific Ocean gleamed, and clouds burned strontium on the horizon.

My ears protested our altitude shift for a minute, then popped, and relief came as we shot down toward a double row of lights. The plane bounced gently once on the runway and coasted to the row of private planes where a burly man with orange batons guided us to an empty space. Our headlights caught him in a flash-frame, his head thrust forward, like a gorilla's, arms and batons waving. Then he glided back toward the runway, listing to one side like a ship sailing into the wind, the whirling batons reminding me of a bird's wings.

We gathered our stuff and carried it for what seemed like hours, through growing darkness to the terminal. At customs, I wrote my occupation on the form, *Artista*, the intention being there, at least, if not the substance.

Blaine rented us a new powder blue Volkswagen bug. *Beautiful cars*, I thought, *especially the eyes—so innocent and vulnerable.* Blaine drove ours directly to Señor Frog's for supper, and we took the last available table. I ordered a turtle steak that was too tough to chew, but the Negra Modelo was nectar from the gods, full of tiny explosions that burst on the roof of my mouth. Two guitars wandered around the restaurant and sang, while a twelve-year-old beat drumsticks on a board, sprinkling polka dots all around the room.

"Otra cerveza, por favor," I managed to say, and thought, *Gimme shelter!* as I watched visible currents of energy connect everything into one viscous whole. Transparent people breathed each other in and out, trailing molecules and agendas. I could see right through them.

"Hey, Bro, what do you think?" Blaine asked.

Is this a trick question? I wondered, as the words arrived in three-dimensional waves and I had to sort them out, make them fit my tongue. "There's a lot . . ."

"Turtle steak not so good?"

"Tough . . . my mistake." The gross matter on my plate held no interest.

"Want something else?"

"Nah, I'm okay." *It's an understatement*, I thought. *I'm universal.*

Later, after checking into the hotel, we drove east out of town and parked. On the beach, a long crescent of diamonds stretched back toward Acapulco, a million jewels filled the sky and the ocean glowed. We smoked a fat J and soaked it all in—the balmy night, the briny smell of the Pacific, the sound of pulsing waves, each grain of sand a link in the universal chain.

Much later, I thought about Aiyah and celebrated our union the way I did every night.

———————

The next morning, I unpacked the watercolors I'd brought and began a small study of beach cabañas, focusing on the big shapes. Skipping the pencil part, I started in with the brush dipped in color, working quickly and easily, convinced that painting was something I was meant to do. It was only a sketch, but the process of putting paint on paper felt like freedom made solid. Afterward, my blisters screamed and my stomach growled, so I took an aspirin and a chance, eating cheese and bean tostadas for lunch. Then I spent the afternoon learning the basic moves of beach volleyball from a squad of athletic Californian women—bump, set, spike and block.

At first, the net itself was my opponent, entangling me at every opportunity and thwarting all my best efforts. I liked the sand and grit, though—a good thing since it covered me from head to toe. My brother, by contrast, was in his element, not a grain of sand on him. The net was his friend. After one of the games, Blaine asked, "Hey bro, could you do me a favor?"

"Probably, what do you need?"

"I'd like to get romantic with one of the bikini chicks. Could you stay clear of our room for a while?"

I grinned, "Sure, I'm fine here. I'll make you a deal, though. I need to borrow a hat."

"A deal it is. Thanks, man."

He flipped me the baseball cap he'd been wearing and left the beach with a slim brunette who was one of the most active players. I appreciated the beauty of the players' forms and their movements, but I felt Aiyah's presence in the core of my being, so I wasn't attracted the way my brother was.

After heating up in the sand, I body surfed for a while, focusing on my center of gravity between navel and pubic bone. That point of contact with a wave became my whole universe until the wave released me and I tumbled into chaos. Exhausted after riding a hundred waves, I crawled, like evolutionary man, out of the ocean and into a lounge chair only to be gripped by a vision of my mystery woman.

> Walking away, through a doorway, glancing to one side, a bag over one shoulder and long hair loose, she's wearing a dark skirt and red sleeveless blouse. The sun catches her beside a marble sculpture that's surrounded by a vine-covered turquoise fence. She turns to look back—green-amber eyes. She's middle sized, spirited and strong. Her voice is honey and melted butter.

Blaine caught me napping. "Hey Cliff, wake up, it's about time for supper. There's a restaurant one of the girls recommended, La Mar. They have good seafood."

I rolled onto my side to hide an embarrassing erection. "Um, how'd it go?" I squinted up at him.

"Lovely. I owe you one."

I gathered myself and followed my brother back to the room for a shower. Later, over shrimp enchiladas at the *La Mar*, Blaine discussed plans for the next day. "I'm meeting Ricardo tomorrow to make arrangements, then I'm going to the airport to fuel up the Cessna, get it ready for the trip back to Texas." He gave me one of his arched-eyebrow looks. "By the way, did you forget to mention to the folks that you were coming to Mexico with me?"

"Um . . . when did you talk to them?"

"I called Dad just before we went to the airport. He didn't seem too pleased that you were . . . 'sneaking off.' Those are his words."

"Well, I did talk to them, like I said I would."

"You finessed me, bro. I thought you were getting permission."

"Sorry. I meant to, but I sort of left in a hurry." It *was* an answer of sorts, but I'd dodged the real issue. A guy doesn't like to admit he's afraid of his father.

For two more days I swam, played volleyball and painted fishermen with their nets drying beside overturned boats. Time passed without notice, my brush danced a rhythm across the paper, and I rode a wave of creative joy. Colors appeared, rendering silhouettes of men at work, set against a luminous backdrop. Nothing spectacular, but the results pleased my eyes and satisfied my need to mark the passage of time.

"The heck with beer, I'll try a piña colada," I said later, as my brother and I mounted bar stools at the hotel's cantina. My blisters had started to heal, and wearing shoes for a change, I felt more civilized.

"You'll have to watch it with the sweet rum drinks," Blaine advised. "They're like race cars with no brakes."

I tasted my drink and cut to the chase. "When are we flying the weed back?"

"Well," he said. "I'll be flying under the radar for a day and a night. I thought you could stay here, get in some volleyball action. The girls say you're getting better at it."

Smooth move, brother, I thought. *You've benched me for the big game.* "So, I'm supposed to play with the girls while you do the deal?" I felt a tightness growing in my chest, and my disappointment threatened to turn into anger. "I'm not a kid, Blaine. At least let me help."

"Calm down, little bro." He tipped his frosted mug and took a sip of beer. "I need for you to keep an eye on the rental car 'til I get back. That's a big help."

I had a thought. Maybe he was trying to protect me from the most dangerous aspect of his business. Whatever his motive, he'd obviously made his decision, but I still couldn't let it go. "The car can take care of itself while it's parked."

"Cliff, there's no room for another passenger," he explained. "Ricardo's coming with me."

"Why's *he* going?"

Blaine sighed. "I'm helping him out of a jam. Someone tried to kill him last night, and he needs to emigrate to the States. We're driving him down to Zihua tomorrow in the rental, so he won't be seen in the airport. I'll leave the car with you and catch a ride back to Acapulco for the plane. You and Ricardo can meet me the next day, help load the plane. Then, after I fly out, you can drive the car back here and I'll see you the next morning at the hotel. "

————————

We hadn't met yet, and I already hated Ricardo for usurping my role as co-pilot. When we picked the man up several blocks from the hotel, he offered his hand. "How do you do, Cliff?" He winked, took my shotgun seat and left me to sprawl in the back of the Bug.

On the west side of Acapulco, the civilized world quickly yielded to one composed of rocks, trees and asphalt, but I got an occasional glimpse of ocean and beach through the open window. Blaine was immaculate in his polo shirt and wire rimmed shades. I sported a palm tree t-shirt and hibiscus flowered jams with a draw string. Ricardo wore a starched dress shirt. When he turned toward Blaine to talk, I studied his profile and dodged the ashes blowing from his cigarette.

His nose extended from his forehead, straight and sharp, and his clean-shaven chin jutted in a parallel plane. I could imagine him with a conquistador's helmet and a curly beard, holding a pike. Except his silver wire-rim glasses ruined the soldier image. They were spectacles in the truest sense of the word, with filigreed gold panels at the hinges. I caught snatches of his monologue, mixed with a flutter of wind. "Trouble before the Olympics . . . *el gobierno* attacking the students . . . demonstration . . . *simpatico* with the students . . . make a deal . . . I go free . . . *gobierno* wants the names . . . so I disappear." He made a 'poof' with his fingers.

By that time, I was leaning forward, my head stuck between the front seats, inhaling his words along with *Delicado* smoke as he continued, "The *gobierno* and the fucking *comunistas* make bad air for me in Mexico. I can't go to airports. Federales, you know. But the air is fresh in *los Estados Unidos*, no?" He looked at me, then Blaine, expecting an answer.

"It depends on where you go," Blaine laughed.

The talk went on and on like that, so after a while I leaned back and took a nap. When I roused, Blaine had parked on the beach facing the Pacific Ocean. Ricardo hopped out and went off in search of someone he knew while I sat in the car with Blaine and watched a half-dozen shirtless men towing a small shark to shore. On the beach a sagging basketball hoop hung waiting for a game, and eden-like vegetation smothered the hills surrounding the calm violet-green Zihuatanejo bay.

Ricardo returned with bottles of sparkling water and a bagful of tamales and the three of us strolled along the shore looking for a good place to stop and eat. The lady with the machete stood in front of a wooden table, her long multi-colored dress concealing a body of extreme proportions. Beside the table, leaning against a pile of coconuts in the husk was a sign that read, *la sirena gorda*, the image of a corpulent mermaid carved above the words.

The edge of her big knife gleamed—evidence of a recent sharpening—as she beckoned us to her table and pointed at a coconut. Blaine produced pesos and she hid the money somewhere in the folds of her dress. Abruptly, she lifted the machete and brought it down with a deft and mighty whack! I jumped back and Blaine laughed. He'd seen it all before. A hunk of husk fell away from the end of the coconut and with it, a tiny sliver of shell. She tilted the big nut, stuck a straw through the small hole she'd made in the nut and handed it to Blaine. I got the next one. Ricardo tactfully declined the offer and spread out tamales on the table. There were no chairs, so we stood and feasted.

I have to say that fresh coconut milk is not my favorite drink, but I sucked it down anyway. The lady took the emptied coconut and whacked it again, cleaving it into equal halves. Using a shoehorn, she reamed the meat from the husk with a pop, leaving it loose in the shells, and handed it all back. Smiling again, she pushed the salt-shaker and hot sauce bottle toward us, then pulled two small yellow limes from nowhere. She quartered them and put them on a small plate, then set the machete on the table, folded her arms and watched us expectantly. Under her scrutiny—and the looming threat of the big knife—I felt obligated to eat it all, a daunting task for the uninitiated.

La sirena undeniably had a kind of abundant beauty. It was easy for me to visualize her diving and surfacing, frolicking among the turquoise waves, cinnamon skinned and bare-breasted, complete with a porpoise's tail. *Artistic vision has its merits*, I though. But then I experienced a ripple of trepidation, imagining her as a siren from *The Odyssey* with the machete meant for me.

I tried the chunky coconut meat plain, then with lime, added salt, and finally went the distance, drenching it in hot sauce. The more I chewed the flesh, the bigger and drier the wad in my mouth got, but my effort earned a celestial smile from the machete lady. It's a good thing we had tamales to go with the coconut. They were moist and filled with an odd assortment of vegetables and meat. One had a whole chicken wing in it, bones and all.

"*Estilo Oaxacaña.*" Ricardo shrugged. "Oaxacan cook." Then he lit a cigarette and turned to me. "Master Clifí I think *la sirena* likes you. A woman like that can make you forget your troubles. You get lost in the mountains of flesh. Maybe if one time you enter her, you can never leave?"

I said nothing, trying to quell my imaginings of being attacked and consumed by an extra-large mermaid. I actually felt small for a change, and Ricardo's use of the Spanish version of my name, Clifí, further diminished me. Cliffy is what I'd been called as a kid.

Ricardo laughed, thinking he'd made a good joke. "This food making me thirsty, amigos. I hope Rodrigo has some cold beers."

———

CHAPTER 21
CLIFF

The relative lightness or darkness of
something is called 'value' in the
language of art. In the old days, it was
called 'tone,' but that's confusing.
Value is important in every thought you
have and every stroke you make.

A polka rhythm drew us into the shade of a palm-thatched pavilion
on the *playa principal* where Blaine and Ricardo ordered bottles of
Pacífico, and I got a Fanta orange. Ricardo lit a *Delicado*, crossed his
legs, and predicted the future of Zihuatanejo. "The government plans
a new city there." He waved his cigarette behind his head, indicating
a general inland direction. "Hotels, restaurants, night clubs, airport.
Zihua, my friends, is soon the place where rich peoples go, so all the
people here get money to spend."

As he spoke, a stocky, dour-looking old man slipped into an empty
chair. He was weathered as a piece of driftwood and wore dingy
muslin clothing to match. I gathered he was the marijuana grower and
tried to shake off my uneasy feeling about the man. Ricardo
pronounced his name, Veek-tore, but said it really fast with a half-roll
on the 'r,' something I would keep trying, but fail to master.

"The new plan for Zihua brings the trouble to the peoples," Víctor said.

"What troubles?" Blaine asked, taking the argument seriously. "I understand life will change if development comes here, but why is that bad?"

Víctor's hands spread wide. "Farmers need a fair price for the crops, protection for the forest. *El gobierno* let the *capitalistas* steal the trees and pay farmers nothing for vegetables and fruits. People want schools, but *el gobierno* wants them *estúpido*, so people don't complain. Now comes imperialist dollars from *los Estados Unidos*. The people become servants. *Es muy malo.* Today, the people are poor but proud and free. Tomorrow, *no mas.*"

Ricardo broke in to explain. "My uncle is *sympatico* with the men in Guerrero, *don Belín. El partido de los pobres.*"

"*Mira,*" Víctor said. "At one time, Lucio Cabañas is the best Mexico has. Fights for the people, for justice. A teacher."

Ricardo took up the narrative. "Two years ago, *el gobierno* orders shooting at a peaceful school meeting, killing seven. *Tío* Víctor's son is one of them. Lucio Cabañas escapes to the mountains to fight the oppressor."

A silence ensued before Blaine said, "The Party of the Poor are the good guys."

Víctor grimmaced, "Is no more good guys. Echeverría brings the violence. Is like a sickness everyone catches. Cabañas makes war on *el gobierno* and *poco a poco*, the good men turns bad—rob, kidnap, murder—all because Echeverría disappears the good people."

The old man spat and reclaimed the conversation in his slow, emphatic way, without mentioning his son's killing. "I fight for the *independencia* all my life."

Víctor went on to tell us he'd grown up in Zihua, harvesting coconuts. As a teenager he fought with the Zapatistas alongside his father in the 1910 Revolution. After military service, he'd come back to Zihua to work on the waterfront and stake a homestead claim. Sometime along the way, he found time to build a house in Zihuatanejo.

The sky had dimmed to an indigo ceiling with a rose glow in the west, so a string of faded Christmas lights provided the only illumination as Víctor wrapped up the monologue. "I grow *mota* for the people—marijuana. I pay the money I owe for the farm. Honest work, *sí*. Now, the other farmers join the cartel." He shook his head. "Criminals, bad as Echeverría and *el gobierno*. The life I have here is finished, *señores*. The *revolución* is dead."

The old man scowled and stared into his beer, as if he could find a solution in the amber liquid. The proprietor of the little cantina had been lurking around behind his counter pretending to be busy, but I'd seen him eavesdropping on our conversation. Suddenly Víctor slapped the table hard, lept up and turned around. The bartender shot out of there like a flushed quail, and I fell off my perch backward, punched by adrenaline. I scrambled to my feet, but just as quickly, the old man relaxed.

Blaine threw some pesos on the table and said, "We'd better get going."

We walked to the car and Blaine drove us to a looming edifice cloaked in darkness—Víctor's house. Inside, a lantern came to life, creating a pool of yellow light on a weathered table. I was tired, and my feet hurt like hell, so I left the three men and went to find a bed. As I climbed the stairs, I saw Ricardo slip Víctor an envelope.

———

In the morning, Víctor gave Blaine a ride to the airport in Acapulco, three hours away, to get the Cessna. Ricardo disappeared on some mission up the beach. The next day Blaine would be flying back to meet us at a cornfield where we'd load the weed. The residual smoky aroma and primitive vibe in Víctor's place was unsettling. Something lurked in that spooky old house, almost visible in the corners, avoiding the light. I shook my head like a dog with ear trouble, trying to rid myself of the spectre, then picked up my watercolor box and bolted for the door.

The girl by the avocado tree sold me a couple of sweet rolls, then one of the motorized canoes ferried me to *las gatas* beach. I found a cluster of untrimmed palm trees that struck me as a good subject to paint. The trees' edges met the sky in pleasing abstractions. Beards of old bleached-out fronds hung beneath fresh green ones, contrasting with the darker oaks. An irregular strip of white sand stretched across the foreground.

If my imagination had permitted it, I would have painted *la sirena gorda*, the huge coconut lady, but I couldn't imagine how to paint her. Instead, I opened my box and slipped out a fresh sheet of paper taped on a piece of cardboard and looked at the scene in front of me. Taking note of the big shapes, I began to splash faint patches of ochre, cobalt and green onto the white paper.

Pigment flew, a dark mass of oaks appeared, and palm fronds emerged from that shadow. Satisfied with my vignette, I ran to cool off in the ocean and swam freestyle until I was out of breath. I came up for air amid a pod of scuba divers and joined them, submerging and emerging, cavorting like a dolphin until late afternoon when they had to go.

Starvation finally took me back to the *playa principal* and a restaurant. I risked enchiladas with crumbly cheese on top, garnished with avocado and cherry tomatoes. While I sopped the remains with a corn tortilla, old man Víctor shuffled up wearing an upside-down smile, and ordered a beer.

"Fried bananas?" the waiter asked, and we both shook our heads, "No thanks."

I sipped a cold Negra Modelo, beginning to enjoy the taste, while the old man drank in silence and avoided my eyes. Deep creases ran beside his nose and stubbled chin, emphasizing the turned-down mouth. Steel-gray hair trailed away from his low forehead in all directions. Thick eyebrows crowded together against the high bridge of his nose. The overall impression was one of menace and anger and age. Without speaking, we drained our bottles, paid our checks and walked silently from the cafe to his house in the gathering dusk.

The sweet-acrid smell of wood-smoke greeted us at the door, merged with a musty animal scent. Víctor pulled a rolled-up envelope from his pocket and smoothed it on the square wooden table. A fireplace was centered at one end of the room, and at at the other, a staircase lead up to a darkened hallway. In a corner, on top of a small chest, was the photo of a young man in a stand-up cardboard frame— possibly a graduation photo. When I lifted it to get a better look, Víctor rushed to my side, grabbed the photo and turned it toward the wall. I stiffened when I saw the butcher knife in his hand. Then, as if nothing had happened, he brought a kerosene lamp to the table, placed the knife beside the envelope, and collapsed in a chair.

"A long day," he said. "My head hurts . . . Too much talk."

Still shaken by the suddenness of Víctor's action, I wondered why he was so determined to keep the photograph hidden? Obviously, he didn't want to discuss it. At the bottom I'd seen the inscription in Spanish, *gracias del Partido de los Pobres.* I wished I could have discussed everything with Blaine—the crazy old man, the bartender, the knife, the photo—but I was on my own, there. The Party of the Poor was on my mind, but I wasn't about to bring up a controversial subject with Víctor.

"Ricardo's your nephew?" I asked, still hesitant to meet his eyes.

"My sister's grandson, *el cabrón*" Víctor reached for the envelope lying on the table.

"Sounds like he has big plans for Zihua."

"Always big plans." Víctor spit on the floor and his voice rose in volume. "Ricardo lies and lies . . . and lies more." Then, with a hiss he spoke a riddle, *"La hierba no es la mota."*

I translated the words to myself, "The grass is not the grass."

With a movement both deft and violent, Víctor grabbed the knife, slit open the envelope and buried the blade in the table, rattling the air. I winced. Through slits of vision I saw the man change into a tiger. No—a Mayan jaguar, stone-faced. A tooth gleamed in the flickering light. On the table, the knife handle still quivered.

The old man extracted a piece of paper from the envelope and read. After a minute, he looked upat me. "Letters come from my Sister Carlota in San Miguel. Carlota sees nothing, so a girl writes the letter and sends to me. The letter says, 'Send money.'"

I turned from the table and opened my eyes wide, fingered the chip carving around the edge of the table, and avoided looking at the knife. Some insane desire to be helpful prompted me to say, "Ricardo's flying with Blaine tomorrow to San Miguel. I guess he could deliver the money to your sister for you."

The old man reached over the table and grabbed my shirt front, his face twisted into a fierce grimace. "You don't know Ricardo."

Tiny droplets of his spittle misted my face and I pulled back, filled with dread, glimpsing the jaguar again. He let go of me and continued, "Ricardo goes to Cuba when the *revolución* begins, only seven years past. Returns, *differente*. Hard, like this knife." He extracted the butcher knife from the tabletop and ran his thumb along the edge. "Is a long story."

The old man followed me across the room, placed the knife carefully back in the drawer it came from. "Ricardo is no more the *idealista*." He approached me, no longer the jaguar, and his voice softened almost to a whisper. "Careful with Ricardo, Clifí. Guard your money." He poked my chest but wore an impassive expression. Then he said, "Big day mañana."

No argument from me. The beer had made me sleepy, and I was ready to let my mind go blank. I made a mental note to tell Blaine about Víctor's warning. Then I scrunched up, ignored the scratching and bumping sounds in the ceiling, and fell into a restless sleep.

———

CHAPTER 22
CLIFF

Art can be made from the contrast
between light and dark, red and green,
soft and hard, textured and smooth or
slow and fast. Nothing more is needed.
This contrast becomes the true subject
of the work, even when something
realistic is portrayed.

Tigers were chasing me again. No way to escape, but I kept running, and they were always right behind. I woke up puzzled why tigers were making pig noises. Then from my shuttered window the sound came again. It *was* pigs—real ones. Outside, one of the local kids held a stick, herding three squealing animals along the path beside my room.

Ouch! "Close the shutter, Cliff," a too-bright sun yelled at me, the bed called me back, and I took a minute to stare at the ceiling and gather myself.

Up above, among the clay tiles, I made out the shape of an iguana. Then another. The pair hugged a hewn rafter and looked around, completely at home. One of them eyed me. "Did you sleep well, *señor* human?"

Yes, very well, mister iguana, I thought, feeling comforted by the presence of the huge lizards. I was their guest here, not the other way around. At least they weren't chasing me.

My host brought a cup of lukewarm coffee so sweet I had to gulp it down.

"Víctor!" I hollered, "This stuff is dissolving my teeth. Did you put sugar in the pot?"

He was all smiles, for a change. "We leave at one hour, *más o menos.*"

As I finished my bean tacos, Ricardo showed up mysteriously for a quick cup of coffee. An hour later the three of us were headed west between the ocean and the green hills, flying down a dirt road in the rented VW, and with Víctor at the wheel, my worries of the night before were dispelled by the blinding light of a new day.

"You always drive this fast?" I shouted from the back seat.

"Better go fast." The crazy old man fishtailed around another curve. "No bumps."

Behind us a huge cloud of dust hovered, leaving a record of our passing. I hung on to the dash and leaned into the curves while cornfields flew past in a blur. Without warning, Víctor slammed on the brakes, and the car did a one-eighty, sliding off the road and harvesting a dozen cornstalks. When we opened our doors, a silent campesino appeared with a straw hat and a machine gun. We got out. Someone else took over the wheel and sped away in the car. Ricardo took off down the road on foot.

Three rows deep into the corn, eight fat burlap bags waited for action. The old man pulled a wad of *colitas* out of the first bag and began rolling a mega-number, using paper he tore from inside the bag. Now we had only to wait. The blisters on my feet were killing me—I'd forgotten to apply bandages before leaving the house.

Without thinking, I accepted a hit off the cigar Víctor had rolled .. . and then another. Something nagged at me, some memory, but it refused to surface. My situation was so strange that only parts of it registered as reality—the quiet voices nearby speaking Spanish, the wasps that made occasional sorties in my direction, the bright green intensity of head-high corn.

It seemed right to be helping supply the growing population of dope-smoking Texans with relief from their pain—the resisters, protesters, dodgers, the disenfranchised and the oppressed. It was damn-near heroic, helping Blaine get this crop delivered across the border. I could almost hear people cheering, but I couldn't for the life of me dredge up whatever it was that I'd forgotten.

Mysteriously, the pain from my blisters vanished. I let the blue paper from my wallet unfold itself and take me to the mistress of the waterfall. Her words stared me down, daring me to solve the riddle, but the 'name of the wind' had me stumped. I shut my eyes and reached across the whole length of Mexico to that farm outside Austin, feeling for her, willing her to think about me.

After a while, I heard the faint sound of a plane and stretched to see, but there was nothing yet. Maybe I'd heard an insect. The intermittent drone continued, and we kept our eyes to the northwest, toward the mountains while we sat and shared the endless joint. The two guards with machine guns were out of sight somewhere. Víctor talked quietly about his children while I swatted horseflies. Finally, bursts of Spanish erupted among the cornstalks. I heard the word *avion* and stood up to look around. Sure enough, in the blue shadow of the near mountain, flying low, I saw the silver gleam of Blaine's aircraft.

With Ricardo's help, our guards dragged the loaded bags closer to the roadside. The approaching plane made half a turn and dropped quickly to land, kicking up a cloud of dust. It rolled to a near stop not ten yards from where we stood and slowly turned around in place. Ricardo stepped up to the passenger door and pulled some wedges from the plane. Then he chocked the wheels as the engine slowed to idle, the dust cloud wafted into the corn field, and the door opened. Blaine handed Ricardo a thin briefcase and hollered, "Better get those goats off the road. I'd hate to hit one."

A man ran down the road waving his arms at the offending goats and I rushed to drag another feed sack from the edge of the road. Blaine opened a draw string, revealing parcels wrapped in brown paper. He handed the top two packages to me, ripped open a third one and pulled out a handful of dry honey-colored flowers. After squeezing and sniffing the product, he smiled and gave a 'thumbs up.'

"Never hurts to check the merchandise" he yelled, stuffing the kilo back in the sack. Ricardo descended from the plane and passed the briefcase to Victor. I re-filled the bag and tied the drawstring. Then I dragged it to the plane and squeezed it in behind the front seats with the other bags. There was no room to spare. When Ricardo pulled the wheel-chocks and climbed back in the cockpit, a feeling of dread overwhelmed me—a fear I'd forgotten something really important. But the moment passed, the door shut, and the engine revved up. I squinted into the surreal glare as the plane roared away, scattering goats and dust in all directions. The whole operation had taken less than five minutes.

Someone brought the car back and hopped out, handing me the keys. Víctor melted away into the cornfield without a good-bye, leaving me alone with the VW. I sped off down the road toward Acapulco, driving the same way Víctor did, eliminating the bumps. It was a three-hour drive to the hotel in Acapulco. Somewhere along the way I slipped into a daydream about sea turtles and volleyball. Then the scene shifted to the cockpit of an airplane.

Throttle down, flaps down, I land on a dirt strip and taxi to a cluster of buildings. Machine-gun fire shatters the quiet. Uniformed men run in front of the airplane, making motions. They drag me out of the cockpit and I fall into a pit of darkness.

I hit the brakes as the two-lane highway reappeared in front of me and windmilled the wheel one way, then the other, until I could bring the car to a halt on the shoulder. I'd drifted across the centerline into the left-hand lane. *Not good to daydream while driving,* I shuddered. Luckily, there'd been no traffic coming the other way. Ahead, I recognized the outskirts of Acapulco. Rattled by the incident, I pulled the crumpled bag of pot from my pocket, tossed it out the window, and headed for the hotel.

The beach was too breezy for volleyball, so I body surfed until nearly dark. After a shower and a Pacífico in the bar, I wandered in search of a plate of bean tacos with salsa fresca and sat down to supper about the time my brother would be unloading kilos in west Texas. My mind flirted off and on with the vision that nearly got me killed. I figured Víctor's machine-gun toting campesinos had prompted the daydream. My body retained a sensation of hands grabbing me, but I wrote it off as paranoia. *What else could it be?* Ultimately, I found my bed and submitted to mindless exhaustion. As old man Víctor'd predicted, it *had* been a big day.

————

CHAPTER 23
MARIAH

For an artist, or anyone for that matter,
the question of priorities often comes
up. How to fill your day, or your life?
Say you have a jar filled with a mixture
of pea gravel, sand and rocks. Dump
out the contents and sift into the three
separate components. Now, put it all
back in the jar. What will you put in
first?

Max and I pile out of his bread truck at Sunflowers to find Cindy standing on the porch by the door with an overnight bag in her hand, reading something on a ragged piece of paper. Rascal runs to us both in turn, trading licks for rubs and scratches. Cindy skips down the steps hollering, "I thought you were long gone!"

"I won't be staying, Cindy. Changes are in the wind."

"Come in. Come in," she says. "I just got home. Peyton and Otis are off on their dope search, so we're on our own. I'm starving."

Max heads for his hives while Cindy and I plunge into food prep. Hadn't realized how hungry I am, but young ladies are taught not to admit it, so I don't. When we sit to eat, Cindy says, "I've been away, visiting a mechanic in Lockhart. When I got home, I found this stuck in the front door." She hands me a scrap of paper.

For the Waterfall Mistress

I've walked the road
and followed clues with blistered feet
to find a muse
who disappeared without a trace
and all I want
is more of you.
But 'til I see
the essence of your naked soul
you'll always keep
a sacred part of me within.
And I will search
the blue of sea and green of earth
to bring you close,
to feel your face,
and hold your heart again.

Love, the Mer-man

I'm stunned! He wants me. *Mer-man must have found my note at the co-op.* "Hold my heart," he says. *I wish!*

A buzz of electricity is lingering on the surface of the paper. The poem goes into the front pocket of my jeans to be pulled out at random times when I need a smile . . . Like now. I pull the paper back out and read the poem again, close my eyes and center myself below my solar plexus, reaching out to him. Lower . . . lower, then I send a squeeze. *After all, he's seen my soul.*

"I can't believe it," Cindy says. "He's smitten and he's never even seen you. 'Waterfall Mistress,' that's hot." She takes another bite of mashed potato.

"I can't believe it either, and I was there. But it's not fair to pursue it, considering my situation."

My hand goes to my belly, unconsciously feeling for a bulge, not finding one yet. I've already betrayed the mystery man by having incredible sex with Sara. Still, as good as it felt, what happened with her seems so isolated and temporary now—so *functional.* Weird how my ideal of a perfect man trumps the reality of a caring and considerate woman. He *does* hold my heart—already. And I long to be filled up again. *Where in the world is he?*

"All's fair in matters of the heart, darlin'." Cindy quips, breaking into my reverie. "Besides, he's probably got baggage too. You know—communists in the family, serial killers, bodies in the basement. Believe me, it's fair."

Serial killers? The thing is, I'm desperate to clear my romantic slate for the prospect of a connection with this mer-man guy, but I keep that to myself. Our meal finished, Cindy hands me a joint and a cup of ginger tea with lemon.

"Cindy," I take a drag on the number and slurp a half-mouthful of hot tea before changing the subject. "I'm going to terminate the pregnancy." It's hard for me to say, even to her. I slurp some more and squelch my self-revulsion, gathering courage. "But I want to look Blaine up and tell him, before I go through with it. I owe him that much. I was hoping you'd go with me to that clinic in Acapulco."

Cindy is casual, taking it all in stride. She probably gets it better than I do, being the pragmatic one. "Funny you should say that." She reaches out to put a hand on my forearm. "I mean, it's not funny. Look, Mariah, I've been stuck in the same rut all year and I have money saved for a road trip. I need to get out of here." Then she frowns. "Shit. I'm afraid the Corvair won't make it to Mexico."

I catch her hand. "It's okay. I cashed the savings bond. I'll buy a car. I hate borrowing yours all the time."

"Oh no. You were saving that bond to buy land."

"I was." My words are trying to catch up to my thoughts. *Hands on cup. Take a sip. Mmm, warm.* "I need to take one thing at a time, first things first. This obligation has me hung up. I'll need transportation to find Blaine. After dealing with him, I'll be able to concentrate on finding my perfect place . . . and this mystery man."

"Outta sight. Then let's do it!" Cindy screams. "Isn't the spring of the year when they say kings and serving wenches go off to war?"

No argument from me, even though spring *is* behind us—summer's here in spades. And I'm not planning on a war. Just a little vacation with a purpose.

Cindy snaps her fingers. "There's a man I know with a beetle for sale cheap. He said it needs a little work."

We leave a note for Max and go see the car, try it out. The guy guarantees the motor for ninety days, so now I own a dark blue bug with a white front fender and a missing rear bumper. With the muffler shot, it makes a little noise. Well . . . a lot of noise. In fact, it sounds like I'm rocket powered. At the inspection shop I get a wink and a sticker anyway. Gotta get some music in this machine. Maybe I'll break down and buy a muffler, too, so the cops won't stop me. I've named the rig *Betelgeuse*, after the star.

I'll get the title changed and new license plates, but it'll take most of the week to get a muffler and eight-track tape deck installed. Other repairs will have to wait.

———

CHAPTER 24
CLIFF

*If everything in a scene is gray, then
something with more color intensity
will stand out. Or if all the edges are
relatively soft, then something with a
hard edge will get your attention. Same
with value contrast, something light
against dark or dark against light. The
focal point will always be the thing
that's different.*

Blaine was supposed to fly back to Acapulco over night and meet me at the hotel the next morning, but he never showed up. I applied a salve and fresh Band-Aids to my blisters, pulled on two pairs of socks, laced up my Chuck Taylors, and followed my nose to a cup of coffee, for starters. I could have done without the hint of cinnamon, but the coffee served its purpose and I went looking for the telephone office. By the time I found the place nestled beside a church, it was nearly ten o'clock. The operator tried to connect several times with the emergency number Blaine had given me, but she never got through. I didn't even have a name, just the number.

My burning feet propelled me around the mercado and cathedral, over to the harbor, back to the Mercado and down to the beach, but no details registered. I imagined engine failure and border patrols, guns and airplane crashes. A cosmic guillotine seemed poised, waiting for me to stick my neck under the blade. Somewhere I picked up a roasting ear, smeared hot sauce on it and ate as I walked, leaning forward and dabbing my chin with a napkin.

I panicked when it dawned on me I'd forgotten to warn Blaine about Ricardo. Víctor'd said not to trust his nephew with money, and something else—*La hierba no es la mota.* "The grass is not grass," whatever that meant. I pictured Víctor with the photograph and the knife, and realized I had no idea what violent extremes he was capable of. All I knew was that Blaine was in trouble. I checked back at the hotel for messages, then called the contact number again with no luck, every thirty minutes until the man working the switchboard started to mutter and roll his eyes. Finally, I apologized and handed him some extra pesos that he stashed right away.

I should have known something was fishy with the deal. It just about killed me, wondering what had happened, but the last thing I wanted to do was call my folks. I'd neglected to tell them I was going to Acapulco with Blaine, and I couldn't imagine talking to Dad again, considering our last confrontation. I almost didn't call. When the operator made the connection, Mother answered on the first ring and I breathed a sigh of relief.

"Clifford! Where are you?"

"I'm in Acapulco."

"Is Blaine with you?" she asked, her voice trembling.

"No. That's why I called. Have you . . . "

"Oh God," she screamed.

"What's wrong, Mom?"

"His plane wrecked. The bodies. . . two of them. . . I thought you . . . I was afraid . . ."

That's how I found out my brother was dead. And Mom thought I'd been killed, too. I heard her sobbing, even through the noisy connection, and wished I could give her a hug. Stunned, I remembered Blaine waving from the cockpit, seeing the wings dip left and right after takeoff, watching him disappear, just a gleam of sunlight between two hills in the distance.

Mother's voice again. "Oh Cliff, I can't . . ." More sobbing. "Listen, your uncle is right here. Let me give the phone to him."

"Hi, son," My uncle said, claiming me for his own. "When's the last time you saw your brother?"

With my heart jumping out of my chest, I flashed on the scene etched in my brain—air too thick to breathe, dust from the airplane, goats and rifles . . . "In Zihuatanejo," I croaked, vocal cords not cooperating. "He was taking a guy to the States, then flying back to Acapulco."

I gulped air. It *was* the truth, without the incriminating parts.

"Let me get this straight. He was taking a passenger from Zihuatanejo to the States."

"And they were stopping in San Miguel de Allende for fuel. That's all I know."

"So you don't know if they stopped there or not?" he asked.

"No," I said. "Only . . . that's where the guy lived."

"Cliff, I'm going to drive down to Mexico tomorrow. I'll stop somewhere for the night and arrive in San Miguel the next morning. Think you can meet me there?"

"I guess. If I can catch a bus."

"You have enough money?"

"I think so."

"Listen, so far, nobody in San Miguel knows who you are. Let's keep it that way. You need to fly under the radar. We don't know who all's involved here."

"I get the picture. I haven't told anyone my name."

"Good. Why don't you think of an alias to use. Meet me at the bus station at noon, day after tomorrow. All right?"

"Sure, I'll be there, one way or another."

"Here's your mother." My uncle signed off.

"Clifford," she said, "When your uncle gets down there, you do exactly what he tells you."

"I will." My heart was still beating in my throat. I wanted to give her some comfort, there just wasn't any comfort in me to give. So I settled for, "Take it easy, Mom."

Silence.

"There's probably a good explanation," I added, thinking, *It doesn't matter anymore. I've been a careless, mindless shit. I should be the dead one.*

There was more silence, then mother said, "Maybe there is. I hope so. . . . Cliff, I've got to hang up right now and call your father. Call me back tomorrow."

"Okay. I love you, Mom."

I tried the emergency number one more time without expecting any results, and I got none. The number was out of service.

———————

When I extracted the car from its parking place, my watercolor box was missing from the luggage compartment under the hood—*stolen*, I figured. I'd been counting on painting to relax my mind. Of course, losing my paint box was a small matter compared to losing a brother, but in a place full of thiefs, I should have been more careful. Should have locked up the damn thing. It looked like there'd be no relief from the horror of what I'd done or the remorse I felt about it. In addition, there was money to worry about. I needed to return the car and find a cheaper place to stay, then find a way from Acapulco to San Miguel the next morning.

The man at the rental office was difficult. When he talked on the phone, his Spanish was fast and fluent, but he spoke English with a Chicago accent, throwing *youse guys* around like spare change. *A Chicano hybrid,* I thought, *Mexican American, or maybe Puerto Rican.* I avoided the creepy eyes.

First, he wanted the papers, so I showed him Blaine's rental contract. He asked where Blaine was, then asked to see my visa. I told him, "Back at the hotel," hoping he'd accept the answer for both questions. Then, he wanted to inspect every square inch of the car, including the trunk. Especially the trunk. He manhandled my travel bag and even asked where my other luggage was, like he was conducting some kind of criminal investigation. There was something familiar about him, the way he carried all his weight around on one leg. The way his shaved head was shoved down between his collarbones. My skin crawled, being around him. I couldn't wait to get out of there, but I stood my ground.

Funny thing, when I unfocused my vision and let his body go fuzzy, a huge hawk hovered over me, predatory, and I heard the flapping of wings. I wanted an incantation, some magic spell to zap him with, make him go away, but no luck. When I focused again on the man's features, they still pulsated, and darkness surrounded him. The creep finally finished with me, signed off on the car and I skedaddled with a bad taste in my mouth.

I found a budget hotel away from the beach, and the porter there sold me two joints for a dollar, so I walked down to the shore, tied my shoes together, slung them around my neck and found an unpopulated spot to smoke. Nothing short of good weed could quell the anxiety I felt, and nothing at all could stop the tigers from coming at night. I longed to go back to some safer past, when my life was under control and my brother was safe.

To be honest, though, I'd never really had control of my life, and Blaine hadn't been safe for years. There was no safe place for me to to go, either, so I let my feet take me ankle deep into the Pacific, where the emptiness stretched on and on and where my tears and molecules could mingle with the ocean and stars. Chest heaving, I scooped up a handful of briny water and tasted it, then closed my eyes.

> There's pain in my head. Voices in Spanish, then hands on me. "Belín! Belín! Wake up!"
> "Ricardo! What happened?" The voice echoes in a cavern-like place. Ricardo looks fuzzy, glowing around the edges.
> He whispers, "We are prisoners, Belín."
> *Slam!* The door opens. A uniform, an ugly face, saying something about *el aguacate*. I know that word— avocado.

The last wave shocked me back, drenching my shorts, while the conversation still rang in my ears. I'd spaced out and drifted into the surf during the weird event with my brother, the second in a span of two days. *Am I losing it?* I wondered, unable to tell if what happened was real or not.

My wet shorts were real, for sure, so I veered toward the shore, feeling a glimmer of hope about Blaine. I followed the beach a long way before turning back, long enough to revisit the night in Texas with Aiyah. I could almost feel her wrapped around me, gently squeezing. With her memory came stillness, breath, and peace. The words of Donovan arrived in sync with the waves, *Way down, below the ocean, where I want to be, she may be*, the song propelling me all the way back to my room. Tigers came again in my sleep. This time they morphed into stone-carved jaguars, guarding a Mayan temple.

CHAPTER 25
CLIFF

What is the shape of negative space?
We sometimes forget it's every bit as
important as the positive. A classic
example is two heads facing each other
in silhouette—the negative shape is a
vase. You can focus on either positive
or negative space, but not both
simultaneously.

Third day after the plane crash

   The stinking bus was ready to leave at eight am, and I boarded
with the goats, the chickens and a sense of urgency. Occupied with
all the sights and sounds inside the vehicle, I didn't notice we'd left
the highway until the bus clattered to a stop beside an ancient adobe
building where an elderly couple with two large bundles stood
gathering dust. The driver leapt out, grabbed their bags and slung
them into the baggage compartment. Then we waited while the old
man helped the old lady take one calculated step after another. *Oh
hell,* I thought. *I caught the wrong bus.* It was a local route. Might as
well have been riding a burro . . . or a turtle.

Time had come to a stop. They finally boarded, but my anger at myself and the world ate up miles of slow and dusty road. The anger eventually gave way to fear, and fear gave way to emptiness. In the midst of that void, I finally remembered where I'd seen the jerk from the car rental agency. When Blaine and I landed at the airport in Acapulco, he was the phantom with batons who'd guided us to park the Cessna. *That guy gets around*, I thought, and half-expected him to be lurking when the bus arrived in Mexico City. Something else nagged at me, too—a nebulous thing that lingered on the edge of consciousness. *Something Ricardo'd said, maybe?*

Anyway, I survived the trip, to the D.F., as the locals call it, and when an express bus rolled into the station, sleek as a Greyhound, I boarded and rode in comfort the rest of the way to San Miguel. Arriving just before dark, I found a modest room, then ate and crashed. I never thought about calling my mother back.

———

Fourth day after the plane crash

Next morning, I ran through the cobblestone streets with my shoulder bag flapping and arrived at the bus station with time to spare. Shoeshine boys hated me for wearing my Chuck Taylors and failing to give them work. A six-year-old sold me two dozen packets of chewing gum while other kids played in the side streets and avoided being run over by crazy drivers.

Finally, a yellow Toyota pickup pulled up to the curb, scattering the children, and my uncle waved from the driver's seat. I threw my bag in the bed and got in. Inches away, half a dozen kids mashed their faces against my window. Uncle Nel tossed a handful of coins out the window on his side, and money bounced down the street while the mob swarmed away in pursuit.

My uncle greeted me with a sideways hug. " Have you eaten, Cliff?"

I shook my head. "Just coffee."

"Let's get lunch. I know a place."

Three blocks off the central square, he turned onto a narrow street and stopped at the curb. A young man stepped out of a doorway, laughing, and ran around to open Uncle Nel's door.

"Hola Noe. ¿Cuídete la troka para mí, por favor?" My uncle pronounced the name *Noe*, like it rhymes with *Joey*. He jingled the truck keys and held them up. *"Quiero hablar mas tarde."*

With a surprised grin, Noe nodded and took the keys, then shook hands with my uncle and made the Toyota disappear around the corner. I took a good look at Uncle Nel—sport coat, khaki slacks and short-brimmed straw hat, rimless glasses—and felt a little shabby in jams and t-shirt as we entered the restaurant. Gauze-draped windows illuminated the cool interior and dozens of candles cast pools of amber light on the tablecloths. To one side, a young woman flipped tortillas on a grill. We stopped at the bar and I asked for a *tamarindo*, a soft drink concoction made from tamarind pods. Uncle Nel ordered a tequila on ice, with a twist of lime

"How did you meet Noe?" I asked.

My uncle said, "I got him this job when he was seventeen. That was ten years ago. I had an idea he might still be here."

"You mean he's older than I am?"

"He must be twenty-seven or eight by now. It's the good skin genes—makes up for his other problems. Noe got meningitis when he was a kid. He's really deaf, but only pretends to be mute."

"So he communicates with sign language?"

"He can, but he prefers to use index cards. Gives you one or two to write on if he wants to talk to you. He can also read lips, but you have to be facing him."

"I still can't believe he's older than I am."

"It's true. Oh, by the way, your mother asked me to give you this." He handed me an envelope and took a healthy swig of his drink. Inside the envelope was a hand-written note from mother, wrapped around three hundred dollars in twenties, enough to last me a all summer. 'Be Careful, Cliff, I miss you and can't wait to see you. We'll talk soon. Love, Mother'

"She just wants to know you're safe, Cliff. Call her."

"Oh shit, I forgot."

My uncle gazed at me intently. "Your father wants me to bring you home right away."

"I'm not going back there just to go to jail."

He squinted one eye and the other opened wider. "I don't think that will be necessary. Look, Cliff, your father really wants to kick your butt, but at the same time he's trying to save it. He's working on getting your indictment dropped."

I let out a long breath. "I guess I'm lucky he's my dad."

"You bet your sweet ass you are."

He tilted his head down in a 'serious' expression. "Listen, your parents think that pot belonged to the two guys that stole the plane. They're not exactly naïve. They're just afraid Blaine's no longer with us."

"I know, I'm scared too, but I can't believe he's dead."

"Cliff, some things they don't understand."

"I know. I'm one of those things."

My uncle polished off his drink and we moved to a table where he ordered for us. I hoped he was through with the lecture, but he wasn't. I suppressed a sigh as he held out his right hand, showing me for the hundredth time the stub of his third finger. I felt a sympathetic twinge in my own hand, same finger.

He said, "When I got this finger shot off in the Philippines, I could have taken the morphine my medical unit issued, but I didn't want to get hooked on it, so I snuck out of the infirmary and smoked pot with the girls in a whorehouse. It helped with the pain and helped me relax. After the war I came home and forgot all about it. What I mean to say is that I don't think marijuana is evil. The problem is, it's against the law, and that makes you a criminal when you use it."

I'd sort of nodded and "uh-hum'd" my way through the one-sided conversation, unable to argue with the voice of reason, but feeling uncomfortable with the subject.

Uncle Nel said, "You know, you'll have to face your father sometime."

That made me even more uncomfortable. "I know, but first I'm going to find Blaine, dead or alive."

"I don't blame you," he nodded. "I volunteered to come down here as a favor to your mother, but, between you and me, I never intended to try and force you to go back. The truth is your father needs you out of the way right now. He just doesn't need the embarrassment of a scandal involving his family."

"I won't do anything stupid."

"Look, this isn't your fault." Uncle Nel glanced toward the door, "But until we know more about what happened here, we should try to avoid attracting too much attention."

Yeah, right, I thought, *with a new canary yellow truck and all.* I overcame my instinct to reply with sarcasm and said, "Oh, by the way, I picked an alias—I'm going to be CJ."

"Good, you could use my last name. 'CJ Holt,' how does that sound?"

"Well, at least it rhymes with Colt I could write Western novels with a name like that." I said, hoping a little humor would lighten the tone of our conversation.

My uncle laughed but stayed with his serious train of thought. "We'll need to get you a haircut and find you some better clothes, CJ. To keep you out of the public eye, after lunch we'll drive over to Guanajuato.

The nachos came, sizzling in a round steel platter set on a larger piece of wood. Each chip had a puddle of refried beans topped with cheese and a slice of pickled jalapeño.

"¡Plato caliente!" the waiter exclaimed, presenting the loaded platter with one hand and distributing our plates with the other.

He got a "Gracias" from us both. I was starving.

Before we cleaned the platter, our waiter was back, mashing avocados at the table-side and serving guacamole with slices of lime and more tortilla chips. Then shrimps *en brochette* arrived in flames. Finally, we had a chicken-filled chile relleno with red sauce and pecans, a wedge of crumbly cheese served on the side.

Noe came to our table, conversed in sign language with Uncle Nel and pointed at me. He was impeccably dressed, from the starched collar to the polished penny loafers sporting real American pennies and taps on the soles. His gold tooth added an element of precious metal. In flickering candlelight, fine wrinkles around his eyes confirmed that he was older than he looked at first. I thought he'd make a great subject to paint—shaved head classically shaped, skin a burnished copper and eyes showing lots of white around the irises.

Noe pulled a small spiral notebook out of his back pocket, sat down to write a note and handed it to my uncle. Then he turned to me, touched his lips and wagged his finger back and forth, shaking his head at the same time. He held my gaze for a second, then winked, slapped me on the shoulder and slipped away, his polished head gleaming in the dim interior.

Uncle Nel explained, "He doesn't want you to let on that he can speak."

"I got it."

"Good. Noe will make discreet inquiries to find out if Blaine's been seen around here or if he's in jail. Let's go, I've made reservations for us at the Hotel La Rosa. I used to stay there years ago. First, though, we'll go for a drive."

Outside, the sunlight was painful. Noe flipped me the keys and solemnly accepted a tip from my uncle. I noticed a small enameled American flag pinned to his collar. Noe bowed and held a mock military salute as I drove the Toyota away toward the railroad station.

"What's with the flag pinned on Noe's collar?" I asked, holding my eyes on the unfamiliar road.

"He wants to emigrate. Wanted me to smuggle him into the U.S. when he was just a teenager." Uncle Nel directed me to the Guanajuato highway before he nodded off. It's too bad. He missed some beautiful scenery.

First stop in Guanajuato was the barbershop. I spotted one of the universal red-and-white striped poles and parked the Toyota. We ducked under the low door frame and Uncle Nel gave moral support by getting a trim and a shave himself while I suffered a shearing. Afterward, almost as bald as Noe, I felt more alien than I had at the bus station—but at least I smelled good drenched in sandalwood.

Khaki slacks, with no cuffs, were altered on the spot. Next came the hand-tooled black belt and matching wallet, black loafers (no pennies), and two short sleeved shirts, subdued prints with *agave* motifs that looked more Hawaiian than Mexican. I insisted on square-cut bottoms so I wouldn't have to tuck them in. I could go shopping for sandals and a hat the next day, but I refused to throw away my old Converse All-Stars. A guy has to draw the line somewhere.

After rousing the proprietor from his siesta at the bar next door to the telephone office, Uncle Nel indulged in a quick pick-me-upper and bought me a Pepsi. At four, we went into the office and he pre-paid the call. "Easier," he said, "to sign off when the operator says it's time."

Mother answered, sounding distraught, with an update on Blaine's status. "The investigation is secret until the bodies are identified," she said. "His dental records have to come from the Air Force, and it's taking longer than expected."

The strain in her voice tugged at my heart and I wished for a way to comfort her, but there was nothing to give, not even empty words. I ached for her, and I ached for my brother. *At least he hasn't been confirmed dead,* I thought. I evaded Mother's questions about coming home and managed to say, "I love you," before the operator cut us off.

The back of my neck itched with stray hairs from the recent barbering and I would have gladly traded for a new skin right then— preferably tanned and blemish-free. Maybe stretched over a more muscled-up physique, with shoulder length hair like a rock-star. Unfortunately, I was stuck with my pale skin and closely trimmed self.

Back at the hotel in San Miguel, Uncle Nel was ready for another drink, so we strolled onto the patio and found a table and a waiter. I had no desire to keep up with his drinking, but made a token gesture and ordered a Negra Modelo. We looked out on the glowing roofs of the town, elbow to elbow, and my uncle got right down to it. "Cliff, it's time for you to come clean, I need to know what's really going on here."

"All right," I said, "but I'm CJ, remember." The shadows had grown long, and velvety clouds built overhead while the western sky turned to honey. A faint rumble of thunder rolled over the mountain behind us as I spilled the beans.

"Blaine and I went to Zihuatanejo with this guy Ricardo, then I stayed one night with his uncle while Blaine went back to Acapulco for the plane. The next day Blaine came back and we loaded the plane with weed. They took off, headed for San Miguel on the way to Texas, and left me with the old man again. That's the last I saw of Blaine."

"Why did he stop here in San Miguel?"

"For fuel. Ricardo lives here, remember. I told you on the phone."

"CJ, the sheriff in Pearsall told Wayman some of the bags in the plane were filled with hay."

"What?" I was unable to process the information. The kilo Blaine and I checked was definitely not hay. Then Víctor's words, *La hierba no es la mota* came back to me, suddenly making sense, and my knee jerked, de-stabilizing the table. My beer teetered precariously and my hand lurched for it, sending the bottle rolling off the table, and crashing to the floor, spilling *cervesa* as it went. "They screwed us!" I said, jumping up from my seat. "Víctor told me not to trust Ricardo with money. He said, 'The grass is not the grass.'"

"Did Blaine know about that?" my uncle asked, using both our napkins to mop the spill.

"I forgot all about it," I said, full of self-revulsion, and shook my head, thinking, *I'm an idiot*. "I meant to tell him," I admitted, trying to snort back tears as the flood came, but to no avail.

I covered my head and hunkered, elbows on the bar, while huge sobs racked my chest. The waiter who came to sweep up the remains of the bottle just stared at it, then stared at me, askance. I suppose he thought I was nuts, crying over a spilt beer like that.

But it wasn't funny. As I stared bleary-eyed at my uncle with my chest heaving, the guilt clinched me in a hammerlock. "It's my fault," I wailed. "I got him killed."

———

CHAPTER 26
MARIAH

Connect the pattern of shadow
everywhere you can. Paint the dark
shape a little bigger than you see it. It
should look like nothing but darkness.

On Tuesday morning at Sunflowers, I hear a scream from the kitchen. "Mariah! the plane crashed!"

The Sunday *American Statesman* is spread on the table and Cindy is pointing to a headline on page two. "It's Blaine's," she says, and my heart sinks as I grab the paper and read, all the while thinking, *now I'll never get to tell him about what's-her-name.*

Cessna Crashes in Frio County

On Friday, May 23, two passengers were killed when a single engine Cessna 210 crashed into a ranch house in Frio County, causing a conflagration. The home, owned by Vernon Cole, 63, was destroyed when impact from the plane ignited a fuel storage tank. Mr. Cole was present at the scene and reported the incident to Frio County authorities. According to Sheriff John Pierce, identification of the deceased is pending, and the FBI has taken over the investigation. The aircraft was registered to retired Major Blaine Grayson, a war hero who flew 67 missions in Vietnam between 1965 and 1967. Major Grayson was awarded the Air Force Distinguished Service Medal and the Purple Heart.

"Cindy, where is Frio County?" I sniffle, "I need to talk to Vernon Cole. He called Mother. Said he wants to talk to me.

Cindy produces a map. "Looks like an hour and a half away. It's down past San Antonio."

"I've got to see where that airplane crashed."

"Sure, babe. When are we leaving?" she asks. *"We"—she said. I adore this woman.*

"Tomorrow morning."

"I'll call and get off work. I'm coming with you." She's already picking up the phone.

No argument from me. Cindy is one hundred percent into the whole odyssey. She's decisive when I might tend to waver, but cautious when I get impulsive. It's a good balance, and I'll be glad to have her with me.

She's finished with her conversation, so I dig out the phone number mother gave me for Vernon Cole and give him a call. No answer. The rest of the day is filled with preparing *Betelgeuse* for a little trip. Sweeping and washing the interior, washing the outside, getting the oil checked, buying gas, and sweet talking the old bug. After trying Mr. Cole's number twice more with no luck, we decide to go see him anyway.

———

The sheriff is in his office in downtown Pearsall.

"John Pierce." He stands to greet us. The ten-gallon white hat remains on his desk, upside down. I'm glad I wore jeans and my western shirt with the pockets. I feel right at home here. I'd like to steal the sheriff's hat, though. He keeps stealing glances down Cindy's cleavage. Her blouse is less modest than mine. And her figure's more abundant.

When I ask about the plane crash, he's all business. "I'm sorry. That's an ongoing investigation. I've been ordered not to give any details, so my hands are tied."

"Well, it's just that Blaine Grayson is my, um, fiancée. I need to know if . . ."

"Ma'am, the identities of the deceased have not been determined. What I *can* tell you is where Vernon Cole lives. Or used to. The aircraft came down on his house."

———

When Cindy and I cross the cattle-guard and pull up to the pint-sized aluminum travel trailer, Mr. Cole is standing in the doorway, wearing jeans and cowboy boots, snap-button shirt and a grin like Steve McQueen. There's a twinkle in his eye and wrinkles around it. The stubble on his jowls matches the stubble around his ears. The bald head is pale compared to the weathered face. He's another hat-wearing man.

"Vernon Cole, ladies." *Did we cross the border into 'ladies' country while I was daydreaming or something?*

After we introduce ourselves and state our intentions, Mr. Cole asks, "Mind answering a question to confirm your identity, Miss Justice? You see, I have confidential information."

"Call me Mariah, please. What's the question?".

"Where did you meet Blaine Grayson?"

"In New Orleans."

"Where in New Orleans?" he asks.

"Um, it was in Audubon Park."

"Okay, Mariah, you pass the test." He motions us inside the cramped space and offers us each a can of Coke from the fridge. "Your mother is real nice, by the way. She's worried about you, though."

"I believe that's the job description of motherhood—being worried," Cindy chimes in.

"I reckon it is." He scratches a sideburn. "You see, it's like this. Don't tell the sheriff I mentioned it." He pauses to lock eyes with each of us in turn. "I took somethin' from the wrecked airplane . . . Well, actually, I found it under a tree that night and before John Pierce got here the next mornin', I decided to remove it from the scene." He reaches in a cabinet under the counter, drags out a soot-covered box and sets it on the counter. "This here is a thirty-caliber cartridge box, standard for the military. Account of my leg, I didn't go into the service. A rodeo bronc stepped on it back when I was seventeen. Messy break. Didn't heal straight. They said I couldn't march . . . I was a little old for the infantry, anyhow."

I'm thinking, *Mr. Cole is going to talk all day and into the night if I let him, lonely old coot,* so I ask, "Excuse me, could you please show me what's in the box?" as sweetly as I can.

"Why, yes ma'am." He turns back to the box and opens the lid. "After all, I been savin' it for you. I had to let the box cool off 'fore I could open it. The gasket melted in the fire, but the box got throwed clear when the wings was torn off the plane, so the insides didn't burn. Weren't no hurry, you see, I had the place all to myself. The deputy waited in his car up by the highway."

Mr. Cole reaches into the scorched cartridge box like a magician and extracts another box, this one cardboard. He lifts the lid and pulls out a blue and white ribbon with a medal hanging down, then hands it to me for a closer look. The twelve-pointed gold star looks like spokes on a wagon wheel without a rim. Between the spokes are twelve white stars. In the center of the medal is a blue disk. The thing is gorgeous.

"Air Force Distinguished Service medal," he announces, and hands me another medal from the box. "This one is the purple heart. When I seen what was in the box, I knowed I'd best keep it all here 'til I could get ahold of you." I'm eyeing the envelope, about to reach for it when he says, "I read the will that night by flashlight. Wore out the 'D'cell batteries." Mr. Cole grabs his hat and reaches for the door. "Ladies, there's more space outside for visitin.' This here temporary home of mine is kinda cramped. Leave your drinks here in the fridge and bring this stuff with you if you like. I figure it's yours now."

I grab the box and we troop ouside, so the old boy can lead us on a tour of his spread. The old man's right leg is more bowed than his left, and he leans to the left like the right one hurts when he puts weight on it. I know what to do. I could give him an adjustment to straighten his back and rotate his hip. Temporarily, it would help, but I know the atrophied muscles wouldn't hold the bones in place. In a day or two he'd be right back where he was before. Instead, I do reiki, allow the healing power of the universe flow through me and into him from a short distance. It must hurt him to walk. Every step.

His threadbare flannel shirt is neatly tucked into a wide leather belt with stitching around the edge and 'Vernon' tooled into the back of it. The jeans are too long and worn to a scallop at the bottom in back by his boot heels. I've finally figured out how he got my parents' number. I gave it to Blaine when we left New Orleans and he kept it in his cartridge box.

"America owes a debt to Major Grayson." Mr. Cole stands up straight, his voice solid and deeps, like he's making a speech. "He served his country, and no need for any dirt to come out. I figure the general population don't need to see what's inside the box. Besides, ain't nothin' wrong with marijuana. God made it just like he made Johnsongrass, or oak trees, horses, cattle, you and me. Shouldn't be no law agin' it."

I agree, of course. In fact, I'm wishing for a joint right now. The effect of the one Cindy and I smoked on the way here has worn off. It seems strange that Mr. Cole would tamper with evidence in a crime scene, but that's not my area of expertise. Besides, who am I to question *his* ethics? I empty the contents of the box on the rock, and he points to one of the items—the red book.

"Speakin' of Johnsongrass reminds me." His voice takes on a conspiratorial tone. "That there journal of Major Grayson's has the inside story about Lyndon Johnson. You ask me, Mariah, that shouldn't be public knowledge. Too embarrassin'." Mr. Cole started to say more, then stopped and reached in his shirt pocket. He produced a small white can with red lettering, popped the top off and tipped brown powder between his lower lip and teeth. "Lyndon's almost a neighbor," he says, lip bulging with W.O. Garret snuff. "Ranch family. Good people."

"Why did you keep the cartridge box, Mr. Cole, instead of letting the sheriff have it?"

"Sheriff would'a confiscated it for evidence, now wouldn't he? You see, the sheriff and me, we go back aways. Don't you be tellin' him I said so, but he's a fine man. I just couldn't hand him the medals and the journal. He might keep it locked up for years. The next of kin might want the medal. Might want to know somethin' 'bout the good major." He takes off down the path, sort of throwing me the words over his shoulder as he walks. "There's a tag inside the lid with your momma and daddy's phone number. There's a note for you in there, too, so I reckon you're the closest kin to Major Grayson, what with that child you're a carryin'."

The lump of snuff makes Mr. Cole's words hard to understand, but fortunately he has finished speaking. He stands, nods and takes time to spit before disappearing up the creek. I'm beginning to like the old gentleman—a jewel in the rough. But I can't figure how he knows I'm pregnant. Must be clairvoyant or something.

Inside the yellow envelope is a scuffed-up card. On one side is a photo of water and sand with people on a beach. Blank on the other. There's a note in there too, a folded piece of stationery, embossed with a gold border. The note reads:

Dear Mariah,

I am sorry this letter is coming to you under unfortunate circumstances. If you are reading this, then something's gone wrong and I didn't make it. Since we met in Audubon Park, I have never given up thinking we would one day end up on the beach together in Zihuatanejo. I could kick myself for letting you go so easily.
If you are able, go there and see George. Remember what I said about cats?
Also, I made a down payment on that apple orchard in Arkansas (see documents). If I am not around, I would like for you to have it, although you will have to make yearly payments. It may be your perfect place.

Love, Blaine

Well, I'll be . . .

Blaine must have written the letter just before his last flight, knowing something might go wrong. If neither body is his, and he's alive, I shouldn't be reading this. I shouldn't be party to these tender feelings from him, not without the man himself being here to deliver them. Still, I drink them in like a pining maiden. The tragedy is a lead weight sitting on my chest, squeezing the air out. Cindy and Mr. Cole have wandered off and left me to cry in the shade beside this little trickle of a creek.

The 'Love' is a nice touch, but we never did have what I'd call a romance. I take note of the Arkansas apple orchard but focus in on the part about the beach. I wonder what kind of showering facilities they have in Zihuatenejo? And cats? That must be his code name for the beach. I remember talk about playa de las gatas, Cat's Beach. But why wouldn't he just say what he meant? *Because he wanted to keep the location a secret, silly.* I can feel the ocean's tug, both subtle and insistent, pulling me southward.

I wander up toward the old windmill that's spinning at a steady rate in the welcome breeze. A long pump rod travels slowly up and down, making a faint clank in a regular tempo. A necessary movement. Water flows from a pipe and the stream swells with each stroke of the rod. What would this country be without water wells?

After a bit, I find Cindy beside the wreck.

"This must have been the kitchen over here. That looks like the remains of a wood-burning cookstove." She's pointing at a collapsed jumble of iron. "Mr. Cole is kind of old-school, isn't he? Look at this glob of glass. Jelly jars, it looks like, melted down like the Wicked Witch of the East. Or was it the West?"

While she rambles on, I'm inspecting the wreck, imagining Blaine seeing the crash coming, how it felt, knowing you wouldn't make it. There's no sign of him, but there's not much airplane left either, just parts. The place feels like a funeral without a casket.

Mr. Cole appears beside a scorched tree trunk, wiping his chin with a red bandana. "Wasn't him in that wreck, Mariah. You know that, don'cha." He fixes his steady gaze on me. . . For some reason, he sounds sure.

CHAPTER 27
CJ

*Sometimes it's better to give up trying
to figure things out. Relax, don't press
too hard. Clarify your questions and let
the solutions reveal themselves.
Remember to trust the process.*

Fifth day after the plane crash

Before Uncle Nel arose the next morning, I extracted myself from
the hotel and investigated the city, unaware I was about to catch a
glimpse of my future. The guilt over my role in Blaine's fate had my
spirit chained, but my sore feet were free to roam, so I went on my
planned mission to buy a pair of sandals and a hat. I joined the
gathering throng on the streets of San Miguel where people were
buying and selling everything, it seemed, except *huiraches*. Staying
on the sidelines, I checked them all out, expecting anyone to be an
enemy.

The artist stood on the sidewalk less than half a block from the indoor *mercado* with a canvas perched on the three-legged easel in front of him. As I passed and glanced at his painting, I had to step into the street to get by. He was chattering away in Spanish to a group of kids and wielding his brush at the same time, oblivious to the city buses, trucks and foot traffic in the street. Amazing.

His subject was the market itself. Through a translucent canopy, sunlight poured onto an array of orange and yellow fruit. Two people occupied a shadow. A little girl stood in front, pointing at a glowing peach. His brush danced lightly, pricking the canvas with a deft touch here and there. All this registered in three heartbeats while I evaded the gathering around him and continued down the street.

Through an archway I glimpsed brightly colored bedspreads, pots in all sizes, glazed and unglazed, some in jarring colors and others muted in hue. Then came a frontal assault of cups, bowls, candles, images of Jesus, tobacco, candy, pastries of all kinds, not to mention silver jewelry and leather in all forms. Signs were everywhere, hand-written, and pictures painted on the wall, as if anyone could be an artist. *What a concept*, I thought. *Maybe they could.*

The *huirachi* shop offered a variety of styles. When I selected a pair, the vendor looked at my feet and shook his head. He looked over his merchandise and picked out another pair, handed them to me. I tried them on, and my toes heaved a sigh of relief, so I bagged my socks and sneakers and paid the man.

Returning to the market, I passed a dark niche, then backed up a few steps to take a second look. Cotton dust lingered in the air, bearing a scent of sunshine and warmth and blankets were stacked to the ceiling. I asked the vendor, *"¿Hay serapes?"* and, without a word, the smiling lady pulled out a stack, and right away a green one called my name. All cotton first off, fringed, with a dark blue stripe between vertical bands of cool green. Two accents of turquoise about an inch wide ran the full length near the edges. It was bigger than the one I'd lost, and when slipped over my head, it came down to my knees. Perfect, all cotton, and cheap.

This time the artist was alone on the sidewalk with an empty easel, puffing on his pipe when I approached. American, by the looks of him. Sandy mustache, ruddy complexion, soft-soled suede shoes. The painting was nowhere in sight, so I asked if he'd finished it.

"Yep. I sell most of them," he said, eyeing my serape appreciatively as he loaded bottles and rags into the pockets of his stool and deftly folded the easel's legs and lid. It took him all of two minutes to pack up his stuff.

"So, you do this a lot?" I asked.

"I come here often this time of year. Only in the mornings, though. Too hot later, and the market starts to close up around lunchtime. Speaking of which, I was just thinking about some *tacos de carne asada*." He grabbed the handle of his easel. "I know a place down the street here. Come along if you want."

I followed him to a hole in the wall a block and a half away. The restaurant had a tiny table and one chair on the sidewalk beside the door. On the table, a bottle of hot sauce and an old cut glass saltshaker. The artist set down his burdens along the stucco wall in front of the café and held out his hand. The top of his head came to my neck, making him five foot seven or eight, and what he lacked in height, he made up in girth.

"Charlie," he grinned through his mustache and his eyes crinkled at the edges with lines of humor.

I took the proffered hand and replied, "Cli . . . um, CJ." A teenager brought out another chair and we sat down.

"*¿Cerveza?*"

"Too early for me. I like the hibiscus tea, though."

"*Una agua de jamaica y una cerveza Pacífico,*" he nodded to the waiter. Then he pulled a pipe from his pocket and began to pack sweet-smelling shag into the business end. I gazed up the gray cobblestone street at the bluegreen patch of foliage against a plastered wall. Closer in, a red geranium spilled from a big pot. When the boy returned with drinks, Charlie rattled off our order in Spanish and looked at me. "Been here long?"

"Since yesterday."

"By yourself?"

"My Uncle met me here."

"College student?"

"I'm starting this Fall . . . Well, my plans may have changed."

The artist lit up and puffed twice on his pipe before setting it down. "You like my painting?"

"I did, what I saw of it. I wish I'd seen it finished. It's oil, isn't it?"

"Um hmm . . ." He sounded distracted.

"I'd like to try oils," I said, taking the plunge. "Before coming here, I painted boats in Acapulco," I said. "In watercolor."

Something about the man's presence gave me confidence and made me honest with myself. I'd been thinking my watercolors had been stolen from the rental car, but then I remembered seeing the box on the table my last morning at Víctor's house. That's where I'd left it.

Our food came, plates of soft tacos piled high with meat and covered with shredded cabbage and white queso. Then another plate of sliced avocado with sections of lime. Charlie shook out a liberal amount of red chile sauce onto his food and I followed suit. We feasted without words until he finished his *cerveza* and raised his bottle to order a second.

"You're welcome to come by the studio and see what I've been up to. I'm heading that way when I finish this beer." He indicated the bottle and took another drink.

"Thanks, but I've got to get back right now," I said. "My uncle's expecting me."

"Any time." He knocked ash out of his pipe onto an empty plate. "Most days I'm either at the market or in my studio. Go eight long blocks straight up the street here. Turn left at the *Tortilleria Los Primos*. Mine is the second house on the right. Studio's in the back of the house. Ring the bell. It might take a minute for me to answer. If I'm in the studio, Rosita will probably answer. Bring your watercolors. I'd like to see them."

He stood up and stuck out a hand. "Nice meeting you, CJ." Charlie peeled off some pesos and threw them down on the table. He pocketed his wallet, and I jumped up to shake hands. Without a backward glance, he snatched up the easel and stool and took off. I counted the money on the table and realized he'd bought my lunch and left a generous tip too.

I hollered after him, "Thanks for lunch, Charlie."

He just raised one hand, waved, and continued up the street.

––––––––––

The encounter with Charlie miraculously transformed San Miguel from a sinister place to a welcoming one. My spirits lifted and my shoulders dropped from around my ears to their normal place. I'd been holding a lot of stuff inside. But I didn't dally. I bought a canvas hat with a braided leather band on the way to the hotel, where I found my uncle sitting on the hotel patio reading the local paper, his murky drink sweating on the table.

"I met an artist at the market. He bought me lunch"

He looked at me and smiled. "Let me guess. About fifty years old, short, with a big mustache, maybe on the chubby side?"

"How'd you know?" I asked, surprised by Uncle Nel's description.

"That sounds like Charles MacRae, my old buddy. I was planning to look him up. He came here in the early 50's to attend art school. He was so good, by second semester they asked him to teach. That's when I bought the paintings that hang in my living room. We used to fish together up in Tampico, but I haven't seen him in years.."

Uncle Nel took a long swallow of his drink and I caught a whiff of gin. He stood up to leave. "Do you know where Charlie lives?"

"He gave me directions from the market."

"Why don't we pay him a visit, CJ? He may be able to help us find your brother."

"Okay. Did you find out anything from Noe?" I asked.

"He showed the photo around town, but nobody recognized Blaine."

I'd convinced Uncle Nel the yellow truck was too conspicuous for us to drive around town, so he loaned it to Noe, and we hiked the twenty-five blocks from the hotel, tiny angels blessing us along the way from niches beside carved doorways. By the time we were halfway there, the new *huaraches* had rubbed my old blisters raw, and I was sorry I'd insisted on walking. I think my uncle was sorry, too, by the splotches on his face and his heavy breathing.

I hobbled along on stinging feet with sandals in hand, hardly noticing my surroundings, until we reached the Los Primos tortilla factory. From there, the aroma of hot *masa* chased us halfway down the block to a wrought-iron gate.

"This must be it," I said and opened the gate, sandals in hand.

Centered in the stone façade of the house was a wood paneled door clad with the same wrought-iron pattern as the gate. A matching railing rimmed the gallery above, and above that, the roof was tiled in traditional terra-cotta. *These are well-off people,* I thought.

Uncle Nel rang the bell, and a minute later a middle-aged Mexican lady appeared. She wore a white lacy top and a colorful print skirt. Her dark hair was piled up on her head, elevating her stature, and gold hoops hung elegantly from her ears. An attractive woman.

"Buenas tardes, señores," she greeted us with a rich musical alto voice, and added in English, "May I help you?"

"Buenas tardes, señora. Me llamo Nelson Holt, y *este es mi sobrino,* CJ." My uncle spoke Spanish in a fluent baritone, introducing us and asking for Charlie. *"Venimos para visitar con señor* MacRae, *si es possible."*

She looked quickly at the sandals in my hand, at my bare feet, then back at my face. "I'm Rosita MacRae," she smiled. "I'm glad to meet you both. Please come in."

Surprised by her perfect English, I ducked under the low lintel and followed my uncle into a front sitting room with plants in pots, lots of windows, and two straight Mission Style chairs.

"Please sit, I'll bring Charlie." The lady said and disappeared.

Voices came from the back of the house, then quick heavy steps moved toward us. I stood as the artist emerged from an arched opening.

He turned to Uncle Nel, "Well, for Pete's sake. Nelson Holt!"

"Charlie, it's been a long time," My uncle replied. The two men grabbed each other in a huge bear hug and pounded each other's back.

Charlie said, "That was quick, CJ. I didn't expect you for a day or two." He looked down at my bloody feet and asked with a grin, "New *huaraches*?"

"Um hm," I nodded.

"Well, come in, come in." He turned and led us into the next room where the pretty lady waited beside an empty fireplace. "Please, let me introduce my wife, Rosita. Sita, my old friend Nelson Holt and his nephew, CJ, the artist."

We shook hands with Rosita and exchanged greetings all around. Then she went off to the kitchen and Uncle Nel commented, "You old scoundrel. She's a beauty, and speaks English like a native."

"Sita's not Mexican," Charlie said, "although many people think so, since she has the complexion and speaks Spanish fluently. She's actually a Cajun, from outside New Orleans."

As brought each other up to date, I learned Uncle Nel had met Charlie in San Miguel de Allende after the war, before Charlie married Rosita. Our hostess returned with drinks and some medical supplies. Then she knelt in front of me, broke a huge succulent leaf and squeezed a clear jelly onto my feet. "Aloe Vera will make it feel better," she said, and instant relief spread from my toes to the back of my head. Rosita gently massaged the pulp into my throbbing feet and wrapped them in gauze while I watched an orange and white cat across the room, licking its paw.

We finished our drinks, and Charlie invited us to see the studio. He led us past a staircase, down a hallway to the kitchen, a tall, bright room stretching across the full width of the house. A ceiling fan slowly spun, and and multi-paned windows looked across a shady courtyard. The two men continued through the French doors and beyond a stone fountain to another two-story stone building nestled among a cluster of trees. As I followed slowly on bandaged feet, Charlie threw an invitation over his shoulder, "Take your time, CJ."

I hobbled through the garden, where bird of paradise and other tropical plants grew in chest-high pots. Giant wind chimes hung from high limbs laid down a foundation of sound, and the sweet-sour notes of ripening fruit added a hint of fermentation. I dragged open the dark studio door and was greeted by the fragrance of cherrywood tobacco mixed with linseed oil.

The artist's resonant voice came from across the room. "An instructor of mine once said there are two kinds of art, sensory art and imaginative art. I do the sensory kind."

Light drifted down from three high windows through a haze of pipe smoke, giving the open space an illusion of texture and weight.

Oil paintings glowed like jewels on the light gray plaster walls.
Charlie indicated the array with his pipe stem. "Imaginative art
requires a different kind of vision. I'm merely a journalist, making
observations. There are no great thoughts in my work. Each piece is a
study in the way light reveals a natural form. I'm essentially a
copyist, recording my life at one particular place and time. Aristotle's
word was 'mimesis.' It means 'to imitate.'"

The lush colors and bold strokes of his paintings drew me like
magnets. I'd been carrying a mental image of an artist being someone
dependent on a rich imagination, full of weird images, experiencing
the sweet torture of alienation. But when Charlie essentially said
there's no need for the torment, I took a quantum leap in my
understanding of art. Making observations was the key.

Uncle Nel shook his head. "Your art is more than mere
journaling, Charlie. I see the intimacy, the care, the closeness of your
observation, the *insight*. You see *into* your subject." He caught my
eye and pointed at two of the paintings on the wall. "See the way the
glare looks on those houses nestled among the trees. That's visual
poetry, the work of a man who not only *looks* at the world, but who
actually *sees* it."

"You are too kind, my friend. I find that when I paint, like you
said, I really do *see* the world around me." With an amused look in
his eye, the artist spilled words in a slow, rolling Carolina drawl, dark
and viscous, like molasses. "I've practiced quite a bit, you know, and
it takes very little to interest me. Inspiration is everywhere, all around
us. An old stone bridge, vapor rising from a hot-spring, hand dyed
silk, an oak tree just before sunset. These are all things I love, and
therefore good subjects for art." Charlie's words seduced me, and my
overriding concern about my brother was pushed aside as my
emotions and my intellect pleasantly converged. Uncle Nel went to
the house in search of a drink and Charlie let me browse his artwork
at my own pace. In a small room off the main one there were more
paintings—all nudes. I took a deep breath as I looked around, then a
great weight lifted off me. I hovered in the sacred space, floating an
inch off the floor, surrounded by icons in homage to Woman, each
done in black, white and flesh tones with a touch of red or gold.

It seemed as though the artist had deliberately obscured the face
but left just enough detail to preserve an air of mystery and allure—

an ear, a nose, maybe one eye, together with more erotic parts. I yearned to know more about the particular lady he'd depicted. What overwhelmed me, though, was a sense of the naked body's wholesomeness. Surrounded by Charlie's artwork, I felt more human and more vital, the frankness of the images acting on me like a truth serum.

By the time the artist appeared at my side, I'd made the connection. "It's your wife."

"Yes," he said. "She says these paintings show her the way she sees herself, soft and abundant. Romantic, but also powerful."

"I wish I could paint like that," I said.

"Well, I could show you how, but it takes persistence. There's a lot to it. By the way, when are you going to show me your watercolors."

Internally slapping my head, I admitted, "I forgot them in Zihuatanejo." But actually, I felt relieved that I wouldn't have to reveal my amateurish sketches to the master.

"Well, another time, then," he said, as we left the studio behind.

———

We found Rosita sitting in the kitchen with my uncle, who turned to me. "CJ, I'd like to have a private talk with Charlie, do you mind?"

"No, of course not," I replied, but I did mind, since I knew they'd be talking about me.

"You could help me water the plants," Rosita smiled.

"Sure."

She indicated the door and I followed her into the garden. She bent to pick up an oversized green pitcher and dipped it into the shallow pool around the fountain, disturbing a pair of birds cavorting in the water. Then she led me to various thirsty plants, explaining, "The rainy season has just begun, so it doesn't rain dependably yet, and I've been watering religiously."

Ferns in pots, cannas in red and yellow, beginning to bloom. Celestial blue flowers on a mid-sized tree beside the studio. Succulents spilling from niches in the wall. As we moved from plant to plant, I sampled their smells and learned their names—jacaranda, bromeliad, cosmos.

In the process of bending and kneeling among the aloes, Rosita's loose-fitting blouse allowed me glimpses of her breasts. I saw a bare nipple, dark against the white glow of fabric, and the sight aroused me. Blood left my head and rushed to other places, leaving me dizzy with the beauty of nature and woman. I tried to avert my gaze, but the attempt was futile. Rosita noticed me looking, of course, and I blushed.

"Oh." She placed a hand at the neckline of her blouse. "This is the way I dress at home. It's okay. A woman's breast is beautiful, no?"

I was unable to meet her eyes, so I continued to study my foot, the rocks, the plants, a tree trunk, the sky. I took deep breaths, and thought about airplanes and *campesinos* with machine guns while we examined more specimens. After a while we found ourselves back at the French doors.

When I walked into the kitchen, Charlie studied me for a moment. "CJ, how did you get mixed up in all this?"

After a pause, realizing Uncle Nel had told Charlie everything he knew about my brother and me, I looked him in the eye. "I was with some people who got busted for pot, and I lost my job over it. I came to Mexico with my brother to lay low for a while and try not to embarrass my dad."

I honestly don't know why I said that about my dad. Before that instant, it had never occurred to me that his needs had anything to do with my coming to Mexico. Maybe it was true, though. Maybe that's part of the reason I flew the coop.

Charlie frowned. "I expect your father is more than embarrassed, thinking he'd lost both his sons."

Rosita came to my rescue, changing the subject. "CJ, how can we help you?"

"I don't know," I said. "I've got to find out what happened to Blaine. If he's still alive, he'll try to contact me."

"Does he know you came here to San Miguel?" Rosita was taking bowls from the refrigerator and setting them on the counter.

"No," I said, surprised by the question. I hadn't thought it through. "I guess he wouldn't know how to find me here. We were supposed to meet in Acapulco."

Charlie scratched his head. "Well, if he did land in San Miguel, maybe he's still around somewhere."

We agreed to get together again the next day for lunch and hitched a ride with Charlie back to the hotel in the 'Woodie,' his long green station wagon with brown wood-paneled sides. It was a surfer's dream.

––––––––

CHAPTER 28
MARIAH

*Be sure to slip a whisper of light into
your shadows, a touch of the cadmium
to make them transparent.*

Rascal the Lab has been trained not to jump on people, so when Cindy and I pull up to Sunflowers after our trip to Pearsall and open the Beetle's doors, he jumps all over himself. I kneel to give him a good rub and we take off running for the creek. Rascal wins the race, takes a quick dip and meets me on the bank before giving himself a thorough and necessary shake. In the bargain, I get a shower and a much-needed laugh.

Back at the house, Cindy is stirring up a meal of fried rice and veggies, Rascal is sprawled at my feet and I'm settled at the table with all Blaine's stuff staring me down. The *Last Will and Testament* states that he's leaving me all the contents of his cartridge box including the deed to a piece of land in Arkansas. It doesn't feel right, though, for me to get all that when his brother Clifford only gets a crashed airplane. And the medals? What about them?

In his journal, on the first page, hand-printed in all caps with a slant, is the word *LOG,* and under it, *BLAINE GRAYSON, 1968-1969.* On the next page is the first entry: *May 1968, Johnson Ranch.* Flipping through, I find entries from May, September and October 1968, each with densely written paragraphs full of quotes from meetings he had with LBJ last year.

On the page after the Johnson transcriptions is a series of dates and places, beginning with *Washington.* Next is an abbreviation—*T.,* then *Austin, New Year's 1969.*

I hesitate to turn the page, knowing that New Orleans will probably be next. Sure enough, New *Orleans, Feb.* That's all. No notes about me, like I didn't even exist. Two weeks of nothing. *Really?* Then *A., Mar* and *Z. Apr.* The paragraph that follows the April entry catches my attention, *CIA involved with Echeverría and Delgado in Guerrero. Tension between Victor and Ricardo.*

Now I'm worried, thinking Blaine may be alive and in trouble somewhere. *CIA involved* does not bode well. So, if the *Z.* is for Zihuatanejo, *A.* might be Acapulco. The *T.?* Probably somewhere else in Mexico. The third to last entry is *Austin, May,* then *A.* again, and *Z.* It looks like he *did* have a mission besides pot running. But who are all these people? And which one will lead me to Blaine? For some reason, 'Go see George' flies in and out of my sleep-logged brain.

While I'm searching the journal for clues, Otis and Peyton roll in from west Texas empty-handed. The pilot didn't show, and they'd apparently waited all night at a ranch with four barrels of aviation fuel and several bottles of whiskey, the remnants of which clung to both guys like a second skin. I back off, giving them plenty of space and relate my experience with Mr. Cole at the crash site. Then I tell them, "According to the newspaper, the bodies haven't been identified yet, so I'm holding out hope that Blaine wasn't one of them."

"If it wasn't Blaine," Otis asks, "then who were the guys they scraped out of his burned-up plane?"

"I guess we'll have to wait and see," I reply, but it's not my style to wait.

Cindy has banished Peyton to the showers, and Otis will be next, thank our lucky stars, so we've put dinner on hold. It's a good thing. My stomach is not ready for food. Peyton emerges from the bathroom in shorts and a cloud of steam, his auburn hair dangling wet on his chest. He stops at the fridge for a cold Pearl before taking a seat at the table and shaking his head. "This dope shortage is making an alcoholic out of me."

I take a seat beside him and ask, "What was west Texas like?"

"Sam's place is a moonscape." Peyton downs half a beer in one swallow. "I don't see how he calls it a ranch. The only thing he raises there is dust."

"No cattle?"

"Only a rumor. I was there two whole days and never saw a single cow."

When Otis finally drags his steaming body to the table, we pass the serving bowls around. The food is uplifting, if the conversation is not, and thanks to soap and hot water, sitting next to the two men is tolerable for me. So is sleeping on the couch, since I'm pooped. The long lost Bruce has apparently returned to claim the bed I recently vacated.

———

CHAPTER 29
CJ

One of the simplest intentions of an
artist is to record experiences based on
observation, in an act of 'visual
journaling.' This practice is the essence
of sensory (lyrical) work. Making an
honest response to a moment in time
strengthens the artist's ability to 'see.'

Seventh day after the crash

The morning after meeting Charlie and Rosita, while my uncle slept, I went to the hotel courtyard and drew in my sketchbook, surrounded by three centuries worth of stone and plaster. Russet and slate accents crusted the pale gray wall and a chipped place revealed the rock's raw citron core, ripe as a melon. It was a painter's dream in tertiary color. I could have kicked myself for leaving my watercolor box at Víctor's.

Still, drawing has its own appeal, especially the pace of it. Giant agaves and aloes spied on me while I worked, watching my every move. My tool took on a rhythm of its own and produced a drawing that shimmered, dreamlike, as if seen through a curtain. Where fleshy leaves overlapped, or cast shadows on the wall and floor, I let the pencil linger and twirl, imparting energy to the drawing—but softly, as though my hand had touched the wall on the precise place my eye lingered.

The wall moves, and I move with it.
Feeling cold and heavy, I cup water in my hands for
the man on the floor to drink.
It's Ricardo. He's moaning. Odors of urine and
molasses assaults my senses.
A sparrow flutters under the eave, where a narrow
beacon of light penetrates the dim interior of the
dungeon.

A spot of drool marred the paper where I'd passed out with my face in the drawing. I'd come to, confused about what had just happened, and while I sorted it out, my uncle arrived waving a telegram. "Good news, CJ! The bodies have been ID'd. It wasn't Blaine."

I took a deep breath and let it out slowly, saying a quiet thanks to God, the Universe, and whoever else might be listening.

Noe showed up with the Toyota on his way to work and drove us to Charlie's house, where he dropped us off. Charlie motioned us inside, saying, "Just in time," and we followed the aroma of cumin and garlic to the kitchen.

After reporting his news about the bodies, Uncle Nel embarrassed me by saying, "Charlie, CJ needs a place to stay for a while."

"Well, why not here with Rosita and me?" Charlie's eyes twinkled.

On cue, Rosita came inside smiling with an array of flowers and went to the sink.

"You're sure about this?" asked Uncle Nel, looking at Charlie.

"Absolutely." He turned to Rosita. "Sita, can CJ have the extra room upstairs?"

"CJ, we would love to have you stay with us," she smiled.

Charlie and Calico disappeared outside while Rosita filled water glasses and arranged the table. "We're having *pozole verde* for lunch," she announced. "I made a big pot."

In a few minutes our host came back inside with an armload of cucumbers and a cat, trailing scent of pipe tobacco. Uncle Nel pulled a note from his pocket. "By the way, Noe got us a list of names. At the bottom is 'Silva hacienda, airport, and *halcones*.'"

Rosita gave him a concerned look. "Did you say 'Silva'?"

"That's what it says." My uncle studied the paper in his hand.

Charlie stopped rinsing the vegetables in the sink. "We know the place," he said, over his shoulder. "And there are two brothers in the family. Sergio and Ricardo Silva. "

Bingo, I thought. *Ricardo is a match*. The search was beginning to narrow.

Charlie set a platter of sliced cucumbers with mint and sour cream on the table then took a chair while we joined hands for a silent prayer. Rosita had served the pozole in bowls with a pile of shredded cabbage and slices of avocado on top—a green soup, all around. A stack of hot tortillas sat on the table under a metal cover with steam coming out the top. While I devoured one of the tastiest lunches I've ever had, Charlie filled in some background for us.

"The hacienda has been here since colonial times. Now it's just a small holding with a big house and some pasture. There was trouble there a couple of years ago. We heard rumors that Ernesto Delgado was involved. He's an American military contractor."

"This could get nasty," Uncle Nel broke in. "*Halcones* means falcons, hunters. Even though he didn't die in the crash, Blaine may still be in jeopardy." He turned to Charlie. "This Silva place. What do you know about it?"

"I know both of those brothers are pilots, for one thing, and I believe there's a dirt landing strip there," Charlie said.

While his thumb and forefinger inspected his chin for stubble and I attempted to dispatch my soup before it got cold, Calico ran a slalom course around my ankles, a form of seduction that involved the bowl of *crema* on the table. I wasn't falling for the cat's gambit, but I'd fallen for another kind of seduction—getting my hopes up after hearing Blaine didn't crash the plane—and logic argued that my brother was neither alive nor free. *We're wasting our time,* I thought. *Blaine was already dead when his airplane crashed. The hijackers would have killed him when they took the plane.*

Rosita had been listening quietly. "We know the housekeeper for the Silvas. She used to work for us here when I taught full time at the Institute. We became close friends, but I don't see her much anymore."

Uncle Nel wiped his fingers on a napkin. "We need to talk to your friend. She may be the only warm body available who might know something."

"It's not an easy thing to do." Rosita made a face. "Juana's husband dominates her. He doesn't like for her to associate with us. The grandmother, *señora* Silva, is blind," she added. "Juana comes to church and sometimes I sit with her while the grandmother sits with another woman. Juana never says much, and after the Mass, she always leaves immediately."

This is no coincidence, I realized. The blind lady must be Víctor's sister, Carlota, the one who'd asked him to send money.

"Do you think you could talk to Juana discreetly?" Charlie asked Rosita.

"At church this evening, we could sit together and pass notes." Rosita twisted a lock of hair on her forehead. "That is, if she comes."

My thigh muscles twitched, ready for a good run, but I couldn't leave. I jumped up to help clear the table, scraped some leftover *crema* into Calico's bowl, and started washing dishes. My uncle discovered a beer in the refrigerator, and with Rosita's go-ahead nod, he opened it.

"We have some unanswered questions," he said, leaning against the counter, facing the rest of us and counting off on his fingers. "First, who took the plane? Then, when and where did Blaine get separated from it? Did he leave on purpose or was he forced? And where is he now?" Four or five fingers worth of questions.

Charlie said, "Sita, maybe you could ask Juana if an airplane landed at the Silva place last week, and if so, find out who was in it."

Noe honked once outside and Uncle Nel left to take a siesta at the hotel. After we finished cleaning up, Rosita sat down in front of me with a roll of light gauze, made a poultice with aloe vera, and wrapped my feet again, her touch doing wonders for the pain and easing my mind. I took a couple of aspirin before going upstairs to take a siesta myself and found Calico already curled up on the bed, waiting.

———

I woke up later that afternoon, lying on my side with a cat nestled behind my knees and a leaf pattern shifting on the window curtain. Rosita had established me in the front room upstairs, among the treetops. It was a comfortable room, even with the too-short bed. Dragging the crumbs of sleep from my eyes, I came downstairs to find the house empty and Charlie puttering around in the shed beside the studio. He was inspecting an old battered twin of his French Easel.

"That looks like an antique." I said, taking in the spattered blue and cordovan paint on its lid.

"It's one of the first that Jullian ever made." He set the easel on a bench and worked the tarnished brass hardware, lifting the lid to reveal tubes of dead paint and a variety of equally dead insects. "CJ, your uncle and I have been kicking around a plan," he said, inspecting a folded-up leg that looked broken. Then he asked, "How would you like to be my apprentice? Learn to paint in oils. It will be a good cover for you while we go out looking for your brother. You can use my name and we'll pass you off as my nephew. Would you be okay with that?"

"I'd be more than okay with it," I said, my pulse kicking up a notch. A guy can't have too many uncles. Besides that, I was anxious to try oil painting.

Raindrops began to thwack the paving stones, so I carried the relic into the studio. The repair required drilling and gluing, attaching metal straps and screws. Charlie had done it all before. We clamped the artifact and left it to dry, looking like a wounded hospital patient in traction, then hustled to the house ahead of the afternoon downpour.

Uncle Nel had returned in a jolly mood after his nap and happy hour. Rosita brewed a pot of tea and we all sipped Orange Pekoe with mint at the kitchen table while she briefed us on her meeting.

"Juana and I sat near the back. Doña Carlota sat with a friend of hers, across the aisle, two rows behind us. I felt like a child again, passing notes in church. She said Sergio and another man arrived at the hacienda on Thursday in a Federale car, parked in the garage and spent the night. On Friday she heard a plane land. There was loud talk in the house afterward."

Uncle Nel leaned forward and scratched his ear. "No sign of Blaine, I guess?"

Rosita shook her head. "Juana heard the plane take off, then much later Ramón took Ricardo and another man away in the jeep. It could have been Blaine, she doesn't know."

"Who's Ramón?" Uncle Nel queried.

"Juana's husband, the Silva's caretaker. The ranch manager."

Charlie scratched his chin. "Suppose Sergio found out the airplane would be landing there to fuel up, so he set up an ambush, hijacked the plane and flew it to Texas with the payload? Maybe he was planning to trade the dope for guns. Who knows? Probably wouldn't be his first time."

Uncle Nel took a swig from his flask. "That makes sense if Sergio is one of the dead men. But if he is, then where's Blaine?"

"That's the question," Charlie nodded. "And what about the Feds? If they were involved, and one of theirs went missing, the place would be swarming with them."

"They may not be involved," said Uncle Nel. "I bet someone borrowed a Federale car and a uniform for the job."

"Can we go visit this hacienda?" I stood up, ready to start the search right away. The connection with Ricardo was clear.

"What if your brother doesn't want to be found?" Charlie countered.

I refused to accept that. After all the talk about the plane landing at that hacienda, I was itching for action.

"We need to proceed with caution." Uncle Nel said, slurring his words and adding to my frustration.

Charlie preened his mustache. "Whoever drove that car away after the plane took off may still be hanging around." He turned to me. "Is there anybody you know of besides Ricardo who can make a connection between you and your brother?"

"No one around here." I said. I'd come to San Miguel incognito, as planned.

Noe banged on the kitchen door, and Rosita greeted him with a peck on the cheek. He handed her a stack of tortillas, then left with Uncle Nel.

Charlie turned to me. "Why don't we go talk to Ramón tomorrow? We'll make it a painting excursion."

"Exactly what I was thinking."

It had been a week since the plane went down—way too long. It was time to move. We gathered our supplies into a wheelbarrow and took off down the street to the garage.

"What's in the box?" I asked.

"It's a 4x5 camera with a 200 mm zoom lens. I hope it will provide some answers for us."

"It looks professional."

"I bought it in France about the same time I bought your easel. They don't make 'em any better than this." He looked over my stuff and asked, "Where's the sketchbook I gave you?"

"Upstairs. Do I need it? I thought we were going to paint."

"It helps to make a plan, draw a thumbnail or two."

We wheeled the empty barrow back to the house where I ran upstairs and came back with my sketchbook. Charlie flipped through it, lingering on the one with giant aloes—the one I'd drooled on. "Nice, but don't see any thumbnails."

"What's a thumbnail?"

"Sometimes," he said. "I have ideas faster than I can execute them, so I make a series of small drawings, bigger than a postage stamp but smaller than an index card. It's a way to save an idea for later, when you may not have any. And when you're painting on location, it saves time. You make corrections and work out problems before you start painting."

"Why don't you take photos of a scene then go back to the studio and paint in comfort?" I asked, remembering my fight with the gnats the day James Conner vandalized my car.

Charlie chuckled and fiddled with his pipe, finally got it lit and took a slow drag. "The pictures come from here." He tapped his head. "And here." He pointed two fingers at his eyes and laughed. "Maybe they come from here." He slapped his belly. "One thing I know for sure is they don't come from a camera. I've never in my life used a photograph to make art. You see a lot of work that's done that way, and it looks flat, hard-edged, with no light in the shadows. A photograph will lie to you about values and depth. There may be a certain level of competence in that kind of painting, but when it's done without any direct interaction, there's no soul in it. Art is about making a connection with the world outside yourself and illustrating that connection."

He was sincere about art, and his knowledge was rooted in experience. I was ready to accept everything Charlie said as truth, but I would eventually come to disagree about the photo thing.

———

CHAPTER 30
MARIAH

A clumsy tool may produce the best art.
In order to avoid tightening up, you
might try drawing with a stick, using
strong coffee instead of paint.

I need to find out what's on the the film from Blaine's cartridge box, and I know Sara has a projector in her studio. When I call, she says, "Come on over."

At her place, after an awkward hug, I hand her the film. "This was in the wreck, inside a cartridge box of Blaine's, along with his journal and some other stuff."

Sara takes the reel, and I feel the heat radiating from her. She shifts a table away from the wall, plugs in her small projector and threads the film, then goes in her kitchen for a bowl of peanuts and chocolate chips. With all set, she hits the light and we enter a world of flickering black and white.

The first scene unfolds with two men in peasant clothes, unloading wooden crates from the back of a truck. One man is thin. The other is bulky, with his head thrust forward like a turtle's. Looking at him, I shiver, even though it's hot in Sara's place. Some people just exude malice, and it's not just his posture, I tell myself. Something else. He looks like the kind of guy who'd shake your hand and crush your fingers together just for the fun of it.

Cut to a grainy shot of a dark interior, rifles arranged in rows. Cut again to the thin man, sneaking along an alley. Next, he walks up to a building surrounded by palm trees. He exits the building to help turtle-man herd a dozen ragged men with their hands tied, wearing blindfolds. They're being chased with a cattle prod into the cargo door of a green airplane.

Sara stops the film, turns off the projector light and turns to me. "What do you think?"

"This is disturbing, Sara. It's one thing to watch a movie you know is fiction. You know, they can do terrible things, and you know it's not real. But this *is* real, and I'm getting scared."

Her hand goes to my arm. "Blaine mentioned an airplane called *The Avocado*, used to execute dissidents."

Sara starts the projector again. In the next scene, the plane lands and taxis to the same building where the prisoners were loaded. Two men emerge, laughing. The thin man and the round-backed man who makes me shiver.

"We just watched a disappearance, Mariah." Sara's voice is strained. "They murdered those men in blindfolds. There's a civil war in Guerrero, near Acapulco. The guerillas are hiding in the mountains. The Mexican government accused them of being communists. Some have been executed, and the CIA is helping. It's a covert operation."

"Sara, I haven't read the whole journal yet, but I think Blaine was trying to persuade LBJ to pull the CIA out of there."

"It's likely. I think this film is part of a documentary he was working on."

In the last scene, the thin man is crouched on a fire escape wearing jeans and a dark shirt with a white band around his upper arm. He's holding a rifle, taking aim at something, and I notice the scar on his left cheek. The gun discharges. The camera pans around a crowd of people running between buildings into a vast open area. Next, we see a tumbling image and finally nothing but sky until the screen goes blank and the film rattles.

I shudder as Sara reaches to turn off the projector. I wonder what happened to the photographer—nothing good, with that camera pointing to the sky. I can only imagine what Blaine was doing with the film. He was a good man, a military man, committed to making the world a better place, and he felt guilty for his part in Vietnam. *Had he been trying to compensate for that?*

"This whole thing is bad news, Mariah. You need to be careful. That last scene with the people running? That was shot at the massacre they had last year in Mexico City before the Olympics. I recognize some of the buildings. And the guy with the rifle? There's a brigade of assassins that wear those white armbands." Her hand comes to rest on my knee. "I imagine right now Blaine's laying low somewhere until the smoke clears."

"Where would he hide?" I ask, covering her hand with mine.

"Anybody's guess." She locks eyes with mine and leans forward. The softer half of me wants to stay and be soothed, but the other half is turning to steel. I stand up abruptly and grab my bag.

She startles, "Don't you want to have dinner?"

"It's okay, I think I'll head for Sunflowers. My stomach can't handle food right now." *I haven't even touched a chocolate chip.*

"Do you want me to make a copy of this film?" Sara asks, holding it up. "I know someone with the equipment."

I pause, mid-exodus. "That's a good idea. How quickly can you get a copy?" I ask, already moving toward the door.

"Should be ready tomorrow."

"Sara, I'm going down there," I declare, and feel the tension in my neck release.

"I figured you were. Wish I could go with you." She's found something on the floor and bends to pick it up. I watch her stride for the trash can, toss something in. Then she turns to face me. "Drop by tomorrow evening. I'll have the copy ready."

We say goodbye from across the room. There's a a drop of water on her cheek, making a highlight. *A tear?* I'm unwilling to risk touching her again—it's too tempting.

————

At Sunflowers, the shadows have grown long, and Cindy is dodging a kamikaze June bug on the porch, while cicadas and bullfrogs play a serenade further afield. Rascal is curled up at her feet, nibbling on his leg.

I scramble up the steps and take a seat. "Cindy, are you ready for Mexico?"

"Honey, is the Pope Catholic?" She grabs my hand and squeezes hard. "I'm ready for action."

"Let's get our shots and visas tomorrow," I say, laying a newspaper on the table and unfolding the Texas map. "There's a curious article in this paper about a small plane being shot at in Hebbronville the same day of the plane crash. I want to stop there and see what we can find out about it."

Cindy finds it on the map. "Hebbronville is between here and Laredo, sort of. It's on the other side of Pearsall. It'll take a while to put the house in order and check with Max and Otis about feeding Rascal." At the sound of his name, Rascal perks up, and Cindy reaches out to scratch his ear.

I'm standing already, anxious to get a move on. "I just have to finish packing the car and I'll be ready."

Cindy looks worried for a second. "You think *Betelgeuse* will make it?"

"I might need to fix the wipers first."

"Hell, girl, no need. It never rains in Mexico."

The *Beetle* had performed perfectly on the trip to meet Mr. Cole in Pearsall. No reason it won't make a longer trip. What to take is the problem. Naturally, my first inclination is to take all my worldly possessions. *Who knows what I might need for the coming odyssey?*

Cindy is all for sparse and stoic. "If we have money, we can get anything we need."

She's probably right, so I agree to travel light. We won't be needing formal wear. Clam-diggers, shorts, the denim skirt, a few tops, some underwear, and I'm set. Traveler's checks from the bank. A new swimsuit. I'll take Blaine's journal and a copy of the film with me. The other contents of his box will remain here in Grandma's chest for the duration. If that man's still alive, he can come get his stuff later.

I need to find a guy named George on Cat's Beach in Zihuatanejo. And the sisters in Acapulco await. I sense their benevolent presence, offering a solution to one of life's classic dilemmas. But how can I break it to what's-her-name that her lifetime is not fated to be? It will take all the courage I can muster. Letting her go is going to be the hardest thing I've ever done.

———

CHAPTER 31
CJ

*When you work from observation of the
world around you, the amount of
information can be overwhelming.
When you try to put it all into the
rectangle of your paper or canvas, you
are faced with the question, 'Where
does the picture stop?'*

Eighth day after the crash

I got ready without shaving, and we plowed into the clear morning
like a pair of sodbusters, with Charlie driving the Woodie toward the
Silva hacienda. Rendered in a sepia monochrome, he wore baggy
pants made of unbleached muslin and a matching pull-over shirt with
a leather cord laced below the collar. The suede vest almost came
together across his middle, well-worn *huaraches* covered his feet, and
a straw hat sat crookedly on his head. Charlie was a painting come to
life.

My outfit was a newer, unstained version of the master's wardrobe, my hat a spotless canvas one like fishermen wear, a green feather stuck in the band to match my new serape. I must have looked like an adolescent bird trying to attract a mate.

With the master at the wheel, I made thumbnails of three roadside scenes in my sketchbook, each one taking less than five minutes to finish. I looked up when Charlie eased off the road at a turnout and killed the engine.

"Isn't this spot kind of exposed?" I asked.

"I was hoping we could hide right here in plain sight," he said, indicating the panorama with a sweep of his arm.

"Like a purloined letter," I quipped.

He glanced at me with a look of approval. "Right, CJ, there's no need for the whole world to see us."

He re-started the wagon and drove another hundred yards or so, turned down a gravel track and parked beside a low bluff. We were hidden from the highway, at least, and the hacienda was visible below.

"I thought we were going to talk to Ramón. Why can't we just go to the door and ask him about Blaine and the Silva brothers?" I asked, grabbing my easel from the luggage compartment.

Charlie struck a match to his freshly packed pipe. "We'd better evaluate the enemy before we attack, don't you think? See what we're up against?"

Why we couldn't just *do* something without always needing to do something else first aggravated me no end, but I gave in and trundled after him. I set up my easel and focused on painting the main house at the Silva place. A collonade on the near side intrigued me, and behind it, I glimpsed a bit of green poking up and out—maybe an interior garden. Arched windows and doors lent an ancient character to the building, marking it as a cousin to many I'd seen in San Miguel proper. After a while it became clear I'd made it too small and placed it too low on the panel.

"You can fix that with a rag and turpentine," the master said, responding to my groan. "You know you could have avoided the problem by doing a thumbnail first." He grinned and tilted his head, obviously amused at my incompetence.

I pushed the blob of brown paint up toward the centerline of the panel and saw an immediate improvement in my design. For a minute the composition locked into place, and knowing what I wanted to capture, I made a mark for the horizon.

Charlie nodded his approval. "One way to approach landscape is to work back to front or from the top down. Start with the distance and finish close-up."

I thought about that for a minute. "So, the sky next?

"Yes, since it's the farthest visible thing. Try starting with a medium-value mixture. Be sure it's dark enough. You can lighten it later if necessary."

———————

I found some measure of peace mixing paint and applying a pale tint of ultramarine to my panel, oblivious to everything but my paints and my subject. In a while, the roar of an approaching vehicle claimed my attention, and seconds later, a dirty white jeep bounced into view and skidded to a stop beside us. A man jumped out, strutted up to Charlie, held his chin high and inspected the Jullian easel with Charlie's painting.

His shiny belt buckle was the first thing I noticed, followed by his black slacks, shined shoes, and a crisp white long-sleeved button up shirt, open at the collar. The way he held his head up, back arched and belly forward reminded me of a bullfighter. I remember thinking how incongruous his clothing was with his vehicle. The jeep had holes in the fenders and door bottoms where the metal had rusted through. And there was the rifle, an old lever-action Winchester, that he held in one hand by his side.

He swung the rifle around toward us. *"¡Es usted!"* he began in Spanish, frowned, and switched into English. "Señor MacRae, what you *do* here?"

Charlie smiled, "Good morning, Ramón, I'm painting a picture. This is my nephew, CJ . . . um, MacRae."

I nodded, and he gave me a cursory glance without offering to shake hands. I stood by my easel, slowly rising onto the balls of my feet, then settling again, remembering what Rosita had said about the man beating his wife. My legs felt like they might cramp at any moment. The rifle muzzle twitched, pointing first at Charlie, then at me, then off somewhere into the distance, like it had a mind of its own.

Ramón had obviously come prepared to run us off. With an angry expression, he stepped back from Charlie's easel, while I entertained a fantasy about smacking him like a horsefly.

"What this?" He asked, clearly uncertain about what he saw on the canvas.

"It's a study of the yucca plant," Charlie explained, "the sunlight on one side against the shadows behind and below."

The bullfighter stood tall in his straw cowboy hat, the Winchester bobbing in his hand. "I manage the *rancho*. You come on private property, *señores*. Now is the time you leave."

Charlie swept his arm around, standing his ground. "I didn't know this was Silva land. There's no sign and no fence. I thought it was public property."

"All Silva land." Ramón waved the Winchester in a broad arc in front of us, indicating that the property extended everywhere. "A fence on the other sides. No need here."

Charlie changed the subject. "I haven't seen Don Sergio in some time. How is he?"

"Fine," the man said, eyes sliding into that lying spot, high and off to his left. "Don Sergio is fine!"

"Maybe he took a trip in an airplane," Charlie prodded. "I understand one landed at the Silva airstrip last week and took off again the same day. A Cessna."

"Don Sergio is not your business." The man curled his lip and pointed down at the ground. "You don't stay here."

"Okay, we'll leave, but I want to finish my painting first. It'll only take two hours, maybe three."

Ramón's expression darkened, but he seemed to be considering the request while he strutted in a circle, examining us. Eventually, he threw his shoulders back and gave the order. "Two hours." He held up two fingers and stuck out his chin. The rifle swung around to point at our feet. "Stay here. No trespass!"

"Thank you, señor.' Charlie gave an abbreviated bow. "We won't be a bother."

The bullfighter glanced into the chasm in front of us and pointed with his chin. "*Mira*, the arroyo. Careful you not fall in. Is much danger!" he warned. "*¡Peligroso!*" With an evil grin he turned away, climbed into the jeep and roared off, as though he had someplace to go.

It took a while for my pulse to settle. Charlie took the opportunity to re-kindle his pipe, and we went back to work. He told me to squint at the subject so the relative values would be easier to identify. I tried it, and found the sky was brighter than the land. The stone buildings were darker than either, with bright spots where the sun hit, and the trees by the house and skirting the hill were darkest of all. In a few minutes, we saw the jeep come to a stop across the arroyo beside the main house.

"There's something amiss down there," Charlie said. "That's for sure."

I looked up from my landscape. "Maybe it's Sergio that's amiss. He's gotta be the one who crashed the plane."

"Ramón sure is touchy about him," Charlie said. "Did you see him get all puffed up when I mentioned Sergio?"

"He blew up like a balloon. I thought he was going to pop."

"He's a terrible liar."

"I wanted to kick his ass clear into that canyon down there."

The artist's eyebrows lifted a hair. "Well . . . there *was* the gun."

"There was that," I allowed, picturing the wavering rifle and suppressing a giggle. "Maybe we should say the Lord's Prayer, ask forgiveness for tresspassing."

"You can say it for both of us," Charlie said. "But his attitude made me want to keep on trespassing."

"Amen to that," I concluded.

He turned to look at my easel. "How's the painting going?"

We were standing about twenty feet from my painting. "It doesn't look like anything from here," I declared.

"You want to have a compelling design when viewed from this distance," he said. "Something to grab your attention. Sometimes, when we observe one area too closely, we tend to lose sight of its relative value compared to the whole picture."

"So how do you fix it?"

"Brighten the light areas and darken the darks."

For a little while, I focused on resuscitating my painting and forgot all about Ramón. A sublime sense of amazement enveloped me, as though I'd been absolved of sin and finally reached the promised land. But the feeling didn't last long, and my impatience returned.

Later, as we sat in the front seat of the Woodie with a bag of tamales and a thermos, I asked if we were staying all day.

"I thought we'd do another painting after lunch."

"What about Ramón?"

"We might linger here a bit longer and let our friend worry about us," he said, "Let the pressure build. Maybe he *will* pop."

But the joke was no longer funny. We finished eating and returned to our easels. I let my eye rove across the rugged terrain, using my newly acquired technique of squinting, so the shadows became unified and the landscape was transformed into a blur of lights and darks. That's when I saw the flash. When I opened my eyes wide, the spot sharpened like a shard of broken glass among the shadows on a low hill, maybe a mile away. Then the spark faded to a twinkle. I thought most likely it was a random piece of metal catching the light, but I was hoping for a signal from Blaine.

"Charlie!" I yelled, "Something's blinking out there across the pasture. We need to move in closer."

I pointed out the spot and Charlie started unpacking his tripod. "The camera will put us up close. Very close." He took his time fiddling with the antique 4x5. It reminded me of cameras I'd seen in episodes of *Gunsmoke* or *Maverick* on television. I half expected to see him pull a black cover over his head and activate an explosive flash.

After focusing the instrument, he said, "Take a look, CJ."

Through the eyepiece I saw a rusty metal roof, a square-shaped white spot among the trees, beside what looked like a stone wall. In my bones, I felt Blaine's nearness, and had to restrain myself from running down there to see if he was in that building.

We watched for another thirty minutes but saw no more flashes.

"Why don't you pack it up while I take another shot," Charlie said, adjusting the camera.

Finally! I thought. Needing no encouragement, I packed the Woodie with our stuff, and before long, we were driving down the highway, looking for another access to the ranch. I had a good sense of where the reflection had come from and pointed out the old gap gate hidden in the sticker bushes beside the road.

"That'll have to do," he said, and continued driving. "Looks like we can walk in from there."

"Aren't we going in?"

"Let's get the photos developed first and see what we're dealing with. Then we'll come back better prepared."

I stewed over the delay all the way back to town, desperate to do something, hating the voice of reason. Charlie parked on a narrow backstreet and disappeared into a hole-in-the-wall camera shop. I waited in the wagon and tried to make my eyes zoom in on objects down the street like a two-hundred-millimeter lens does. The process calmed me down.

As we drove to the house, I considered whether artistic principles could be applied to solve the problems of life. I would never have seen that flash if I hadn't been squinting into the shadow at the time. Seeing had always been spontaneous for me, like breathing, but I'd always let it do its thing and used my ability without conscious interference. To think sight could be controlled to produce specific results was a new concept—and a powerful one. Maybe I was destined to become an observer of life. Not some kind of action hero, but simply a witness.

———

CHAPTER 32
CJ

Rather than produce images that
confirm our preconceptions, the artist
may choose to shift our point of view
and lure us into unanticipated growth.

After we dropped off the film with shots of the Silva barn, I took refuge in the studio with a cat and a cup of coffee, revisiting Charlie's artwork and feeling grateful for the nourishment. One painting of Rosita with a shovel in the garden gave me goosebumps, and like a dust mote, I hovered among the beams of light and lingered to absorb the almost painful beauty of it.

Following the sparrow up and out through a crack, I
fly free of the dungeon and look down on a tin roof, a
mountain. In the distance is a city of tile roofs and
gilded spires—San Miguel de Allende.

"Supper, CJ," Charlie hollered as the studio door scraped open. Calico leapt off my chest, but not before sinking a claw in it, and I found myself alone on the cold stone floor, looking up at the ceiling.

I have a memory of myself as a toddler, maybe three years old. My mother used to take me into our backyard when she hung out clothes. I would sit beside the clothesline post and fly, going straight up maybe twenty feet to hover and look down at our yard, our fence, the house and the neighborhood. Then I would float back to the ground by the post.

What had just happened felt like that.

In the kitchen, five black and white photos were spread on the table for all to see. Noe and Uncle Nel pored over them while Rosita distributed coffee. One photo showed the barn, blending into its surroundings, with the dark metal roof nestled into a dense stand of ancient live oaks. Tree branches hugged the earth, obliterating the building except for a short section of pale stone wall. Another showed the back panel of a white jeep, barely visible through the trees, confirming that our friend Ramón had been there.

Rosita brought a supper of tortillas and beans to the table, and while we scarfed it down, Charlie took the lead making a plan. "Sita, could you drop us off at the Silva's gate?"

"Why don't we ask Noe to drive?" she suggested. "I'd like to go with you."

Noe nodded and mimed turning a steering wheel back and forth. He was way ahead of us. Charlie hesitated a second, then grinned through his mustache, "Okay, Noe drives. Let's finish up here and get our equipment together."

I found out that by 'equipment,' Charlie meant a .45 automatic for himself, a shotgun for Uncle Nel, a flashlight, a come-along, and a length of stout sisal rope. I would carry the come-along and Rosita would handle the flashlight. Charlie would take the rope.

They didn't provide me with a gun. I guess they figured I was an unknown factor in the rescue business, and they were right. Still, I was uncomfortable without a weapon, so I went to the garden shed and found an axe. Nice and sharp—just right for a boy scout like me.

I hurried to the house, snagged my serape and found everyone waiting outside by the wagon. Noe drove, Rosita took the shotgun seat, and I sat in back between the two old men. Our equipment was stashed in the cargo space behind us. We expected only three people to be at the Silva place. Juana, who was on our side, or at least neutral, the old lady, who was infirm and confined to the indoors, and Ramón. Unless Ricardo or the missing Federale showed up, Ramón would be our only opponent. He did have the Winchester, but according to Rosita, he usually stayed indoors at that hour with Juana. We could only hope. And Blaine would be alone in his cell at the barn—if he was there at all.

With the sun down, the altiplano cools off quickly, and I was glad I'd remembered my serape. A lonely cloud-draped full moon watched us pile out of the Woodie to inspect the barbwire gap. Noe had instructions to circle around in one hour, then after that, every fifteen minutes. I straddled the top wire and stepped over, holding the top two wires for the others to crawl through. Cattle had eaten the pasture down, and except for the occasional cow-pie, walking was easy as we followed the sandy ruts of the little-used road.

Surrounded by the spicy aroma of arid brush-land, we plodded on, exposed by intermittent moonlight, when suddenly the road erupted in front of us with the sound of hooves and bawling cattle. We'd surprised a small herd sleeping in the middle of the road. Surprised us a little bit, too. The cows loped off a ways, then slowed to a walk before returning to their customary route, and we followed them.

At first, I didn't notice the building, obscured as it was by drooping oaks, but then a wide-open doorway appeared and we shooed the cattle through the stone structure and out the other side. Charlie disappeared and the rest of us stopped in the middle of the barn surrounded by the sweet smell of molasses and the taint of something else. No light penetrated there, so Rosita switched on her flashlight for a second, revealing a hayrack that ran the length of the building on one side. On the other side was a stone wall with two doors, one with a hasp and lock. Uncle Nel stood with his back to the locked door and motioned Rosita and me against the wall. The light went out.

"Blaine!" he called, in a loud whisper. We heard a shuffling noise, then, "Mmmmh," the voice coming from the other side of the door.

I jumped, surprised at hearing him so close, knowing he was there, gratified that his anguish—and mine—would soon be over.

"Hang on, Blaine," I whispered. "We'll get you out." *Why are we whispering?* I wondered.

"How the hell are we going to get this door open?" Uncle Nel queried the darkness.

Charlie's voice echoed, "That's what I'd like to know. I could shoot the lock, but it would raise the whole neighborhood."

"I have the axe." I said, feeling the ancient hasp and wishing for a crowbar. "It'll make some noise, though."

"Okay," he said. "Just do it quickly."

"Rosita."

"Yes CJ."

"Would you shine the light on the door, please?"

The hasp was attached with heavy bolts. The hinges were broad iron straps mounted on the face of the door, strong enough, but they were attached with old nails. It looked like they could be pried loose.

"Shit!" someone said. Rosita had turned the flashlight toward the floor, illuminating the piles of manure we'd all stepped in. "Shit," everyone said, almost in unison, and the reek of fresh cow patties enveloped us.

"Mmmmph!" The voice erupted again from the other side of the door.

I slid the axe blade behind the end of the hinge and twisted.

Squeak.

More twists—more squeaks.

I had gained a quarter inch of slack as the nails began to loosen, but I was impatient with the gentle approach. "I'm going to whack it," I said, visualizing the place to strike in the darkness.

I focused on the gap where the hinge met the door, braced my leg against the stone wall, then swung hard, heard a 'clank!' and the axe stuck in solid wood. I freed it and after two more swings, the nails gave up, and the door loosened.

The bottom hinge was more trouble, and I nearly sliced my ankle when the axe bounced off the hinge. For a moment, I considered the axe's potential, pictured blood flowing, then erased the image. With a final blow the door fell, and I jumped aside as a body tumbled out. The man scrambled away on hands and knees, but Rosita kept him illuminated with the flashlight.

"That's not Blaine," I said, unable to believe my eyes.

Charlie grabbed the man's ankles. Rosita trained the light. Uncle Nel leveled the shotgun and yelled, "Hold it, or I'll shoot."

The man stopped struggling and sank to the ground.

Charlie hollered, "Ramón!" He cut the gag off our captive's face while Rosita removed the lashings that cut into his wrists. My heart rate spiked. The shotgun didn't waver as Uncle Nelson asked the question that was in all our minds.

"Where's Blaine?"

"Gone," Ramón said. "*El Norteamericano* attacks me."

"It's no wonder he did." Charlie poked him in the chest with his automatic. "You're lucky to be alive, mister. How long have you been here in this room?"

"I here long time."

But it couldn't have been more than a few hours. I was surprised at how small and thin Ramón seemed, sitting in the dirt, compared to his inflated presence earlier that day. I had the urge to give him a good stomping, but he seemed pretty beat up already.

"Who took the airplane, Ramón?" Charlie asked.

"*Los Federales* come with the machine guns."

Then the questions came, one after another.

"Where were you when the plane landed?"

"With the cattle, señor."

"And you work for who?"

"Don Sergio."

"Where is he?"

Ramón shrank even more, writhing, reptilian, and shrugged his shoulders.

"Is Sergio working with the Federales?" Charlie asked, keeping the pressure on.

He shook his head, "No."

"Did you talk to him after the airplane landed?"

"*Sí*, we talk."

"When?"

"Same day."

"What did he say?"

Ramón blew out a breath and leaned to one side. "Say, wait for he comes back. Keep *don* Ricardo *y el norteamericano* here."

"He left you alone to guard Blaine and Ricardo?"

"*Sí.*"

"Then he left on the airplane and never came back?" Charlie let up, looking away. Rosita's flashlight was getting dim and my concentration lagged.

"No, *señor*," Ramón said, dejected. "He don't come back."

"Who went with Sergio in the airplane?" Charlie persisted.

Ramón hesitated before finally muttering, "El . . . el Federale."

"They went to buy guns, didn't they?"

Ramón ignored the question.

"Where's Víctor?" I butted in. "This is his sister's ranch."

"Víctor don't come here."

The flashlight batteries were almost gone. Using the rope we'd brought, I bound Ramón's hands and feet together behind him, maybe tighter than before, considering I still wanted to beat the crap of him. A search of the room we'd broken into yielded nothing but some eating utensils, a near-empty bucket of water and a stinking makeshift latrine. Also, in the last dim glow from the bulb, we read a message on the wall. "BG," followed by a dash, then "OK."

"It's a message from Blaine." I traced the letters scratched thinly on stone before the light went out.

In the doorway of the barn, Uncle Nel hovered over the cringing figure of our captive. "Blaine must have been stuck in here since the hijacking." He said. "Assuming he escaped today, that's almost a week."

Charlie turned away. "We'd better go."

We left Ramón tied up. Rosita gave the man a cup of water, and I resisted the urge to kick him—but just barely.

"Ramón, you're a shitty excuse for a human being," Charlie declared, expressing my sentiments precisely.

———————

On the way back to town, there was time enough for me to reflect on how close the axe had come to taking off part of my foot, and to think how close I'd come to kicking a man when he was down. How much potential harm there was in that axe—and in me.

We dropped Noe and my uncle at the hotel, and I drove to the garage. As the three of us walked around the block to the house, a solitary dog barked. None of us noticed the person huddled in the shadows until Charlie almost stepped on her.

"What the . . . ?"

Rosita knelt in front of the cowering woman and pulled aside the scarf that covered her head and most of her face.

"Juana?"

The women spoke quietly for a bit before Rosita helped her up and led her inside. Juana was hunched over as though bracing herself against some strong wind. They disappeared into the bathroom and eventually the torrent of Spanish words slowed to a trickle and they joined us in the living room. Charlie poured everyone a shot of Kahlua while Rosita explained, "When Ramón didn't come home tonight, Juana became frantic. She came here because she didn't know anywhere else to go."

Charlie nodded. "And you told her we found Ramón."

"I told her he is tied up at the barn. She's okay with that for the time being."

"I'll bet she is. What did you find out?"

"A man came yesterday to tell *señora* Silva that Sergio was killed in an airplane accident. When the man left, Ramón began drinking and last night he beat Juana up. She's been waiting at the gate for a couple of hours. She's afraid he will beat her up again."

I studied the unfortunate woman, her black eye and the bandage high up on her cheek. One whole side of her face was puffed up. Never having seen a woman damaged like that, I looked away. Acid rose up in my throat, and I bolted for the kitchen and a glass of water. I almost jerked the back door off its hinges going for fresh air. *How could someone do that to a woman?*

Alone in the garden, running through my short list of profanity, I fantasized about things I'd like to do to Ramón and walked off my rage until a dog barked nearby and broke the spell. When I came back in the kitchen, Rosita was translating Juana's account of the day the plane landed.

"She heard the airplane, then gunfire. Ricardo and Sergio came in the house and went to the cellar. Later a *Federale* brought a *norteamericano.* The plane took off an hour later and Ramón drove Blaine and Ricardo to the barn."

The women conversed in rapid Spanish for a minute. "There was a mess in the cellar," Rosita said. "Someone had been sick. After the men left, she cleaned it up."

Ricardo, I thought, remembering my vision of Ricardo, sick with Blaine taking care of him.

"Would you ask if Sergio spoke to her before he left?' Charlie asked. "If she knew when he planned to come home?"

After another conversation with Juana, Rosita said, "He told Ramón he would return the following day." That squared with what Ramón had told us. Sergio must have planned to mop up the loose ends at the hacienda when he came back, including Blaine and Ricardo.

"How about the Federales?" Charlie pressed on. "Can she describe them?"

The woman responded, but I wasn't paying full attention when Rosita translated. "Juana said one man stooped and walked with a limp . . . Charlie, she's afraid of her husband."

"She needs to stay with us tonight, don't you think?"

"Yes, definitely." she said, "I'll make up the other guest room for her."

When she took Juana upstairs to bed, Charlie stood and stretched his back. "It's been a long day, CJ. It won't hurt Ramón to sleep alone in the barn tonight. He won't go far. Not the way you tied him up."

I couldn't have agreed more about Ramón. My mind was still on his wife's face, and her life—how shitty it must be. That's when I made the connection. She had to be the girl Víctor had said wrote letters for his sister. I'd been thinking 'girl' meant someone young, and Juana had to be over thirty.

———

Early the next morning, I drove back to the Silva place in silence, wondering if Juana could be trusted. I knew Ramón hadn't come clean. He'd blamed the hijacking on the Federales, but it didn't add up. If they'd been working with Sergio, then where were they now?

Rosita got out at the house, and I scared up a pair of jackrabbits on the way to the barn. Charlie and I found Ramón about a hundred feet away from the building, beside the dirt track, where he'd rolled himself into a ditch. Still tied up and stinking of animal waste, he wouldn't stop whining about *el nortemericano* stealing his jeep and his rifle. We threw him in the wagon, and took him to the house.

It was a nice place—traditional, finished in dark wood and plaster, illuminated by a twinkling wrought-iron chandelier. A crucifix hung on the wall. No sign of the old woman. A scent of lemon polish came off the heavy dining table where I took a seat, and Rosita produced glasses of water with lime. She even found some cold beans and tortillas for Ramón. I wouldn't have bothered. Being in the same room with him kept my adrenaline up and my right leg bouncing.

Charlie had lingered on the porch to have a smoke, and when he came in, his voice rang against the plaster walls, causing me to jump. "What happened to the American, Ramón?"

Ramón fixed his eyes on his hands and huddled low in his chair. "I know nothing, señor."

"You held him prisoner here for most of a week. You have to know *something*." Charlie said. "Where did Sergio go?"

I figured it was a trick question. Ramóns gaze drifted toward a spot on the ceiling that he found particularly interesting. "I don't know."

Maybe that was true, but he knew Sergio was dead. He must have known Sergio stole the plane, who was with him, and what was in it, too. I wondered who Ramón was covering for, and whether he was working with the Federales.

Charlie changed tack. "You kept Ricardo prisoner here, together with Blaine?"

"Sí, señor! Don Sergio gives orders. Don Ricardo *está* enfermo. Bad. I bring el dóctor." Ramón mimed giving himself an injection in the hip. I didn't trust the man for the most part, but if this part of his story was true—if Ricardo had been a prisoner and sick enough to need a doctor, then he couldn't have helped hijack the plane. Lots of *ifs*.

Rosita entered the room and reported, "I looked in on the *señora* Silva and told her Juana would be back tomorrow."

"What you do with *mi esposa?*" Ramón asked.

"Your wife is safe, Ramón," Rosita scowled. "No thanks to you. Your wife will stay at our house tonight. We have photographs of her showing the damage you did. If it ever happens again, *señor* MacRae and I will bring the police and testify in court. You will not harm Juana ever again, you understand?"

He nodded.

"Furthermore, we have evidence that you kidnapped two men and held them prisoner for five days. Do you understand that?"

Ramón sulked like a little boy being scolded by his mother. He was obviously worthless as a source of information. *And even less value as a man*, I thought.

"*Sí señora,*" He straightened and tried to puff himself up. "My jeep and my rifle—*el nortemericano* steals them."

Without a trace of her usual smile, Rosita said, "We can give no assurance that you will ever see them again, Ramón."

Charlie broke in and added a long warning in Spanish with an ominous tone. I couldn't translate, but it sounded like, "If you ever do anything to harm your wife again, I will scramble your miserable testicles with eggs and feed them to the hogs."

———

CHAPTER 33
MARIAH

*A good design will have the ability first
to attract, then hold a viewer's
attention. The artist uses a medley of
artistic elements to achieve this
result—value, color, texture, edge,
balance, rhythm and thrust, not to
mention content, emotion and intention.*

Traffic noise and slamming doors wake me up at Motel 6 in San
Antonio. The pancake house next door indulges us with all the butter
and syrup we can slather on our pecan waffles and I have to resist
licking my plate. Cindy wants to see a historic mission before we
head for Hebbronville, so after visiting the clinic for shots, the
consulate for visas, and the car agency for insurance, we take the
afternoon to explore the city's relics.

The time-worn, walled-in quadrangle at San Jose Mission inspires me. "Cindy, just imagine a huge garden filling all this space with corn and beans and squash. The deer would need ladders to get inside."

"And the human bandits too."

Around the perimeter are monks' cells, with some of the original hand-made wooden doors almost intact. The walls seem ancient, but the place was built just over two hundred years ago. Not ancient, exactly, in terms of human civilization. We go inside one of the dark little rooms and look back out at the rectangle of light. Cindy is freaked out by the cramped space. "Imagine their sexual frustration, Mariah. I wonder how they handled it."

"I suspect, being alone in the little room, they did themselves."

"It's not supposed to be allowed," Cindy says. "Vows of celibacy, you know."

"That doesn't count, doing yourself." *I'm relatively certain, anyway.*

"The hell it doesn't!"

Cindy's the expert on religious things not strictly Methodist, so I let the comment go unchallenged and look out the open doorway. Across the field, a small hawk throws down on a careless rodent, then flails the air, flapping skyward. Nearby, another small creature rattles out a mechanical noise—a locust, maybe. I imagine two hundred years of prayer, and power floods my belly, like a transfusion, filling me to the base of my spine. I soak it up until I'm brimming with energy. I could do *reiki* here for hours, non-stop.

"It seems lonely inside these walls," Cindy laments, running her hand along the age-polished stone. "Well-kept but sterile, somehow."

"They didn't have politics and daily news to interfere with natural rhythms. There must have been a great feeling of camaraderie, living self-sufficiently in a cooperative spiritual community, isolated in their own little world."

"Hell, Mariah, they were all Indian slaves, a conquered people, for Christ sakes, except for a few priests. Who do you think built all this?"

I refuse to be disillusioned about the place, no matter what she says. Whoever the inhabitants were, I'm a little jealous of them, living surrounded by vaulted ceilings and high arches, cool in the blistering summers, soaking up solar heat in winter. The time-blackened stone must have glowed when it was all new and white, like a fresh love.

———————

After changing clothes at the motel, we're off to the famous San Antonio River walk. At one end is the Tower of the Americas—a great phallic shape with a spaceship on top—left over from last year's Hemisfair.

Cindy stops to look at the skinny monster. "Texas sure is proud of itself."

"Sure is."

"I like the old stuff better."

"I agree. That mission was a treat." I'm clinging to my utopian vision of life two hundred years ago, but Cindy has no idealistic bones in her body. "

"Yeah," she says, "It's amazing what you can do with slave labor."

"Those weren't slaves," I protest. "They were inspired by God. The workers volunteered."

"If you say so."

An assortment of bridges and boats entertains us while the sun goes hiding behind buildings and trees. The cooler air is a relief, drying our perspiration and stimulating our appetites. Cindy's yellow sun dress has put her right in the party spirit. I present a more sedate exterior in my denim skirt and button-up blouse. Inside, though, I'm buzzed, walking the sunken landscaped trail next to the river, complete with bridges and trees.

Friendly people spill out of cafes and linger in doorways, under stone arches. The Casa Rio restaurant serves tamales and *chile-con-queso*, a puffed tortilla, thin as paper and crunchy-gooey with cheese. Dessert is a sugary praline with a pecan half on top—pure alchemy.

Drinks are bought and consumed, dancing is done, and a good time is had, with no obligations. I'd hate to be caught down here after dark, though. As the shadows lengthen, I'm leery of slipping into an alien world, where priorities are different, laws are scarce and things might get out of control. Reminds me of New Orleans.

"I love the music," I comment, "except for the accordion." *Not my favorite instrument.*

Cindy agrees, "You can throw it under a bus for all I care."

"This taste of Tex-Mex is great, but I can't wait to see the real Mexico." I yawn, beginning to think about sleep.

The Mariah in me likes surprises. She enjoys confronting the unexpected, taking chances. The Mary Ellen part wants order within all the chaos. Beauty amid shabbiness. She wants control. I keep going back and forth between them, first trying to impose order on my life, then getting bored with it. I don't think there is a solution, but for the moment I feel like Mariah again.

———

Next morning finds us driving through the endless sticker-bushes of South Texas. Cindy seemed to enjoy the historical places we saw, despite her skeptical nature. She would have stayed to visit all five of the old missions in San Antonio, but I have a mission of my own down in Acapulco with the sisters, and it won't wait. Sheriff Sanchez greets us in Hebbronville and takes us into his tiny office under the jailhouse. He's a smiling Buddha-shaped man wearing a lived-in gray uniform and a sidearm, safely buttoned down. Sanchez stands beside his swiveling desk chair and waits to sit, while I take the only other chair, leaving Cindy to stand in the doorway. I feel instantly at home.

"How may I help you ladies?" He asks, making eye contact with me and holding it.

"I'm looking for a man whose airplane was stolen. It crashed up north of here, in Frio County. I read something in the news about a plane that tried to land here last week." I haven't blinked yet and Sanchez hasn't either. *It's a contest.* "I read that somebody shot at it," I add.

"Ah. The Cessna. Ah, yes." Sanchez, with hands behind his balding head, leans back in his swivel chair, turns toward the window and looks up in the sky.

I won the contest, so I get to blink.

"I shot the airplane myself." he says. "Border patrol sent a message, suspecting it may have been stolen, heading this way. It came here unauthorized across the border, so I waited, and when it touched down, emptied my weapon." Sanchez pats his holster. "Scared them off. I missed the pilot, though. Missed all the vital parts." He laughs. "They were trying to sell marijuana and send guns to Mexico, you see, and Mexico already has too many guns. They don't need no more down there. Later the Cessna crashed and burned." Sitting up straight and crossing himself, Sanchez adds, "Good riddance to the gun smugglers."

Smiling, he looks me in the eye. "And this friend of yours. He is also a gun smuggler?"

"I don't know." *What else can I say?* "He'd better not be. He's the father of my baby." I pat what's-her-name ever so gently and ham it up a little, reaching for sympathy. Feels ironic, though, trying out the role of motherhood in public while planning to end the pregnancy. "He doesn't know yet. He's a veteran." *Truth sometimes is the most effective persuader.*

Sanchez turns serious. "The day before the Cessna tried to land, I confiscated five crates of rifles, two Thompson machine guns, and two grenade launchers at our little airport here. Unfortunately, all the perpetrators have escaped."

"Sheriff," I ask, "Who were the guns for?"

He sucks air and takes his time letting it out. "We don't know the destination of the guns. Could be Central America. Could be Mexico. There is a civil war in Guerrero, but nobody speaks of it. Peasants wanting better prices for their crops. Better education. If the guns were meant for them, I would deliver them myself, personally. Their cause is righteous. The government in Mexico is not so good, ladies." Sanchez maintains his steady gaze.

"Is there anything you know about the pilot?" I ask.

"I found out this man, Mr. Grayson, filed a flight plan from Austin to Acapulco. The airplane landed in Acapulco. When it left Acapulco, a flight plan was filed for Guadalajara, round trip. It never landed there. The FBI took the case. Told me I was done with it. This is all I know." His hands go palms-up at his sides. "Now I can go back to writing speeding tickets, arresting minors in possession of alcohol and chasing hippies stealing peyote from the ranches around here.

Doing serious work." I believe Sanchez is being sarcastic, but he's hard to read. He stands, reverting to his amiable self, and holds out his hand. "The best of luck finding your friend."

He's dismissed us, so we take our leave. Outside, I turn to Cindy. "That was no help. I can't believe Blaine was involved in gun trafficking."

"He said the plane only touched down without stopping." Cindy takes the wheel of the Beetle. "Maybe Blaine never got this far."

"That's what Mr. Cole thought. Blaine was hijacked somewhere in Mexico. I'm sure of it . . . unless . . ." *He wouldn't have let someone else fly his plane, would he?*

"Mariah," she says. "This thing with the guns is a worry."

"I know. I guess I don't know him that well."

With the help of a thin doobie, I manage to put my cares aside for the rest of the drive and Laredo comes to meet us, it seems. We've been counseled not to eat raw vegetables on the other side of the border, so our last meal in the States is a large chef salad. After turns in the shower and at the mirror, getting all shaved, primped and plucked, we are ready for whatever happens. Cindy is unconscious in the blink of an eye, but I get hooked on the stupid late-night television, unable to sleep, anticipating tomorrow's adventure. *Must be the full moon.*

———

CHAPTER 34
CJ

*If you don't know how to proceed, turn
the canvas toward the wall and work
on something else for a while. Later
you can look with new eyes. Sometimes
you have to wait to find things out
instead of figuring them out—accept
the mystery and let solutions reveal
themselves.*

Two days after our long night at the hacienda, I ran up the hill and
back, racing daylight all the way to Rosita's garden, where the
salmon-pink light shifted to silver, my breathing slowed, and my
heart opened. Amid the hum and twitter of airborn creatures, I
focused on the spectacle around me, imagining how it might be
painted, how I would mix the colors, how they'd look on a canvas. I
could no more have summoned another link with my brother than I
could fly, but without warning, the connection came again.

A familiar jeep labored through the gears, cracking
and popping its way up a hill, the driver intent. . .
Blaine. . . Ahead, a curve in the road. The sign reads,
'Salvatierra.'
There's a mountain, with farmland all around. Wind in
my face. Vibration of the steering wheel. Thatched
roofs appear. Wattle-and-daub shacks . . . Dim figures
. . . A burro and cart, a boy driving . . .
The jeep sputters and dies, then it's quiet. Out of gas .
. . Top of the hill, shifting into neutral . . . A little push
. . . There it goes, bouncing once, twice, it disappears
deep in the valley. . . I hear a distant crash.

The sound of that crashing jeep stayed with me as I returned to the
awakening day. 'Salvatierra' felt like a command to get busy and
save the Earth. In the studio shed, I found Charlie's grinding stone
and sharpened the axe I'd abused at the Silva's barn. Sparks flew and
my feet pumped. At least the axe was saved, and to some extent I was
healed along with it. But I still couldn't settle, and the urge to keep
moving sent me off through the stone-paved back streets of San
Miguel. I avoided the military outpost, the police station and both art
schools, just to be safe and fly under the radar. At the Hotel La Rosa,
I found Uncle Nel packing to leave.

"I'm taking on a lot of grief by leaving you here, you know. Your
mother wants you home, period. Your dad's ready to wring your
neck, but to tell the truth, I think he just wants you to stay out of
trouble."

"I'm sure. That sounds like Dad." I said, wondering how long I'd
be able to outrun my fear of facing him. What I'd say when we met
again.

Uncle Nel threw some pesos on the bed and snapped his suitcase
shut. "I'll do my best to stall them. Probably best for you to become
invisible here. Stay in the studio with Charlie, out of the public eye.
Avoid gatherings. Fly under the radar, CJ. We don't know what kind
of hombres Blaine's involved with." He winked and picked up his
suitcase. "Best wait for Blaine to get in touch with you."

At the truck, he repeated the Mexican salutation he'd taught me,
loosely translated as "I wish you health, love and money, and the

time to enjoy them." I shook his four-fingered hand, and I watched him drive away, feeling lucky to have an uncle like that. And feeling hungry. The strange session with Blaine had left me drained and famished, so I grabbed a couple of *empanadas de queso* at the café by the clock tower. Then, keeping to the backstreets, I trudged up the hill to my room and took a nap that lasted the rest of the day and on through the night.

———

CHAPTER 35
CJ

*Look at the shadow and squint until the
shadow on the form merges with the
shadow cast by the form. Paint the form
shadow and the cast shadow as one
shape and one value. Then ease your
light into that shadow. It takes darkness
to make the light really shine.*

June

Noe had arranged to keep an eye on the Silva place by contracting with Juana to deliver groceries twice a week. Uncle Nel was keeping tabs on the grapevine in Texas, alert for news about Blaine. He'd promised to send Noe a telegram if he heard anything. Charlie and I stayed close to the studio and developed a daily routine of making art and trying to stay out of trouble.

After one especially delicious breakfast of huevos rancheros and sopapillas with cinnamon and honey, we set up easels in the garden by the studio and prepared to paint a landscape. First, I drew a thumbnail with the plastered studio and its wooden porch toward the top of a vertical rectangle. Then I traded sketchbook for easel and began mixing a color world of green and tan, added turpentine and splashed wet paint onto my panel. I watched the paint drip, liked what I saw, then grabbed the painting and held it face-up while the syrup set.

Charlie was analyzing the shadows around the studio. "Look at the parts," he said. "You have shadows on the objects themselves." He swiped a short vertical stroke with brownish paint on his panel. "Also, you have shadows that objects cast on the ground or other objects." He made a horizontal stroke with the same color.

"Now put the parts together. Let the shadow on the form merge with the shadow it casts. Squint your eyes until you can see the overall pattern of light and dark. This is the abstract design, the arabesque, or the gesture of the scene. It's a dance in two values."

"OK," I said. "I can see the light pattern."

"Now reverse your vision into the dark."

For a minute, I consciously focused on the negative space in the scene, connecting the dark shapes. "I think I've got it now," I said.

"Hold onto it, don't let go. Now, think about pattern of shadows as one unified thing—one homogenized piece of darkness—and paint the dark pattern. It takes patience. Later, you will look for light in the shadow, but first you have to create the shadow."

On the panel he joined the two strokes, and they became one shape.

"What color is it?" I asked.

"Excellent question." He looked up and smiled.

"Brown?" I answered.

"For our purpose, there's no such thing as brown," he explained. "It's either yellow, red or green. Ask yourself the question, 'What's the nearest color?'"

"I see bluish purple under the trees," I reported. "Under the porch of the studio, it looks redder."

"Then paint it that way," Charlie ordered. "Remember, the shadow has space in it. Make it transparent."

So I mixed Ultramarine and Alizarin Crimson with a little turpentine and lightly stroked some paint on the panel, surprised by how black the mixture looked.

"This looks too dark," I said, afraid of using too much pigment.

"It's funny," he chuckled, "You never find out what's far enough until you've gone too far. But that's how you learn, CJ. Be bold."

Charlie's platitudes sounded like they'd been stolen from a Country Western song, but I could relate. The advice had to do with more than just painting a picture. I'd been half-scared to make a move of any kind or in any direction since Blaine's misadventure, but I was itching to get on with it, to make some kind of progress. Any kind. *What the hell*, I thought. *What's the worst that could happen?*

From where I stood, the upstairs gallery cast shade on the whole side of the studio, including the dark wood of the door. When I squinted, the door disappeared into the darkness surrounding it, details vanished, and colors emerged. Still squinting, and looking closer, I spotted pinpoints of red and orange where the wood seemed to glow, like fire in the shadow. With that observation came a rush of pleasure, and for the first time, I believe I saw the landscape the way an artist does.

"I get it now, Charlie," I said, adding a dab of cadmium red to my dark mixture. "Darkness is a *thing*. I thought it was nothing, but it's kind of like evil being more than just the absence of good, darkness has its own substance."

"And same way evil often has an element of good in it, shadows have luminosity," Charlie said. "It's not surprising that it took you a while to get it, CJ. Everyone can see the trail of light, but you have to suffer the shadow in order to make the light shine. Eat your vegetables before you get dessert. Trust the process."

———

CHAPTER 36
MARIAH

*Up close, see the paint. From a
distance, see the picture. Impressionist
art usually resolves best from fifteen to
twenty feet away. At a closer distance
the painting becomes a surface,
featuring the textures and rhythms of
individual brushstrokes.*

June

Up before the sun, with coffees in hand, mine decaf with sugar
and real cream, we cross the border like it isn't there. *Sergeant
Pepper's Lonely Hearts Club Band* leads the way, and I get high with
a little help from my friend. The little car ticks along at fifty miles per
hour, but Cindy informs me it sounds faster if you say eighty
kilometers per hour. She's a math person. And a map person, thank
goodness. I'm a driving person—for now at least.

"How long do you think it will take to get to Acapulco?" I ask,
dreading the appointment with *las hermanas*, but anxious to get it
over with.

"It may take a year in this rattle-trap." Cindy finds it necessary to
disparage my car at least once a day.

"Hey, don't be putting down the *Beetle*." I've shortened *Betelgeuse*
to *Beetle*, except for formal occasions. I have a proprietary interest,
but I won't let Cindy's snide remarks distract me. "Really, how long,
Cindy?"

"Let's see." She checks the map. "Almost nine hundred miles. Looks like two days, Mariah. Maybe two and a half, with all the little towns and the crooked roads."

We're going through flat country now, with the vegetation you'd expect of an arid climate. Cacti appear by the roadside, and mountains make a dusty blue perimeter. "What a nice setting for a huge bowl of pollution," I observe.

"Monterrey is a smudge on the desert," Cindy declares with authority, "but a perfect place to top off the gas tank."

We were warned not to run out of gas in the middle of nowhere. After the pit stop—and I have to emphasize the 'pit' part—we take a good look at the map. There are two ways to go. South, just missing Mexico City, or the longer route west to Mazatlan and down the coast. We decide the more direct route will save time, and forty-five stinky minutes later we've passed through Monterrey into open country again. We pass our last joint back and forth as the *Beetle* enters a long stretch of arid country, a bug creeping across a barren slab. I'm amazed that so much of the earth can be covered with nothing but dirt.

Cindy has taken the wheel, giving me a chance to review Blaine's red journal. One of the April 1968 entries has me puzzled, so I read it out loud, "'LBJ says Echeverría is a heartless son of a bitch. Those poor bastards with the Party of the Poor in southern Mexico ran the Russians off. They're not communists, for God's sake. They're poor farmers who want a decent price for their crops and education for their kids.'" The journal is written in blue ink, but there's a note written in black, squeezed in under the LBJ quotation, like it had been added later. "Get this, Cindy, 'Natán Perez killed by *halcones* in 1967. Víctor's son. With help from the CIA. Resistance turns violent.'"

"Who's Víctor?" Cindy asks. "And what's *halcones*? Some kind of disease?"

"I don't know. Blaine was into smuggling weed. He never said anything to me about Mexican politics." *But what if these notes refer to the people in the film I watched with Sara? The round-backed creep and the skinny guy?* In the Spanish-English dictionary Cindy brought along, I look up *halcón*, falcon, and wonder what I'm getting myself into.

I like being useful, and helping people. That's why I studied physical therapy in the first place. But can Blaine *be* helped? He seems set on a path that can't be changed. *So, why can't I stop arguing with myself about him?*

I put down the journal, decide to enjoy the trip, and lose myself in the blue haze that recedes to the horizon. It's almost possible to imagine the Sierra Madre going all the way to the southern ocean—a skeleton beneath the sparsely vegetated land.

"Cindy, travelling brings a bigger perspective, don't you think? I'm starting to see the bones of things."

"What things?"

"Well, These mountains for instance. They look like the backbone of Mexico."

"Like we saw on the map?" Her brow wrinkles, and I'm afraid I'm not getting through.

"Like that, but in 3D," I say.

"O . . . kay . . ."

When we reach the outskirts of San Luis Potosi, enchiladas are calling, so we stop to eat. Then we find a decent hotel with a friendly and talkative clerk.

"*Señoritas,* you stay some time?"

"We're going further South," I tell him.

"Ah . . . to Mexico City!"

"No, to Zihuatenejo, actually." I make the correction, wondering why I bother.

A distressed look appears on his face. "But nothing is there. You go see Acapulco. Is very nice."

"Maybe for a day," Cindy joins in.

He is a nice man and we don't want to be rude, so it takes some time to free ourselves.

"Anything you need, *señoritas,* you come to me," he says with a big smile.

"Thank You." (in chorus)

Back in our upstairs room I'm stretched out on the bed. "That guy reminded me of a little boy. I think he just wanted some attention."

"Yeah, Mariah," Cindy smirks. "More like he wants a date. I thought you were noticing the bones of things. Didn't you see the bulge in his pants."

"Oh. You think?" *Am I being naïve again?*

"We're cute. We're American."

"I suppose the guy likes the road-weary windblown look."

"I think he likes young and alive." *She's cynical, but probably right.*

I'm looking out the window through the thin curtains at the neon Pepsi sign across the way. "Are you picking up on these pieces of corporate America everywhere?" I ask. "Look at the soft drink signs all over the place where capitalist greed has invaded Mexico."

"Like Coke bottles on the march?"

"Exactly," I say.

"Some kind of dark force?"

"That's what I'm saying." I like how Cindy matches me, thought for thought. "It's an insatiable beast that eats up the people's teeth."

"I believe they had sugar here before Pepsi Cola. And capitalism, too, for that matter. Everywhere you look people are in business, selling something."

She's so logical it's maddening, but I won't give up the argument. I'm on a roll, starting to work up a head of righteous steam, and enjoying it. "Look how the profiteers are taking advantage of these people, squeezing them for every last *centavo*. Think of the hovels they live in compared to the houses we've passed, with bars on the windows and glass embedded on top of the walls. The rich live in constant fear of someone taking their stuff."

"So that's why you paid to park in the hotel garage instead of on the street?"

"Yeah, well . . . Here in Mexico, I guess *we're* the rich people."

"Remember *Pogo*? the cartoon?"

"I have seen the enemy, and he is us?"

"Ironic, isn't it?" Cindy takes great pleasure in keeping me honest.

I pile the braid on top of my head and take a shower. Low pressure and hard water give me fits getting the soap rinsed off, but sleep comes easy. I forget about politics and dream of launching into the surf on a floating log . . . and meeting a mer-man in the water.

———

CHAPTER 37
CJ

At first, you'll strive to 'get it right'
each time you approach the easel and
the subject. After a while, though, you
need to 'let go' and just make a
painting.

Noe was out of pocket somewhere for a few days and I hadn't heard from Uncle Nel yet, so trusting Blaine to take care of himself, I concentrated on mastering Charlie's principles of painting. Early one morning, we drove down by the lake, where the prickly pear cactus grew into fifteen-foot trees. Right from the start, I struggled, with the water of the lake glaring silver in the background and posing the unanswerable question, *How do you paint a glare, anyway?*

Discouraged by the impasse, I took a walk toward the water and smoked part of a 'J' before returning to stare at my work, then at the master's. I watched him put the finishing touches on his painting—a nice close-up of the cactus, yellow flowers and all, with a bit of water behind—a visual poem.

"I like it," I said.

"Thanks, how is yours going?" he asked, while continuing to scan his work.

"Not so well. I'm afraid I'll going to screw it up."

He turned, holding a loaded brush in his hand. "You think getting high helps with that?"

I shrugged my shoulders. "It helps with my anxiety."

"What anxiety?"

His question sent me into questioning mode, and I went through the possibilities—fear of painting a horrible picture, fear of the tigers in my dreams, fear of the cops, fear of death. In the end, I faced my real fear. "I'm afraid I'll forget something really important, like I forgot to warn my brother about Ricardo."

"That's totally understandable," he said. "And significant."

"When I smoke, the fear goes away, and I feel free."

He took out his brier and lit up a plug of brandy-soaked shag, then gazed at the horizon and produced a series of smoke signals before going on.

"Freedom's a tricky thing. Lots of ways to lose it. You can even lose it without being aware it's lost." He cocked his head, reminding me of a puzzled collie or airdale. "Everyone has a load to bear, CJ, and we all look for relief. For me, painting eases the pain. When I pour all my faculties into it, the anxiety takes care of itself."

Surprised that Charlie, who was solid as a rock, had his own anxieties, I watched the smoke from his pipe drift away in the gentle breeze and said, "I know. Painting usually works for me too, except times like today when I get stuck."

"So, you *do* get high on painting?"

"Sometimes," I said. "I haven't really thought about it."

"Well, pick your poison. You may find it can be as habit-forming as pot is."

After lunch we parked by the railroad tracks and went hiking along the dirt embankment with our easels on our backs, following the rails, surrounded by the smell of creosote. The right-of-way cut through a low ridge at one point and the track lay between two twenty-foot high banks. It was a dreary stretch of land.

"There's something out here I want you to see." Charlie said, as we dodged ant hills and swatted gnats. "Last year, Sita and I went to a wedding and met Neal Cassady, the guy who drove the bus for Ken Kesey's Electric Kool Aid Acid Test. Also, the hero of Jack Kerouac's *On the Road*. It was early and Cassady was plastered. Later, they said he was on Seconal, I don't know."

Charlie peered at me. "CJ, I've never talked to anyone so quietly desperate . . . Cassady enunciated his words as though each one had special meaning . . . And there were spaces between them. I'll never forget what he said that night, 'I . . . live . . . for . . . all . . . of . . . us.' I suppose he was trying to explain why he needed to burn his candle at both ends. Cassady had a certain kind of poetic wisdom, but it didn't translate to a strong self-preservation instinct.

"It was a cold February night. After the party, he came down here by himself, passed out beside the tracks and never woke up. They found him the next morning."

We'd stopped beside a cross with plastic flowers hung on it. Someone had made a shrine, a *descanso*, like the memorials you see beside the road all over Mexico. Some of the flowers looked old, some new. At first, I thought, *how trite*. Charlie wiped the dust from one cluster of flowers as a mourning dove sounded off from a clump of mesquite trees down the way. I looked at the lonely stretch of track, then back at the sad little memorial, and my impression of it softened to *how appropriate.* I hadn't read Kerouak, and I didn't know anything about Ken Kesey, but I focused on one bright yellow silk lily in the *descanso*, and thought *That man should have stayed away from downers and stuck with LSD.*

Charlie wanted to do another painting, so I set up my easel on the bank above the tracks. Despite the tokes I'd taken on the joint, or maybe because of them, anxiety still lurked like a sneaky dog waiting to bite my ass. But the tightness binding my shoulders and neck began to dissipate as I squeezed out dollops of deep yellow, burnt sienna and ultramarine. The palette knife moved around of its own accord, picking up dabs of color and mixing fresh hues on the oval board. Another pile of paint. And another . . .

When the horn blew, I jumped, tripped over an easel leg and rolled halfway down the embankment. The palette took flight, doing a somersault, and I must have screamed. The diesel engine flew by in a blur of green and orange, and then behind it, two or three passenger coaches—stripes of black and brown. Somewhere I saw the letters. F *de* M. *Ferrocarril de Mexico*. When the last car passed, I took a few deep breaths to savor the quiet and for a minute, I went to that other place.

> On foot, following a mountain road in the cold light of
> dawn. White goats climbing a bluff across the valley.
> Pines and lush pasture below. Dew on the grass. A
> cornfield. . . Now thunder. Lightning. A barn where I
> find shelter.

I came back from my brother's life, took one look around, and cracked up. By some strange twist of fate, my palette had made a perfect dive and come to earth facing the sky. It had been too long since I'd really laughed, and I made the most of it.

Charlie hollered, asking if I was okay.

I answered while gazing down at the little shrine by the tracks, thinking how solid and predictable life seems sometimes, then how fragile and precarious it can be without a moment's notice. After a while I stood up, dusted myself off and picked up the lucky palette before climbing back to where my easel waited. Still grinning, I picked up a brush, my dignity regained, and cut loose on the eleven by fourteen-inch panel, making rhythmic strokes of paint until the palette was empty. On my panel was a dynamic abstraction of the scene. It felt so good, I flung my brush all the way to infinity.

We were walking slowly back to the Woodie along the right-of-way, easels and stools in hand when Charlie set his burdens down and turned to me. "You know, CJ, I've been thinking. We have the annual studio open house coming up. Would you like to be part of it? Show your paintings along with mine?"

"Of course! If there's room," I said, excited and skeptical at the same time. On some level I knew it was a diversionary tactic designed to distract me and give me a break. But it was a chance to prove myself. "Are you sure?"

"Wouldn't be asking otherwise." He pursed his lips, causing his salt and pepper mustache to wiggle around his nose. "It's a formal occasion. Rosita sent out invitations, and some people will be coming from out of country. We can get you some business cards and have you a tux made."

"Formality is not my strong suit," I said, realizing I'd made a bad pun. "I'm more of a jeans and t-shirt kind of guy."

"We dress up so the client will believe we're successful," he chuckled. "It's an illusion."

Hard to tell if he was serious about that or not, but I guessed the artist needed to be framed as well as the paintings. Spit-shined for public viewing.

"That must be expensive," I said.

"Not really, not here. Besides, I think you'll find it pays for itself."

That comment turned my head around. Instantly, I felt guilty for taking a free ride from my mother and from Charlie and Rosita. I knew he wasn't hinting at anything, but I decided right then and there to start paying my own way and stop living on handouts.

————

CHAPTER 38
MARIAH

*Sometimes you simply need to shut
down your own voice and listen for
guidance.*

What's-her-name is on my mind this morning. There's no place for judo in the motel room, so I stretch and then sit in meditation, contemplating my navel. My belly is a centimeter fatter, but I'm not really 'showing.' I do what Max taught me. I close my eyes and imagine myself encircled by white light. Then I up the amperage. Suddenly I'm aware of what's-her-name inhabiting my abdomen, sending a strong signal.

"Mom."

"Hello?" *Is that a voice?*

"That's too bright. It's supposed to be dark in here."

I tone down the white light.

"That's better. You don't have to call me what's-her-name, you know."

"What do I call you then?"

"Hannah. That's my name."

Oh shit. I wasn't prepared for her to have an identity. *Now what?*

I start chanting OM, Hannah joins in, and together we wake Cindy up.

"All right," Cindy protests. "Enough, already. I'm at your mercy. I'll confess, but no more chanting, please."

I stand in a flash. "Hannah and I are hungry, girl, let's get some breakfast." It just popped out, from I-don't-know-where.

She gives me a long look. "Okay, I'll be quick."

I put on the same clam-diggers and tennies, with a fresh scoop-necked blouse, this one raw silk in a deep gold earthy tone. Cindy's wearing jeans and t-shirt with an embroidered vest in purple and green. Together we look like Mardi Gras.

Next door, the restaurant serves huevos rancheros with fried potatoes and chorizo, serve-yourself salsa fresca, *frijoles* and fresh squeezed orange juice. Last week it was hard to face food in the morning, but this is a good day for me, so the aroma is appetizing and the taste, delicious. Cindy brought the map so we can peruse our route for the day. The plan was to continue south to Acapulco, where *las hermanas* are. That was the plan.

"Let's go through Toluca, instead," I say, "and turn west at Taxco. If we by-pass Acapulco, we'll get to Zihuatanejo quicker."

Cindy is the best friend I'll ever have. She accepts me at face value, and you can't beat that. She has grasped the significance of by-passing Acapulco with aplomb. *I love this woman.* As Max would say, "She's a peach with aplomb."

"Looks like it starts to get interesting from here to Zihua," she notes. "I'm not into the bright lights so much, anyway."

"Me neither. I just hope that road's paved."

CHAPTER 39
CJ

*To see as an artist, it may help to
dispense with willful pursuits and
submit to the influence of nature.*

After over a week of total abstinence, my head started to clear of
the cannabis residue. One day before dawn, I took a long walk down
to the lake, then sprinted for half a mile as the sun rose, scaring the
quail and cottontails, until blood pounded in my ears and all thoughts
were gone. When I showed up at the studio, ready to paint as usual,
Rosita was there, dressed in a long maroon terry cloth robe, talking
quietly with her husband. Assuming she would be our model for a
change, I expected alizarin crimson to play a big part in the
morning's painting. I stepped up to my easel, and the master
approached his, but I was totally unprepared for what happened next.

Rosita turned toward the east window that faces the garden, unfastened her robe, and let it drop to the ground. A shaft of sunlight bathed the front of her body and turned the surrounding motes of dust into an array of jewels. Starved for oxygen and flooded by a wave of emotion, my brain called for deeper breaths. From somewhere I heard a chorus of angels, singing hallelujahs. I picked up a big brush, dipped it in turpentine, crimson and sap green, and made a series of broad strokes, letting the paint drip in places. The aggressive odor of distilled pine sap charged the atmosphere, and a world of color appeared on my panel. The dripping stopped when I turned the panel horizontal and I set it on the floor to dry while our model rested.

I addressed my palette. Burnt sienna with a touch of ultramarine for shadowy places. Plenty of ochre and cadmium, both yellow and red, for mid-tones. More yellow and some white added to half of that mixture for the color of sun-bathed flesh. Thanks to the hundreds of tubes in Charlie's stock, I'd started to feel about paint the way pioneers in the old West must have felt about land—that there would always be plenty of it.

When Rosita stepped into her pose again, I drank in the sight, aroused and fully alert, Working from shadow into light, I applied paint to panel. The color was good, and the shapes, right, so I began to refine the details, taking three steps back to observe, then three forward to make a stroke, the dance all-consuming.

After a while, fear set in. I had dabbed on a lot of paint, leaving globs of paint that looked like chocolate chips with little peaks. The figure seemed hard and masculine. Teetering on the edge of despair and afraid to make another stroke, I confessed to Charlie, "I'm in trouble, here."

Once again he had a technical solution. "Let's consider your approach," he smiled. "It looks like you may have been attacking the canvas at a perpendicular angle, like a sword fighter. This is a friendly subject. Treat it gently. Align yourself with the picture plane and take a parallel approach. Try leading with your hand and letting the brush follow. You'll find the surface texture of your painting changes dramatically with the brush angle."

A lightbulb flashed in my head. Charlie meant for me to paint with a light touch. I could hold the brush with my fingertips the way Edna Faye had taught us to draw with a pencil.

"What should I do with this?" I asked, looking at the mess I'd created. "Wipe it all off?"

"Soften it, CJ, so the paint looks more like skin. You've seen me scrape the panel with a knife, then give it a pass with the soft blender, leaving a ghost of the image. You can rescue that discarded paint and reuse it," Charlie advised, indicating my palette. "Divide it into three piles. Add green to one, red to one and leave one alone. Then make lighter and darker versions of each pile. Work on the palette for a while until the colors come alive and you feel ready to paint again. Trust the process."

I followed Charlie's advice, scraped the panel down until a ghost of the figure remained—as though seen through a veil of gauze. I analyzed Rosita's skin tones and mixed three rows of paint, one greenish, one golden, and one reddish, each row with three distinct values from almost black to nearly white.

Rosita fell naturally into classic poses, invoking a timeless atmosphere of beauty and immediacy. Charlie arranged her with red or black fabrics and white pillows, under the north light of the big window. There were no props, just the naked lady, surrounded by color. She was very round in many respects. The dark hair that was usually piled on her head came down almost to her waist. Her skin glistened like a well-baked pastry, skin so smooth that in the light I could see a halo of fine hairs glowing on her cheek and chin, a little thicker on her upper lip.

I was taken with her body, her essence. Not the swell of breast or hips, the crease of backside or patch of pubic hair, but the complete sum of parts. I was aroused, and felt guilty about it. Nevertheless, I looked without restraint, as though I'd been thirsty for the sight of her my whole life. And I didn't rush, but observed slowly and carefully, receiving her gift reverently, internalizing the vision. While immersed in that process, I began to perceive Rosita's essence. The brush became an extension of my hand and I laid a secret *I love you* on the canvas with the paint.

I had no idea how to go about painting her, no real training, but the paintings happened anyway, and for a time my pulse beat in harmony with all creation, and I breathed the substance of beauty. Sometime during the session, we included a prop, a long-stemmed goblet, which added a narrative element to the lyrical nature of our compositions. There were tracks of dried tears on my face, and a taste of salt in my mouth when I came around hours later. I'd completed three small studies.

"Charlie," I said. "For a while there, I think my brush was singing."

"Oh, no wonder." He observed the dagger-like filbert I held. "You've been using the 'sing-ing' brush. Easy to confuse them and pick up the wrong one." Dead-pan, he took the brush and handed me another, a thin round one about three-quarters of an inch long. "You need the 'sign-ing' brush." His eyes twinkled. "Sign your paintings, CJ. We're finished for the day."

I signed my studies and thanked Rosita for modeling, already beginning to miss the spectacle of her flesh but feeling much, much better about myself.

When I thanked Rosita, she said, "It has been a pleasure, CJ." She turned her head slightly to the side, her dimples showing. "I felt beautiful today." As though she could read my thoughts, she added, "There will be other times, you know. Charlie has a commission to paint a series of nudes for a client in California, so we have more sessions planned. He thought you were ready for some passion in your painting and I agree. The creative power comes from Eros, you see. An artist loves the world—and the world will also love the artist."

She leaned her head closer. "But you know what Charlie always says, 'Don't forget to breathe.'" She grinned and punched my shoulder.

———

CHAPTER 40
CJ

*When painting a nude, give all the
parts equal attention. Faces, breasts,
legs and butts are all relatively easy to
paint, but hands, especially, take time
and attention, as do feet, elbows and
ears. Look at those details on a piece of
figurative art and you'll know what
you've got.*

A couple of days after the session with Rosita, Charlie and I were looking over the body of work that we'd selected for me to show. Leaned against the wall just inside the studio door were three of the watercolors I'd rescued from Víctor's house, together with my best oils—a combination of landscapes, still lifes and nudes. There would be room to hang twelve in all.

Charlie said, "These are lyrical pieces of art, CJ. Pure poetry." Then he indicated the last two studies I'd done of Rosita. "But in these, the goblet takes us into the realm of symbols, the idea that a woman has choices, accepts a particular role in life—sometimes for the better, sometimes for the worse. There's a hint of mystery in your latest paintings. There's a story there, maybe a rite of passage."

Charlie found his pipe, took a long draw, and exhaled a stream of blue smoke. With a wistful expression, he said, "When I was a teenager, my mother and I went to a museum in Kansas City where we saw a huge painting, entitled *Brutality*, by John Patrick. The scene was set against a Paris skyline. On the left side, a man restrained a rearing horse with a rope while hiding a big stick beside his leg. There was an ugly expression on his face. The horse was terrified. That painting won a prize in the Paris Salon back in the 1880's. Not long afterward, Paris passed its first animal cruelty laws protecting workhorses from abuse."

"It sounds powerful," I said, trying to imagine the scene and get my head around the idea of an artist being a hero.

"Patrick's work is an example of art where the social narrative made a difference in the world." He inspected a spent tobacco ember in his pipe. "I don't think my own art really makes a difference for anyone."

"It does for me," I said, with honest appreciation.

My mentor nodded, then caught my eye. "Thanks, CJ, that means a lot."

"You know, you should write a book." I said.

"No, *you're* the one who should write the book."

"But you have all the answers."

"And you have all the time. Besides, I don't have all the answers."

"At least you have all the questions," I allowed.

"That's the truth," he chuckled and cocked his head. "What are you going to call this book of yours?"

The notes I'd made in my sketchbook filled page after page, without even touching many of the principles Charlie had taught me. I realized the book was already underway. The first chapter would be about the importance of observation—of paying attention. I remembered my father always exhorting me with those same words, "Pay attention!" Then I considered how different Charlie was from Dad and said, "I think I'll call it A Coward's Guide to Oil Painting."

———

The girl who brought cheese samples was the daughter of a friend of Rosita's who lived out in the country. Patrice was French and pretty and seemed sort of quiet and shy on first impression. I'd seen her delivering butter and cheese around town with her mother. Charlie had gone on some errand in the Woodie and I'd been putting wires on the backs of my picture frames, getting them ready to hang. When I came into the kitchen, Rosita introduced us and I took a taste of cheese, appreciating the flavor and unique texture of the Muenster variety. It melted in my mouth and I moaned, getting a sideways glance from the cheese girl.

"It is very good," Rosita said, "but perhaps too soft for tacos. Do you have something that is easier to grate?"

"Yes, ma'am. We have another variety that's aged longer. It's drier, but I have none with me."

"We'll have someone call at the dairy for it, then. I hope you'll come to the open house, Patrice. CJ will be exhibiting his paintings alongside my husband's."

Rosita suggested I show Patrice the studio, so I took her through the garden, observing the French braid, the elegant neck, the bright blue blouse with buttons down the front. Short gray skirt, brown calves and ankles, feet with red painted toenails and sandals that matched the skirt. A beautiful girl, from head to toe.

The old studio door, stuck from humidity, shrieked when I jerked it open, and we stepped inside to find my nude paintings of Rosita lined up against the wall where I'd left them sitting in plain sight. Embarrassed, I tried to distract her by pointing out one of my best landscapes, framed and ready to hang, but while she marched around the studio inspecting everything, she kept looking back at the nudes.

Suddenly, she turned toward me and grabbed my arm, her eyes narrow. "You know a *cia* watches this house?" she hissed, the corners of her mouth turned down.

"No. What's a *cia*?"

She glanced around, as if someone might be listening and enunciated. "C . . . I . . . A. He's like this." She bent her head forward, hunching her shoulders while leaning to one side. "Like a bull, but broken," she added, then poked me in the arm and started to turn away.

"Wait, Patrice." I reached for her shoulder. "What do you know about this man?"

She put a hand on my chest, and her eyes widened. "He is here on the street when I come, parked in the same red car I see at that airport. He goes away fast when I see him."

"What airport? You mean the one at the Silva hacienda?" I asked.

"No, the airport in Acapulco. The car is there yesterday when we send my père to Paris."

I flashed back to that airport, to the man with the batons directing us to park the Cessna. To his posture and his limp. *Uh oh.* Patrice brushed her hip against me, and I stiffened. She pointed back at my paintings. "You sell your naked pictures?"

"Um, I hope so," I nodded, distracted, my mind on the CIA man, knowing that his showing up again was no coincidence.

She poked my chest. "You must do *me* next time, painter man."

I gulped, thinking about doing her, what she meant. We'd reached the modeling stand that Rosita used, with the pillows and blankets. She hopped up and sat down on a pillow, leaning back and posing in imitation of one of my paintings she'd seen.

I stared, trying to reconcile the residual image I had of Rosita with the presence of Patrice, lying there with an impudent look on her face. She fixed me with a steady gaze and began to unbutton her blouse. Slowly. One button at a time. Then she sat up and shrugged, allowing it to slide away. Underneath was a silky thing that floated upward with her fingertips, liberating her breasts.

Cool light from the high windows streamed down on her flesh, laying a film of blue on the creamy skin beside her near nipple. An ache of pure beauty jumped across the distance between us. The pulse in my neck raged. Elsewhere, too. When she stretched and arched her back, looking at me again, I must have unconsciously moved closer, flying under the radar.

She held up a hand, palm forward. "Stop!" so I stopped.

"No touching, not here." She smiled and poked my chest again. "I know a place."

Somehow, I found the voice to ask, "Where?"

"At *la grutta* . . . on Tuesday morning . . . nine o'clock." Her eyes opened wider and I nearly fell into them. Parted lips, the color of her toenails, revealed her teeth, small and sharp. I begged my eyes to stay on her face, but my vision took in the broader view.

I had barely croaked, "Nine o'clock," when a banging sounded outside the window and broke the spell. Someone was beating on something out there. Patrice became modest, and next thing I knew, she had the blouse on and was headed for the door. I followed.

Patrice jerked the door open, colliding with Rosita.

"Oh!" The two women exclaimed in unison.

Rosita recovered first. "Patrice, your ride is here."

"Oh, thank you, Mrs. MacRae. I better go." She trotted briskly away and disappeared around the side of the house.

"She is pretty, isn't she?" Rosita asked.

"Yes." I couldn't deny it.

After supper that night, I holed up in my room with a cat and a notebook and wrote down everything I could remember that Charlie had said about painting, adding several chapters to *A Coward's Guide*. Hours later, with my head swimming in the flood of painting lore, I drifted into Blaine's world again.

> One foot, then the other, hits the muddy ground. I hear
> sucking sounds. Following this fence around a
> cornfield. Row after row. Shoes heavy with mud.
> Head aches. Eyes hurt. There is pain in my belly.
> More plodding steps. Trembling from the cold, I look
> up at an angry sky, veer into the pine trees and
> collapse.

I'd knocked the notebook to the floor, startling myself into full consciousness. The pain, the cold, and the collapse had me worried that easy living and the effort of daily painting had distracted me from what was really important—my brother's plight. He needed help, and I needed to to find him—*mañana*, though. Suddenly famished, I raided the refrigerator for chicken enchiladas, ate them cold, then descended into a deep, dark void of sleep that lasted through another jaguar-infested night.

———

CHAPTER 41
MARIAH

*When you look at a subject in nature
that's earth colored and gray, after a
while the subtle colors begin to emerge.
Look for soft rose or violet hues in the
sand, a brighter yellow in the edge of
the cloud, a piece of purest blue high in
the sky.*

I've been in beautiful places, but the sheer scale of this place
bewilders me. Blue-green spits of land enclose Zihuatanejo Bay and
welcome us to a womb-like harbor that offers to protect us from the
ocean's extremes. The wooden boats drifting toward shore remind me
of a silent film I saw projected on a coffee-house wall in Austin. In
the film, a half-naked primitive woman languidly paddled a canoe
through a dense atmosphere, surrounded by ethereal light. The air is
clear, but somehow this place feels like that.

When I stop at the beach and turn the motor off, Cindy turns to
me. "If I'm not mistaken, Mariah, we've just discovered paradise."

It's true. The water has me under it's spell, and my eyes can barely take it all in. "If I ever have a house, I want to paint it this color blue."

"Look at those boats!" she exclaims, eyeing the primitive watercraft alongside the floating wooden pier. "We must have time-travelled."

"Wash your car, lady?" The boy is eight years old, maybe ten. I stare at him, uncomprehending. "Wash your car. One dime."

Bug carcasses decorate the front of the Beetle, grossing me out. A dime seems pretty cheap for a car wash, so I make the offer, "OK, a dime now and a dime when we get back."

"Your daddy didn't raise no dummy," Cindy quips.

I lock the car, feeling righteous about supporting an up-and-coming local entrepreneur. "I'm glad the car's getting washed. It hasn't had any attention since Texas."

"I think he meant *watch* the car. Like *guard* it, not wash it," Cindy explains.

"Oh . . . It *did* sound like too good a deal," I laugh. *I guess I still have a lot to learn.*

We select a highly recommended room on the edge of town. I pay for a week in advance and our smiling landlady shows us the well and the outhouse. No electricity. I'm unfazed since this is normal for me, after months on a bus, but not Cindy, so I have to show her the ropes. Well, there's only one rope—the one for the well bucket. After retrieving the car, we find a garage in town that agrees on a price to watch it *and* wash it. Our landlady serves supper of Spanish mackerel with shredded cabbage, tortillas, lime and hot sauce. Sleep is welcome.

Next morning, we get around late, but eventually don swimsuits, hats and cover-ups and walk down to the beach. The dugout canoes come and go, and the captains check us out. One of them is very helpful, offering to take us to *Playa de Las Gatas*. Amazing how the little outboard motor powers our floating log, like a tugboat pushing a barge on the Mississippi.

The man we find at *Las Gatas* beach is wiry, compact and blond, mid to late thirties. It's a wonder the sun here doesn't bleach everyone's hair to white. George's bizarre pale tresses have been left to their own inclinations, resulting in a lopsided afro. I'm finding it impossible to hold eye contact, since the hair bounces whenever he moves his head, even when he talks.

"Blaine Grayson sent me a message to come see you," I say, after introductions.

"Come in, come in. Welcome," he smiles and comments, "A friend in the hand is worth two in the bush." For that, he gets a sideways stare from both of us.

He's led us into his abode and school, such as it is, where scuba tanks and gear, snorkels, swim fins, life preservers, and all sorts of fishy things sprawl in ordered chaos. Signed photos commemorate the visits of famous and not-so-famous people. Flotsam and jetsam dangle from the walls, among lengths of rope and hanging nets, decorating the place like a disorderly seafood restaurant.

"Sorry about the mess, the maid's on vacation—an extended one," George laughs. "Get you something to drink?" A red metal ice chest keeps Fanta cool as well as Dos Equis. He offers one in each hand for our examination.

"No thanks, not right now," we say.

"I have fruit—papaya and mango."

"Mmm. Okay, maybe mango."

"Coming right up." He produces knife and fruit, then demonstrates how to fillet a mango. In less than a minute, we have a plate full of peeled slices and a wet towel to wipe our hands. The fruit is ambrosia.

"By the way, would you like to partake?" He's holding up a cannabis cigar.

I would, of course, like to partake, but the place is so magical, and I feel so good already. Besides, I have a mission to accomplish. I need to quiz him about Blaine. "Well, maybe just a hit or two."

Needless to say, one hit leads to another, and we all end up skinny-dipping together, playing with an old volleyball, acting out what Cindy calls George's predictable male fantasy.

"This is fun," he says, teeth glowing like opals in the afternoon light. "It's usually pretty quiet around here."

Although we left all our stuff back at Zihua proper, Cindy and I accept the invitation to stay the night. After dinner, we take a few more tokes on the potent Guerrero weed and with Dos Equis in hand, enjoy a Pacific sunset, knee-deep in the ocean. George explains about the little sharks called *las Gatas* that live in the bay. *I can't believe he's telling us now, after we've already been swimming in it.* Now I have the shudders.

"Don't worry, they're vegetarian," he says, "They can't eat homo sapiens." But the voice comes from a far-away place, like an echo, and I'm edging toward shore. I stop where the surf is safely ankle deep, but I can't keep my eyes off the surface of the water, scanning for little fins until darkness falls.

It's true, though, what people say about the phosphorescence in the ocean at night. It is sublime illumination. It is stardust. I have to keep reminding myself that I'm looking for Blaine. If not for him—and the sharks—it would be easy to just relax and let time go by.

CHAPTER 42
CJ

*A variety of forces will conspire to keep
you from making art. The person who
ultimately succeeds in becoming an
artist is the one who perseveres.*

That last telepathic session with Blaine worried me, so I told
Rosita about the strange visions.

Her eyes widened. "That's extraordinary," she said. "And what
did you learn?"

"Well, he pushed Ramón's jeep over a cliff and took off on foot . .
. And I think he's hurt or sick."

"So, lacking physical evidence of his whereabouts, your spirit
seeks out his spirit."

"I guess you could say that," I said, "Or else his seeks out mine."

But the spirit of Blaine was elusive, as spirits will be. It lurked in the shadows all that day and wouldn't talk, so the three of us tried to tease it out over dessert at Rosita's kitchen table, accompanied a shot of Kahlua. Calico found my lap and curled into it, while in flickering candlelight, we invoked the spirit. At first, we got no reply. Not a sound except the buzzing of insect wings and the occasional far-away trumpet of a mariachi.

My own spirits soared on those brassy notes, and my yearning to effect a contact with my brother intensified. With the warm kitchen wrapped around us like a cocoon, my thigh began twitching in pre-cramp mode. The energy of my jumpy leg may have amplified the cosmic vibrations in the room, but the table seemed to shake with a presence, and I half expected my brother to appear.

Instead, I went to him.

> My thighs cramp, something's splitting me in two.
> The long ears of a horse. No, a mule. I shift onto one
> butt-cheek, then the other, tryto evade the ridge of
> backbone between my legs. But it's no use. Nothing
> helps the incessant pain. A bottle appears in my hand,
> and I take a swig. It goes down smoothly and takes
> away the pain. A river winds ahead through a steep
> valley and I follow it toward its source as the sun sets.
> A sign reads *el Río del Oro*—the River of Gold.

"CJ? You OK?" Soft voice, feminine, friendly.

My focus returned gradually. Rosita was peering into my eyes, her hand on my arm. Disoriented, I blinked several times and lifted my head from the table.

"Where did you go?" she asked.

"I . . . umm . . . I had another communication with Blaine."

"Would you like to talk about it?"

I nodded. There was no doubt in my mind that I had inhabited Blaine. That I had travelled to where he was and felt what he felt. "It's like I was him . . . riding a mule with no saddle. . . it hurt . . . I drank something from a bottle . . . medicine."

Just then, a knock came from down the hallway, and while she went to answer the door, I readjusted to the 'real' world. Seconds later, Noe waltzed into the kitchen and handed me a telegram from Uncle Nel. I opened it and read aloud, "B called. Has hepatitis. Says don't worry. Dad getting call traced. News—bullet holes in B's plane—Rifles seized at airport. Call parents."

Unfortunately, there was no info about Blaine's whereabouts, and "don't worry" always meant "worry" in my experience, but the telegram confirmed what I'd just felt with him. He was in pain.

"What's hepatitis?" I asked.

Rosita said, "It is a serious illnes that affects the liver. He will have been very sick and weak, possibly for weeks."

"I can't relax with him stuck in limbo like this," I said, my voice unsteady. "I need to find him."

"I understand, CJ. How may we help?"

"I don't know. I've got Víctor pegged as the rat that packed the kilos, but he didn't steal the plane. He was with me when Blaine flew off. And Ricardo was locked up with Blaine. Now we know Sergio was the thief . . . but on TV, the outlaws always know about a shipment of gold before they hold up the stagecoach. I figure Sergio knew ahead of time that Blaine was landing at the hacienda." I paused as my thoughts caught up with my words.

Charlie leaned forward and gripped the table. "Who do you think tipped Sergio off?"

"Well," I said, "Víctor and Ricardo both knew the plan days before we loaded the plane. Either one could have told him, I guess. Although it just as well could have been Ramón or Juana. They might have overheard something and passed it on."

Charlie paced the floor, hands in his pockets. "CJ, gun-runners are not forgiving people. You don't suppose Sergio planned to rip off his contact in the States, do you?"

"I doubt it. Probably didn't know he was hauling Johnsongrass."

Suddenly Charlie stopped and turned. "In that case we have two rats here. One that switched the kilos and another that stole the plane."

Rosita had been puttering around in the kitchen, listening and not contributing. She came to the table with glasses of lemonade and asked a question I hadn't considered, "Would bullet holes make the airplane crash, or could someone have sabotaged it?"

I looked at Charlie.

He looked back. "Maybe there were three rats."

Rosita adjusted a hair pin and asked, "And which rat got paid for the marijuana?"

I pictured the day of the hijacking, the airplane landing, the cloud of dust and the bags of kilos. "Ricardo gave Víctor a briefcase full of money when we were loading the kilos," I said, and right away knew someone would have to pay Víctor a visit. If I couldn't find Blaine, maybe I could find the money. I'd try to catch Víctor alone at his house in Zihua if possible, but I'd need more than luck to survive the interview. I'd need Noe's help. I kept the half-baked plan to myself and thought, *no problema, find the River of Gold and save the Earth.*

———

CHAPTER 43
MARIAH

Keep focused on a positive outcome.
Let intention be your guide. Don't
waver. Sometimes that is all you need.

Cindy has caught George's eye, so while they cavort in the *cabaña*, I'm walking the beach, looking for shells, and keeping my own counsel. I could get used to living here, so clean and natural compared to the Galveston beach. Thankfully, people have not managed to dirty it yet. Maybe this *is* the perfect place.

"Yikes!"

The jellyfish I almost stepped on is beached and lifeless, but still capable of a nasty sting. I stare at the transparent body and will myself to focus on my surroundings as the gently surging tide lures me into the water. *Stench of dead fish, fading with distance. Gulls squawking up above, planning a sortie. Woman wearing a green headscarf, walking toward me.*

Hannah says, "Thanks, Mom," as I put space between us and the jellyfish. She craves the ocean, her element—wet and salty, with the constant pulse of waves beating a steady rhythm. *Perhaps we've come all the way to this southern coast to get what* she *needs*. I know this is what *I* need.

My number one jiu-jitsu move is a gentle sit-down throw. If someone attacks from the front, I grab one of their forearms with both hands, then sit in place and roll onto my back, throwing both legs up, presumably into the person's chest. With no sparring partner available, I practice my part on the beach, until it flows, and I can either right myself in one continuous motion or continue with a back flip. Hannah likes the movement, especially without the bumps and jolts.

When we've had enough, the ocean gives me a rinse, and I trudge through the soft sand to George's place, prepared to find out what he knows about Blaine. The sweet smell of burning weed reaches out and I hear giggles in the bedroom, so I knock and yell, "Hey, did you save any of that for me?"

I hear, "Just a minute, Mariah."

I realize too late that my question might be misinterpreted. Oops! I've sworn off orgies for the forseeable future. *Just one guy (the right one) will be sufficient, thank you very much.* Besides, I haven't been invited.

The door opens, and a half-smoked joint appears, attached to a hand. Taking the roach gingerly, I say, "Thanks," and hurry out to the patio where I take a seat beside the wooden cartons of empty long necks, under the coconut fronds, and inhale deeply.

Way down the beach a hovering flock of gulls dips and rises, mini points of light that appear and disappear. Beneath them, a dark speck inches along at the water's edge, eventually turning into a bicycle and rider, wobbling and making dubious progress. But what is the shiny thing in front?

Cindy and George emerge from their love nest wearing disgusting grins and skimpy swimsuits, their hair tousled and their faces glowing.

"Who's that?" I ask, pointing at the shrieking gulls and the stoic rider pedaling toward us. He's young, possibly twelve years old, almost as thin as the spokes on his bicycle. The mysterious shiny thing is an aluminum box attached in front of the handlebars.

"¡Señor Jorge! Tengo pescado fresco," the boy shouts, competing with the gulls for volume and closely matching them in pitch. I'm wishing I knew a little more Spanish.

"This is Juan Carlos, bearer of our dinner, I hope." George lifts the lid of the box and smiles. "Bringing his brother's catch to my door."

The smell of raw fish is soon replaced by the aroma of wood-fire and sizzling oil. The table is set, and dinner served—perfectly grilled mackerel with sliced onion on top, shrimp on a skewer, a covered plate full of tortillas, hot sauce, slices of lime and a shaker of salt. We're sitting at the table under straw-colored palm fronds, *al fresco*. A Beatles tape plays on the battery-powered stereo, dragging from time to time. It's my first real chance to ask George about Blaine.

"Do you have any idea where Blaine was going when he left here?" seems like a good starting place, but George just shakes his head, and I follow up with, "Do you know if's coming back?"

"Well, he might come back any time." George is not really paying attention. He's chewing . . . and smiling. Blaine's note in the cartridge box read, 'George will know,' but he doesn't seem to. *Maybe he doesn't know he knows?* Anyway, he rallies to say, "I remember Blaine's words exactly. 'George,' he said, 'I have a job to do. I may be gone for a while.'"

"And you haven't seen him since, what was it, March?"

George is shaking his head. "Well, just the once. I was in the village picking up mail, and I saw him with another man. A Mexican. They didn't see me though. They were in a hurry."

"Did the Mexican have any distinguishing features, like a limp?"

George discovers the prawn in his hand and takes a bite. "Not that I noticed."

"Was he fat or thin?"

"Slender, about like me. Oh, and he wore glasses."

Finally, I stop beating around the bush. "Blaine was collecting information about the CIA's activities in Mexico. I know he had meetings with LBJ about it, and I'm worried he's mixed up with gun runners."

George nods and mutters, "*El Aguacate*" under his breath.

"Did you say *Aguacate*?"

He looks around as if ears might be hidden in the palm-thatched ceiling. "It's an airplane that makes people disappear."

———

CHAPTER 44
CJ

*The goal here is to paint a picture, not
to save paint. Be generous and mix
plenty before beginning. That way, you
won't have to break your rhythm later
to stop and mix a color.*

The jaguars returned in my dream last night, and for once, I
climbed on one for the ride. Jaguars travel fast, let me tell you. The
strange communions with Blaine had me believing he was in pain
and in trouble. I had to do something, but I hated bringing danger to
Charlie and Rosita—they were too nice. They were also too slow. If
I'd waited for them to come up with a plan, it would have taken
weeks.

Old man Víctor was the one who'd tended the marijuana field, so
he was the one who no doubt had switched the kilos. He gave me the
heart-stopping willies, but I knew he was the key to finding Blaine
and his money. Consulting the atlas again, I found the *Río de Oro*, a
river flowing deep in the Sierra Madre del Sur, and that convinced me
that my little side-trips into Blaine's consciousness were relevant
after all. On the map, the route southwestward from San Miguel
glowed like a golden thread.

I found Noe standing alone in front of Los Nopales. He was the very picture of nonchalance, whistling off-key with his hands clasped behind his back—a capable man and already a trusted friend. When I squinted, he swelled to twice his size, green-gold, with many arms like some Hindu god. Reassured by the image, I opened my eyes wide, so he'd shrink to his normal dimension. I wanted him with me when I confronted Víctor. Noe had a gun.

"Noe, I have to find Blaine."

He nodded rapidly and grinned.

I searched his face and he searched mine.

"He's sick," I said, "but I think he may be going to Zihuatanejo," making sure I got all my syllables articulated.

More nods from Noe.

"Can you take me there?"

A wrinkled brow, sideways look, then more nodding.

"Now?"

He shook his head and surprised me by croaking, "*Mañana,*" the effort making his eyes bulge.

I jumped. "Can we go early?" I asked and got nothing but a blank look, so I tried in Spanish, "*¿Temprano?*"

He nodded vigorously and held up five fingers.

"Five o'clock in the morning?" I shouted, incredulous, thinking we should be leaving at seven-thirty or eight.

Noe grabbed my hands and nodded again. He repeated the five-finger thing and pulled out his trusty spiral notebook, making a crude drawing of my neighborhood with an 'X' on it.

"Okay, the *tortillería* at five o'clock." I held up five fingers this time. "Bring your pistol."

There was more nodding and a salute.

That evening I looked over the road map, then left an inadequate note for Rosita and Charlie, who were in Mexico City for two days buying things for the open house. I hated leaving San Miguel without consulting them, but I had already postponed taking action for too long. There was nothing to pack, really. It would be an early morning, so I set the alarm clock and tried to sleep, going in and out of consciousness for most of the short night.

At 5 am I was standing in the darkness, wearing t-shirt and jeans, Converse All-Stars, and my new serape. The aroma of hot masa had me wishing I'd eaten breakfast and I'd almost decided to knock on the tortillería door and beg for food when Noe arrived. The tiny green TR4 convertible impressed me at first, until I saw there were no glass covers over the headlights and no bulbs.

I indicated the empty sockets. "No lights, Noe?"

He pointed at his watch, shook his head and shrugged—there'd been no time to fix them. He flung open the door, I folded myself into the tiny car and we took off with Noe jamming gears. Leaving San Miguel behind in the moonlight, we headed south on Highway 51 at eighty kilometers-per-hour, the pre-dawn air howling over the windscreen like a polar storm. I defended myself with my serape, wrapping up like an enchilada and scrunching into a fetal position. Somehow, I slept, but fitfully, dreaming in fragments about falling off a cliff and reaching for Patrice's breast.

The Triumph was hugging a hairpin curve when I woke up. A leg cramp compelled me to stretch both legs over the side of the car and kick my feet. Noe took the cue to make a pit stop in the middle of nowhere. On the horizon, a sliver of molten sun emerged from the pink mist and lingered a minute before breaking free, and the day shifted quickly from rose to silver.

I asked, "How far have we come, Noe?"

He checked his watch and said, "One hour, *mas o menos*," cranking the words like a ratchet.

"You've got your gun, right?"

He pulled up the cuff of his pants, showing me a tiny derringer strapped to his shin. Then he jerked his hand up with the derringer cocked and aimed at me. He was grinning like a hyena. I held both hands up, then two thumbs up for a smooth move, but my confidence sagged. It looked like a toy gun, and we were entering a war zone.

Noe took off again, focused on the road ahead. With his antique goggles and leather vest, he looked like the intrepid bi-plane pilot chasing the Red Baron. Soon, a warming draft of air brought the scent of pine and a roadside sign announced 'Salvatierra.' Confident we were on track, I stayed busy ogling roadside attractions—mules tied behind fruit trucks, garbage in all forms, junked cars, parked semi-trucks, and burros grazing beside the road.

Hazy mountains loomed ahead, hummocky and mysterious. I braced against the dash and door as we tunneled our way through the tree canopy. Traffic nonexistent, Noe took the curves at maximum speed and downshifted like a pro, while I sat with knees in my face, butt slung forward and head down. When we stopped at an intersection for gas and tacos, I spilled out of the car and staggered in circles, trying to get my land legs back. Noe pointed at me and turned the wheel back and forth, his eyebrows raised.

"Me?" I asked.

He nodded and rolled his hands in a forward motion, so we rolled on, this time at a much slower rate, but on a flatter and straighter road. Farm and ranch country. We got into more varied terrain with rusty-looking pine trees around Patambo, and when we crossed the *Río de Oro*, it felt so good I almost forgot to worry about the upcoming show-down with Víctor.

When I turned the wheel over to Noe again, he brought us through a series of thirty kilometer-per-hour switchbacks—stacked together, steep grades, deep canyons—with no guard rail. Then we came down off the Sierra alongside another river, and into the coastal flat west of Zihuatanejo.

———

CHAPTER 45
MARIAH

*When the sequence of question and
answer has been uninterrupted and an
artist achieves momentum in the
process of painting, a 'rhythm of
application' is apparent in the finished
work.*

Mañana has turned into several days' worth of *mañanas*. While
my agenda is on hold and my tan deepens, the ocean is trying to
restore my sanity, and I'm allowing it to have its way with me. I've
even accepted the little vegetarian sharks. After all, everyone in the
world breathes in and out at the same time, more or less. All the
critters too, for that matter.

Why do we have to go to work? Hassle with bosses? Hurry up and
finish assignments? Why not just *be*? I can't sit and meditate in the
sand because of the sand fleas, but I can sit in the surf, get in sync
with the waves. Sometimes, in unguarded moments, my mer-man
arrives, serving up a cocktail of arousal and peace, with a dash of
peril. The nectar he offers lights up chakra after chakra, all the way to
the bottom, and I savor the sharpness of it. But I know it's silly to
obsess on a mythical creature who made anonymous love to me in the
dark. *Did that really happen? . . . Maybe I just wanted it to.*

La bahía is smooth as glass this morning, reflecting a cloudless sky. I've already slogged through sand, practiced my forms, and rinsed off when George shows up, panting. He's surprisingly lucid and energetic, having foregone the usual morning doobie for some reason and taken an early run on the beach. "Gotta stay in shape, Mariah," he grins. "A diver needs his wind, you know."

So does a lover.

"You seem to have a lot of wind," I laugh. The only thing keeping me from dropping out and becoming a full-time beach bum right now is the obligation I feel toward Blaine. After all this is over, if I find him, and if he asks me nicely, maybe I *will* go to Arkansas, live on his land. Maybe destiny wants me there. But first, I'm going to find him and let him know about Hannah. Then I'll be free, no matter what he does.

"George, I've been thinking about something Sara said. She thought Blaine would be in hiding, laying low, but that's really not his style. If he's alive, he's already following plan B. I bet he's getting together another deal."

"You know, you're probably right. When Blaine stayed here, he swam a lot. We'd play basketball sometimes at the *playa principal*, eat something at the cantina, have a few beers. It was sort of a routine. Then he would disappear for a few days. Later, he'd come back like a tom cat, pretending he'd never left. I figured he was getting laid somewhere."

Suddenly, George's face transforms as though he's achieved satori. Years fall away. His eyes become lighthouse beams. "Víctor!" he says. "Now that I think of it, Blaine must have gone to see Víctor, the man with the field of gold. I hear it's guarded by *campesinos* with Tommy guns and zombie goats."

"Zombie *what*?" I ask, confused.

"Dead zombie goats. That's what I hear anyway—from the locals. Besides the house in town, Víctor owns a farm way out in the country." George heads across the deep sand toward his house and I fall in step beside him.

"Does he grow weed at this farm?" I ask, thinking I need to see the place.

"Probably nearby, so he can keep an eye on it." George follows me inside and wanders the room, looking around as if there might be a marijuana field hidden in some corner.

I take another shot in the dark. "What do you know about *el Partido de los Pobres* and the peasant uprising here in Guerrero?"

"Don't know much about them, but I think Víctor does. His son was a member." George gives up his search and starts rustling up breakfast, squeezing orange juice and stoking the fire, a sublime smile on his face.

"Who can resist fresh grilled mackerel and tomatoes?" he says, wielding the spatula. "That which we call a fish, by any other name would taste as sweet."

He's still beaming when I ask, "George, is it possible to talk to this Víctor guy?"

"Sure, we'll go *mañana*."

I decide to be patient for one more day, then we'll have to do something, even if it's wrong.

———

CHAPTER 46
CJ

*Forget what you know. Paint what you
see. Be faithful and answer the
questions one by one. Is it redder or
greener? Lighter or darker? Harder or
softer? The questions you ask are not
difficult, but they are specific ones, and
you need to sustain the chain of
questioning for as long as you can.*

It was almost noon when we stopped in front of the two-story
house in Zihua, and by then, the butterflies in my gut felt like
helicopters. I dreaded how Víctor would react to our unannounced
visit, and if Noe hadn't already turned off the TR4's ignition, I'd
have told him to keep driving. I remembered Víctor's tendency
toward violence, and was glad my partner had come armed. Noe
pulled up his pants leg, un-strapped the pistol, and slid it into his
pocket. I took a deep breath and strengthened my resolve. The front
door swung open as we approached it.

"Clifí." Victor offered his hand, showing no sign of surprise.

The sound of my real name shocked me at first, even in the
Spanish version, *Clifí,* so I hesitated before I recovered my manners
and shook his hand. "Víctor, this is my friend, Noe."

The old man smiled and turned to Noe, who made a show of brushing his hands on his shirt before extending a hand. "*Mucho gusto*, Noe," Víctor pronounced the name with an accent on the second syllable and a short 'e,' No-*éh*.

Noe patted his chest and bowed deeply. He pointed first to his ear and shook his head, then to his mouth and shook his head again, indicating he was deaf and mute. He had his own reasons for maintaining silence, and I didn't question his judgement. Víctor's smile was a surprise, incongruous with his hard-lined face. When I squinted at him, a brilliant green-gold penumbra edged his form, vibrating against the violet background, reminding me of Noe's aura.

"*Bienvenidos,*" Víctor said. "Come in."

I followed the two men inside and Noe pranced around the room, examined relief carvings on the table edge and chair backs, felt the texture of the stone walls, and generally acted the conquering fool, appraising his newly-won turf. He approached a pot that hung in the fireplace, picked up an implement, lifted the lid and inhaled deeply. I was embarrassed by this intrusion, but Noe nodded, unabashed, a dreamy look on his face.

"Amigos." Our host executed a barely perceptible bow. "A meal is ready."

Víctor brought plates, spoons, and a bottle of mescal to the table, as if he'd been expecting us, and I worried, *What am I doing here? What if he poisons us?* While we sat and ate and drank, he asked the question I'd come to ask *him*.

"Clifí, what news you have from don Belín?"

"None. I'm looking for him. You know Sergio stole his plane and crashed it? Sergio and another man were killed."

The old man held my gaze, "Sorry about the airplane, amigo. . . Not sorry about my nephew Sergio . . . a bad man." He waved his hand in the air between us. "But I know nothing of this."

I found it hard to believe that he didn't know about the crash, but I had little experience in judging whether someone was lying or not. His face looked as sour as it had the last time I'd seen him, but he seemed genuinely puzzled.

"I thought Blaine might come here," I said.

He chewed his mouthful of stew and took his time answering. "Yes, is possible. I wait for him here." He kept studying my sidekick, like Noe was the answer to some unspoken question. I'd been all psyched up for a battle, so Víctor's attitude confused me. He didn't act like a man who'd stolen an airplane and helped kill his nephew, but how was I to know what he was capable of?

Víctor seemed to come to a decision, and said, "Your brother heals with a *brujo* in the mountains. He gives me a message for you if you come here. He gets well. No worry." The old man stood and went to the ornate cabinet on the wall. Sitting on top, still turned facing the wall, was the photograph he'd taken away last time I was in the room. I tensed as he opened the fretworked door and brought out the watercolor box I'd forgotten.

"You forget something the last time you here," he said, handing me the box.

"*Gracias*, Víctor," I said, opening the lid.

Taped inside was one of my paintings. It hadn't been that long since I'd made the little study, but seeing it gave me a pang of nostalgia and the desire to paint. When I showed them my other sketches in the box, Noe nodded appreciatively, the old man smiled, and the tension in the room eased.

Víctor held up one finger and went out the door, returning with three cool cervezas and setting them on the table. He took a seat and a long pull on his beer, then wiped his mouth with the back of his hand. "Now I tell a story."

"Born the year 1900." He slapped himself in the chest. "I fight the *revolución* with my father and Zapata in the battle of Chilipancingo. My father dies in the battle."

Noe jumped up and executed a deep formal bow. Then he gave a military salute, holding it while Víctor's story continued.

"I go with *mamá* to live with my sister, Carlota and her husband, Herman Silva in *la ciudad* Guanajuato. I call my sister *Tota*. I am *Bico*." He crossed his fingers. "Since childrens, we are close like this."

Víctor focused on the three sweating bottles of *Pacífico*, then gazed upward at the ceiling beams. He seemed to look both inward and far into the distance at the same time, and while he spoke, I looked into that same distance, imagining the scenes he described.

"Herman fights in the *revolución* with Álvaro Obregón, and Obregón grants Herman the *hacienda* with a big house near San

Miguel for his service. The family moves to San Miguel. I stay in Guanajuato, go to university, not far away." Víctor scowled and shook his head. "When *mamá* dies, I come here to Zihua. I don't see my sister for twenty years. The mother of Sergio and Ricardo dies at the birth of Ricardo, so Tota cares for her grandsons at the hacienda."

Noe jumped up and ran to the front door, the fireplace and around the table. Then he galloped up the stairs and disappeared. I heard a clatter and bang, and Noe came running back down trailing a red blanket and a long sword. He stood facing the old man, giving him his undivided attention, the sword's tip resting on the floor.

Víctor ignored him and continued, "The father favors Sergio. Ricardo is more intelligent, Sergio stronger. The brothers fight, and Sergio wins. But first, Ricardo marks him with a knife, here." He indicated his left jaw. "When the boys are older, *un accidente* with the auto takes the father and the grandfather. Tota suffers the loss of her eyes. I go see her in San Miguel one time, but I live here with Lupe, and we have three childs, so I don't help my sister."

Noe twirled the blanket like a bullfighter's cape, making pirouettes in the middle of the room while brandishing the sword and somehow keeping an eye on the old man's lips. The old man went silent, and his face darkened. He reached for the mescal bottle, took a swig and chased it with beer. "Ricardo goes to *la universidad*, then Cuba, for the *revolución*. Before that, Ricardo has a soul."

"What happened in Cuba?" I asked.

"A woman happens. Luz Martinez." Víctor stopped to study the ceiling for a while. Noe deftly folded the blanket, wrapped it around his waist and began to saunter around the room swaying his hips, imitating a woman.

"Luz works for the newspapers," Víctor said, "and teaches English to the peasants. Joins the rebels to fight Batista. When Castro tricks the people, takes the government, declares Cuba is *comunista*, Luz joins the rebels to fight Castro. Is a secret."

With the sword and the mock skirt, Noe ran around the room, acting out the Cuban revolution.

"Some of the rebels were against Castro?" I asked. "That's crazy. How did they know who was on which side?"

"*Sí, es un problema*," Víctor said, nursing his *cervesa*.

Noe stopped running for a minute to pick up the blanket, which had fallen off. He wrapped it back around his waist while I tried to wrap my mind around the political tangle with Ricardo in Cuba.

"How does Ricardo fit in?" I asked.

"Ricardo works for the Mexican newspapers, writing stories on Cuba, on Castro, the *revolución*, and the *comunistas*. He meets Luz and the two become secret lovers."

Noe was back on the job with puckered lips, kissing his own hand, the wall, and finally the top of Víctor's head before he was waved off, and our storyteller proceeded. " Luz works for Castro. Is a teacher. Discovers Castro's plans, informs the *banditos* a way to surprise Castro's men. Many is killed."

Noe had one hand on his hip, holding the makeshift skirt in place and one hand above his eyes like a visor. He was sneaking around the room, pretending to look for something, and I finally got it. "Luz was a spy."

"*Sí*. Castro captures Luz and executes her for spying." Víctor paused to dramatize, chopping the side of his neck with the edge of his hand. "Ricardo escapes."

Noe leapt suddenly in the air, waving the sword like a cossack and brought it down to the floor with a violent slash, stopping just short of whacking the stone surface, miming the unfortunate woman's execution.

I said, "I can see why Ricardo was pissed off."

Víctor said, "No one is innocent, Clifí. Maybe in the beginnings, but war changes everything. Many peoples think Castro wins in Cuba because the *norteamericanos* fuck up. And now the *Cia* works here in Mexico. Same fuck up. Telling lies. Making the people disappear." He spat on the floor.

"But what does all this have to do with Blaine?" I asked, pacing the flagstones.

"Clifí, your brother and Ricardo tries to stop the *Cia* helping *el gobierno* here in Mexico. But a man who touches the darkness becomes a part of the shadow. When you battle with this power, Clifí, you never prevail. You hope only for the way to persist."

"We used to be the good guys," I lamented.

"Well, amigo, in war, no one is good guys." He reached out and patted me on the shoulder. "But you are a good guy. *¿No?*"

He grinned or grimaced, I'm not sure which, and wiped his mouth. I stared at the label on the mescal bottle, *400 Conejos*, finished my beer, got a cup of water. I was beginning to think Víctor might be one of the good guys. I should have mentioned something to him about the creepy-eyed guy *cia* that Patrice had identified, but I'd shoved that whole subject to the back of my mind, and the four hundred rabbits residing in the mescal bottle helped to keep it there. They also helped me find courage to bring up the issue on my mind.

"Víctor, there was something funny about the *mota* we loaded on Blaine's airplane. My uncle said those kilos were packed with hay."

Noe stopped playing guitar and slid his hand in his pocket where the little pistol was concealed. I'd never actually seen him shoot the thing. He was competent at so many things, I just assumed he'd be accurate with it.

Víctor only hung his head and nodded.

I pressed the issue, "You loaded those bags with Johnsongrass."

We all watched a mouse dart across the floor, skitter into a corner and disappear. Víctor took another drink of mescal and wiped his mouth. His voice softened as he spoke, "Yes, the fault is mine." He covered his grisly head with his hands. "Is like this, Ricardo and Sergio make a deal for selling *colitas* to Belín, but the crop is not ready in time. Ricardo makes the plan—fill the kilos with *hierba*, so I make kilos, some *colitas*, some *hierba*. Now my debt to Ricardo is paid. I keep my farm, Ricardo gets the money, and Sergio gets dead." Víctor slapped the table.

That got my attention. The old man's ferocity had almost gotten to be endearing—almost.

"Víctor, was that part of the original deal?" I asked. "Sergio getting dead?"

He leaned forward and grabbed my forearm, breathing mescal fumes into my face. "Look, Clifí, Ricardo hates his brother—all his life." He released my arm and slapped the table again. "Ricardo tricks him."

"How?" I asked,

Víctor shrugged his shoulders, his eyebrows impersonating wooly worms. "The airplane suffers a crash, no?"

"Yes."

He shrugged again and tapped his head. "Ricardo is *intelligente*. Maybe makes trouble with the airplane. Then, maybe he says, 'I'm sick. Can't fly. You fly, Sergio.'"

I saw how the plan might have gone down. Ricardo was in Acapulco a day or two before the flight to Zihua—before he got sick. There would have been an opportunity for him to mess with the Cessna and make sure Sergio flew it. But there was another question I'd been afraid to raise.

"What happened to the money, Víctor? You said Ricardo got the money, but I saw him give you a briefcase when the plane landed."

Víctor answered, without hesitation. "Is not money you see in *la cartera*, but the papers for my house in Zihua, my farm. Now I owe him nothing. Ricardo has the money, Clifí."

It all seemed so clear for a change. There *were* three rats.

Víctor looked pained. "But no one gets the *mota, verdad?* Don't worry. I fix with don Belín. The crop now in the field is mine, not Ricardo's. I grow it for don Belín to sell, amigo. Pay him back, so he buys a new airplane."

Víctor stood framed in the darkness of the doorway, and for a minute vanished into the surrounding void. The negative space around him was a deep chromatic black, made of all colors at once and yet no color. The old man was a paradox, both fierce and vulnerable, all in the same package. Here he was willing to cheat Blaine so he could get the title to his farm back from Ricardo, but also willing to furnish Blaine with hundreds of kilos of quality weed to make up for the deception. I believed he was telling the truth.

Noe had found a guitar and sat stone-faced, playing three-note riffs in tremolo while I returned to the mezcal bottle for a shot. I realized I'd arrived in Zihua before my brother. He was still on his way, and it would take him a long time to get here riding a mule.

Our host shifted around the room, glowing with an inner light, orange-red, like sunset on the ocean. He opened a drawer in the chest against the wall and removed something, then looked at Noe and asked, "*¿Requerdes a tu madre?*"

A strange question, I thought. He was asking if Noe remembered his mother.

Noe muted the guitar and shook his head.

"Was her name Gabriella?"

Víctor must have switched to English for my benefit.

Noe nodded, set down the guitar and stood up.

"Gabriella Fuentes y Solana?"

"*¿Como?*" Noe bleated like a goat, straining with effort. "How?" he'd asked Víctor .

"Because I know her, I know you also."

Noe's eyes got big, and his voice plaintive. *"¿Como?"* he wailed,

Víctor took a deep breath, approached Noe and said, *"Porque eres mi hijo."* Then he embraced his son.

I was just as surprised as Noe. We listened in shock to the ensuing tale of romance and loss, years before Víctor's marriage. Gabriella had discovered she was pregnant. Her parents were strict Catholics and Víctor, being a devout athiest, had refused to convert. They, in turn refused him access to Gabriella and sent her to a convent to have the child. She'd died when Noe was born. But Víctor, the child's father, had kept up with his development, learned of his deafness and sent anonymous gifts to the grandparents in Mexico City until the boy matured. The grandparents had both died of influenza when the epidemic came and Víctor lost touch.

The old man produced a photograph and handed it to Noe, a clue it was time for me to leave father and son alone. "I'm going to turn in for the night." I said and stood up too quickly, the rabbits having taken their toll.

Víctor held me steady. "You know the bed upstairs, amigo."

Noe put away the guitar and we all went out back to pee. I heard Víctor say to Noe, "No need for the *pistolito*, hijo," but of course, Noe didn't hear. The comment made me curious how Víctor knew about the derringer, but I let it go.

Víctor pressed something into my hand. "Clifí, my sister, Tota gives me the keys when Sergio is born. One is for the cellar door in the Silva hacienda, where Ricardo and Sergio keep the money. One is for the tunnel to the cellar. You find a door in the stables. Now is the time for using the keys." His hands squeezed mine with emphasis. "You get the money for don Belín. You go get the money. But leave *un poquito* for Tota, *por favor*."

CHAPTER 47
CJ

*It's good to vary your method on a
regular basis. Avoid getting stuck in a
rut. If you tend to begin your paintings
with a wash, then start with a stroke of
charcoal. Instead of making a full-color
block-in, try painting in monochrome.
Allow yourself to be surprised by what
you create.*

I woke up to an ache in my head and a stubble on my chin. Instead of dying of thirst, I decided to go for water and found a note on the table beside my paint box. *"Voy al campo. Mi casa es su casa."* The old man had gone to the country and left us breakfast on the fire. Noe and I rolled tortillas around our potatoes and chorizo and contemplated our future. I'd have to go back to San Miguel without finding Blaine, and Noe would have to wait for an extended reunion with his new-found father. He had the car to return, and I'd promised to help prepare for the studio open house.

Strange how I was already thinking of Charlie and Rosita's place as home. In keeping with my desire to protect them, I left a message for Víctor and Blaine to contact me through Noe at Los Nopales. Keys jingled in my pocket, reminding me of the night before, and I pulled out a matched pair of three-inch bronze antiques. Each key had a loop handle and a long round shank with two prongs on the end. I shivered, vaguely remembering Víctor handing me the key-ring, and the words, "You go get the money, Clifi."

I grabbed my watercolor box before heading out the door. It turned out that Noe had 'borrowed' the car without the owner's permission, and was under the threat of losing his *cojones* if he didn't get it back before the man noticed it was gone. Understandably, he was in a hurry to get on the road, but I lobbied for a quick wade in the ocean, first. We parked at the basketball court where three little kids were trying to heave a coconut husk through the hoop. Out on *la bahía*, a launch angled through light chop toward the beach, bringing a single rider. She was light-skinned, and something about the single braid sparked a recognition. *One of the legendary fat mermaids*, I guessed, as Noe whistled softly and made hand signals describing the female form. We both grinned, watching the dugout approach.

The rider pivoted on the thwart and scoped us out for a minute, as though sensing we were looking at her. Or maybe she was eyeing the TR4—it *is* a cool car. I jogged to the shoreline and slipped off my sandals, then tossed my shirt and wallet in a pile. I walked out calf-deep into the water as the floating log lurched to a stop beside me.

After some small talk, I discovered the mermaid was on the same mission I was. She suddenly asked, "How's the water?"

"It's azure." I'd never said the word before, and it snuck out of my mouth without permission, making her eyes sparkle and crinkle at the edges. *She must have been dieting*, I thought. *She's not corpulent at all.* I admired the shimmer on her green one-piece suit while she hopped out and splashed ashore. I watched her go, thinking I'd never see her again.

Then she threw her bag on the sand, spun around and waded back to me.

———

CHAPTER 48
MARIAH

Unwavering intention held closely, like
faith, will ultimately take an artist to
the end of the journey, although the
final picture will often be other than the
one imagined.

I've set out for Zihua proper to check on the Beetle, pay for the
extra days and pick up some things at the rented room. Actually, I'm
killing time until George takes us to talk to Victor. I'm pressing for
tomorrow. The wind has come up and my shuttle is bouncing through
a light chop on the way to the *playa principal*. Two guys check me
out as we slow down and glide toward the beach. When I step out of
the boat, one of them is standing ten feet away in the water. I start to
leave, then turn back, on the spur of the moment. I don't know why
I'm emboldened. Maybe it's because he doesn't know me, but I go
ahead and ask, "What brings you to paradise?"

"I'm looking for my brother. How about you?"

"Actually, I've lost track of someone too." *And I'm losing myself in his eyes.* "His name is Blaine Grayson."

"That's . . . my brother," he stammers.

"Blaine Grayson is your brother?" I ask, my voice rising.

He shushes me with a finger to his lips and glances both ways. "That's right."

"Any luck finding him?" I ask, my hand instinctively going to the pouch with the opal in it.

He glances at his feet. "No, no luck." Then his eyes meet mine again. "So how . . .?" He falters, mid-sentence and I see I may have to help him out.

"He never said anything about having a brother."

"How do you know him?" he asks.

It's a fair enough question but a loaded one, and it's my turn to hesitate before answering, "I knew him in New Orleans." *I knew him all right—in the Biblical sense, but that's not something I'm planning to share right now.*

His face screws up in consternation. "So . . ."

I change the subject. "How's the water?"

He looks out toward the horizon like he's looking for Atlantis, or Nirvana, and is yearning to go there. "It's azure," he says.

Without waiting, I dive into the clear water and swim hard until I need to come up for air. Surprisingly, he's kept pace. Stopping a body-length away, he sputters, standing chest deep in the froth of low-breaking waves. "Did you give up?" he shouts. *Another loaded question.*

"On what?" I holler back.

"On Blaine."

"Do you ever ask easy questions?"

There's something attractive about him. He's not beautiful—that's not it. Kind of thin, not much body hair, patchy stubble of a beard. But magnetic for sure. *Is this a recurring theme? Why do I keep meeting dream guys in the water? Why do I forget to ask their names?*

———

CHAPTER 49
CJ

*You may find that a single carefully
observed detail will give more impact
than a whole litany of description.*

She dived in the water and I followed. Looking back, I remember the eyes and voice, and the little leather bag nestled between her breasts. I could draw her face from memory, but I can't remember much of what she said. The picture was embedded, though.

I saw droplets of water and glints of highlight as though spattered on a canvas panel. *This is how I would paint her*, I thought, *all wet from ocean water and sparkling in the sun, using shades of terra rosa, turquoise, ochre and malachite.* Real, but more than real . . . perennial. A warm glow came off her . . . magnetic. I knew those bottomless eyes, but I couldn't place them.

"I have to get back to San Miguel by six o'clock," I said, thinking it was crazy to leave her standing there. "Why don't you come with us?"

She peered at the TR4 on the beach and laughed, "Oh sure. Where would I ride? On your shoulders?"

I had no answer to that, but the thought of her sitting on my shoulders with her legs wrapped around my neck was arousing to the point of embarrassment and it's a good thing we were chest deep in the Pacific.

She shook her head and the wet braid followed. "Just kidding. I have my car."

"You could follow us," I said.

"I *do* need to talk to you." Her eyes fastened on me. "I'm keeping some of your brother's things back in Texas. Look, there's something I need to do here. A guy I need to see. After that, I'll meet you in San Miguel, if I can find it."

My infatuation subsided with the mention of my brother. I had more questions to ask her, and I probably could have gotten answers then, but Noe was jumping up and down and playing a polka on the horn. He drew a thumb across his throat, followed by the 'circle up' sign. My time was up.

I turned to the girl, said, "I've got to go," and swam for shore. She followed, and I pulled one of Noe's *Los Nopales* cards from my wallet and handed it over. Then I tilted my head toward the TR4 and said, "Noe will know how to find me."

"Okay." She glanced at the card and back at me. "I guess I'll see you there."

I jogged to the car where Noe was jumping up and down, scooped up the kids' abandoned coconut husk, and in one motion, from twenty-five feet, I launched a hook shot and made a basket. It was only on the ride back to San Miguel that I realized I'd forgotten to ask her name.

———

CHAPTER 50
MARIAH

*In composing a picture, it is good to
leave a space for rest—a patch of
blue—where the eye can pause before
moving through the rest of the work. A
famous violinist once said that many
people know how to play the notes.
Only a master can play the rests.*

Urgent alarms disrupt the canopy over the patio while Cindy,
George and I are eating breakfast. Debris pelts us from above,
landing in the bowl of peaches and threatening our scrambled-egg
tacos. A dark-winged hawk accelerates into the cobalt sky, reminding
me that under the placid veneer of our oceanside Eden, the tooth and
claw of a primal struggle goes on. After a respectful silence, the
would-be prey resume their concert in unison, if not harmony,
celebrating a restoration of the status quo.

Cindy has found her own equilibrium here with George. But me? I'm not complacent. Inertia has hold of me, my opal is trying to burn through its pouch, and a nagging sense of duty has conspired to make me pushy.

"When are we going to look for Víctor?" I ask, standing to clear the dishes. "I mean I could space out here forever, but my money will soon be gone and I *did* come down here to find Blaine. I don't think he's going to find *us*."

Cindy and George look at each other, then he says, "Sure, why not today?"

"What do we need,?" I ask.

"Well, we need shoes," George says.

"That's all?"

Half an hour later, the launch takes us to the main Zihua beach where the usual activity is in full swing. Someone has found a real basketball, fixed the goal, and four teenagers are playing a noisy game of horse. Past the margin of palms and other vegetation, the natural world gives way to a human one both precarious and dingy. A tin roof shanty town emerges, stripped of vegetation, and destined, it seems, to poverty. Dust from the unpaved street rises to coat the windows, and old heavy-set women sweep the dirt in front of painted doors. I wonder where the men have gone.

"Zihua means 'the place of godesses.'" George tells us, "The town's logo is a fat mermaid—sailors, you know, they've been coming here for centuries."

I glance back at the woman we just passed and wonder if she knows how to swim. Moving along briskly, we overtake a shaggy burro laden with multicolored blankets. The adorable animal is standing by a drab stucco building that's pasted with posters and painted with signs. We've discovered *el Mercado*, a place overflowing with restrained abundance.

Spilling out of dark arcades are chiles and tomatoes, onions, garlic braids, coconuts and all kinds of fruit. My eyes dance from one treat to the next, intrigued with novelty, dazzled by the variety and color. I have a sense of standing still while the promenade of visual accents passes us by, but my feet tell me that we are still walking.

A stinky fish market is next, *el Pescador*, complete with squid and oysters and children with flyswatters, chasing manic swarms of flies.

It's kind of gross. *And here I fancy myself a country girl.* Under a thatching of palm fronds and signs announcing Corona Extra, is a bar with a parrot stoically guarding the portal. Already open at this hour, the bar lacks customers. Across the street two men in chairs try to look respectable, but their eyes are fixed on the dark recesses of the cantina. *Probably planning their attack.* As we pass, I catch the scent of stale beer, disinfectant, and a faint whiff of manure.

Up the street, an ancient woman with her hair in a bun wields a fierce broom, marshalling the packed dirt on her stoop, keeping a stray chicken at bay. The stucco houses are painted terra-cotta orange with deep maroon accents or turquoise against pale lemon yellow. Some have pots of flowers, but the soil itself seems sterile, unable to support vegetation.

On a side street is a two-story stone house with no trees, but signs of a garden in back—our destination. First order of business is a pit stop in the garden where for a moment I lose my sense of time and place. A trace of my dream guy is present in this place. A scent, maybe, or something more ethereal.

I long for the feeling of completeness I had with the mer-man, his friendly presence. For good measure, I give the phantom a squeeze and feel a shock of solidification, as though he's right here, engorged member and all. His words come to mind, "You'll always keep a sacred part of me within." Cindy and George have gone around front, so I stay with him for a little while beside the banana tree, beset by quick, quiet convulsions while he tugs on my ponytail.

The house is empty.

"I was afraid of this," George frowns. "We'll have to go to Víctor's country place where his family lives, but it's another ten kilometers west of here. Anyone up for a hike?"

"How long will it take?" I ask.

"All day to go there and back. We might want to stay over."

"Why can't we drive in the Beetle?"

"We could, but it takes longer to drive the long way around than it does to walk, and the road is awful now that the rains have started."

Back at the market we stop among the purses, scarves and piñatas to purchase a netted *bolsa* and some gifts for the family we're going to meet tomorrow.

"We'll have to find another method of packing supplies," I say, hefting the oversized bag full of stuff.

George agrees, "We'll come better prepared mañana."

While working out our itinerary, we've accumulated a small band of children, the usual strange combination of bold and shy. When I look at them, they giggle and run, then quickly catch up as soon as I look away.

"I know these kids," George explains. "I usually talk to them and give them a coin or something. They're probably afraid to approach me because of you two."

Cindy has a camera. They allow her to take pictures and receive too big a tip from her before we retreat. Their eyes bulge.

"That's too much." George cautions, but too late. The five-peso note is flying down the street like a battle flag and the kids are off to attack the market. I have no doubt they'll conquer it.

———

CHAPTER 51
CJ

*Sometimes Providence gives us a day
that is good for 'finishing,' when our
task seems almost to complete itself.
Take advantage of those days to work
on several stubborn pieces that have
been thwarting completion.*

Sunday morning, I got up at dawn. Charlie and Rosita were in
their room as usual, doing morning meditation, and I was reluctant to
disturb them. I didn't intentionally leave them out of the plan. It just
happened that way, and once the plan was in motion, there was no
time to clue them in.

On the streets, only laborers, shopkeepers and peddlers were out
and about, all purposeful, accompanied by church bells chiming from
three directions. They ignored me while I scaled the stone wall under
the big mesquite and eased behind the row of apartments. Light shone
through a curtain in the square window of Noe's cubicle, illuminating
the steps as I crept down to his lair. How Noe knew I was there, I
have no idea, but as I reached out to knock, he opened the door and
waved me into his cramped lodgings. A kerosene lamp glowed on the
table and the odor of petroleum permeated the space. There was no
coffee pot that I could see, but Noe produced two cups of the
steaming brew, another of his magician's tricks.

A stack of three-by-five index cards waited on the table with a pair of pencils. I was glad there would be no miscommunication, and Noe wouldn't have to strain to speak while we worked out a plan. We each took a chair.

I picked up a pencil and wrote, "Blaine's money is stashed in the Silva's cellar. I want to sneak in and get it back. No help from the MacRaes."

"Yes, good idea," Noe wrote. "Best do before Ricardo comes home."

"Good. I have the keys."

He nodded and wrote, "What to do with Ramón?"

"Can you distract him?" I wrote. "Get him out of the house?"

He glanced at the ceiling and looking back at me, nodded, then watched me jot the question that had been on my mind. "Can you get a better pistol?"

Noe moved his head from side to side as though he was having a hard time making up his mind. I knew he was attached to his derringer, but I wanted more firepower on our side.

He finally nodded and gave the sign for forty bucks. I sipped my coffee and jotted, "Okay. You go in the front and I go in the back."

"*Bien*. I have a new car," Noe wrote.

"Perfect. Can you be ready tonight?" I asked, dispensing with writing on cards.

Noe gave a thumbs-up and watched my face closely.

"Rosita picks up Juana at 6:30 to go to church. We follow Rosita there and wait at the wire gate until they leave. I go to the hacienda on foot. You go in the car, lose Ramón and come back for me in one hour." I said, holding up a finger.

"I lose him at the house of his girlfriend," Noe wrote, then he rasped, "Haha."

"Okay, I'll meet you at 6:00 in front of the park." I slipped him three twenties and left.

———

Charlie and Rosita had gone somewhere, so to kill some time, I went to the studio, scraped down my palette and set out fresh paint.

One unfinished piece called to me. I'd frozen up in the midst of asking the endless questions Charlie had me ask, "Redder/greener, harder/softer, lighter/darker, etc.

"Give it time," he'd said. "Work on something new. Let your momentum build. Then, when you feel ready to finish, just do it."

I gave the dried panel a wash of varnish and asked, "What do you need?"

The answer was, "Help!" so I reminded myself to ask a more specific question. "Are the darks dark enough?"

The image was a bowl of fruit. The shadow under the bowl had been indicated, but not really painted, so I deepened the shadow with a semi-transparent mixture of dark blue, dark red and a little deep yellow. I almost got stuck, but then I remembered what Charlie'd said about mixing color. I made a lighter version of the shadow color and repeated the process to make another, still lighter hue. With the three piles of pigment, I re-painted the bowl, using a full range of values. For the final touch, I placed a highlight of thick, almost white paint in just the right spot, prompting a wave of emotion.

I closed my eyes and the waterfall mistress joined me. It seemed that in spite of all that had happened, she wouldn't let go. I reached for her ponytail, shut my eyes to savor the time, and made contact. The gentle embrace grew firmer and tighter until I heard the faint echo, "I have to go," and we separated once again. After a few seconds, I opened my eyes and appraised my painting. Judging it a success, I 'fixed' several more paintings the same way. The modifications all took place in a very short time frame, and it turned out to be a good day for 'finishing.' I made a judgement, acted precipitously, then walked away.

———

Evening thunderclouds had stacked up over San Miguel, threatening a shower, and the sky was dark as dusk, but no rain had fallen yet. Twenty blocks of zigzag through the streets took me to the park where I lay down on a bench to catch my breath and dozed for a minute. The ancient black Mercedes that crept to the curb and startled me looked like Nikita Krushchev's ride, except it had a taxi sign stuck on top. Noe wore a crisp black chauffeur's uniform with gold piping and a matching officer's hat. He pulled back his jacket to show me the butt of a slim automatic tucked into a shoulder holster. Noe grinned and his gold tooth sparkled in the fading orange light. It was a perfect disguise.

We took the long way around to the Silva's pasture gate, and the sky was even darker when Noe let me out. Still no rain. I straddled the wire, trotted toward the buildings, and crossed the cattle guard as Noe's headlights turned into the driveway and lit up the front of the house. I watched from behind the bole of a giant mesquite while Noe honked three times, got out and stood at attention by the passenger's door. While the Silva's dogs raised a ruckus, I waited for the front door to open, the damp neck of my sweatshirt magnifying the chill in the air. I hoped Ramón would be easily distracted, and worried that he'd be suspicious later. Then I decided there was no need. I'd be in and out, and he'd never know about it.

Right away, the skinny bullfighter appeared in the yellow glow of the porch light. He hurried down the steps and strutted up to the Mercedes. Noe held the passenger door open while they engaged in a brief conversation. Ramón glanced back at the hacienda, hesitated, and ducked into the car. Noe took the wheel and crept slowly back to the highway before turning toward town.

I knew the basic layout of the compound from our previous visit. The old lady was in the house somewhere, but aside from her, the coast was clear. As I approached the stable, cast shadow swallowed up forms and bushes kept shifting positions in the breeze. I threw valium fortified sausages to the dogs, and a hinge creaked nearby, so I flattened against a wall and held my breath for a count of two hundred. After that the dogs were quiet, but my heart sounded like a Harley.

One key opened the door in the stable . According to Víctor, a tunnel led from there to the hacienda cellar where the Silva brothers stashed their money. I shoved the door open and cursed when a long splinter jammed into the soft spot between my thumb and index finger. I yanked it out and shot a beam into the gloomy passage, then switched the flashlight off, trusting memory to guide me through the tunnel.

Right away I stepped into something slimy, skidded, and banged my head on the ceiling. I ducked and splashed through puddles, soaking my shoes, but eventually came to the cellar. The other key worked, the door opened, and I shone the flashlight into the room. Blaine's money belt lay in the center of a small table, folded neatly— empty. Encouraged that I was in the right place, I strapped it around my waist and redirected light on the table.

Be methodical, I thought, but it didn't happen that way. The single drawer came all the way out when I pulled on it, spilling staples, paper clips, a gold-plated ball point pen along with a checkbook, the big kind, spiral bound, with three stubs to a page. A quick search revealed that the last two checks had been written by Ricardo three days before the hijacking. One stub had a notation in Spanish. *Pemex*—eight hundred fifty liters of aviation fuel. That was expected. He'd prepared to refuel Blaine's plane at the hacienda.

The other stub read, *Servicios Aviones, Acapulco*. Clipped to the stub was a receipt for sale of a fuel guage for a Cessna 210D, signed by Ricardo Silva. Stuck in back of the checkbook was an owner's manual for the aircraft, English version, with Blaine's name written on the front. Flipping through it, and finding a dog-eared page with a diagram of the fuel gauge and description of how it worked, I thought, *Bingo*. Together with the receipt and check stubs, this confirmed that Ricardo was at the hacienda just before the plane was hijacked, he'd taken Blaine's manual, and he'd probably screwed with the airplane. The bastard was rat number two, all right, and probably number three, also. I'd lost track of all the rats.

I pocketed the paperwork and searched for Blaine's money. The table had no secret compartments and the floor looked solid, so I started with the wall on the left side of the door, inspecting the mortar between bricks. The surface was tight as a vault, with no gaps or seams. When I reached the corner, I thought I heard one of the floorboards creak above my head. Cringing, I turned off the flashlight and listened to my breathing. I counted to three hundred and heard nothing else, so I shone a light on the back wall. Near the ceiling, a foot or so from the corner of the room, the mortar looked slightly different—lighter in value and newer, maybe.

The rickety table allowed me to climb up and get a closer look at the wall, and a crack all the way around one brick gave away the hiding place. With some wiggling, the brick came loose to reveal the packets of hundreds, held together with rubber bands. A set of keys was there also, identical to the ones in my pocket. I left the keys where they were and loaded the money belt before easing the brick in place.

On my way back down, some clumsiness of mine, or weakness in the table, caused it's leg to give way with a crash, and I collapsed along with it. The flashlight sailed against the wall and everything went dark. I sprawled on the floor, cringing from the noise. There was no damage to me except for a minor bump on the chin but the table would never be the same. I had the goods on Ricardo, and I had the money. It was time to exit, so I abandoned the dead flaslight and scrambled my way out of there, worried about the racket I'd made. The old lady was blind, but she could probably hear just fine.

Running crouched through the void with hands in front of me, scraping my knuckles on the sides of the tunnel, I stayed low and tried to anticipate the turns I'd made coming in. With a splash I slipped and fell, twisting an ankle. Then I was up and at the exit, sooner than expected. Craving fresh air even more than light, I threw open the door, and it slammed behind me as I stepped into the open.

The shots erupted like thunder and lightning. A short burst from the barrel of a submachine gun—four or five rounds. Blood and a sudden bone-deep pain sprouted from my hand. I squinted at the tiny witch standing on the path not ten feet away, her fat weapon aimed at my belly. She'd missed my torso, but barely, and blown away the ring finger on my right hand. *Carlota!*

"*Señora*," I gasped, grabbing my bloody stump of a finger and looking around for a way of escape. "*Por favor, no me mate. Víctor me mandó.*" I was on autopilot speaking to the blind gunslinger, my Spanish flowing like arterial blood. "Please, don't shoot. Víctor sent me."

"*Creo que no le mandó mi hermano. Creo que se mandó usted mismo, para robarme.*" She spoke slowly enough and simply enough that I got it. She didn't believe Víctor had sent me. She thought I was a thief. I had to admire her intuition. She was right-on about that. From my adrenaline-charged memory, I retrieved the pet name Víctor had called her when they were children.

"Señora, Tota. *Soy* amigo de Bico." I had my mental fingers crossed, since my literal ones were busy, or bloody, or missing. I thought the old hag's expression softened when I used her pet name for her brother, but the gun barrel did not waver.

"Bico," she said, free hand on her heart. "*me haces falta.*" She *was* missing her brother.

The Spanish continued to roll off my tongue. "*Mire,* Señora, Tota. *Permítame enseñarle. Víctor me dió las llaves. Mire.*" I'd continued my appeal, saying, "Let me show you the keys Víctor gave me." I extracted the ring with my left hand, jingled the keys and tossed them by her feet. I thought there'd be a chance to run as she squatted down, but the gun barrel stayed fixed on my midsection while she picked up the keys. Without eyesight, the lady still had an unerring sense of where I was. Exactly. While I applied pressure to the stub of my finger and blood dripped on the ground, she felt each of the keys slowly and carefully, facing me with the gun the whole time. Then she spoke.

"*¿Y qué se encontró usted en la bodega?*" She wanted to know what I found in the cellar.

I squeezed my throbbing hand, took a deep breath. There would be no do-overs. It was tournament time—the finals. I squinted at her, and searching for a scrap of light in the shadows, I glimpsed the faintest pinpoint of silver at her throat—some kind of necklace. The silver glow surrounded her whole tiny essence.

I opted for the truth, and using my best Spanish, said, "Your grandson Ricardo robbed my brother and hid the money here. I found it in the cellar." I pulled a single packet of bills from the money belt, probably two thousand dollars. "*Con permiso, señora Tota, quiero darle el dinero.*"

"*Póngalo en la tierra, con las llaves.*" She pointed with the weapon, meaning 'throw it on the ground.'

I threw the packet at her feet. "*Son cientos,*" I said, "*de los Estados Unidos.*" American hundreds.

She reached down and carefully thumbed the stack of bills.

"*¡Ándale, pues!*" She motioned me away with the back of her hand, and I needed no more encouragement. The machine gun swung around, still aimed at me. Holding my ruined finger, I ran zigzag, just in case, with Ricardo's grandmother acting like an elderly hispanic

Annie Oakley. The valium-doped dogs roused enough to yowl a time
or two as I streaked across the pasture, putting distance between me
and grandma Tota, running partly to get away, partly to burn the
adrenaline. As I ran, she emptied the clip of the M3. At what, I don't
know. I was out of range, but I sped up, anyway, despite the sprained
ankle. The hand would need to be looked at, and my dark gray
sweatshirt and bluejeans were a bloody mess, but I had the money
and I definitely hadn't been ID'd.

Stopping at the barbwire gate to rip a bandage from the sleeve of
my shirt, I breathed some of the finest air I'd ever breathed, with a
hint of sage or chamisa, one of those gray-leaved fragrant plants.
Moonlight and stars—those far-away points of light—seemed like
my long-lost friends. Above and beyond the pain, a cosmic surge
overwhelmed me, like the rush I'd felt that night with Aiyah at the
waterfall—an exquisite mixture of excitement, relaxation and pain.
Maybe I *was* cut out to be a thief after all. A nine-fingered one.

I wrapped the hand and crouched beside the fence to wait for Noe.
We'd planned to meet there by the highway after the heist and drive
on to spend the night in Guanajuato, to make sure nobody followed
us back to Charlie and Rosita's house. Noe's part must have gone as
planned, because pretty soon his car slowed down and the passenger
door opened. I jumped up, dizzy from standing too fast, and lurched
at the door, missing it and crashing into the side of the car before
falling into the front seat. The air was cool, but I was soaked with
sweat. Noe drove down the road a piece before pulling over to look at
me, focusing on my bloody shirt, my hand.

"How'd it go?" I mumbled, my hand throbbing like crazy.

He nodded for half a minute then stopped abruptly and rubbed his
thumb and forefinger together, eyebrows arched in a question.

"I got the money." I patted the bulge around my waist.

Noe grinned and drove us toward a hotel and a medic in
Guanajuato.

———

CHAPTER 52
MARIAH

*All of the light areas should fall within
one value range. All of the dark areas
should fall within another.
Make sure the lightest light in the dark
is darker than the darkest dark in the
light, and keep the darkest dark in the
light lighter than the lightest light in
the dark.*

Today we're redoubling our effort to contact Víctor at the country
home where his wife and children live. It's Sunday, and the people of
Zihua are all inside the church as we leave the cluster of tin roofs and
follow the dirt road past the last Pepsi sign into a paradise of flora—
coconut palms and mango trees—with ripe fruit hanging. Glimpses of
la bahía shine through the verdure as we begin to climb on what
promises to be a long and sweaty route.

Gallant George has loaded his backpack with the gifts we bought yesterday for the family—a bottle of Kahlua, an opal necklace, a tiny piñata filled with *dulces*, a leather purse, an embroidered apron, a barette with abalone inlay. I'm wearing my standard clam-diggers and a button-up with pockets. Cindy's in Bermuda shorts and a Hawaiian shirt of George's. He forges ahead, his t-shirt advising us to 'Eat Kelp—Feed the World.' Twice, we take a break and a toke or two, and the morning is all gone when we finally arrive at a village. Our water bottles are exhausted, and so are we.

A procession fills the road ahead with people dressed in black and white, the men with mustachios and hats, the women in black lace shawls. It looks like a silent movie set. We navigate our way around them in technicolor while they ignore us completely.

"Is this just an ordinary Sunday, or is there a celebration?" I ask.

George grins. "Every Sunday is a celebration, because the people don't have to work."

"I bet the women do," Cindy says.

Beyond the village, a lane appears off to the left, and we follow it to a humble home made of wattle-and daub. Everything is lashed together with strips of bark, the palm-thatched roof supported by saplings. The structure looks like something organic, sprouted from a hut-producing rhizome.

Three women graciously welcome us into a kitchen organized around a hearth circle of stones where I see orange coals glowing under the darkened fender of a vintage automobile. The younger daughter flipping tortillas is thin and pretty, in a sober way, dressed in a knee-length skirt and plain white short-sleeved shirt. Her short apron shows signs of a recent encounter with fresh *masa harina*.

I offer my hand to her mother first and then to her, using one of the four Spanish words I know. "*Soy* Mariah."

Her mother shakes hands, but the daughter looks at her hands and then curtsies, "Anita, mucho gusto."

The older sister is seated, or rather reclining. "Gloria, encantada," she waves.

Cindy and George introduce themselves and he asks, "Y Víctor?"

"*No, no está.*" Not here.

"*¿Cuando regrese?*" When does he return?

"*No sé, señor.*" She doesn't know.

George unpacks our gifts and we present them to the women amid squeals and hugs. Gloria, the one confined to a modified chaise lounge, is wearing a peach and beige print dress. Her hair is lighter brown than the others and pulled to either side in braids. Her eyebrows naturally arch high up toward her hairline. Lupe, Víctor's ageless wife, is dressed plainly like her daughter the tortilla flipper, sans apron.

We are expected to eat a simple and delicious meal—squash, frijoles and tortillas, with a salsa that takes the skin off my tongue. I'm still an apprentice pepper-eater, so I put two drops on my beans and stir them up, "Gracias."

Spanish is travelling around the room at a good clip, like a train that has gotten up to speed and has someplace to go. George can almost keep up with Lupe. I don't understand a word, so instead of rolling my 'r's, I concentrate on rolling tortillas with just the right amount of beans and clamp the end between my ring and little fingers to avoid leakage. Cindy is having trouble with hers, though. I can see bean juice dripping from her elbow.

Anita smiles at our ineptness in a good-natured way. Gloria, the older daughter, is more cheerful than Anita—and she's the invalid, sitting in a recliner on wheels. Packed into the tiny kitchen with the rest of us amid hanging braids of garlic and chiles, Gloria seems to have accepted her limitations with amazing grace.

George explains, "Lupe doesn't know when Víctor is coming back. She said we are welcome to stay here and wait for him if you like. We can spend the night here."

Cindy and I look at each other and answer in unison, "Why not?"

"They need some things from the village, and I said we would help them."

"Of course."

Anita is dispatched with funds to get supplies and we pretend to help with cleanup while Lupe efficiently takes care of everything. George leaves to buy a butchered goat. In the garden beside the house I learn the Spanish name for peppermint, *yerba buena*, as well as other names I promptly forget. Lupe has grown the garden mostly for seasonings. There are several kinds of chiles, the fruits both green and red, but I bet they're too spicy for me to touch, much less taste.

Seeing the little herb patch makes my fingers itch to get into the dirt, pull a weed, spread mulch—something. I can hardly stand it, not knowing if and when I'll have my own garden again.

————

With our translator gone on a mission, Gloria entertains us, singing *a capella* folk songs. In the midst of her concert, she shows us characters she's cut from manila file folders and decorated with tempera paint, reminding me of the paper-dolls I played with as a girl. But these are the deluxe, hand-crafted variety, about five inches tall, with felt glued on the back. All the construction must have been done while she reclined in the lounge chair.

A large tan felt board has been attached to the wall beside her to make a stage for the coming drama. She introduces each character in the story with formality as they enter the stage. We first meet Mama and Papa. Then Gloria places a brown triangle, the roof, over them, and a tree beside them to complete the scene. The figures of Gloria, Natán, Anita and little Paulito are introduced in turn, crowding together under the roof that represents the house where we now sit, and I realize that she is dramatizing the story of her family. All have eyes, but no other features on their brown faces.

A purple mountain appears above the roof and to the side. Opposite the mountain, two wavy horizontal lines in brilliant blue— the ocean. Next, Gloria marches out two more brown figures, one with a black hat and no eyes, wearing a frown and shooting a rifle. The other has only eyes, like her family. We learn they are *el halcón* and Lucio Cabañas. She places them on the far side of the mountain. At this point George returns with the goat meat, hangs it on a rack above the fire, and joins us to watch the show.

George says, "Looks like we're going to learn about Víctor and Lupe's son, Natán. He's one of the martyrs of Guererro."

Animated by Gloria, the figure of Natán leaves the family and climbs the mountain. From behind it, Lucio appears and the two greet and make friends. They read from a book Gloria provides. Beside them, she adds a single cut-out of four people who appear to be listening to Lucio. She has given them ears to go with their smiles, but no eyes. The universal sign of justice, a set of scales, is placed above the people.

All this time, Gloria has been humming a soft melody, but it changes to a minor key when *el halcón* appears, followed by a block of gray bodies with faceless heads and rifle barrels pointing. *El halcón* aims his rifle at Lucio and Natán. Natán flops over. Gloria pastes a cross on him and her song becomes haunting.

Now she takes scissors and divides the smiling company of listeners in two. She flies a fat green airplane over the mountain and lands it, picking up half of the company. Then she flies them over to the ocean, and drops them in. They sink beneath the blue waves and the symbol of justice follows them into the water. When I realize I'm seeing a replay of events I'd watched in Blaine's film, and my stomach does flip-flops. It's the same airplane.

Gloria lands the plane and puts white crosses on the men below the ocean, puts a frown on Lucio's face and a smile on *el halcón*. Each member of the family gets a frown. Natán and the other paperdolls with crosses are placed above the mountain—in heaven. The symbol of justice remains beneath the waves.

Gloria sings another lilting song and the show concludes. We applaud and thank our performer. George engages her in Spanish for a minute, then Cindy asks a question.

"George, who is that character with the evil smile and the black hat?"

"That's Ernesto Delgado. He's a hit man for the government," George explains. "*El diablo* is one of his nicknames." I notice Gloria nod and cross herself. Anita and Lupe follow suit.

"Is he real, or is he a supernatural devil?" Cindy poses the question and George has a ready response, surprising me with his clarity, as if practicing his Spanish has awakened a dormant part of him. Prying information out of George when he's high is like shucking an oyster that you have to suck down raw in order to find a pearl. Today, after the long hike, he's a wealth of knowledge.

"*El diablo* is no myth. Not long ago, Cabañas was a teacher in a rural school. The farmers and workers in Guerrero wanted a better education so he organized teachers and became the leader of the socialist students' and peasants' organization, *The Party of the Poor*. The people only wanted fair prices for farmers, fair pay for workers and free speech for all. Natán, represented the coconut growers and helped Cabañas stage a peaceful strike in central Guerrero. Police came to the meeting and shot some of the people, killing three including Natán and wounding several others. *El diablo* was with the policemen."

Watching Gloria's dramatization helped me make a connection with Blaine's journal entry about Natán being killed by *halcones* in 1967. Now George's explanation of the events makes it clear what happened and why Blaine had been interested. Still, it's shocking, and I ask, "The police just shot Lupe's son for making a peaceful protest?"

George gives me a tolerant look "The government here is hard. And the CIA made things worse, training special units of the police and supplying guns. I think that's what your Blaine was looking into."

"Hey, I don't claim Blaine. I'm a free safety . . . But you're right, he kept a journal about it."

"Anyway," he continued, "Cabañas survived and afterward formed the Peasant Brigade of Execution, a group here in Guerrero that fights for justice." Now George turned his head and sucked air through his teeth. "They also rob banks and kidnap people for ransom. You might say Cabañas became an extremist."

"That is so sad." Cindy looks disgusted. "What's with the green airplane?"

George says, "The government uses the Avocado to drop their enemies in the ocean for the sharks to eat."

"That's sick," Cindy says.

I shiver, remembering the line of blindfolded men I watched being loaded into a real airplane, and speculate on who the government might consider an enemy.

"It's lucky that Víctor and Lupe have another son," George says, making a valiant but futile attempt to look on the bright side of the unspeakable outrage. "Paulito is nine, old enough to help with the business. Víctor is a fruit vendor, and Paulito is usually by his side."

How can he be so matter-of-fact when I find the situation so frustrating in so many ways? "Of course, the men go out into the world and the women stay at home." I say, rebelling against the confinement imposed on them, while at the same time, I'm appalled at their complacency with the status quo. "But then, I guess they've never known anything different."

"That's true," George agrees. "Their life is very traditional."

I'm uncomfortable, having a conversation about these women right in front of them—even though they don't understand English—but they don't seem to notice, so I let it go. I've already begun to think about range-of-motion exercises for Gloria, massage and other things I know how to do for her. I may not have enough influence to change the world at large, but, given time, I could definitely change hers.

"It's a tradition, for sure," Cindy says. "They keep everything going. Women are stewards of the blood. Without us, nothing would be possible."

The phrase, "Stewards of the blood," gets my attention, and I give Hannah a pat—my blood.

Now that we've run out of words, I notice the *familia* is preparing to retire for a siesta, so we shut down our conversation and do the same.

———

CHAPTER 53
CJ

*Forget about line at this point and
work on building the form. Keep the
darks and lights separate. Let the
canvas show through some places to
make the painting luminous. Make the
human flesh glow with the color of life.*

I was thankful to have lost only a finger. Although my body ached
in numerous places, over-the-counter drugs took away most of the
pain. My ankle turned black, then purple. My chin was yellowish
with prickly whiskers sticking out of the scab, disturbing enough that
I gave up looking in the mirror for a few days. Shaving, too, for that
matter. But with constant applications of Rosita's all-better salve, my
hand healed in record time. I'd asked the doctor in Guanajuato to
remove the rest of my carpal bone at the joint and use the remaining
skin to make a good covering for the nub, so my hand would look the
same as my Uncle Nel's.

There were loose ends to tie up with Ricardo as well, but the crisis
was over. The money belt became part of my wardrobe, hidden inside
my long shirt tails, and some secretive impulse kept me quiet about
its presence. My plan was to return it to Blaine, but it's funny how
after wearing it a while, I got possessive about the thing, as though its
contents actually belonged to me. Thoughts of easy living snuck in.

Over another gourmet meal with Charlie and Rosita, I parceled out the news from Zihua. "Víctor's planning to give Blaine the entire harvest from his fields to square things up," I said. "He thinks Ricardo sabotaged the Cessna and lured Sergio to be pilot so he'd die when it crashed."

"Whoa!" Charlie leaned back in his chair. "That's a lot to take in."

Then Rosita made the understatement of the year, "This Víctor is a complex character. He seems to have one foot in the light and one in the shadow."

And that pretty well summed it up. While I healed, there was plenty of time to think about light and shadow, good and evil, but there were no easy answers. In art, there can be no light without darkness. I suppose evil is a necessary part of the world. Otherwise we wouldn't know what good is.

One thing's for sure, there was way more to the smuggling business than I'd bargained for. Mortality had always been an abstract concept for me, but my point of view shifted the moment I faced gunfire, and there would be no going back. I'd begun to see life, not as an accumulation of years, but a lease on the future with a limited term. I was tired of sneaking around, and I was desperate to make good use of the time I had left.

I'm a lover, not a fighter, I thought. At least I wanted to be. But the prospect of finding my waterfall mistress was growing more remote with each passing day, and it seemed like I had to work harder to keep the memory of that night alive. Not that my yearning for her had ceased, but there were times when what happened between us seemed like nothing more than a fantasy.

I should've followed Odysseus's example and tied myself to a mast instead of keeping the appointment, but a sexual fantasy is not the same as the real deal. Patrice and I had arranged to meet on Wednesday morning at La Grutta, a local hot spring, so I stashed the money belt in the bottom of a chest in my bedroom and took off on foot. It was a seven or eight kilometer walk to La Grutta, and trickles of sweat had run down my neck and soaked my shirt by the time I arrived, paid, changed into swim trunks and walked down the dirt path to the pool.

No one was around, it being a weekday morning. I was eager to cool off but when I jumped in the waist-deep water, it felt like a warm bath. I passed through an arched tunnel where jewels of opalescent light glowed in the ceiling, and highlights sparkled like polished brass on the liquid blue-green surface of the water. In the most secluded part of the grotto, I found Patrice waiting with reflections rippling over her in waves. I had a fleeting impression she might devour me, like a siren of the swamp.

"For a minute," I gulped, "I thought you hadn't come."

Her chin thrust out and up. "I always come." She stepped forward, entangling me in her tentacles then tightening her grip. I lifted my bandaged right hand clear of the water, bent my knees and sank to meet her, quivering when we touched. She put one hand on my sore chin. I sought her lips and closed my eyes while her other hand went searching and I remembered another lady from another place and time.

Ka-lunk! First the splash, then something struck me on the back below the water line. I jerked around and saw a man standing twenty feet away, grinning. He was bleached, and hairy, and freckled, like my brother. *Damn!* I realized. *It is my brother, throwing rocks.*

"Of all the times to show up," I muttered, but inside I was jumping for joy.

Blaine waved, and Patrice went off screaming a tirade in French, then louder in Spanish, first at him, then at me. My wince turned into a full-on squint until I saw only a fiery essence, spitting sparks that hissed when they hit the water. I'm sure she said things about my mother, my species, and probably the size of my dick, which was rapidly shrinking. She stomped away in chest deep water, elbows flying, making the water sizzle.

Blaine came up beside me to watch her go. "Wow! High-strung, isn't she?"

I watched Patrice splash through the stone arch and disappear, amazed by the transformation she'd undergone.

My brother said, "It may take more than flowers for that one, bro. Jewelry maybe. Say, what happened to your chin? Did she do that to you? . . . And the hand?" He stopped to inspect the bandage taped around my knuckles. "What happened here?"

With my other fist, I swung a roundhouse that connected with the bone in his upper arm.

"Ow!" He winced, backing up a step.

"Where the hell have you been?" I yelled, my heart racing.

Blaine grinned, rubbing his arm. "I heard you came looking for me. After all this time, I thought you'd be glad to see me.".

He gripped my shoulder and I reached out to bear-hug him. "I am, but your timing's the pits."

I stepped back and looked him over. Couldn't say he was tan exactly, more like orange or russet. The sun had brought out pigment in the form of freckles on his face and arms. The beginnings of an afro, bleached almost white, spilled out from under a baseball cap the same ice-blue as his eyes, and a thin blue-green aura surrounded his whole gaunt shape.

"How'd you find me?" I asked.

"Lucky. That Noe fella wasn't at the restaurant, so I was lurking under the arroyo bridge earlier, keeping an eye out. When you walked across it, I followed you here. I had no idea you had a date."

"Look," I said, "There's something I should've told you before you left with the weed. Víctor said not to trust Ricardo with money." I'd been needing to get that off my conscience, thinking it was a big deal. Apparently it wasn't.

He chuffed, "I'll say. The bastard got away with it, didn't he?"

"There's more," I said. "I found out Ricardo sabotaged your plane." For some reason I was hesitant to tell him I had the money-belt, so instead, I quizzed him, "What are you going to do about him?"

"Kill him, most likely."

"Kill him? You're kidding."

Blaine studied the ceiling of the grotto, his cheek twitching. "Depends on what he has to say. I'd like to kill him, but first he has some explaining to do."

I could see he wasn't going to take me seriously, so I changed tactics. "You were supposed to be sick. Victor said you were healing in a cave somewhere."

"After we broke out of the barn, I took Ricardo to a medic. He had acute hepatitis and needed bed rest for a few weeks, so I left him and took off. I wasn't sick, then. It took four or five more days before I got it, then I had to hole up. When he got better, he found me, and we went looking for a plane. Found a free one, courtesy of the Guatemalan government. We've got one more deal going, Cliff. Víctor's giving us his crop."

"Oh crap. You and Ricardo ripped off an airplane?"

"Easy as pie," he said.

"But Ricardo ripped *you* off." I protested, and eased down into the water, neck deep. "I'd be pissed."

"It'll be okay, Cliff. Ricardo and I worked it out. I have to see this through, help him get to the States. He's helping me recover my losses. Then I'm retiring. I love smuggling dope, outwitting the other guys, getting the best deal I can. It's a challenge. But it's no fun to travel when you're broke." He squatted down beside me in the water and the pale blue aura that hovered around him darkened to a dull gray. It felt like he was holding back, not telling the whole story.

"By the way," Blaine said, his voice subdued, "do you have any cash on you?"

"I have a few dollars." I stood and pulled some wet bills out of my jams and handed them over. I couldn't have known he'd hook up with Ricardo again, but I should have known he'd be broke. Blaine unfolded the mess and counted twenty-seven dollars. I felt like running all the way back to the studio. *Time to get out of the water*, I thought.

———

CHAPTER 54
MARIAH

How do you know when the painting is finished? You'll know, when your inner critic stops chattering and your eye is able to move freely over the work without interruption.

Laundry day. Cindy and I have joined Lupe and a dozen village women at the river for a ritual performed the same way for centuries—soap, scrub and rinse. Bubbles drift away in the gentle current, and the ripples of female laughter wash my soul. We've come to help, but I think we're getting in the way instead. After rinsing and wringing, the women carry baskets of wet clothes on their heads in a royal procession. Cindy and I sling our basket between us and clamber up the path with all the dignity we can muster.

Back at the *casita* we find Anita preparing a meal and Gloria practicing scales. Artists at work. They have no advantages in life, yet they exude a natural grace and inner beauty that spills onto whatever they touch. They take note of the leather pouch around my neck and shyly inquire, so I show the girls my opal and point at my belly. They understand I wear the talisman for a special passenger.

Lupe and I are hanging out the laundry when Víctor and Paulito arrive. The Chevy one-ton truck is loaded with bags of onions, and one of the dual tires is shredded, just barely hanging on the rim. Man and boy go to the well and return to the fire with a bucket of water for hand-washing, then lunch is served, and the stalwart family eats without a word or prayer. I wonder if these kind folks are atheist.

My first bite of goat meat taco bites me back with the fierceness of a cornered Chihuahua, but I manage to tame it, throwing down a half-liter of bottled water. Cindy, I notice, has slipped her taco quietly to Paulito, who grins and has no trouble making it disappear. When we've cleared the table, it's siesta time. Chores are suspended, and everyone takes a short holiday. We're clustered in the shade, around the family hearth, seated on empty five-gallon buckets. Lupe serves cinnamon tea and disappears. Gloria, ensconced in her rolling chair, is singing. Paulito strums a three-quarter size guitar in muted accompaniment.

Then Víctor clears his throat and asks me why we came to Zihua. While George interprets, I tell everyone the story about my travels on the Submarine, meeting Blaine in New Orleans, getting pregnant, his plane crashing and me coming here to look for him. I tell them about the film with the two men and the airplane. Then I ask George to find out if Víctor knows anything about Blaine.

After a long consultation in Spanish, George reports, "Blaine is alive and well. He's been with a shaman in the mountains to the north, recovering from an illness. He was investigating *el diablo* Delgado, the man who killed Víctor's son. Sergio Silva and Delgado planned to steal Blaine's plane and trade the marijuana for guns. Ricardo found out and sabotaged the plane, effectively assasinating his brother. Then Ricardo got sick, and later Blaine.

It all makes sense, now. Blaine *did* come to Mexico for another reason besides smuggling. I have a moment of indigestion, whether of food or of facts, I'm not sure, but another swig of water seems to cure it for the time being.

"The struggle is not over," George continues. "Yesterday, someone in a red car shot out a tire on Víctor's truck. He thinks it might have been *el diablo*." Víctor chimed in and George listened intently, then shook his head. "Now he's saying something I don't understand. Something about atonement."

"I was hoping he could lead us to Blaine." I say, getting impatient. "So that's all?"

"Except that he's planning to deliver his onions to Blaine in San Miguel—along with another product."

"When?" I ask, looking back and forth between the men.

"Soon," Víctor interjects, and quickly abandons the scene. Apparently he understands English.

I follow the old patriarch and manage to isolate him beside the little corral where he's feeding two goats branches stolen from an unsuspecting tree. *"Señor,"* I ask, my pulse racing. "Do you mind if I follow you San Miguel?"

"Better you not go."

"Víctor, I have to find Blaine."

Leaving the corral, Víctor walks to the back of his truck and turns around. "Is okay," he says softly. "You wait for me where the highway goes north. Five o'clock. Today. Under the bridge."

I watch the old man pull an aired-up tire from the bed of his truck and set it down beside the rear wheel. With a tire tool, he begins removing the battered tire. I would help. I can change a flat, but I have little experience fixing tires, so I re-join the others and tell Cindy it's time to go.

Coffee is brewed, and George is roused. We ready ourselves and pack what little there is to pack then go in turn to the outhouse. The *familia* is cheerful and loving, giving hugs all around. They are glad, I'm sure, to have their usual sleeping arrangements restored. I double-check my plans with Víctor, then promise Lupe I'll return to Zihua. Gloria accompanies our departure with a folk melody in high soprano, delivered softly, with Hannah following note for note.

I suspect the real reason for my presence here is not locating Blaine but learning how to live. Finding Blaine seems less critical now, and I'm positive that I'll never be with him again. That merman character, though? That's a different story. Maybe he's only a shadow, but he touched me—body and soul—and he writes love poems. Just thinking about him is like going home.

On the hike back to Zihua, Cindy says, "You know Mariah, this is where we follow different paths." I can tell by her serene smile that she's found her own mystery man.

"So, George," I say. "You two have decided to shack up?"

"We like to think of it as 'castle up,' if you please."

"Oh absolutely, I *do* please, and you have all my blessings." I turn to Cindy, noticing her olive skin has already gone deep brown. She's perfectly suited to living on a beach. "I'm going to miss you, though."

The canoe shuttle brings our expedition back to George's beach where I ask the pilot to wait while I gather my stuff and change into my swimsuit. Cindy and George are standing outside.

"You'll come back to visit?" she asks, giving me a hug.

"For sure. You'll hardly know I'm gone."

"Right on!" George approves, and gets his own hug.

I shoulder my bag again and step into the waiting canoe. The water is choppy, and the afternoon shadows are getting longer. This mission feels important. I'm going to get my obligation to Blaine out of the way so I can get on with my life. I wish there was time to get in the water again at the municipal beach, maybe have one more fantasy with the mer-man before leaving Zihua. But there's not. I'll have to hustle.

CHAPTER 55
CJ

*Art provides nourishment for the
people, just as surely as food. First the
artist is fed while producing the work,
then the viewer while appreciating it.
But remember, not everyone will be
hungry for this kind of sustenance.*

Open House Day

On open house day I woke up late, jumped into shorts and shoes
and worked up a good sweat jogging up the hill and back. I arrived at
the house to find no sign of Charlie and Rosita but Juana was there,
dressed in black and white, with stockings and shined leather shoes.
All in all, a different look from when I first saw her cringing in our
doorway—a much better look. Seeing her made me wonder what our
old friend Ramón was up to. *Probably trying to keep his fancy boots
out of the cow pies, the bastard*, I figured.

In the shower, I gave thanks as always for hot water, then scraped off my beard along with some skin. After dressing, I strolled into the kitchen with my face bleeding and found Juana butchering a perfectly ripe papaya. Part crimson lake and part Indian yellow, its waxy color reminded me of a semi-precious stone. The flesh was eminently paintable. And delicious too—sweet and fragrant.

Juana put a piece of paper towel on my bloody chin, then enlisted me to fold napkins, wipe down forks and carry stuff out to the studio. We spread a black cloth on the big table and loaded it with plates and glassware until everything sparkled.

Rosita had left a note, "Please go buy two kilos of cheese for tacos. Take the wagon," so I bounced the Woodie out to the dairy, expecting the worst.

"Oh, it's you again," Patrice greeted me with a flat stare. I'd been hoping she wouldn't be there, or if she was, that she'd forgiven me for what happened at La Grutta. Apparently, no dice.

"Rosita asked me to get two kilos of cheese," I mumbled.

"Oui, of course." She stepped aside for me to enter the premises. "We have three kinds."

"She wants some to grate for tacos," I said.

"The Comté, then. The others are too soft."

Patrice was dressed in a sleeveless blouse, and dark slacks, protected by a heavy white apron, all very businesslike. She hefted a sizeable round of cheese onto a chopping block, then cut off and wrapped two pale yellow chunks that weighed over a kilo apiece. From the corner of my eye, I watched her hands and her mouth, remembering the kiss and looking for the aura I'd seen before, but there was no glow and no color.

I'd paid and turned to leave when the back door of the salesroom opened, and my brother came striding through, all slicked up with shorn hair and a big smile. *I'll be damned*, I thought. Maybe I actually said it.

Blaine looked guilty. "Hey, bro, I need to talk to you."

"I expect so." I hadn't seen him since the grotto incident.

He glanced back at Patrice with a meaningful 'I'll see you later' look and followed me out the door. I tilted my head back toward the shop. "What the hell, Blaine?"

"Oh, you mean Patrice."

"Exactly. Patrice. Have you been here ever since you barged in on us at La Grutta?"

"Yeah, well." Blaine kicked the ground, raising a puff of dust. "When I left the grotto that day, she ambushed me."

"Ambushed?"

"Well, she was hot, and I um. . ." His hands rose from his sides in a helpless gesture.

"You fucked her." I couldn't believe it. "You're still fucking her!" He nodded.

"You son of a bitch. You dick head! You big fucking . . . fuck!" I ran out of words.

"Are you finished?" He asked, blue eyes gazing at me.

"Maybe. Why?" I asked, and walked out of there double-time, releasing a cloud of steam. He'd stolen my date, right when things were getting interesting.

Blaine dogged me all the way to the the Woodie and leaned against the door, blocking my way. "Look, Cliff, I need you to help me get a plane in the air."

I stared him down. The thought of climbing into another airplane nearly brought my breakfast up in my throat. "The last thing I want, Blaine, is to get wrapped up in some small-time Mexican civil war. Haven't you learned your lesson?"

"This is my last trip, honest." He crossed his heart.

"Did you know Víctor stuffed those bags with Johnsongrass?"

"Look, I hate this business," he admitted.

"I thought you loved it."

He winced, then modified the statement, "It's love-hate."

"Why do it, then?" I asked, reaching for the door handle.

"To replace the Cessna and pay off the place in Arkansas," Blaine said, pressing against the door, holding it shut. "Víctor harvested the rest of his crop and Ricardo flew the old C47 we stole in Guatemala to the Silva hacienda."

All I need, I thought, *is another dope deal, right in the middle of my debut as an artist.*

"When do you fly?" I asked, shoulder to shoulder with him.

"Tonight."

"Tonight's the open house at Charlie's studio. I have to be there." I jerked the door open, put the bundle of cheese on the passenger seat and sat down to drive.

Through the open window, Blaine said, "Afterward, then, around midnight. At the Silva place."

I peeled out and drove away without a word, leaving him standing there.

————

CHAPTER 56
CJ

Ability doesn't affect the experience of
making art, only the communicability
of the work. In addition to practicing
self-expression, a skilled artist must
develop a visual language that
resonates with the viewer.

The Open House

I left the dairy and stopped at Los Nopales to check with Noe
before heading back to the studio. He handed me a note saying there
was no word yet from the girl we met in Zihua. I could've kicked
myself for not getting her name. All I had was a tantalizing memory
of her eyes and skin, the way she fit into her swimsuit, and a general
feeling of affinity.

I looked up from the note, and Noe was giggling, miming an
hourglass figure.

"Okay, Noe." He was as trustworthy a sidekick as anyone could
ask for, but sometimes he got under my skin. "The truth is, I'm
looking forward to seeing her again. I like her."

His head bobbed, his eyes went out of focus and he pounded his
heart, signaling he liked her too.

"I'm meeting Blaine at the hacienda tonight after the show," I said. "You might want to stick around."

He nodded vigorously then went back to his post as valet at the restaurant. At the house, I fed Calico, ate a cheese sandwich and occupied myself for a while grating two kilos of Comté for tacos. It was difficult, but I managed left-handed, making good use of my right elbow and forearm to stabilize the grater. After that, I went to help Juana in the studio, cleaning up trash cans and banging dirt from the fiber doormats.

The cellist arrived and began tuning up. Noe came, starched and spiffed, and assumed his station outside the door to the street while I tuned up his guitar. He couldn't hear a thing, but if his instrument was in tune he played like a maestro. At the last minute, Rosita and Charlie rushed in the studio like a gale wind and swept me into the house. She helped me assemble the tuxedo, doing things with the cufflinks and tie that I couldn't have managed by myself, even with two working hands. We got the cummerbund wrapped around my waist, so you'd never know there was a money-belt underneath. It felt awkward, but I wasn't comfortable leaving Blaine's money unattended. Rosita never said anything about it.

My role for the first hour of the event was greeting guests at the front door while Noe parked cars. People came dressed in a variety of finery, with Mexican wedding shirts, tuxedos and short black dresses in abundance. Everyone seemed at ease, something I couldn't claim. My jacket smelled like chemicals, the shirt was stiff with starch, and my pants rode high in the crotch. Maybe alcohol was their secret.

I expected it to be a long night, with the reception lasting until eleven or after, followed by a rendezvous with Blaine at the Silva place, but that first hour passed quickly. To begin the second hour, Noe switched from parking cars to making music with the cellist. His twelve-string rounded out the sound and quickened the pace when the duet launched into *Malagueña*—one of my favorites—stirring up a plaintive but arousing vibe.

When I went to claim a cup of punch, Charlie spotted me and waved me over. He was talking to a broad-shouldered, round-backed man with a flat-top haircut and a bulging six-foot frame stuffed into a blue blazer. He looked Mexican in a European kind of way and spoke with a harsh Chicago accent. I knew I'd seen him before, but couldn't imagine where.

"We sacrifice, maybe one, maybe five, to make it better for a hundred, a thousand, maybe millions," he was saying. "It's a good trade, don't you think?"

Charlie replied, "I suppose so, unless you are one of the five."

"But it's necessary. The revolutions in Mexico will never succeed. Positive changes need to come from inside the established order."

"Maybe changes do come that way, but they don't come fast enough. Someone has to push."

"These agitators make changes for the worse. Ask the French. Their revolution brought Napoleon—with no good end, right?"

"But the students," Charlie protested.

"They have guns."

"No bazookas. No machine guns. No airplanes."

"The society must be protected. The common people."

"The students are common people." Charlie had an earnest look, fueled by the red wine he'd been sampling.

"No, they are intellectuals. They are elites. Not common people." The guy was trying to keep the upper hand, making an argument I'd heard before, but didn't buy. "Protesters interfere with business, with commerce," he went on. "We should drop them all in the lake, fucking communists."

"They just want the wealth to be shared," Charlie said. "The poor people are suffering."

"The poor always suffer."

Like most people, I guess, I had no real understanding of economics or politics. I was trying to keep an open mind, but this guy sounded like a politician to me, with an answer for everything. No heart, though. I don't know where he got off talking about poor people like that.

I wouldn't have known what to say to him, but Charlie had an answer, "The poor suffer at the hands of the rich and powerful. It's what makes them poor."

"You should be better informed." The man turned away and almost bumped into to me. "Ah, the young master. I want to talk with you about some paintings in the little room."

"Okay," I nodded, stunned by his rude words 'You should be better informed.' As I turned away, Charlie caught my eye and patted his ribcage, then raised his eyebrows for some reason, trying to tell me something. I didn't get it, but I obliged the man by giving him a tour of my paintings.

He stood in the exact center of the enclosed space and spoke in a conspirational tone, "I haven't seen your work before."

With limited elbow room, I circled, playing it cool. "This is my first show here. Rosita calls me an emerging artist."

"I expect you will do well, especially with the figurative work. You have a special touch with the nude. These women in your paintings look freshly fucked. I guess artists get fringe benefits." He sidled up to me, licked his lips and said, "I'd like to make an offer on one of your pieces."

"Which one?" My gut rebelled, and it was all I could do to steady my voice and keep from backing away.

There was something weird about the guy—maybe the big pupils, kind of sparkly, or the hair, waxed and combed straight up— something familiar. I kept thinking I should know him. He looked around, then strode up to a painting I'd done of Rosita, checked to see if we were alone and made his offer—one-half the marked price.

"I'll give you cash," he whispered, "You won't have to give the MacRaes a cut."

It was a cheap low-ball offer and a shitty thing for him to do, but I considered taking it. It was my first opportunity to make a sale, and I craved earning my own livelihood.

I blinked. He didn't, and my eyes wandered to the doorway just as Rosita walked by. She waved, jarring my conscience awake.

Just then, two women entered the room, holding glasses of red wine and chatting about Noe's proficiency on the guitar. They began to inspect each painting, taking their time. They were thirty-ish, one a short, rounded brunette, encased in dark satin and dangling jewelry. The other was taller, strawberry blond with a Mia Farrow haircut, wearing a gray knit dress. Both wore heels, making their calf muscles bulge.

After circling the room, the women came up to us. The one with jewelry focused on creepy-eyes. "Excuse me, I'd like to buy some paintings. Are you the artist?"

The man pointed at me.

"I'm CJ MacRae." I swallowed and took the plunge. "I'm the artist." All at once, my fingernails had become very interesting and I inspected them closely for pieces of dried oil paint.

She looked me over. "Well, you do good work for such a young man."

I stood up straight and met her eyes. "Thank you." *What else was there to say?* The compliment felt good, but how was I to know if she was qualified to judge my work. I couldn't tell if my paintings were any good or not. But then, I wasn't qualified to judge her judgment, either. *Go with the flow*, I thought.

"How long have you been an artist?" she asked.

"All my life." I smiled, trying out the chit-chat thing.

She lead me on a circle of the room, pointing out the paintings she wanted to buy while I followed her in a daze.

"That one." She indicated my still life of peaches in a blue bowl before striding across the room and touching a frame. "This one and also . . . that one. I want to take them home in my suitcase. Is that permitted before the doors close on the show? We're flying to Santa Barbara in the morning and we can't stay up too late tonight."

I took two nudes and a still life off the wall and we found Rosita at the sales desk. The women said I'd captured the light in those paintings, but I really hadn't captured a thing. I remembered capturing lightening bugs once or twice, and there was that armadillo I caught by the tail one night at the dude ranch . . . No, I hadn't caught anything. It was the other way around. Oil painting had captured *me*—so much so that I was starting to have notions about staying in San Miguel and skipping out on school in the fall. I looked around the room at finely dressed folk, fine food, good music, and thought, *Painting is what I'm meant to do.*

I remembered to thank my first customers before returning to the little room where the creep waited. No question the guy was jerking me around. I'd already lowered my prices to rock-bottom and taking money 'under the table' wasn't fair to my mentors. Besides, I'd just sold three paintings.

"You made a good sale." He eyed the bandage on my hand.

"Thanks, I'm amazed."

"About my offer?" He pointed to the little nude he'd selected.

"Sorry," I said. "The price stands."

He marched over to the painting. "Tell you what, I'll take it at twenty percent off the marked price."

It was the voice that finally gave him away. I'd heard it at the car rental agency in Acapulco. Same guy. And at the airport, he was the guy with a flashlight who directed planes to park. *What the hell?* I gave him a squint-eyed glance and the whole room went dark, him included. *Trust the process*, I told myself, then focused high on his forehead and took a deep breath.

I said, "I don't think so."

He shrugged. The corners of his mouth turned down and he murmured, "It's your loss." As he made his move toward the door, something bulged under the left arm of his jacket. That's what Charlie had been trying to tell me—the guy was packing a pistol.

He turned, a hand on the door jamb. "By the way, Cliff, how's your brother Blaine? Tell him I've been away for a few days. Had to go to a funeral in the States. Tell him Delgado is back. I'd like to trade a few pounds of coke for some guns. Maybe our boy Ricardo can help. He likes to kill commies." Then he was gone.

Shit! I froze, blown away by the fact he knew my real name. It felt like something evil had climbed up in my underwear and squeezed hard. By the time I recovered my wits enough to go look for him, he was gone. But to be honest, I hadn't tried to catch him. And to be realistic, I couldn't have caught anybody in my shiny leather-soled shoes, even if I'd wanted to. I guess the gun had me a little scared, too.

In the garden, the sound of distant bells punctuated the stillness, promising peace, but my inner state was in turmoil. I needed to tell Blaine about Delgado as soon as possible. Rosita was going out the door as I went in. She handed me a wad of cash and kissed me on the cheek. "Congratulations, CJ, on the beginning of a lucrative career. We just sold four more of your paintings. But excuse me, I have to get some wine from the kitchen. I'll be back in a minute."

"Okay, thanks." I longed for a joint but grabbed a glass and poured myself a whiskey instead . . . and I don't drink whiskey.

———

CHAPTER 57
CJ

*A painter leads the eye of the viewer
through a composition using
directional strokes and trails of light,
ultimately arriving at a center of
interest where the eye will linger.*

I made the rounds with the guests in the studio, nursing my drink and discussing art while the music and other dramas played out around me, so it was maybe half an hour before I noticed that Rosita hadn't returned. Breaking in on Charlie holding court with a handful of guests, I said, "I'm going to look for Rosita."

He nodded and I left, catching Noe's eye as I went out the door. Thankful for the relative silence, I stopped a minute by the fountain to admire the stars and with a touch of envy, avoided a couple necking on the bench. Calico met me at the kitchen door but refused to come inside. Two bottles of rosé sweated on the counter where Rosita must have left them. I stood still, listening to the quiet house. Then someone grabbed my elbows and jerked them behind my back.

"Don't say a word. I have Rosita," I heard at my left shoulder and something hard jammed into my ribs.

I kept my mouth shut.

"Get the jacket off." *That voice is familiar*, I thought, and when he released my arms, I slid the jacket off one arm, jerked my elbow back and stomped his instep. It was a good move, one that I'd used effectively on some of the meaner basketball players during close games. It didn't work. He shoved. I lurched forward and ricocheted off the counter, upsetting a wine bottle and shattering the glass.

"Next time I'll shoot," the creep hissed in my ear, poking my ribs with the revolver. He jerked my arms behind me again and wrapped tape around my wrists and forearms. The cummerbund and money belt vanished. How he managed it with only two hands, I don't know. I was wrestling an octopus.

He grunted, "Move it. Now."

I moved it, and found Rosita trussed up on the floor by the front door. The creep reached down and slit the strap binding her feet. "Get up."

She stood abruptly, looked at me and gave a slight shake of her head.

"Out." He thrust an arm at the entrance.

She fumbled the door open and went out. I followed, and the door shut behind us.

By the curb a familiar maroon '67 Dodge Dart sat idling with the passenger door open and front seat tilted forward.

"Get in," the voice rasped. Rosita got in and slid across the back seat. I got in after her. The guy took the shotgun seat and shut the door. I recognized the driver.

"Ramón, you sorry piece of shit," I shouted, and got clubbed on the head for my effort.

The car took off at a moderate speed. The creep had a revolver pointing at my face. I looked over at Rosita and realized once again how beautiful she was. Steady, competent eyes looked back at me. Reassuring.

When Ramón turned onto the highway, I had a minute to think about where we were going . . . and about the 'disappearances,' when people are loaded on an airplane and dropped in the Pacific. Maybe Rosita and I were destined to be shark bait. *But why us?* I wondered. I tried to get my hands worked around so I could loosen her bindings, but it was no use. Ten minutes later we were parking in the driveway at the Silva place.

The voice turned to syrup. "Cliff, you're going to keep your friend Ricardo company while I do business with Blaine tonight. You're going to be . . . how shall I say this? . . . one of my bargaining chips. I suggest you say a prayer that you're still alive. If all goes well, you may stay that way."

He and Ramón marched us through the front hall and straight to the cellar door. They stopped to wrap tape around my legs, then Ramón pushed me with his boot, and I tumbled down the steps like a lop-sided bowling ball, cracking knees and elbows, trying to keep my head tucked. I rolled against the far wall and the door slammed. A narrow beam of light shone under it, giving body to a world of shadow.

I wished the creepy-eyed bastard hadn't separated me from Rosita, and worried what he had in mind for her. I hoped Noe brought Charlie in a hurry.

"¿Quién es?" I heard.

"Ricardo?"

"Clifí. I am here." He was only a voice on the floor opposite me. "You have a cigarette?"

"I don't smoke," I hissed. "What the hell have you done, Ricardo?"

In a loud whisper, he said, "I don't plan this. I know what you think."

"No, you don't know what I think." My knees throbbed and my shoulders were being gradually dislocated by the tape job, but from what I could see, he was in worse shape than I was, with one of his eyes half-shut.

"Who *is* that creep that threw me in here?"

"Ramón?"

"No, the other creep, Delgado. He's CIA, isn't he?" Impatient, I scooched closer to hear him better.

"No . . . eggs."

"Eggs?"

"*El diablo* works no more for the *Cia,*" Ricardo said. "Works with Sergio. Supplies weapons for the bastard *halcones*. But Sergio is no more." I'd been slow on the uptake. Way too slow. The creep who'd been dogging me since I first arrived in Mexico had been in on the hijacking all along.

"What's he want with us?" I asked.

"The airplane, the *mota*, the money, our life. Everything." He hesitated. "I bring the big airplane from Guatemala with Belín, but he goes to his girlfriend and *el diablo* catches me here at my house. I have no *mota* and no money, so he beats me and puts me here."

"Is anybody with him?"

"Only fucking Ramón."

"Ricardo. About those kilos in the Cessna? Víctor switched the *mota* for Johnsongrass."

"*Es verdad*, he admitted. "The harvest was little. Too early. I say to tío Víctor, 'Use hay, fill the kilos. Put *la mota* on the top, so the bags look okay.'"

"That's fucked up," I said, thinking, *Rat number one just confessed.*

"Yes. But I discover my brother plans taking the Cessna, so I trick him."

"So you *let* Sergio steal the airplane full of hay?"

"Yes, of course," he admitted, and his bright silver aura began to dim.

"How'd you know Sergio wouldn't kill you and Blaine?"

"Is a risk, no? But this is his house. The pig no shits where he sleeps, *verdad*?"

It took a minute to sink in. It wasn't likely Sergio would just fly off and leave a crime scene at his own house. He would have planned to take care of loose ends like Blaine and Ricardo when he came home. And when he didn't come, that had left Ramón hanging, without further instructions about his prisoners. That's why Blaine was still alive.

I craved another shot of whiskey, a joint, anything to take me away from the whole scenario, not to mention the pain. But no. My only resource was Ricardo, a beat-up con man who'd sabotaged Blaine's airplane and taken his money. And I couldn't confront him about the receipt he'd signed from *Servicios Aviones* without giving away the fact that I'd been in that cellar before, taking back what he took from Blaine.

I looked into the dark pit of his soul and said, "You killed your brother."

"Well, the airplane kills him, but I kill the airplane."

So he was the saboteur, I concluded, *rat number two*, and went for a strike-out. "What about the money Blaine gave you for the *mota*?"

"Sergio takes the money," he said, "but he keeps it here in *la bodega*. We get loose, get the money, then we go north with Belín, no?"

I knew there was no money in the cellar because I'd stolen it and then the creep Delgado had stolen it from me. But I didn't care anymore. Like Charlie always said, freedom's a tricky thing. After carrying my brother's money for a few days, it had started to feel like mine. I'd begun to daydream about ways to spend it. Ways to improve my life. Things I could buy. That money had the power to conquer me.

With the belt gone from around my waist, I felt lighter, glad to be rid of it, actually. My eyes shut of their own accord and my mind floated free, travelling on the dim shafts of light that filtered into the cellar through the floorboards above. *Save Rosita*, I swore, *and find some relief.*

> The sharp odor of cheese permeates the atmosphere. Naked flesh, clammy with sweat. The woman's back is arched. She spins around. Patrice. Long hair falls down over me, shutting out the light. I will myself somewhere else. Anywhere.

I came to, on the brink of vomiting, and Ricardo was still yammering on, "I have a plan, Clifí, but the plan goes bad when I come here with your brother in the Cessna." He held up three fingers I could barely see. "One, I plan Delgado dies with Sergio when the airplane crashes, but the plan doesn't work. Another man goes to die in his place. Two, Ramón, *el chingado*, helps Delgado put me here in the cellar with *don* Belín when we bring the Cessna here. Gives us drugs, so we sleep. Three, I am too sick to do nothing." He paused to take a breath before adding, "Now is one too much times I sit here in this damn *bodega*."

"So, how do we get out of here?" I asked, knowing it wouldn't be easy.

"We need the key, Clifí."

I figured the keys were gone from the hiding place where I'd left them weeks before. I couldn't have reached the loose brick, anyway, taped up like I was. And Ricardo was in no shape to help. Surely Charlie and Noe would show up soon. I couldn't tolerate Rosita getting hurt.

"Would Carlota help?" I asked, remembering her fierceness and thinking she might be our last resort. "Maybe she could bring the cavalry to our rescue."

"*Es posible.* Maybe you make a noise," Ricardo suggested.

With nothing else to use for a noisemaker, I hollered myself hoarse, hoping Tota would hear us and do something besides shoot us. There was no response, but the yelling took my mind off the pain in my shoulders for a while.

"Clifí," my cellmate rasped. "Now we kill Delgado."

"Sure thing, Ricardo, but how?"

"Maybe we have help from Víctor. He comes tonight with the *mota.* And your brother comes. Tonight, we fly to Texas."

"What time is it?" I asked, my voice almost gone.

"Twelve, maybe. Belín comes soon."

We could hear voices upstairs. One sounded like Charlie, making a frontal attack, a verbal one, but I couldn't understand what he was saying. Another voice yelled back. There were sounds of a scuffle, bumps and knocks on the floor. Then I heard a shot and Rosita screamed.

———

CHAPTER 58
MARIAH

*With each stroke you take a risk. Fear
may build up and effectively prevent
forward progress, so just remember
you are doing what you love and make
that stroke. You'll find it gets easier
with time.*

It *can* be done—lose a damp swimsuit and gain a pair of pants
without losing your shirt—even inside a VW bug, all while avoiding
the stick shift and the casual voyeur. I'm parked under the bridge
where I can keep an eye on the road and watch for Víctor. *Now, if I
can keep up with that truck*, I'm thinking, as the one-ton flies past at
full throttle, piled high with bags of yellow onions. No evidence of
Acapulco gold.

The Beetle strains in third gear until I intercept the truck, then with
full tank of gas and Cindy's Creedence Clearwater Revival tape to
keep me company, I settle into the rhythm of the road. I know it's
stupid to go blindly into danger like this, but I need to put Blaine
behind me, and this is the only way I know to find him. For now, the
music helps me keep a distance from the matters at hand. It feels
strange, though, driving without Cindy, my intrepid co-pilot. *Good
Golly Miss Molly* is her favorite song.

Night falls, and our headlights cut a meager swath through the surrounding wilderness. I shift into second gear on some of the grades, and slow down to less than twenty miles per hour. Víctor's truck is a turtle going uphill. I hope nothing big comes our way on this narrow blacktop. There'd be no room to pass.

But nothing happens. We make one stop for gas, then hours later, around midnight, Víctor stops at a gate and waits for me to park Betelgeuse and get in the truck.

"*Silencio*," He whispers, his finger to his lips, and with the headlights off, we wobble through a pasture and around a barn. Ahead is a cluster of buildings on a low rise, dark except for a glow on the far side. Víctor makes a right-angle turn and kills the motor, then unscrews the interior light before opening his door.

Beside us a dark shape looms, steep on one end and tapered at the other, like the Rock of Gibraltar. I realize it's something man-made, draped with heavy fabric. Reminds me of dust covers on furniture, only huge in scale. Ahead, dogs have sounded the alert, one with a deep bark and one howling like a coyote.

We're creeping around a low outbuilding when a rigid body slams against my back and a hand goes over my mouth. Tucking my chin, I grab the wrist and forearm with both hands, shift my feet and drop my head to the ground, all a fluid, practiced move. Keeping my butt high, I yank his arm down and twist my head to the side. My opponent flips over my shoulder and lands on his back, the breath knocked out of him.

It worked. The judo throw worked! I truly *am* a free safety! *Good thing he wasn't any bigger.* Víctor is beside me now, whispering rapidly in Spanish, producing a wad of baling twine from his pocket. I help him roll the lightweight man onto his stomach, and we quickly tie his hands and feet. Then hands to feet. The dogs have calmed a bit, but I can hear someone yelling faintly.

Víctor cuts a gag from the man's shirt and secures it with another piece of twine. Finding the back door of the house unlocked, he motions me inside where I hear a man and woman arguing. A gunshot rips the air and Víctor and I dive through separate doorways. My heart pounds and I force myself to take deep breaths, wondering if Blaine is somewhere in the house. *I hope so. We need help.*

"Charlie!" A woman screams. Heavy footsteps run toward us. I shrink back into the darkness and see a fleeting shape pass. The back door slams as the man leaves and we peek out of our holes, like mice, to see if the coast is clear. It wasn't Blaine that ran by, I'm sure of that, the guy was too bulky. In another room, a woman is speaking softly, accompanied by muffled bumps.

Víctor motions for me to stay back and edges down the hall with his knife in front of him, tracking the fresh spatters of blood on the floor. Looks like the man who ran past us was wounded, whoever he was. I follow Víctor, despite his instructions. In the main room, a woman is kneeling on the floor, bent over a gray-haired man, holding his head. His eyes are closed. There's a big automatic pistol on the floor beside him.

The woman looks up as we approach, and someone jumps into our path, crouched low and pointing a finger at us. "Stop!" he yells, in a strange voice. We both stop, put our hands up. But he's not pointing a finger. It's another pistol.

Then he recognizes us and grins, letting the weapon drop to his side. It's Noe, the gold-toothed guy who was with my swimming partner in Zihuatanejo.

"Please help me get Charlie to the car, "The woman pleads, "It's his heart."

Noe picks up the man's gun and heads for the door. Víctor rushes to help the man to his feet.

Outside, Noe is looking around corners, both guns ready, while Víctor helps the heart-attack victim into the back of a surfer wagon. He has a brief exchange with the wife and hands her the big automatic before she takes the wheel.

"I need to get him to the hospital," she says, and drives away.

Víctor turns toward us and says, "Noe."

"Papá," Noe squawks, holstering the gun and bending forward into a formal bow. They have a rapid conversation in Spanish that I can't hope to understand with Noe hacking out the words. Víctor turns to me. "We have danger of the running man. He is wounded in the leg. Noe thinks he goes inside."

"We should split up," I suggest. "There are two of them."

Noe nods.

Víctor pauses on the steps at the entrance, hunting knife in hand, the picture of a freedom fighter from the revolution. Chest out, shoulders straight, he points at Noe and me. "You go in back, look for Ramón. I go for *el diablo*."

Noe and I race around the side of the house at full tilt. He goes in the back door first, crouching low, and runs down the hall. In in the main living room, we find Víctor and a gunman in a standoff. It's like an old western, except Víctor's sidearm is a knife. He's holding it beside his ear, blade between thumb and forefinger, pointed at his opponent. I recognize the guy from the film with the green airplane, the one who lists to one side. The one who makes people disappear.

Noe draws a bead on the gunman, croaks, "*Halcón*," and fires, missing his target.

The man turns and snaps off a shot, hitting Noe in the arm, then a racket in the hallway distracts the shooter for a split second. He turns and plugs Víctor in the chest as the old man's hand comes forward in a perfect arc. The knife floats through the air, end over end, and silently lodged in the shooter's neck. Blood gushes. *El diablo* grabs at the knife in his neck, and drops to his knees, then melts into the floor, his big revolver clattering beside him. Noe lurches for it. Another man races for the gun, too, and I tackle him from behind then sit on him while Noe points two guns at the man's face. It's the same guy Víctor and I'd tied up earlier.

A high-pitched keening comes from the corner of the room where Víctor fell. A tiny woman wearing a black *rebozo* cradles his head. When I reach them, the man isn't breathing. Noe screams, "*La llave*," making a gargling sound, and twists his hand like he's holding a key. He points both pistols at the old woman with Víctor.

I look into her empty eyes and repeat the words, "*La llave*." From her dress, she produces a ring with two old-fashioned keys. By this time the room is quiet, and we can hear a muffled voice in the hallway where the racket came from earlier, before the last gunshot. I take the keys to the first door and yell, "Blaine! Are you in there?"

"His brother," comes an answer. "Get me out of here."

———————

CHAPTER 59
CJ

In the foreground, shadows are darker,
the lit parts are lighter and peripheral
shapes in the foreground are seen as
soft-edged accents, while at the center
of action the subject becomes crisp and
clear.

When a gunshot sounded above us and Rosita screamed, I began rubbing my wrists furiously against the wall. Someone ran across the floor upstairs and I strained to hear the broken words. The gray tape, some kind of tough industrial stuff, finally yielded, and I yanked it off and freed Ricardo.

"We need the key," he insisted, so I allowed him to direct me into the corner and gave him a boost to look in the hidey-hole.

When I lifted him up, the pain hit me like a body-slam. Stitches in my hand had broken open, my knees throbbed, and my shoulders were in agony. Ricardo tossed me the brick and felt around the stash but found no key. I let the deflated man slump to the floor, clinched my teeth and charged up the steps, brick in hand, trying to outrun the pain.

I heard Noe yell, then a single gunshot from a pistol, followed by a louder shot. I slammed the brick on the door latch with all my strength. And again. There was another shot. I banging brick on metal until the soft clay disintegrated in my hand and I crumpled on the landing, defeated.

A high-pitched keening filled the silence, as if coming from the stone walls themselves. Outside the door a woman shouted, "Blaine."

I yelled, "His brother. Get me out of here!"

I stood while a key rattled in the lock and the door swung open, blinding me with light. The apparition standing *contre-jour* might have been an angel. That's what I thought at first, but then I recognized the hazel eyes from the beach in Zihuatanejo. There were tears on her cheek.

"Víctor's dead."

I scanned the room, saw the old man on the floor, and my heart dropped out of my chest.

"Oh no."

The tiny lady who held Víctor's head was emitting a sound like coyotes on the prowl. It was Tota, the one who'd shot off my finger. I looked back at my rescuer. She looked at my maimed hand, at my face. *No makeup,* I thought. *Nice.*

"I'm CJ," I rasped, with what was left of my voice.

"Mariah," the angel nodded, and then reached out to straighten my bow tie.

"Thanks," I rasped, and staggered into the dining room with one question on my mind, *How can a person feel so good and so bad at the same time?*

Noe passed me a bottle of aspirin and I swallowed four. He had a bloody bandage on his arm, but otherwise appeared okay. He pointed at the other man on the floor and gargled, *"el halcón."*

I took a long look at the man with the knife in his neck, the one who'd been stalking me for weeks. *El diablo's* eyes were no longer creepy. Next, I considered his accomplice, Ramón, tied up in a chair, and resisted the impulse to go kick him in the nuts.

"Rosita?" I asked the air, wondering what had happened to her.

"At the hospital," Mariah said. "She's okay. Her husband had a heart attack."

"Charlie!" I whispered. *A mild heart attack*, I prayed miserably, not knowing if there even *was* such a thing. The place had gone silent. The odor of gunpowder lingered, obscuring the lemony, piney scent that I remembered from my first time in that room. I stared at Mariah.

She stared at me. "Where's Blaine?"

I scanned the room, half expecting him to be standing in a corner somewhere.

The electric chandelier twinkled above, as before. The brass vessels still sat on the mission style sideboard. The white tablecloth remained undisturbed on the heavy dining table. Tota was quiet. Noe unwrapped a red cummerbund from around his waist and ceremonially draped it around Víctor's neck. Then he crossed himself, mumbled a brief prayer for the newfound father he'd just lost and picked up the two pistols again. Everyone took deep breaths and looked around.

We heard footsteps on the porch and Noe aimed both guns that way. The front door burst open, and Blaine strode in with a gun of his own, hollering, "What the hell is going on here?"

He stopped to take stock of the situation. Two men lying on the floor, silent and bloody, an old lady grieving over one of them. Ramón, tied in the chair. Noe, pointing two pistols at him, a big revolver in one hand and a smaller automatic in the other, while blood dripped from a wound in his arm. Ricardo, lying on a bench blowing a smoke ring at the ceiling. Me, standing beside Mariah.

Patrice appeared from nowhere and scurried up behind Blaine, rubbernecking the scene as he lowered the automatic.

"Looks like the whole gang showed up." He said. Then he recognized the body of the old man. "Oh no."

I'd completely changed my mind about Víctor since our first meeting. He was an honorable man. Had been, dammit. I took in his body and blood-soaked chest. The face that always appeared angry, now had a satisfied look. Contented, as though he'd reached his goal. But his eyes were glass. Tears flooded my cheeks. Mariah gently closed Víctor's eyes and squeezed my hand.

Blaine wandered over to the dead *halcón*, studied his face and said, "You lose, Delgado." After a minute, Blaine pulled me aside.

"C'mon Cliff, I need you to help load the plane. We're flying to Texas tonight."

"You're kidding," I said, choking on the words, my throat raw. "I've got people to see about."

I knew his plan but wasn't buying it—I had one of my own. Besides, I figured he should have gotten out of the smuggling business while the getting was good. My mind was on Charlie, but I struggled between the impulse to help my brother and the obligation I felt toward Charlie and Rosita. Not to mention Mariah.

"Nope, I'm not kidding," Blaine said. "Ricardo's too messed up, and this can't wait. I need you."

I verified Ricardo's condition with a glance. He was sprawled on the bench by the dining room table, looking ghastly, with his eyes closed and a cigarette smoldering on the floor. Still, I argued my case. "Noe found some speed in the medicine cabinet. Let's dose Ricardo with it, wake him up."

"Okay, give it a try," Blaine said. "That gooney-bird needs a co-pilot."

Patrice was not happy being ignored. While I stood talking with my brother, she wiggled her way to his side and clung to his arm. I had a moment of nausea, wondering how I'd ever been attracted to her. I stretched my arms above my head and breathed deep, trying to regain the use of my shoulders. My guts churned at the carnage in the room but settled a bit when I focused on Mariah. *Some kind of magic,* I guessed.

She stepped up to face us and Blaine stammered, "Mariah! I uh . . ."

"I found you, and you're alive," she said. "I'm pregnant. I have no expectations. Her name is Hannah. Oh, and I have your cartridge box in Texas. Here's your film." She handed him a film reel and turned to Noe. "Let's leave these brothers to do their thing and go see about your friend with the heart attack. I have a car."

Blaine and I watched her go. "Damn!" he said, shaking his head. *My thoughts, exactly.*

———

CHAPTER 60
MARIAH

*You'll want to save the highlights for
last. Add a dash of pure color to the
white and place it carefully. It is the
breath of life, making an eye sparkle or
a river glint.*

Everyone involved at the hacienda has a reason to steer clear of
the authorities, so the police have not been called about the double
homicide. I hate that I couldn't save Víctor—it all happened too fast.
After throwing up my guts in the bathroom, I feel as limp as the
washrag I used to wipe my face. The family . . . oh my God! Lupe,
Gloria, Anita and Paulito. Grief has a grip on my heart.

But I have no time to linger over consequences. Noe, the little deaf
guy, has just come in the front door, needing attention. While I'm
patching up his wounded bicep, he writes a note, asking me to stick
around a bit longer and help wrap things up. Handing me an aspirin
bottle to pass around, he goes to makes a pot of coffee. Blaine's
current flame (and driver) makes her exit with a flounce and a pout,
but no more ado. Blaine throws Ramón in the cellar, locks the door
and we survivors gather for a quick parley.

"This makes twice that Ramón's turned on us," Blaine says, glaring at the cellar door.

"We can't just leave him locked up," I protest.

"He'll keep down there for the time being, until we figure out what to do with him. We need to get this place cleaned up."

So, we do, working the mops and rags, spreading pine-scented cleaner wherever blood was spilled. Breakage is swept away, and the interior is brought to a tentative equilibrium. Now that I've told Blaine what's what, I feel liberated. Strange, I don't even mind following his instructions. Clean-up chores are my first priority, but soon I'm pressed into service outside. The night is cool and quiet, so someone must have fed the dogs.

El diablo's red Dodge is parked in the hacienda driveway. I guess Rosita will have to figure out how to get rid of it. She'll also have to decide what to do about Ramón. The unanimous opinion is that he could stand to spend at least one night in the cellar, and I have no objection, considering I've already had to subdue the guy twice now, using my free safety skills.

Ricardo has revived enough to stumble outside. He wants to go with Blaine on the flight, thinks he can co-pilot. At first I thought he was one of the men in the assassination film, but I've examined him and there's no scar on his cheek, so I'm convinced it was his brother Sergio instead.

I move the Beetle closer to the tarp-covered airplane, dig out my patchwork jacket and a poncho to loan CJ. I hand it to him while he's talking with his brother, then Blaine passes us each a pair of rubber gloves, saying "It won't do to leave any fingerprints on the airplane. This is going to be a one-way trip."

CJ's hand must hurt so I send a short *Reiki* blast his way. He wasn't missing that finger when we met in Zihua. I've asked how it happened, but he says it's too embarrassing to talk about. I haven't revealed that I know his name's Clifford, or said a word about Blaine's will. We each pull on our gloves, take the tarps off and help Ricardo into the plane. When I look up at the monster C47, I can't help but think of that other airplane, the Avocado.

With the help of a wheelbarrow we man-handle and woman-handle the burlap bags of weed from the truck to the plane and Blaine pulls them up through the cargo door. Looking to slow down the freight train of my mind, I break into one of the kilos and snatch a handful of the sticky weed, then stash it in my bag for later.

The last wheelbarrow load to go in is the body of Delgado, *el halcón*, wrapped in a sheet. Blaine wants to dump it in the mountains somewhere, since there isn't an ocean nearby. Noe and I will be driving Víctor's body along with his sister, Tota to Zihua. I dread telling Gloria about her father's death. It's going to be an awfully sad final chapter to her felt-board saga.

CJ and I pocket our gloves and hurry down to the far end of the landing strip to build a fire. Apparently, Blaine will be taking off without headlights, so he needs a beacon to guide him. The oak and juniper-wood make a blaze, and CJ turns to me. "Look, Mariah, Blaine takes my help for granted, but it's my choice. I'm not going with him. I owe more to Charlie and Rosita than I do my brother. Besides, I need to be here, to help you and Noe."

"You have to do what you have to do." My fingers brush his shirt sleeve and there's a jolt of electricity. *Whoa.* With the fire behind him, his burnished silhouette has a magenta glow. He's totally focused on me, drawing me in, but I resist the urge to melt and instead tell him my plan.

"After this, Noe and I are going to Zihua to help Víctor's family."

"I've got two hundred bucks to give them," he says, patting his pocket. "But can you give me a ride to the hospital first? I need to check on Charlie."

"Of course."

"Then count me in," he says.

I offer my hand. "Let's do it."

————

CHAPTER 61
CJ

*You'll know you're finished with the
painting when you're certain another
brush stroke will make no
improvement. Sometimes you may have
already made one stroke too many.*

I downed a cup of coffee laced with tequila and climbed up into
the cockpit to see if Blaine needed anything. I found him holding a
flashlight, fiddling with the C47s instrument panel.

"No lights?" I asked, surprised that my voice still worked.

"The mechanic was going to look for replacement lights, but I
asked him to focus on the engine, the batteries and the flat tire."
Blaine indicated the faint glow of a few ancient bulbs in the
instrument panel. "The essential stuff all works, and the batteries are
charged. I don't need lights anyway when I'm in the air, I've flown
plenty of black-out missions in one of these babies. I do need a fire at
the end of the strip, though, so there's a target to aim for on take-off."

We'd already loaded the airplane with some two hundred fifty
kilos of marijuana, and the body of *el diablo*. The hawk would never
hunt a rebellious peasant again. Noe and I threw together a makeshift
coffin for Víctor and loaded it into the back of his truck, then Noe
stayed to arrange bags of onions around the coffin while Mariah and I
hustled to build a fire at the end of the runway.

We scrounged some kindling and piled on dead branches from the oak and juniper trees beside the strip, avoiding the thorny mesquites. Mariah put a flame to the bonfire, rolled a joint and lit that, too, before asking, "What now?"

"I guess it's time to get out of this place," I said, my voice hoarse.

She took a hit from the joint and held her breath. "Noe's planning to drive Víctor's truck back to Zihua, with the body. Tota is going, too."

I shook my head. "I don't think Noe's wounded arm will take all that downshifting."

"That leaves either you or me." She flicked ash off the number and handed it to me as I contemplated driving a lumbering one-ton flatbed through the tight switchbacks on the road to Zihuatanejo. I took a toke and held it in while Mariah went on, "That truck is half bear and half snail. Going downhill, it jumps out of third gear and you have to wrestle the stick. Uphill, it creeps along at twenty miles per hour."

Spouting a stream of smoke, I joked, "It may take both of us. I can wrestle the snail part and you take the bear."

She gave me a shove and claimed the 'j' again. "Some joke," she said. "The snail part's easy. *You* can wrestle the bear." The firelight cast a highlight on her earring, reminding me of one I'd seen before, and the fringed jacket rang a distant bell.

"We make a good team, Mariah." I said, beginning to relax as my pain diminished.

She released a cloud of smoke and laughed,"You 're right. We found Blaine, didn't we?"

"I don't know," I said, handing her the joint. "I think *he* found *us*."

"After all the trouble we went to." Her eyes danced, and I saw the little girl in her, the precocious, mischievous one who'd hide where you'd never find her and chase you down when you were 'it.' While I watched, Mariah turned to pure gold. She matured before my eyes, becoming old and wise, but still beautiful, and I remembered something she had said. To look at her, I wouldn't have thought she was pregnant. I could have pursued the thought further, but I didn't. It felt like enough to have a new friend and trustworthy comrade.

She touched her chin, then reached out and found my arm. "You know, we'll have to come up with a good story to tell the doctors about Noe's gunshot wound." She passed me the joint in the darkness. "Like maybe it was self-inflicted."

"You think they'd believe Noe shot himself with his own gun?" Coughing out a lungful of smoke, picturing Noe with his arm in a sling, I felt a wave of gratitude that my buddy hadn't taken a vital hit like Víctor did. I pulled off the bowtie that hung loose on my collar and tossed it in the fire. I would have discarded the stupid leather-soled dress shoes and gone barefoot, except the altiplano had it's own brand of cactus and such, not to mention mesquite thorns.

"Nothing would surprise me at this point, CJ." Mariah turned her head sideways. "You know, your timing was perfect back there. You bought Víctor enough time to throw the knife before he was shot. If you hadn't banged on that cellar door at the exact second you did, we'd probably all be dead."

The rainy season hadn't fully kicked in yet, and the bonfire wood was dry. The flames soon leapt fifteen feet into the air, high enough for a beacon, surrounded by a world of shadow. Mariah and I jogged blindly back to the airplane in the darkness, holding hands. The C47's cargo door was illuminated by the headlights of Víctor's truck. Noe, up to his usual antics, was rodeo-riding the truck's hood. With his good arm he was swinging Blaine's money belt like a whip. He must have taken it off the dead man when I wasn't watching. He grinned and tossed it to me, fully loaded.

Just in case of emergency, I pocketed three bills before securing the belt under my shirt and putting the clumsy gloves back on. There'd been a kind of *snap* or *pop* when I let go of Mariah's hand to catch the belt. The small explosion had sent waves through me and left my skin vibrating.

———

CHAPTER 62
MARIAH

*Be prepared to paint a masterpiece
today. At the same time, be prepared to
burn the work. With an attitude that
embraces this paradox, the artist has a
chance for success.*

CJ and I sprint all the way back to the plane and arrive breathless,
still holding hands. No sign of Blaine, so I assume he's inside the
plane. Noe is sitting on the hood of the old flatbed truck, riding it like
an elephant handler and beating the fender with a piece of leather I
recognize as Blaine's money-belt. He throws it to CJ, who straps it
around his waist, under his shirt. I have to shake my head.

Blaine pokes his nose out the airplane door and looks around, his
gaze landing on Noe. The little guy jumps down from the truck and
goes into a pantomime about flying and playing the guitar and pretty
senoritas. He seems to be making a heart-wrenching effort to
convince Blaine to take him to the U.S.

But Blaine says, "No, maybe next time. You stay here and get that arm looked at right away," Then he disappears again inside the plane.

Noe takes it pretty well, considering, but I can tell he's disappointed. When we get our heads together for a minute, he writes a question in his notebook, and I give the question a voice.

"CJ, are you going to tell Blaine about the money belt?"

"I'm not planning to," he says, just before his brother reappears.

Blaine gives CJ a signal to spin the propeller on the right engine, so he ducks under the fuselage and I follow him to the far side of the plane. He's hurt, and he can't get the thing to spin so I have to take over, spinning it fourteen times, so the oil will circulate. We jump back, Blaine hits the starter and the engine catches with a deafening roar, disrupting the night. On the other side, I repeat the process. Engine number two cooperates and the decibel level doubles. After a minute, Blaine appears at the cargo door and gives me a two fingered salute. He motions at CJ to follow and they disappear inside the airplane.

CHAPTER 63
CJ

*There are times when you're aware
only of your subject and materials, and
the awesome beauty of life is
overwhelming.
There are other times when your paints
and brushes thwart you at every stroke,
when the color won't work, when
you've forgotten to ask for guidance.
These are the core experiences of art.
Sometimes it's harmony, and
sometimes a struggle, but in either case
art is about a profound connection
between the artist and the outer world.*

My shoulders were all but useless, so Mariah had to spin the props
on the C47. Blaine wanted to tell me something, so with the fire
blazing some thousand yards away and propellers whining, I climbed
in the plane again, bashing my head on the door frame. Ricardo was
still inert in the co-pilot's seat. Reaching down and lifting an eyelid, I
realized he'd passed out again from the painkillers he'd taken, so the
speed wasn't working. I felt a hand on my shoulder and flinched, then
Blaine leaned close and spoke in my ear.

"Listen, Cliff, there's no time to waste. Ricardo's comatose and I need you to co-pilot. We're running late. As it is, we'll be crossing the border right at dawn." I froze in place, stunned, while he gave the order, "Turn on the flashlight and shine it on the instrument panel."

In the throes of cognitive dissonance, I jumped up and trained the flashlight on the guages. The co-pilot's seat-back vibrated under my bandaged hand and the noise inside the prop-driven aircraft rattled my brain. *Damn!*

I threw the flashlight in the seat and ran back to the cargo door, unbuckling the money-belt as I went. Mariah stood with a five-gallon bucket full of water, ready to put out the fire after takeoff. I threw her the belt and shook my head. She nodded slowly and a stab of longing nearly ripped me open. We shared eyeballs for a second before I jammed the door in place and made my way to the front of the plane.

I dragged an unconscious Ricardo from the co-pilot's seat, and took his place. Blaine adjusted the prop angle and fuel mixture, then throttled up. Props shattered the air, engines roared, and we began to roll toward the fire at the end of the strip, a mere pinpoint of light. The blind take-off had me clinched like a fist as we accelerated. The old plane rocked, tilted and bumped its way up the field, gaining speed until we abruptly parted with Earth and angled up into the night sky. As we climbed, stars shimmered above us, a dim landscape emerged below and the air cooled quickly.

———

CHAPTER 64
MARIAH

*It's fine to aspire to greatness, but
you'd better not become attached to the
idea. Focus on making the moment
great.*

It's hard to believe they're gone. With considerable effort, I
lumber down the strip with a water bucket, changing hands every few
steps. All that's left of the fast-burning beacon fire is a bed of coals.
Setting the bucket down, I kick the stray embers together into a pile
and drip a stream of water around the perimeter, gradually moving to
the hotter center. My tennies crunch on charcoal and steam rises,
threatening to choke me, until finally the bucket is empty and the fire
is out. After hours of furious action and ear-splitting noise, all is
quiet.

But this is not over. I run back to find Noe waiting, with the truck
running and Tota sitting stone-faced beside him on a twenty-pound
bag of onions. They're headed to the San Miguel hospital to see
about Charlie and get Noe's arm looked after before they head south
to Zihua. I can't get my mind off of Víctor's family. Paulito, poor
kid. He was his dad's sidekick, apprentice farmer and fruit peddler.
How will the family make it without a father?

The money-belt wraps around my waist, invisible with my jacket buttoned, but it feels like a corset and a huge responsibility. Without saying anything, CJ made my mission clear when he threw it. The money goes to Víctor's wife, Lupe. Kind of heroic on CJ's part, letting it go that easily . . . or else kind of troubling. I don't know, but for now, I'm going with heroic. I remember the first time I saw the belt, in Blaine's room in New Orleans after we'd made love. Seems there's some kind of symmetry now, with it snugged around Hannah and me. Like the completion of a cycle.

But, as I jump in the Beetle and follow the old Chevy, I feel deprived. Working with CJ almost seemed like a partnership for a minute there. One with possibilities. The jolt when he let go of my hand nearly knocked me down and now I'm wired to a new frequency, like I'm magnetized. He'd better take good care of himself. I think I'm gonna be needing him.

———

CHAPTER 65
CJ

*Sometimes an artist must dissociate
from empirical facts, let the divine light
shine through and paint that.*

Far below, a few scattered lights indicated the road to Torreon. I sat in the right-hand seat with a flashlight between my knees and tissue paper stuffed in my ears, gradually getting accustomed to the noise of the C47 and resisting the overwhelming desire to rip off my stupid gloves. For a while I watched Blaine's every move at the controls. To communicate, we had to scream at each other, and my voice was gone, so the time passed with few words.

The temperature plunged as we climbed. I rummaged for wool blankets, threw one over Ricardo and scrunched up with mine, wrapping my arms around my knees. Then a deep indigo haze settled around me while the night's events replayed in my head.

I should have pegged creepy-eyes as an enemy from the time he harassed me at the rental car office in Acapulco. Although his body lay in the back of the plane, *el diablo's* spectre still lurked in my psyche. I half expected him to rise up from the dead and grab me, right where I sat. I should have warned Charlie and Blaine about him . . . and told Víctor.

Every step of the way since arriving in Mexico, I'd skipped over some important fact and ignored some real danger. By omitting the negative space from the picture, I'd failed utterly at helping my brother and my friends. I'd left a lot behind, too, all on the spur of the moment, and every minute was taking me further from my new life as an artist, from Charlie and Rosita, my buddy Noe, and from Mariah. I hated leaving her in the lurch, after declaring I'd help her drive to Zihua with Víctor's sister and the body. When it came down to the nitty-gritty, some kind of blind loyalty to Blaine, some mindless blood-bond had trumped everything else I wanted.

One thing I was glad about though. Mariah had the money belt, and I trusted her to do the right thing. All that dough rightly belonged to Víctor's family after the sacrifice he'd made, taking a bullet for his family and mine. I figured he'd done a service for all humankind, for that matter, by taking out Delgado.

With that matter settled in my mind, I drifted off to that familiar place in a Texas lake where the waterfall mistress and I were joined in body and soul. For a time, I pictured Mariah's face on her, and in my fantasy world, the two women became one.

Hours later we'd risen to six thousand feet again while crossing a mountain range near the Texas border. The chore of dumping the *halcón's* body fell to me, with Ricardo in a coma and Blaine busy at the controls. I did the job in a hurry, shivering with cold, kicking the bundle out the door while gripping the frame with one hand, turbulence trying to whip me out along with the body. I threw the door shut and sat down with relief, my right hand throbbing, and I must have passed out

In a minute I roused myself. The wind screamed around the cargo door, louder than before as I scrambled back to the cockpit. As soon as I sat down, Ricardo appeared, wearing a parachute on his chest, holding a revolver and giving the sign for money with his thumb and forefinger. I realized he'd been faking it all along.

One word at a time, Blaine yelled, "There. Is. No. Money. You. Ass. Hole!"

"Your gun and jacket. No funny business." Ricardo shouted, his gun hand shaking. "Now we change the course, *amigos*." The bastard actually smiled.

Blaine held both hands up and shouted, "There. Is. No. Gun!"

Ricardo felt around Blaine's waist while holding the pistol to his head. He came up with the film reel Mariah gave Blaine and pocketed it. Then he frisked me, his hand still shaking. *He's cold and he's left-handed,* I thought, trying to figure a way to get the pistol.

Blaine made eye contact, then glanced at the flashlight between my legs. I can't explain it, but the cabin seemed to heat up for a second and I knew I had to make a move. Blaine took off his jacket and our hijacker started to put it on, changing gun hands. The second I saw the pistol go into his right hand, I hit the switch on the big flashlight, reached out and shoved it in his face, keeping my eyes focused into the night sky. My brother came out of his seat swinging like an attack dog. A shot was fired, fiberglass shattered and wind whistled through a long diagonal hole in the left window. The flashlight tumbled from my hand and darkness prevailed.

Blaine yelled, "Fly the plane, Cliff!" and I heard nothing else but a series of bumps while the two men wrestled into the back of the plane. After that, there was nothing but engine sound—no more gunshots, at least. I felt a wet spot as I took the pilot's seat, so I tasted it. *Blood!*

I recovered the flashlight, and hoping the plane would fly itself, I went back into the cargo area, shining the light. Nobody in sight and the cargo door open. *Blaine!* I thought, *Hang on, bro.* Ricardo had our only parachute.

My brother's voice came in my head again. "Fly the plane, Cliff."

While I played with the flaps to adjust altitude, dropping little by little, it seemed like the plane was really flying me. A tall peak loomed on the left, more mountains rising up behind it. Before long, an orange glare streaked across the right wing and into the cockpit, announcing dawn. I knew I was close to the border.

We'd been cruising at six thousand feet when Blaine disappeared. *Could he have gotten the gun, grabbed hold of Ricardo and pulled the rip cord?* I wondered. *Could he hold on while the chute opened?* I had to believe he'd held on. If he'd fallen to his death it was all my fault. I knew I hadn't latched that cargo door properly after dumping *el diablo.*

At four thousand feet, the Rio Grande snaked into view. It was a bright pink slash, broken and perforated, appearing and disappearing all across the horizon in front of me. I dropped altitude faster, leveling off at thirty second intervals, crossing the river at two thousand feet. I was in Texas—over it, at least. On my right, everything seemed flat, relatively. Still some rough country ahead and to the left. I started an even more rapid descent, scanning the terrain, and veered slightly to the right, afraid to try a real turn. That's when I remembered to fasten my seat belt.

The approaching Earth scared the shit out of me. *How can I steer the plane straight enough to land on the highway down there?* I asked myself. Hard ground was frightening. I wanted to just keep flying. No choice, though. Another mountain threatened, straight ahead.

I crossed the highway at an angle, dropped to a couple hundred feet above ground and took several deep breaths, scouring the landscape. I went for the flattest place, keeping the nose toward the ground by sheer force of will. Instinct wanted it up and pointed toward safety, but I knew better.

With my eyes shut there was nothing but engine roar and a great void. I opened them and saw the most beautiful sight imaginable, a land bathed in gold and silver with a world of blue up above. In that moment, I fell in love with the Earth . . . with Heaven . . . with the airplane.

When the airspeed dropped to eighty knots, the engines sputtered, and I remembered something Blaine had said earlier about landing a C47. "Nose up, power down." *Trust the process, CJ.*

Feeling the weight of the plane in my gut, I never realized I'd failed to drop the landing gear, but it wouldn't have changed anything. I must've pictured a belly landing from the second I took control. The fuel gauge was below the last hash-mark, riding on empty. Maybe the airplane wouldn't explode on impact. As the ground approached, I adjusted the flaps, and the nose came up, then I cut the power to both engines. I didn't know what else to do.

CHAPTER 66
CJ

*One principle often overlooked by
beginning artists is the receptivity of
the ground. It makes a difference
whether the painting surface is
absorbent or sealed, textured or
smooth. It affects the viscosity of the
paint and therefore the rhythm of
application. It influences when you can
make the next effective stroke. In all, it
determines from the beginning what the
ultimate outcome will be.*

I'd just crossed the second highway when the tail hit the ground.
The nose followed with a whump! and I bounced hard in the seat.
Like fingernails on a blackboard amplified a thousand times, the
plane screamed across the desert floor, lurching up, down and
sideways. The landscape ahead rushed at me—not so flat as it looked
from the air. I held on and wondered, *Where are the fuel tanks?*

Finally, the screaming stopped. First the airplane's. Then my own.
A little smoke streamed from the left engine, but I could see no fire.

I was lucky. Feeling like I'd landed, not on earth, but in the open
arms of God, I unbuckled my seat belt and went to check again if my
brother was miraculously inside the plane, maybe in the head, doing
his business. But he and Ricardo were long gone. The cargo door was
still wide open and the cargo was still strapped to the floor. I
contemplated the stack of weed for a second or two, then opened a
bag, snatched one of the kilos, and made a fast exit. No way I could
get hundreds of pounds of marijuana safely delivered. This was the
middle of nowhere, the only sign of civilization a solitary windmill a
mile or so away.

I hustled to get clear of the plane and stopped for a second to admire the streaks of amber and cerulean that presided over the barren landscape. Then I addressed the voices in my head. The greedy one was saying, "There's a hundred thousand dollars worth of weed in the plane—get it stashed somewhere." The more practical one was saying, "Just take the kilo and walk away from here." The voice of self-preservation said, "Take a quarter ounce and throw out the stems, so you can eat it all if necessary."

I chose option number three and did it quickly, shedding the rubber gloves and sticking them in my pocket with the small packet of weed. The soft earth welcomed my feet as I sprinted for the highway, poncho flapping. I reached the asphalt and looked both ways, my heart still beating like crazy, and stuck out a thumb. The golden sky reminded me of Mariah's aura when she stood in the doorway at the hacienda after rescuing me, and I felt the same kind of ache I'd felt after spending a whole half-hour merged with the waterfall mistress.

A car pulled over a couple hundred feet past me and started backing up, so I ran. In the distance to the north, I heard the chopper approaching and got in the car, gulping air. Through the back window I watched the helicopter bank and circle the spot where I'd left the plane. My ride was going to San Antonio, and that was good enough for me.

The End

Acknowledgements

This novel has been a group project. I provided the through-put, but others have given me shoves, both gentle and vigorous, to get me to the point of publishing.

First credit goes to my partner, Anne Titus—friend, wife, consultant, inspiration, lover and ultimately editor of my book.

I could not have written *A Coward's Guide to Oil Painting* without Nancy Hartney, Su Raymond and the Dickson Street Writers, who suffered with me through the early drafts.

In addition, thanks to my old buddy Greg Thomas who told me, "I think you have a book," when it was still a shitty first draft wanting to be a novel.

The following people contributed
in a valuable and timely way:
Terry Dushan
Octavio Logo
Steve Folkers
Masie Cochran
Kate Lacy
Tony Cohan
Timothy C. Tyler
Molly Gibson
William Beaver
Harry McDermott
Nick Nicholson
Steven Schneider

And last, I want to thank those I accidentally forgot to mention.

MM Kent

CPSIA information can be obtained
at www.ICGtesting.com
Printed in the USA
FSHW022214150620
71213FS

9 781735 081212